Many Windows

Many
Windows

22 Stories from *American Review*

Edited by Ted Solotaroff

HARPER COLOPHON BOOKS
Harper & Row, Publishers
New York, Cambridge, Philadelphia, San Francisco
London, Mexico City, Saõ Paulo, Sidney

Copyright acknowledgments appear following page 346.

MANY WINDOWS. Copyright © 1982 by Ted Solotaroff. All rights reserved. Printed in the United States of America. No part of this book may be used or reproduced in any manner whatsoever without written permission except in the case of brief quotations embodied in critical articles and reviews. For information address Harper & Row, Publishers, Inc., 10 East 53rd Street, New York, N.Y. 10022. Published simultaneously in Canada by Fitzhenry & Whiteside Limited, Toronto.

FIRST EDITION

Designer: Abigail Sturges

Library of Congress Cataloging in Publication Data
    Main entry under title:

    Many windows.

    (Harper colophon books)
        1. Short stories, American.   2. American fiction—
    20th century.   I. Solotaroff, Ted, date.
    II. American review (New York, N.Y.: 1973)
    PS659.M27   1983   813'.01'08   81–47803
    ISBN 0–06–090923–4 (pbk.)

82 83 84 85 86 10 9 8 7 6 5 4 3 2 1

Contents

Introduction

THE TWENTY-TWO PIECES of fiction in this collection were chosen from the two-hundred-odd that appeared in *New American Review* (later *American Review*) during the eleven years of its run. I have excluded from consideration those that have been published in book form, such as *The Cat in the Hat for President* and *Catholics*, and those that went on to lead a different life in novels, such as *Portnoy's Complaint, Hermaphrodeity, Mawrdew Czgowchwz, Ragtime, Wrinkles, Even Cowgirls Get the Blues, The Public Burning*, and so forth, where they are still readily available. From the others, I've tried to select pieces that represent the range of fiction we published, that play off each other in ways that make for an interesting and useful collection, and that still bowl me over.

There is perhaps nothing as instructive about one's taste as choosing from works one had already chosen, five or ten or fifteen years ago. In general, I find that my taste has tended to become more conservative than that of the inquisitive and venturesome editor and his colleagues at New American Library who began *New American Review* in 1967. Partly that's a function of role. When *NAR* began, we made a point of emphasizing its catholicity, believing that as a paperback magazine, it could survive only by appealing to diverse tastes and interests while maintaining its standards of quality. Hence we published a fair amount of experimental as well as more traditional fiction; took chances with various stories that tested the barriers of erotic description and language, which were only beginning to weaken; gave a certain advantage to manuscripts that were telling of the political, social, and cultural upheavals of the times; and in general tried to make our fiction conversant with our essays, which were mostly topical ones, most of them bearing the imagination of alternatives that was abroad in the land.

All of which was not simply a matter of marketing calculation. *NAR* tried to establish a footing between the traditional culture and the counterculture; our purpose, as it evolved in the late 1960s, was to try to apply the critical standards of the former to the ideology and sensibility of the latter, and occasionally vice versa. In fiction, this mainly meant publishing work that was articulate and whose point of view and effects were earned by craft rather than asserted by rhetoric; while at the same time recognizing that new modes of expressiveness test and alter one's notions of the articulate and the earned.

This is to put these matters, though, in a more schematic and balanced way than the actual process of editorial judgment allows. It assumes that your taste is sufficiently sure and flexible and objective to be equal to every manuscript that comes your way. Sometimes you think it is: at least you know that you have to publish this narrative, however unconventional—or conventional—it may seem, if you're to go on making sense of what you're doing; you know you won't publish that one for the same reason, no matter how fashionable—or unfashionable—the author or the writing may be. Those are the easy ones. The hard ones are those that drive you to your fence and sit you down on it. The author may simply have a more subtle imagination than yours— and one that doesn't leave tracks. Or he may take you, however resistantly, into a place so sordid or depraved that your respect for narrative power tells you one thing and your disgust another. Or you may think a story is terrific up to the end but that its end is too obvious or obscure, though its author stubbornly doesn't. These are only a few of the cases where your decision-making process falters into doubt. It may be that the bottom line of how you really function as an editor is to what you give the benefit of your doubts. That may also be the bottom line of what makes your magazine continue to be interesting, because benefits of doubt are where the risks are, and as our poetry editor Richard Howard liked to remind me, "only the risky is truly interesting."

During the years I was editing *NAR/AR*, the benefit of my own doubts tended to go to the less known, the topical, and the innovative. This was in keeping with its claim to being a "magazine of new writing," but it was also consonant with a stage of my own journey. Like many intellectuals of my generation, I was reevaluating a good many of my values, and trying to create some space for growth that had been taken up by careerism and a faith in authority—other traits of my generation. With respect to literature, I came off some of my graduate-student elitism and tried to develop the idea that literature was too important a democratic resource to be left to the literati. By the same token, I felt that the heavy hand of the modernist tradition that academicism had laid on the norms of literary value needed to be resisted and that, in Auden's words, "new styles of architecture, a change of heart" should be encouraged. This made me open to the plain-speech style and democratic vistas of the new generation as well as to its cultural eclecticism, its expansion of consciousness, its relaxation of forms and categories to free up energy, and so forth.

Well, the counterculture has been over for a decade or more, and I'm fifty-three now and growing conscious of the selectivities that come with aging. As in other matters, my literary interests have less to do with inquisitiveness and more with sustenance. The fictions I've wanted most to include in this collection are not especially topical or innovative, or else these qualities are subsumed in more general and less easily defined ones. Perhaps the closest I can come is to say that their consciousness of life and their artistry are seasoned—not as a salad is but as wood is, as character is. They have a genuine subject, a complex situation or course of events taken at the full. This sense of plenitude, of having much to say and tell, comes from a subject that is deeply held, steeped in feeling. Hence the pressure of the narrative seems to come naturally to it, a function of the inwardness, of the dream energy pressing for expression, and of the narrative art that concentrates and empowers this energy as a magnifying glass does the sunlight.

Sometimes the resulting intensity is immediately evident, as in Gilbert Sorrentino's "The Moon in Its Flight"—a *cri de coeur*, sounding down the corridors of memory, of an unconsummated and still unfinished love affair between a Catholic street kid from Brooklyn and a Jewish princess from Mosholu Parkway: "I don't even know where CCNY is! Who is Conrad Aiken? What is Bronx Science? Who is Berlioz? What is a Stravinsky? How do you play

Mah-Jongg? What is schmooz, schlepp, Purim, Moo Goo Gai Pan? Help me." The strength of the narrator's experience, its erotic tenderness, longing, and pain, are witnessed by the extraordinary vividness of details with which the girl, himself, the setting, the time—everything—are remembered. The truth of the ache is in the tone of the writing—nostalgia screened by chagrin, wonder by anger: this complexity being further evidence of the force and depth with which the emotion of the story is held. This is the voice of a man who is writing for his life, in the sense that once into the experience, his life will make no sense until he manages to deliver it.

A number of the other stories have a similar declarative intensi- ty: Robert Stone's "Aquarius Obscured," Leonard Michaels's "Getting Lucky," Harold Brodkey's "Innocence"—another re- membrance of young love, which has "the authority," in Brod- key's words, "of being on one's knees in front of the event." But there are other registers of the narrative voice which bespeak the same generative attachment to the subject, the same sense of ne- cessity that this much, at least, must be said. William Gass's "In the Heart of the Heart of the Country" is written in spare, objec- tive vignettes of dailiness in a small town in Indiana that is slowly failing even as its life goes on, just as the narrator's mind goes on observing even as his spirit sinks in longing and grief. In this case, the emotional burden of a broken relationship, one between the middle-aged narrator and a young woman, is not front and cen- ter; it is rather like an ache in the back of his descriptions of the town's neighbors and landscapes, commerce and socializing, edu- cation and religion. The urgency of the narrative, parodoxically enough, lies in its control—the slow-breathing control of a man trying to hold himself together, not an actor, but a patient in whom little is going on save pain and the influx of the world. What is so remarkable is the poise with which Gass holds the narrative on the interface between the personal and the phenom- enological in a kind of diminished curiosity, the grief and the observation validating and deepening each other.

Grace Paley's "Faith: In a Tree" is another example of a dis- tinctive voice narrating a social scene, specifically the Greenwich Village scene of young mothers without husbands. Comic rather than elegiac, Faith's voice is indefatigably gregarious and subtly lonely, a kind of inspired gossip. With her savvy eye and impetuous heart, she provides the minutes, as it were, of the Saturday-afternoon conclave at the Washington Square sandbox. At the center of the action are needs that none of the stray men who come by are likely to fill, just as Faith's consciousness circles around and around the hole left by her transient husband.

A writer seized by his or her subject in the ways I have been trying to suggest is likely to produce a movement against or beyond the conventions of narrative—a bold adaptation of the form to the pressure and reach of the content. In Grace Paley's story, the first-person point of view is summarily stripped of its limitations, and lines of telepathy are set up to handle the incessant flow of information and communication that animates the scene. Along with its charm, the device expresses the helpless intimacies of this circle of Village women and children where everything hangs out. In Gass's story the innovative stroke is the deliberate elimination of any overt narrative development, to accord with the patient-like passivity of the speaker and the sense of entropy at work in the community, and by extension, in the heart of the country. Toward the end of "The Moon in Its Flight," the narrator abruptly invents—or is it an invention?—a scene of consummation ten years later, when he and Rebecca accidentally meet again at the lake. He speaks of this scene as "the literary part of this story," the implication being that fiction will now provide what life has withheld. On the other hand, he speaks of Rebecca's having "gone out of the reality of narrative," the implication being that what follows did happen but is too melodramatic to be believed. I don't think that Sorrentino means the ambiguity to be resolved one way or the other, for the story is not only about desire but also about art: the transactions that imagination carries out in both realms, if indeed they are finally separate realms in this case.

To my mind, this is the true province of innovation and experiment—not for its own sake but for the subject's sake, provided the subject is a genuine one. A sign of a genuine subject, as I've suggested, is the strength, vibrancy, and resilience of feeling it releases into the prose itself; another sign is the complexity it sustains—the doubleness of vision that literary art mediates and resolves into a rich fusion of situation and context, action and meaning. In García Márquez's story of a senile angel who is found lying moribund in a villager's chicken yard, where he is successively marveled over, exploited, and then ignored, the natural and the supernatural keep touching down in each other's realm in silly, surreal, and indomitably innocent ways. "His only supernatural virtue seemed to be patience. Especially during the first days, when the hens pecked at him, searching for the stellar parasites that proliferated in his wing, and the cripples pulled out feathers to touch their defective parts with, and even the most merciful threw stones at him, trying to get him to rise so they could see him standing." In García Márquez's hands, the material turns into myth before one's eyes and finally into a parable of the soul's bedraggled journey through the world. There is an interesting reverberation between this tale and Andrew Fetler's "To Byzantium," a story that dramatizes the progress and pathos of a pious Greek Orthodox priest, his church, and his family, amid the religious inanities of Los Angeles.

Philip Roth's "'I Always Wanted You to Admire My Fasting'" begins with an essay that presents two views of Kafka—the familiar, crippled refugee from his own desires and the "writer, father, and Jew" who came out of hiding in the final months of Kafka's life, when the force of his terminal illness liberated him. Then, in his own masterstroke of daring, Roth gives his subject twenty-five more years of life and turns Kafka into one of those displaced Middle European intellectuals who peopled the Hebrew schools and Friday-night tables of America in the 1930s and 1940s. Another turn of the screw of Kafkaesque irony produces this figure of forlorn dignity who briefly courts Roth's spinster aunt to an inevitable outcome and dies eventually in a sanatorium in New Jersey, as totally obscure as he had wished.

Roth's piece is first a biographical study and then a story, or rather, it comes together finally as a hybrid form perfectly adapted to the subject at hand—a life so patterned by irony, so strange in its outcomes, that it beggars any fictional version of it: that is, other than Kafka's own. In the following pages you will find other transactions going on between the modes of fact and those of fiction. A few years ago, when the "new journalism" was all the vogue, its practitioners, led by Tom Wolfe, were applauding themselves for their acquisition of the techniques of the novelists, whom they aimed to supplant as the principal chroniclers of the age. Meanwhile, without much publicity, fiction writers were making their own raids across the dwindling frontier between the realms of factuality and fiction, including what alleges to be one or the other. In an age given over to various channels of public disinformation, ranging from presidential press conferences and State Department white papers, to the institutional ad and the product commercial, the novelist finds a particular opportunity and even a necessity for the kinds of lies he tells, his "false documents" being in the interest of freeing inquiry from the "factual" lies and blandishments of the regime. As E. L. Doctorow wrote in *AR* 26, "The novelist deals with his isolation by splitting himself in two, creator and documentarian, teller and listener, conspiring to pass on the collective wisdom in its own enlightened bias, that of the factual world."

The pages of *NAR/AR*, issue after issue, contained experiments with tellingly "false documents." Donald Barthelme's study of Robert Kennedy is a kind of synthetic journalism, a collage of real and invented newspaper clips designed to portray Kennedy as a contemporary "representative man," in Emerson's term, the complete media figure: "a pastless futureless man, born anew at every instant. . . . Nothing follows from what has gone before. He is constantly surprised. He cannot predict his own reaction to events. He is constantly being *overtaken* by events. A condition of breathlessness and dazzlement surrounds him." Kennedy himself is speaking, paraphrasing the French structural critic Georges Poulet Why not? All sources of imagery are available to the man who is making his self completely dissoluble in his image. Another kind of false document is Max Apple's wholly imaginary account of the career of Howard Johnson in "The Oranging of America"—a genial condensation of the American dream in its capitalist phase. The religion of consumerism finds its quintessential figure in Apple's pseudobiographical account of this visionary of mobility and prophet of profits, who carries out his mission in a customized Lincoln equipped with an ice cream freezer for testing his product, a map for charting his ministry, an office for his helpmate, and eventually a cryonics freezer in tow for prospective resurrection.

There are more seemingly traditional stories here, such as William Mathes's "Swan Feast," Dinah Brooke's "Some of the Rewards and Pleasures of Love," Vassily Aksyonov's "Little Whale, a Varnisher of Reality." But they are no less powerful for that, and being fully imagined and boldly executed, no less new. Originality in fiction is less a matter of the subject or the means than the quality of the experience. There have been many stories of violent hunters and amorous cripples and politically terrorized writers. But such is the energy of vision in these stories and such the focusing power of their incidents and images that whatever banality we may feel is quickly burned away and the imagination comes into its own. "Wash Far Away," John Berryman's story of a man teaching *Lycidas* in the midst of World War II, is obviously written close to the bone of an actual experience. George Dennison's story of a prodigious high jumper who takes up ornithology seems as purely imagined as a dream. Yet both writers are pursuing the same mystery—the nature of genius—and from their different directions, both manage to touch her hem.

Henry James said that "the house of fiction has many windows." Yes, and there are many more today than in James's time. It's now more like a high rise apartment complex, so many are in residence there, so numerous are the points of vantage and view. Most of the accommodations, though, are smaller, and skimpier, more provisional and transient, than in James's time. So it seemed to me during the years I edited *NAR/AR*, when I continued to be struck by the number of gifted new writers who came, as it were, from out of the blue and who, after a story or two, perhaps a novel, often disappeared back into it. The same might be said of *NAR/AR* itself: it came out of the vast realm of American possibilities with a few questions on its mind, hung in there for a decade or so, and then went the way of much of the writing and spirit it tried to welcome and give a home to. In an age whose universal is change, virtually everything becomes ephemeral and mutable or at least begins to seem so. Reading through the files of *NAR/AR*, I was surprised to feel as often remote as nostalgic. But then I would come upon another story that was still fully alive, still enduring, and whenever possible, I've put it in this collection.

—Ted Solotaroff

Many Windows

Innocence

HAROLD BRODKEY

1. Orra at Harvard

ORRA PERKINS WAS A SENIOR. Her looks were like a force that
struck you. Truly, people on first meeting her often involuntarily
lifted their arms as if about to fend off the brightness of the apparition. She was a somewhat scrawny, tulip-like girl of middling
height. To see her in sunlight was to see Marxism die. I'm not the
only one who said that. It was because seeing someone in actuality who has such a high immediate worth meant you had to decide whether such personal distinction had a right to exist or if
she belonged to the state and ought to be shadowed in, reduced in
scale, made lesser, laughed at.

Also, it was the case that you had to be rich and famous to get
your hands on her; she could not fail to be a trophy and the
question was whether the trophy had to be awarded on economic
and political grounds or whether chance could enter in.

I was a senior too, and ironic. I had no money. I was without
lineage. It seemed to me Orra was proof that life was a terrifying
phenomenon of surface immediacy. She made any idea I had of
psychological normalcy or of justice absurd since normalcy was
not as admirable or as desirable as Orra; or rather she was normalcy and everything else was a falling off, a falling below; and
justice was inconceivable if she, or someone equivalent to her if
there was an equivalent once you had seen her, would not sleep
with you. I used to create general hilarity in my room by shouting her name at my friends and then breaking up into laughter,
gasping out, "God, we're so small time." It was grim that she

1

existed and I had not had her. One could still prefer a more ordinary girl but not for simple reasons.

A great many people avoided her, ran away from her. She was, in part, more knowing than the rest of us because the experiences offered her had been so extreme, and she had been so extreme in response—scenes in Harvard Square with an English marquess, slapping a son of a billionaire so hard he fell over backwards at a party in Lowell House, her saying then and subsequently, "I never sleep with anyone who has a fat ass." Extreme in the humiliations endured and meted out, in the crassness of the publicity, of her life defined as those adventures, extreme in the dangers survived or not entirely survived, the cheapness undergone so that she was on a kind of frightening eminence, an eminence of her experiences and of her being different from everyone else. She'd dealt in intrigues, major and minor, in the dramas of political families, in passions, deceptions, folly on a large, expensive scale, promises, violence, the genuine pain of defeat when defeat is to some extent the result of your qualities and not of your defects, and she knew the rottenness of victories that hadn't been final. She was crass and impaired by beauty. She was like a giant bird, she was as odd as an ostrich walking around the Yard, in her absurd gorgeousness, she was so different from us in kind, so capable of a different sort of progress through the yielding medium of the air, through the strange rooms of our minutes on this earth, through the gloomy circumstances of our lives in those years.

People said it was worth it to do this or that just in order to see her—seeing her offered some kind of encouragement, was some kind of testimony that life was interesting. But not many people cared as much about knowing her. Most people preferred to keep their distance. I don't know what her having made herself into what she was had done for her. She could have been ordinary if she'd wished.

She had unnoticeable hair, a far from arresting forehead, and extraordinary eyes, deep-set, longing, hopeful, angrily bored behind smooth, heavy lids that fluttered when she was interested and when she was not interested at all. She had a great desire not to trouble or be troubled by supernumeraries and strangers. She has a proud, too large nose that gives her a noble, stubborn dog's look. Her mouth has a disconcertingly lovely set to it—it is more immediately expressive than her eyes and it shows her implacability: it is the implacability of her knowledge of life in her. People always stared at her. Some giggled nervously. *Do you like me, Orra? Do you like me at all?* They stared at the great hands of the Aztec priest opening them to feelings and to awe, exposing their hearts, the dread cautiousness of their lives. They stared at the incredible symmetries of her sometimes anguishedly passionate face, the erratic pain for her in being beautiful that showed on it, the occasional plunging gaiety she felt because she was beautiful. I like beautiful people. The symmetries of her face were often thwarted by her attempts at expressiveness—beauty was a stone she struggled free of. A ludicrous beauty. A cruel clown of a girl. Sometimes her face was absolutely impassive as if masked in dullness and she was trying to move among us incognito. I was aware that each of her downfalls made her more possible for me. I never doubted that she was privately a pedestrian shitting-peeing person. Whenever I had a chance to observe her for any length of time, in a classroom for instance, I would think, *I understand her.* Whenever I approached her, she responded up to a point and then even as I stood talking to her I would fade as a personage, as a sexual presence, as someone present and important to her into greater and greater invisibility. That was when she was a freshman, a sophomore, and a junior. When we were seniors, by then I'd learned how to avoid being invisible even to Orra. Orra was, I realized, hardly more than a terrific college girl, much vaunted, no more than that yet. But my god, my god, in one's eyes, in one's thoughts, she strode like a *Nike*, she entered like a blast of light, the thought of her was as vast as a desert. Sometimes in an early winter twilight in the Yard, I would see her in her coat, unbuttoned even in cold weather as if she burned slightly always, see her move clumsily along a walk looking like a scrawny field hockey player, a great athlete of a girl half-stumbling, uncoordinated off the playing field, yet with reserves of strength, do you know? and her face, as she walked along, might twitch like a dog's when the dog is asleep, twitching with whatever dialogue or adventure or daydream she was having in her head. Or she might in the early darkness stride along, cold-faced, haughty, angry, all the worst refusals one would ever receive bound up in one ridiculously beautiful girl. One always said, *I wonder what will become of her.* Her ignoring me marked me as a sexual nonentity. She was proof of a level of sexual adventure I had not yet with my best efforts reached: that level existed because Orra existed.

What is it worth to be in love in this way?

2. Orra with Me

I distrust summaries, any kind of gliding through time, any too great a claim that one is in control of what one recounts; I think someone who claims to understand but who is obviously calm, someone who claims to write with emotion recollected in tranquillity, is a fool and a liar. To understand is to tremble. To recollect is to reenter and be riven. An acrobat after spinning through the air in a mockery of flight stands erect on his perch and mockingly takes his bow as if what he is being applauded for was easy for him and cost him nothing, although meanwhile he is covered with sweat and his smile is edged with a relief chilling to think about; he is indulging in a show business style; he is pretending to be superhuman. I am bored with that and with where it has brought us. I admire the authority of being on one's knees in front of the event.

In the last spring of our being undergraduates, I finally got her. We had agreed to meet for dinner in my room, to get a little drunk cheaply before going out to dinner. I left the door unlatched; and I lay naked on my bed under a sheet. When she knocked on the door, I said, "Come in," and she did. She began to chatter right away, to complain that I was still in bed; she seemed to think I'd been taking a nap and had forgotten to wake up in time to get ready for her arrival. I said, "I'm naked, Orra, under this sheet. I've been waiting for you. I haven't been asleep."

Her face went empty. She said, "Damn you—why couldn't you wait?" But even while she was saying that, she was taking off her blouse.

I was amazed that she was so docile; and then I saw that it was maybe partly that she didn't want to risk saying no to me—she didn't want me to be hurt and difficult, she didn't want me to explode; she had a kind of hope of making me happy so that I'd then appreciate her and be happy with her and let her know me: I'm putting it badly. But her not being able to say no protected me from having so great a fear of sexual failure that I would not

have been able to be worried about her pleasure, or to be concerned about her in bed. She was very amateurish and unin-
formed in bed, which touched me. It was really sort of poor sex;
she didn't come or even feel much that I could see. Afterwards,
lying beside her, I thought of her eight or ten or fifteen lovers
being afraid of her, afraid to tell her anything about sex in case
they might be wrong. I had an image of them protecting their
own egos, holding their arms around their egos and not letting
her near them. It seemed a kindness embedded in the event that
she was, in quite an obvious way, with a little critical interpretation, a virgin. And impaired, or crippled by having been beautiful, just as I'd thought. I said to myself that it was a matter of
course that I might be deluding myself. But what I did for the
rest of that night—we stayed up all night; we talked, we quarreled for a while, we confessed various things, we argued about
sex, we fucked again (the second one was a little better)—I treat-
ed her with the justice with which I'd treat a boy my age, a
young man, and with a rather exact or measured patience and
tolerance, as if she was a paraplegic and had spent her life in a
wheelchair and was tired of sentiment. I showed her no sentiment
at all. I figured she'd been asphyxiated by the sentiments and
sentimentality of people impressed by her looks. She was beautiful and frightened and empty and shy and alone and wounded
and invulnerable (like a cripple: what more can you do to a cripple?). She was Caesar and ruler of the known world and not Caesar and no one as well.

It was a fairly complicated, partly witty thing to do. It meant I
could not respond to her beauty but had to ignore it. She was a
curious sort of girl; she had a great deal of isolation in her, isolation as a woman. It meant that when she said something on the
order of "You're very defensive," I had to be a debater, her
equal, take her seriously, and say, "How do you mean that?" and
then talk about it, and alternately deliver a blow ("You can't
judge defensiveness, you have the silly irresponsibility of women,
the silly disconnectedness: I *have* to be defensive.") and defer to
her: "You have a point: you think very clearly. All right, I'll
adopt that as a premise." Of course, much of what we said was
incoherent and nonsensical on examination but we worked out in
conversation what we meant or thought we meant. I didn't react
to her in any emotional way. She wasn't really a girl, not really

quite human: how could she be? She was a position, a specific
glory, a trophy, our local upper-middle-class pseudo Cleopatra.
Or not pseudo. I couldn't revel in my luck or be unself-conscious-
ly vain. I could not strut horizontally or loll as if on clouds, a
demi-god with a goddess, although it was clear we were deeply
fortunate, in spite of everything, the poor sex, the difference in
attitude which were all we seemed to share, the tensions and the
blundering. If I enjoyed her more than she enjoyed me, if I lost
consciousness of her even for a moment, she would be closed into
her isolation again. I couldn't love her and have her too. I could
love her and have her if I didn't show love or the symptoms of
having had her. It was like lying in a very lordly way, opening
her to the possibility of feeling by making her comfortable inside
the calm lies of my behavior, my inscribing the minutes with
false messages. It was like meeting a requirement in Greek myth,
like not looking back at Eurydice. The night crept on, swept on,
late minutes, powdered with darkness, in the middle of a sleeping
city, spring crawling like a plague of green snakes, bits of warmth
in the air, at four A.M. smells of leaves when the stink of automo-
biles died down. Dawn came, so pink, so pastel, so silly: we were
talking about the possibility of innate grammatical structures; I
said it was an unlikely notion, that Jews really were God-haunted
(the idea had been broached by a Jew), and the great difficulty
was to invent a just God, that if God appeared at a moment of
time or relied on prophets, there had to be degrees in the possibility of knowing him so that he was by definition unjust; the only
just God would be one who consisted of what had always been
known by everyone; and that you could always identify a basical-
ly Messianic, a hugely religious, fraudulent thinker by how much
he tried to anchor his doctrine to having always been true, to be
innate even in savage man; whereas an honest thinker, a nonliar,
was caught in the grip of the truth of process and change and the
profound absence of justice except as an invention, an attempt by
the will to live with someone, or with many others without consuming them. At that moment Orra said, "I think we're falling in
love."

I figured I had kept her from being too depressed after fucking—it's hard for a girl with any force in her and any brains to
accept the whole thing of fucking, of being fucked without trying

to turn it on its end, so that she does some fucking, or some fucking up; I mean the mere power of arousing the man so he wants to fuck isn't enough: she wants him to be willing to die in order to fuck. There's a kind of strain or intensity women are bred for, as beasts, for childbearing when childbearing might kill them, and childrearing when the child might die at any moment: it's in women to live under that danger, with that risk, that close to tragedy, with that constant taut or casual courage. They need death and nobility near. To be fucked when there's no drama inherent in it, when you're not going to rise to a level of nobility and courage forever denied the male, is to be cut off from what is inherently female, bestially speaking. I wanted to be halfway decent company for her. I don't know that it was natural to me. I am psychologically, profoundly, a transient. A form of trash. I am incapable of any continuing loyalty and silence; I am an informer. But I did all right with her. It was dawn, as I said. We stood naked by the window silently watching the light change. Finally she said, "Are you hungry? Do you want breakfast?"

"Sure. Let's get dressed and go—"

She cut me off; she said with a funny kind of firmness, "No! Let me go and get us something to eat."

"Orra, don't wait on me. Why are you doing this? Don't be like this."

But she was in a terrible hurry to be in love. After those few hours, after that short a time.

She said, "I'm not as smart as you, Wiley. Let me wait on you. Then things will be even."

"Things are even, Orra."

"No. I'm boring and stale. You just think I'm not because you're in love with me. Let me go."

I blinked. After a while, I said, "All right."

She dressed and went out and came back. While we ate, she was silent; I said things but she had no comment to make; she ate very little; she folded her hands and smiled mildly like some nineteenth-century portrait of a handsome young mother. Every time I looked at her, when she saw I was looking at her, she changed the expression on her face to one of absolute and undeviating welcome to me and to anything I might say.

So, it had begun.

3. Orra

She hadn't come. She said she had never come with anyone at any time. She said it didn't matter.

After our first time, she complained. "You went twitch, twitch, twitch—just like a grasshopper." So she had wanted to have more pleasure than she'd had. But after the second fuck and after the dawn, she never complained again—unless I tried to make her come, and then she complained of that. She showed during sex no dislike for any of my sexual mannerisms or for the rhythms and postures I fell into when I fucked. But I was not pleased or satisfied; it bothered me that she didn't come. I was not pleased or satisfied on my own account either. I thought the reason for that was she attracted me more than she could satisfy me, maybe more than fucking could ever satisfy me, that the more you cared, the more undertow there was, so that the sexual thing drowned—I mean the sharpest sensations, and yet the dullest, are when you masturbate—but when you're vilely attached to somebody, there are noises, distractions that drown out the sensations of fucking. For a long time, her wanting to fuck, her getting undressed, and the soft horizontal bobble of her breasts as she lay there, and the soft wavering, the kind of sinewlessness of her legs and lower body with which she more or less showed me she was ready, that was more moving, was more immensely important to me than any mere ejaculation later, any putt-putt-putt in her darkness, any hurling of future generations into the clenched universe, the strict mitten inside her: I clung to her and grunted and anchored myself to the most temporary imaginable relief of the desire I felt for her; I would be hungry again and anxious to fuck again in another twenty minutes; it was pitiable, this sexual disarray. It seemed to me that in the vast spaces of the excitement of being welcomed by each other, we could only sightlessly and at best half-organize our bodies. But so what? We would probably die in these underground caverns; a part of our lives would die; a certain innocence and hope would never survive this: we were too open, too clumsy, and we were the wrong people: so what did a fuck matter? I didn't mind if the sex was always a little rasping, something of a failure, if it was just preparation for more sex in half an hour, if coming was just more foreplay. If this was all that was in store for us, fine. But I thought she was getting gypped in that she felt so much about me, she was dependent, and she was generous, and she didn't come when we fucked.

She said she had never come, not once in her life, and that she didn't need to. And that I mustn't think about whether she came or not. "I'm a sexual tigress," she explained, "and I like to screw but I'm too sexual to come: I haven't that kind of daintiness. I'm not selfish *that* way."

I could see that she had prowled around in a sense and searched out men and asked them to be lovers as she had me rather than wait for them or plot to capture their attention in some subtle way; and in bed she was sexually eager and a bit more forward and less afraid than most girls; but only in an upper-middle-class frame of reference was she *a sexual tigress.*

It seemed to me—my whole self was focused on this—that her not coming said something about what we had, that her not coming was an undeniable fact, a measure of the limits of what we had. I did not think we should think we were great lovers when we weren't.

Orra said we were, that I had no idea how lousy the sex was other people had. I told her that hadn't been my experience. We were, it seemed to me, two twenty-one-year-olds, overeducated, irrevocably shy beneath our glaze of sexual determination and of sexual appetite, and psychologically somewhat slashed up and only capable of being partly useful to each other. We weren't the king and queen of Cockandcuntdom yet.

Orra said coming was a minor part of sex for a woman and was a demeaning measure of sexuality. She said it was imposed as a measure by people who knew nothing about sex and judged women childishly.

It seemed to me she was turning a factual thing, coming, into a public relations thing. But girls were under fearful public pressures in these matters.

When she spoke about them, these matters, she had a little, superior inpuckered look, a don't-make-me-make-mincemeat-of-you-in-argument look—I thought of it as her Orra-as-Orra look, Orra alone, Orra-without-Wiley, without me, Orra isolated and depressed, a terrific girl, an Orra who hated cowing men.

She referred to novels, to novels by women writers, to specific scenes and remarks about sex and coming for women, but I'd read some of those books, out of curiosity, and none of them were literature, and the heroines in them invariably were innocent in every relation; but very strong and very knowing and with terrifically good judgment; and the men they loved were described in such a way they appeared to be examples of the woman's sexual reach, or of her intellectual value, rather than sexual companions or sexual objects; the women had sex generously with men who apparently bored them physically; I had thought the books and their writers and characters sexually naïve.

Very few women, it seemed to me, had much grasp of physical reality. Still, very strange things were often true, and a man's notion of orgasm was necessarily specialized.

When I did anything in bed to excite her with an eye to making her come, she asked me not to, and that irritated the hell out of me. But no matter what she said, it must be bad for her after six years of fucking around not to get to a climax. It had to be that it was a run on her neural patience. How strong could she be?

I thought about how women coming were at such a pitch of uncontrol they might prefer a dumb, careless lover, someone very unlike me: I had often played at being a strong, silent dunce. Some girls became fawning and doglike after they came, even toward dunces. Others jumped up and became immediately tough, proud of themselves as if the coming was *all* to their credit, and I ought to be flattered. God, it was a peculiar world. Brainy girls tended to control their comes, doling out one to a fuck, just like a man; and often they would try to keep that one under control, they would limit it to a single nozzle-contracted squirt of excitement. Even that sometimes racked and emptied them and made them curiously weak and brittle and embarrassed and delicate and lazy. Or they would act bold and say, "God, I needed that."

I wondered how Orra would look, in what way she would do it, a girl like that going off, how she'd hold herself, her eyes, how she'd act toward me when it was over.

To get her to talk about sex at all, I argued that analyzing something destroyed it, of course, but leaves rotted on the ground and prepared the way for what would grow next. So she talked.

She said I was wrong in what I told her I saw and that there was no difference in her between mental and physical excitement, that it wasn't true her mind was excited quickly, and her body slowly, if at all. I couldn't be certain I was right, but when I referred to a moment when there had seemed to be deep physical feeling in her, she sometimes agreed that had been a good moment in her terms; but sometimes she said, no, it had only been a little irritating then, like a peculiarly unpleasant tickle. In spite of her liking my mind, she gave me no authority for what I knew—I mean when it turned out I was right. She kept the authority for her reactions in her own hands. Her self-abnegation was her own doing. I liked that: some people just give you themselves, and it is too much to keep in your hands: your abilities aren't good enough. I decided to stick with what I observed and to think her somewhat mistaken and not to talk to her about sex any more.

I watched her in bed; her body was doubting, grudging, tardy, intolerant—and intolerably hungry—I thought. In her pride and self-consciousness and ignorance she hated all that in herself. She preferred to think of herself as quick, to have pleasure as she willed rather than as she actually had it, to have it on her own volition, to her own prescription, and almost out of politeness, so it seemed to me, to give herself to me, to give me pleasure, to ignore herself, to be a nice girl because she was in love. She insisted on that but that was too sentimental and she also insisted she was, she persuaded herself, she passed herself off as dashing.

In a way, sexually, she was a compulsive liar.

I set myself to remove every iota of misconception I had about Orra in bed, any romanticism, any pleasurable hope. It seemed to me what had happened to her with other boys was that she was distrustful to start with and they had overrated her, and they'd been overwrought and off-balance and uneasy about her judgment of them, and they'd taken their pleasure and run.

And then she had in her determination to have sex become more and more of a sexual fool. (I was all kinds of fool: I didn't mind her being a sexual fool.) The first time I'd gone to bed with her, she'd screamed and thrown herself around, a good two or three feet to one side or another, as she thought a sexual tigress would, I supposed. I'd argued with her afterwards that no one was that excited especially without coming; she said she had come, sort of. She said she was too sexual for most men. She said her reactions weren't fake but represented a real sexuality, a real truth. That proud, stubborn, stupid girl.

But I told her that if she and a man were in sexual congress, and she heaved herself around and threw herself a large number of inches to either the left or the right or even straight up, the man was going to be startled; and if there was no regular pattern or predictability, it was easy to lose an erection; that if she threw herself to the side, there was a good chance she would interrupt the congress entirely unless the man was very quick and scrambled after her, and scrambling after her was not likely to be sexual for him: it would be more like playing tag. The man would have to fuck while in a state of siege; not knowing what she'd do next, he'd fuck and hurry to get it over and to get out.

Orra had said on that first occasion, "That sounds reasonable. No one ever explained that to me before, no one ever made it clear. I'll try it your way for a while."

After that, she had been mostly shy and honest, and honestly lecherous in bed but helpless to excite herself or to do more to me than she did just by being there and welcoming me. As if her hands were webbed and her mind was glued, as if I didn't deserve more, or as if she was such a novice and so shy she could not begin to do anything *sexual*. I did not understand: I'd always found that anyone who *wanted* to give pleasure, could: it didn't take skill, just the desire to please and a kind of, I-don't-know, a sightless ability to feel one's way to some extent in the lightless maze of pleasure. But upper-middle-class girls might be more fearful of tying men to them by bands of excessive pleasure; such girls were careful and shy.

I set myself for her being rude and difficult although she hadn't been rude and difficult to me for a long time but those traits were in her like a shadow giving her the dimensionality that made her valuable to me, that gave point to her kindness toward me. She had the sloppiest and most uncertain and silliest and yet bravest and most generous ego of anyone I'd ever known; and her manners were the most stupid imaginable alternation between the distinguished, the sensitive, the intelligent, with a rueful, firm, almost snotty delicacy and kindness and protectiveness toward you, and the really selfish and bruising. The important thing was to prevent her from responding falsely, as if in a movie, or in some imitation of the movies she'd seen and the books she'd read—she had a curious faith in movies and in books; she admired anything that made her feel and that did not require responsibility from her because then she produced happiness like silk for herself and others. She liked really obscure philosophers, like Hegel, where she could admire the thought but where the thought didn't demand anything from her. Still, she was a realist, and she would probably learn what I knew and would surpass me. She had great possibilities. But she was also merely a good-looking, pseudo-rich girl, a paranoid, a Perkins. On the other hand she was a fairly marvelous girl a lot of the time, brave, eye-shattering, who could split my heart open with one slightly shaky approving-of-me brainy romantic heroine's smile. The romantic splendor of her face. So far in her life she had disappointed everyone. I had to keep all this in mind, I figured. She was fantastically alive and eerily dead at the same time. I wanted for my various reasons to raise her from the dead.

4. Orra: The Same World, a Different Time Scale

One afternoon, things went well for us. We went for a walk, the air was plangent, there was the amazed and polite pleasure we had sometimes merely at being together. Orra adjusted her pace now and then to mine; and I kept mine adjusted to her most of the time. When we looked at each other, there would be small soft puffs of feeling as of toy explosions or sparrows bathing in the dust. Her willed softness, her inner seriousness or earnestness, her strength, her beauty muted and careful now in her anxiety not to lose me yet, made the pleasure of being with her noble, contrapuntal, and difficult in that one had to live up to it and understand it and protect it, against my clumsiness and Orra's falsity, kind as that falsity was; or the day would become simply an exploitation of a strong girl who would see through that sooner or later and avenge it. But things went well; and inside that careless and careful goodness, we went home; we screwed; I came—to get my excitement out of the way; she didn't know I was doing that; she was stupendously polite; taut; and very admiring. "How pretty you are," she said. Her eyes were blurred with half-tears. I'd screwed without any fripperies, coolly, in order to leave in us a large residue of sexual restlessness but with the burr of immediate physical restlessness in me removed: I still wanted her; I always wanted Orra; and the coming had been dull; but my body was not very assertive, was more like a glove for my mind, for my will, for my love for her, for my wanting to make her feel more.

She was slightly tearful, as I said, and gentle, and she held me in her arms after I came, and I said something like, "Don't relax. I want to come again," and she partly laughed, partly sighed, and was flattered, and said, "Again? That's nice." We had a terrific closeness, almost like a man and a secretary—I was free and powerful, and she was devoted: there was little chance Orra would ever be a secretary: she'd been offered executive jobs already for when she finished college, but to play at being a secretary who had no life of her own was a romantic thing for Orra. I felt some apprehension, as before a game of tennis that I wanted to win, or as before stealing something off a counter in a store: there was a dragging enervation, a fear and silence, and there was a lifting, a preparation, a willed and then unwilled, self-contained fixity of purpose; it was a settled thing; it would happen.

After about ten minutes or so, perhaps it was twenty, I moved in her: I should say that while I'd rested, I'd stayed in her (and she'd held on to me). As I'd expected—and with satisfaction and pride that everything was working, my endowments were cooperating—I felt my prick come up; it came up at once with comic promptness but it was sore—Jesus, was it sore. It, its head, ached like hell, with a dry, burning, reddish pain.

The pain made me chary and prevented me from being excited except in an abstract way; my mind was clear; I was idly smiling as I began, moving very slowly, just barely moving, sort of pressing on her inside her, moving around, lollygagging around, feeling out the reaches in there, arranging the space inside her, as if to put the inner soft-oiled shadows in her in order; or like stretching out your hand in the dark and pressing a curve of a blanket into familiarity or to locate yourself when you're half-asleep, when you eyes are closed. In fact, I did close my eyes and listened carefully to her breathing, concentrating on her but trying not to let her see I was doing that because it would make her self-conscious.

Her reaction was so minimal that I lost faith in fucking for getting her started, and I thought I'd better go down on her; I pulled out of her, which wasn't too smart, but I wasn't thinking all that consequentially; she'd told me on other occasions she didn't like "all that foreign la-di-dah," that it didn't excite her, but I'd always thought it was only that she was ashamed of not coming and that made being gone down on hard for her. I started

in on it; she protested; and I pooh-poohed her objections and did
it anyway; I was raw with nerves, with stifled amusement because
of the lying and the tension, so much of it. I remarked to her that
I was going down on her for my own pleasure; I was jolted by
touching her with my tongue there when I was so raw-nerved but
I hid that. It seemed to me physical unhappiness and readiness
were apparent in her skin—my lips and tongue carried the currents of a jagged unhappiness and readiness in her into me; ech-
oes of her stiffness and dissatisfaction sounded in my mouth, my
head, my feet, my entire tired body was a stethoscope. I was
entirely a stethoscope; I listened to her with my *bones;* the glim-
mers of excitement in her traveled to my *spine;* I felt her grinding sexual haltedness, like a car's broken starter motor grinding
away in her, in my *stomach,* in my *knees.* Every part of me
listened to her; every goddamned twinge of muscular contraction
she had that I noticed or that she should have had because I was
licking her clitoris and she didn't have, every testimony of excitement or of no-excitement in her, I listened for so hard it was
amazing it didn't drive her out of bed with self-consciousness; but
she probably couldn't tell what I was doing, since I was out of her
line of sight, was down in the shadows, in the basement of her
field of vision, in the basement with her sexual feelings where
they lay, strewn about.

When she said, "No . . . No, Wiley . . . Please don't. No . . ."
and wiggled, although it wasn't the usual pointless protest that
some girls might make—it was real, she wanted me to stop—I
didn't listen because I could feel she responded to my tongue
more than she had to the fucking a moment before. I could feel
beads sliding and whispering and being strung together rustlingly
in her; the disorder, the scattered or strewn sexual bits, to a very
small extent, were being put in order. She shuddered. With discomfort. She produced, was subjected to, her erratic responses.
And she made odd, small cries, protests mostly, uttered little exclamations that mysteriously were protests although they were
not protests too, cries that somehow suggested the ground of protest kept changing for her.

I tried to string a number of those cries together, to cause them
to occur in a mounting sequence. It was a peculiar attempt: it
seemed we moved, I moved with her, on dark water, between
two lines of buoys, dark on one side, there was nothingness there,

and on the other, lights, red and green, the lights of the body advancing on sexual heat, the signs of it anyway, nipples like scored pebbles, legs lightly thrashing, little *ohs;* nothing important, a body thing; you go on: you proceed.

When we strayed too far, there was nothingness, or only a distant flicker, only the faintest guidance. Sometimes we were surrounded by the lights of her responses, widely spaced, bobbing unevenly, on some darkness, some ignorance we both had, Orra and I, of what were the responses of her body. To the physical things I did and to the atmosphere of the way I did them, to the authority, the argument I made that this was sexual for her, that the way I touched her and concentrated on her, on the partly dream-laden dark water or underwater thing, she responded; she rested on that, rolled heavily on that. Everything I did was speech, was hieroglyphics, pictures on her nerves; it was what masculine authority was for, was what bravery and a firm manner and musculature were supposed to indicate that a man could bring to bed. Or skill at dancing; or musicianliness; or a sad knowingness. Licking her, holding her belly, stroking her belly pretty much with unthought-out movements—sometimes just moving my fingers closer together and spreading them again to show my pleasure, to show how rewarded I felt, not touching her breasts or doing anything so intensely that it would make her suspect me of being out to make her come—I did those things but it seemed like I left her alone and was private with my own pleasures. She felt unobserved with her sensations, she had them without responsibilty, she clutched at them as something round and slippery in the water, and she would fall off them, occasionally gasping at the loss of her balance, the loss of her self-possession too.

I'd flick, idly almost, at her little spaghetti-ending with my tongue, then twice more idly, then three or four or five times in sequence, then settle down to rub it or bounce it between lip and tongue in a steadily more earnest way until my head, my consciousness, my lips and tongue were buried in the dark of an ascending and concentrated rhythm, in the way a stoned dancer lets a movement catch him and wrap him around and become all of him, become his voyage and not a collection of repetitions at all.

Then some boring stringy thing, a sinew at the base of my

tongue, would begin to ache, and I'd break off that movement, and sleepily lick her, or if the tongue was too uncomfortable, I'd worry her clit, I'd nuzzle it with my pursed lips until the muscles that held my lips pursed grew tired in their turn; and I'd go back and flick at her tiny clitoris with my tongue, and go on as before, until the darkness came; she sensed the darkness, the privacy for her, and she seemed like someone in a hallway, unobserved, moving her arms, letting her mind stroke itself, taking a step in that dark.

But whatever she felt was brief and halting; and when she seemed to halt or to be dead or jagged, I authoritatively, gesturally accepted that as part of what was pleasurable to me and did not let it stand as hint or foretaste of failure; I produced sighs of pleasure, even gasps, not all of them false, warm nuzzlings, and caresses that indicated I was rewarded—I produced rewarded strokings; I made elements of sexual pleasure out of moments that were unsexual and that could be taken as the collapse of sexuality.

And she couldn't contradict me because she thought I was working on my own coming, and she loved me and meant to be cooperative.

What I did took nerve because it gave her a tremendous ultimate power to laugh at me, although what the courtship up until now had been for was to show that she was not an enemy, that she could control the hysteria of fear or jealousy in her or the cold judgments in her of me that would lead her to say or do things that would make me hate or fear her; what was at stake included the risk that I would look foolish in my own eyes—and might then attack her for failing to come—and then she would be unable to resist the inward conviction I was a fool. Any attempted act confers vulnerability on you but an act devoted to her pleasure represented doubled vulnerability since only she could judge it; and I was safe only if I was immune or insensitive to her; but if I was immune or insensitive I could not hope to help her come; by making myself vulnerable to her, I was in a way being a sissy or a creep because Orra wasn't organized or trained or prepared to accept responsibility for how I felt about myself: she was a woman who wanted to be left alone; she was paranoid about the inroads on her life men in their egos tried to make: there was dangerous masochism, dangerous hubris, dangerous hopefulness, and a form of love in my doing what I did: I nuzzled nakedly at the crotch of the sexual tigress; any weakness in her ego or her judgment and she would lash out at *me;* and the line was very frail between what I was doing as love and as intrusion, exploitation, and stupid boastfulness. There was no way for me even to begin to imagine the mental pain—or the physical pain—for her if I should fail, and, then to add to that, if I should withdraw from her emotionally too, because of my failure and hers and our pain. Or merely because the failure might make me so uncomfortable I couldn't go on unless she nursed my ego, and she couldn't nurse my ego, she didn't know how to do it, and probably was inhibited about doing it.

Sometimes my hands, my fingers, not just the tips, but all of their inside surface and the palms, held her thighs, or cupped her little belly, or my fingers moved around the lips, the labia or whatever, or even poked a little into her, or with the nails or tips lightly nudged her clitoris, always within a fictional frame of my absolute sexual pleasure, of my admiration for this sex, of there being no danger in it for us. No tongues or brains handy to speak unkindly, I meant. My God, I felt exposed and noble. This was a great effort to make for her.

Perhaps that only indicates the extent of my selfishness. I didn't mind being feminized except for the feeling that Orra would not ever understand what I was doing but would ascribe it to the power of my or our sexuality. I minded being this self-conscious and so conscious of her; I was separated from my own sexuality, from any real sexuality; a poor sexual experience, even one based on love, would diminish the ease of my virility with her at least for a while; and she wouldn't understand. Maybe she would become much subtler and shrewder sexually and know how to handle me but that wasn't likely. And if I apologized or complained or explained in that problematic future why I was sexually a little slow or reluctant with her, she would then blame my having tried to give her orgasm, she would insist I must not be bored again, so I would in that problematic future, if I wanted her to come, have to lie and say I was having more excitement than I felt, and that too might diminish my pleasure. I would be deprived even of the chance for honesty: I would be further feminized in that regard. I thought all this while I went down on her. I didn't put it in words but thought in great misty blocks of something known or sensed. I felt an inner weariness I kept working in spite of. This ignoring myself gave me an odd, starved feeling, a mixture of agony and helplessness. I didn't want to feel like that. I suddenly wondered why in the Theory of Relativity the speed of light is given as a constant: was that more Jewish absolutism? Surely in a universe as changeable and as odd as this one, the speed of light, considering the variety of experiences, must vary; there must be a place where one could see a beam of light struggle to move. I felt silly and selfish; it couldn't be avoided that I felt like that—I mean it couldn't be avoided by *me*.

Whatever she did when I licked her, if she moved at all, if a muscle twitched in her thigh, a muscle twitched in mine, my body imitated hers as if to measure what she felt or perhaps for no reason but only because the sympathy was so intense. The same things happened to each of us but in amazingly different contexts as if we stood at opposite ends of the room and reached out to touch each other and to receive identical messages which then diverged as they entered two such widely separated sensibilities and two such divergent and incomplete ecstasies. The movie we watched was of her discovering how her sexual responses worked: we were seated far apart. My tongue pushed at her erasure, her wronged and heretofore hardly existent sexual powers. I stirred her with varieties of kisses far from her face. A strange river moved slowly, bearing us along, reeds hid the banks, willows braided and unbraided themselves, moaned and whispered, raveled and faintly clicked. Orra groaned, sighed, shuddered, shuddered harshly or liquidly; sometimes she jumped when I changed the pressure or posture of my hands on her or when I rested for a second and then resumed. Her body jumped and contracted interestingly but not at any length or in any pattern that I could understand. My mind grew tired. There is a limit to invention, to mine anyway: I saw myself (stupidly) as a Roman trireme, my tongue as the prow, *bronze*, pushing at her; she was the Mediterranean. Tiers of slaves, my god, the helplessness of them, pulled oars, long stalks that metaphorically and rhythmically bloomed with flowing clusters of short-lived lilies at the water's surface. The pompous and out-of-proportion boat, all of me hunched over Orra's small sea—not actually hunched: what I was, was lying flat, the foot of the bed was at my waist or near there, my legs were out, my feet were propped distantly on the floor, all of me was concentrated on the soft, shivery, furry delicacies of Orra's twat, the pompous boat advanced lickingly, leaving a trickling, gurgling wake of half-response, the ebbing of my will and activity into that fluster subsiding into the dark water of this girl's passivity, taut storminess, and self-ignorance.

The whitish bubbling, the splash of her discontinuous physical response: those waves, ah, that wake rose, curled outward, bubbled, and fell. Rose, curled outward, bubbled, and fell. The white fell of a naiad. In the vast spreading darkness and silence of the sea. There was nothing but that wake. The darkness of my senses when the rhythm absorbed me (so that I vanished from my awareness, so that I was blotted up and was a stain, a squid hidden, stroking Orra) made it twilight or night for me; and my listening for her pleasure, for our track on that markless ocean, gave me the sense that where we were was in a lit-up, great, ill-defined oval of night air and sea and opalescent fog, rainbowed where the lights from the portholes of an immense ship were altered prismatically by droplets of mist—as in some 1930's movie, as in some dream. Often I was out of breath; I saw spots, colors, ocean depths. And her protests, her doubts! My God, her doubts! Her *No don't, Wiley's* and her *I don't want to do this's* and her *Wiley, don't's* and *Wiley, I can't come—don't do this—I don't like this's*. Mostly I ignored her. Sometimes I silenced her by leaning my cheek on her belly and watching my hand stroke her belly and saying to her in a sex-thickened voice, "Orra, I like this—this is for me."

Then I went down on her again with unexpectedly vivid, real pleasure, as if merely thinking about my own pleasure excited and refreshed me, and there was yet more pleasure, when she—reassured or strengthened by my putative selfishness, by the conviction that this was all for me, that nothing was expected of her—cried out. Then a second later she *grunted*. Her whole body rippled. Jesus, I loved it when she reacted to me. It was like causing an entire continent to convulse, Asia, South America. I felt huge and tireless.

In her excitement, she threw herself into the air; but my hands happened to be on her belly; and I fastened her down, I held that part of her comparatively still with her twat fastened to my mouth, and I licked her while she was in mid-heave; and she yelled; I kept my mouth there as if I were drinking from her; I stayed like that until her upper body fell back on the bed and bounced, she made the whole bed bounce; then my head bounced away from her; but I still held her down with my hands; and I fastened myself, my mouth, on her twat again; and she yelled in a deep voice, "*Wiley, what are you doing!*"

Her voice was deep, as if her impulses at that moment were masculine, not out of neurosis but in generosity, in an attempt to improve on the sickliness she accused women of; she wanted to meet me halfway, to share; to share my masculinity: she thought men were beautiful: she cried out, "*I don't want you to do things to me! I want you to have a good fuck!*"

Her voice was deep and despairing, maybe with the despair that goes with surges of sexuality, but then maybe she thought I would make her pay for this. I said, "Orra, I like this stuff, this stuff is what gets me excited." She resisted, just barely, for some infinitesimal fragment of a second, and then her body began to vibrate; it twittered as if in it were the strings of a musical instrument set jangling; she said foolishly—but sweetly—"Wiley, I'm embarrassed, Wiley, this embarrasses *me* . . . Please stop . . . No . . . No . . . No . . . Oh . . . Oh . . . Oh . . . I'm very sexual, I'm too sexual to have orgasms, Wiley, stop, please . . . Oh . . . Oh . . . Oh . . ." And then a deeper shudder ran through her; she gasped; then there was a silence; then she gasped again; she cried out in an extraordinary voice, "*I FEEL SOMETHING!*" The hair stood up on the back of my neck; I couldn't stop; I hurried on; I heard a dim moaning come from her. What had she felt before? I licked hurriedly. How unpleasant for her, how unreal and twitchy had the feelings been that I'd given her? In what way was this different? I wondered if there was in her a sudden swarming along her nerves, a warm conviction of the reality of sexual pleasure. She heaved like a whale—no: not so much as that. But it was as if half an ocean rolled off her young flanks; some element of darkness vanished from the room; some slight color of physical happiness tinctured her body and its thin coating of sweat; I felt it all through me; she rolled on the surface of a pale blue, a pink and blue sea; she was dark and gleaming, and immense and wet. And warm.

She cried, "*Wiley, I feel a lot!*"

God, she was happy.

I said, "Why not?" I wanted to lower the drama quotient; I thought the excess of drama was a mistake, would overburden her. But also I wanted her to defer to me, I wanted authority over her body now, I wanted to make her come.

But she didn't get any more excited than that: she was rigid, almost boardlike after a few seconds. I licked at her thing as best I could but the sea was dry; the board collapsed. I faked it that I was very excited; actually I was so caught up in being sure of myself, I didn't know what I really felt. I thought, as if I was much younger than I was, Boy, if this doesn't work, is my name mud. Then to build up the risk, out of sheer hellish braggadocio, instead of just acting out that I was confident—and in sex, everything unsaid that is portrayed in gestures instead, is twice as powerful—when she said, because the feeling was less for her now, the feeling she liked having gone away, "Wiley, I can't—this is silly—" I said, "Shut up, Orra, I know what I'm doing . . ." But I didn't know.

And I didn't like that tone for sexual interplay either, except as a joke, or as role-playing, because pure authority involves pure submission, and people don't survive pure submission except by being slavishly, possessively, vindictively in love; when they are in love like that, they can *give* you nothing but rebellion and submission, bitchiness and submission; it's a general rottenness: you get no part of them out of bed that has any value; and in bed, you get a grudging submission, because what the slave requires is your total attention, or she starts paying you back; I suppose the model is childhood, that slavery. Anyway I don't like it. But I played at it, then, with Orra, as a gamble.

Everything was a gamble. I didn't know what I was doing; I figured it out as I went along; and how much time did I have for figuring things out just then? I felt strained as at poker or roulette, sweaty and a little stupid, placing bets—with my tongue—and waiting to see what the wheel did, risking my money when no one forced me to, hoping things would go my way, and I wouldn't turn out to have been stupid when this was over.

Also, there were sudden fugitive convulsions of lust now, in sympathy with her larger but scattered responses, a sort of immediate and automatic sexuality—I was at the disposal, inwardly, of the sexuality in her and could not help myself, could not hold it back and avoid the disappointments, and physical impatience, the impatience in my skin and prick, of the huge desire that unmistakably accompanies love, of a primitive longing for what seemed

her happiness, for closeness to her as to something I had studied
and was studying and had found more and more of value in—
what was of value was the way she valued me, a deep, and no
doubt limited (but in the sexual moment it seemed illimitable)
permissiveness toward me, a risk she took, an allowance she made
as if she'd let me damage her and use her badly.

Partly what kept me going was stubbornness because I'd made
up my mind before we started that I wouldn't give up; and partly
what it was was the feeling she aroused in me, a feeling that was,
to be honest, made up of tenderness and concern and a kind of
mere affection, a brotherliness, as if she was my brother, not different from me at all.

Actually this was brought on by an increasing failure, as the sex
went on, of one kind of sophistication—of worldly sophistication—and by the increase in me of another kind, of a childish
sophistication, a growth of innocence: Orra said, or exclaimed, in
a half-harried, half-amazed voice, in a hugely admiring, gratu-
itous way, as she clutched at me in approval, "Wiley, I never had
feelings like these before!"

And to be the first to have caused them, you know? It's like
being a collector, finding something of great value, where it had
been unsuspected and disguised, or like earning any honor; this
partial success, this encouragement gave rise to this pride, this
inward innocence.

Of course that lessened the risk for this occasion; I could fail
now and still say, *It was worth it*, and she would agree; but it
lengthened the slightly longer-term risk; because I might feel tre-
bly a fool someday. Also it meant we might spend months making
love in this fashion—I'd get impotent, maybe not in terms of
erection, but I wouldn't look forward to sex—still, that was beautiful to me in a way too and exciting. I really didn't know what I
was thinking: whatever I thought was part of the sex.

I went on, I wanted to hit the jackpot now. Then Orra shouted,
"It's *there!* It's *THERE!*" I halted, thinking she meant it was in
some specific locale, in some specific motion I'd just made with
my tired tongue and jaw; I lifted my head—but couldn't speak:
in a way, the sexuality pressed on me too hard for me to speak;
anyway I didn't have to; she had lifted her head with a kind of
overt twinship and she was looking at me down the length of her
body; her face was askew and boyish—every feature was wrin-

kled; she looked angry and yet naïve and swindleable; she said angrily, naïvely, "*Wiley, it's there!*"

But even before she spoke that time, I knew she'd meant it was in her; the fox had been startled from its covert again; she had seen it, had felt it run in her again. She had been persuaded that it was in her for good.

I started manipulating her delicately with my hand; and in my own excitement, and thinking she was ready, I sort of scrambled up and covering her with myself, and playing with her with one hand, guided my other self, my lower consciousness, into her. My God, she was warm and restless inside; it was heated in there and smooth, insanely smooth, and oiled, and full of movements. But I knew at once I'd made a mistake: I should have gone on licking her; there were no regular contractions; she was anxious for the prick, she rose around it, closed around it, but in a rigid, dumb, far-away way; and her twitchings played on it, ran through it, through the walls of it and into me; and they were uncontrolled and not exciting, but empty; she didn't know what to do, how to be fucked and come. I couldn't pull out of her, I didn't want to, I couldn't pull out; but if there were no contractions for me to respond to, how in hell would I find the rhythm for her? I started slowly with what seemed infinite suggestiveness to me, with great dirtiness, a really grownup sort of fucking—just in case she was far along—and she let out a huge, shuddering hour-long sigh and cried out my name and then in a sobbing, exhausted voice, said, "I lost it . . . Oh Wiley, I lost it . . . Let's stop . . ." My face was above hers; her face was wet with tears; why was she crying like that? She had changed her mind; now she wanted to come; she turned her head back and forth; she said, "I'm no good . . . I'm no good . . . Don't worry about me . . . You come . . ."

No matter what I mumbled, "Hush," and "Don't be silly," and in a whisper, "Orra, I love you," she kept on saying those things until I slapped her lightly and said, "*Shut up, Orra.*"

Then she was silent again.

The thing was, apparently, that she was arhythmic: at least that's what I thought; and that meant there weren't going to be regular contractions; any rhythm for me to follow; and, any rhythm I set up as I fucked, she broke with her movements: so that it was that when she moved, she made her excitement go away: it would be best if she moved very smally: but I was afraid to tell her that, or even to try to hold her hips firmly, and guide them, to instruct her in that way for fear she'd get self-conscious and lose what momentum she'd won. And also I was ashamed that I'd stopped going down on her. I experimented—doggedly, sweatily, to make up for what I'd done—with fucking in different ways, and I fantasized about us being in Mexico, some place warm and lushly colored where we made love easily and filthily and graphically. The fantasy kept me going. That is, it kept me hard. I kept acting out an atmosphere of sexual pleasure—I mean of my sexual pleasure—for her to rest on, so she could count on that. I discovered that a not very slow sort of one-one-one stroke, or fuck-fuck-fuck-Orra-now-now-now really got to her; her feelings would grow heated; and she could shift up from that with me into a one-two, one-two, one-two, her excitement rising; but if she or I then tried to shift up farther to one-two-three, one-two-three, one-two-three, she'd lose it all. That was too complicated for her: my own true love, my white American. But her feelings when they were present were very strong, they came in gusts, huge squalls of heat as if from a furnace with a carelessly banging door, and they excited and allured both of us. That excitement and the dit-dit-ditting got to her; she began to be generally, continuingly sexual. It's almost standard to compare sexual excitement to holiness; well, after a while, holiness seized her; she spoke with tongues, she testified. She was shaking all over; she was saved temporarily and sporadically; that is, she kept lapsing out of that excitement too. But it would recur. Her hands would flutter; her face would be pale and then red, then very, very red; her eyes would stare at nothing; she'd call my name. I'd plug on one-one-one, then one-two, one-two, then I'd go back to one-one-one: I could see as before—in the deep pleasure I felt even in the midst of the labor—why a man might kill her in order to stimulate in her (although he might not know this was why he did it) these signs of pleasure. The familiar Orra had vanished; she said, "GodohGodohGod"; it was sin and redemption and holiness and visions time. Her throbs were very direct, easily comprehensible, but without any pattern; they weren't in any regular sequence; still, they were exciting to me, maybe all the more exciting because of the piteousness of her not being able to regulate them, of their being like blows delivered inside her by an enemy whom she couldn't even half-domesticate or make friendly to herself or speak to. She was the most out-of-control girl I ever screwed. She would at times start to thrust like a woman who had her sexuality readied and well-understood at last and I'd start to distend with anticipation and a pride and relief as large as a house; but after two thrusts—or four, or six—she'd have gotten too excited, she'd be shaking, she'd thrust crookedly and out of tempo, the movement would collapse; or she'd suddenly jerk in mid-movement without warning and crash around with so great and so meaningless a violence that she'd lose her thing; and she'd start to cry. She'd whisper wetly, "I lost it"; so I'd say, "No you didn't," and I'd go on or start over, one-one-one; and of course, the excitement would come back; sometimes it came back at once; but she was increasingly afraid of herself, afraid to move her lower body; she would try to hold still and just *receive* the excitement; she would let it pool up in her; but then too she'd begin to shake more and more; she'd leak over into spasmodic and oddly sad, too large movements; and she'd whimper, knowing, I suppose, that those movements were breaking the tempo in herself; again and again, tears streamed down her cheeks; she said in a not quite hoarse, in a sweet, almost hoarse whisper, "I don't want to come, Wiley, you go ahead and come."

My mind had pretty much shut off; it had become exhausted; and I didn't see how we were going to make this work; she said, "Wiley, it's all right—please, it's all right—I don't want to come."

I wondered if I should say something and try to trigger some fantasy in her; but I didn't want to risk saying something she'd find unpleasant or think was a reproach or a hint for her to be sexier. I thought if I just kept on dit-dit-ditting, sooner or later, she'd find it in herself, the trick of riding on her feelings, and getting them to rear up, crest, and topple. I held her tightly, in sympathy and pity, and maybe fear, and admiration: she was so unhysterical; she hadn't yelled at me or broken anything; she hadn't ordered me around: she was simply alone and shaking in the middle of a neural storm in her that she seemed to have no gift for handling. I said, "Orra, it's OK: I really prefer long fucks," and I went on, dit-dit-dit-dit, then I'd shift up to dit-dot, dit-dot, dit-dot, dit-dot . . . My back hurt, my legs were going; if sweat was sperm, we would have looked like liquefied snow fields.

Orra made noises, more and more quickly, and louder and louder; then the noises she made slackened off. Then, step by step, with shorter and shorter strokes, then out of control and clumsy, simply reestablishing myself inside the new approach, I settled down, fucked slowly. The prick was embedded far in her; I barely stirred; the drama of sexual movement died away, the curtains were stilled; there was only sensation on the stage.

I bumped against the stone blocks and hidden hooks that nipped and bruised me into the soft rottenness, the strange, glowing, breakable hardness of coming, of the sensations at the approaches to coming.

I panted and half-rolled and pushed and edged it in, and slid it back, sweatily—I was semi-expert, aimed, intent: sex can be like a wilderness that imprisons you: the daimons of the locality claim you: I was achingly nagged by sensations; my prick had been somewhat softened before and now it swelled with a sore-headed, but fine distention; Orra shuddered and held me cooperatively; I began to forget her.

I thought she was making herself come on the slow fucking, on the prick which, when it was seated in her like this, when I hardly moved it, seemed to belong to her as much as to me; the prick seemed to *enter* me too; we both seemed to be sliding on it, the sensation was like that; but there was the moment when I became suddenly aware of her again, of the flesh and blood and bone in my arms, beneath me. I had a feeling of grating on her, and of her grating on me. I didn't recognize the unpleasantness at first. I don't know how long it went on before I felt it as a withdrawal in her, a withdrawal that she had made, a patient and restrained horror in her, and impatience in me: our arrival at sexual shambles.

My heart filled suddenly—filled; and then all feeling ran out of it—it emptied itself.

I continued to move in her slowly, numbly, in a shabby hubbub of faceless shudderings and shufflings of the mid-section and half-thrusts, half-twitches; we went on holding each other, in silence, without slackening the intensity with which we held each other; our movements, that flopping in place, that grinding against each other, went on; neither of us protested in any way. Bad sex can be sometimes stronger and more moving than good sex. She made

sobbing noises—and held on to me. After a while sex seemed very
ordinary and familiar and unromantic. I started going dit-dit-dit
again.

Her hips jerked up half a dozen times before it occurred to me
again that she liked to thrust like a boy, that she wanted to thrust,
and then it occurred to me she wanted me to thrust.

I maneuvered my ass slightly and tentatively delivered a shove,
or rather, delivered an authoritative shove, but not one of great
length, one that was exploratory; Orra sighed, with relief it
seemed to me; and jerked, encouragingly, too late, as I was pulling back. When I delivered a second thrust, a somewhat more
obvious one, more amused, almost boyish, I was like a boy whipping a fairly fast ball in a game, at a first baseman—she jerked
almost wolfishly, gobbling up the extravagant power of the gesture, of the thrust; with an odd shudder of pleasure, of irresponsibility, of boyishness, I suddenly realized how physically strong
Orra was, how well-knit, how well put together her body was,
how great the power in it, the power of endurance in it; and a
phrase—absurd and demeaning but exciting just then—came into
my head: *to throw a fuck;* and I settled myself atop her, braced
my toes and knees and elbows and hands on the bed and half-
scramblingly worked *it—it* was clearly mine; but I was Orra's—
worked *it* into a passionate shove, a curving stroke about a third
as long as a full stroke; but amateur and gentle, that is, tentative
still; and Orra screamed then; how she screamed; she made
known her readiness: then the next time, she grunted: "Uhnnn-
nahhhhhh . . ." a sound thick at the beginning but that trailed
into refinement, into sweetness, a lingering sweetness.

It seemed to me I really wanted to fuck like this, that *I* had
been waiting for this all my life. But it wasn't really my taste,
that kind of fuck: I liked to throw a fuck with less force and more
gradations and implications of force rather than with the actual
thing; and with more immediate contact between the two sets of
pleasures and with more admissions of defeat and triumph; my
pleasure was a thing of me reflecting her; her spirit entering me;
or perhaps it was merely a mistake, my thinking that; but it
seemed shameful and automatic, naïve and animal: to throw the
prick into her like that.

She took the thrust: she convulsed a little; she fluttered all over;
her skin fluttered; things twitched in her, in the disorder sur-

rounding the phallic blow in her. After two thrusts, she collapsed, went flaccid, then toughened and readied herself again, rose a bit from the bed, aimed the flattened, mysteriously funnel-like container of her lower end at me, too high, so that I had to pull her down with my hands on her butt or on her hips; and her face, when I glanced at her beneath my lids, was fantastically pleasing, set, concentrated, busy, harassed; her body was strong, was stone, smooth stone and wet-satin paper bags and snaky webs, thin and alive, made of woven snakes that lived, thrown over the stone; she held the great, writhing-skinned stone construction toward me, the bony marvel, the half-dish of bone with its secretive, gluey-smooth entrance, *the place where I was*—it was undefined, except for that: *the place where I was:* she took and met each thrust—and shuddered and collapsed and rose again: she seemed to rise to the act of taking it; I thought she was partly mistaken, childish, to think that the center of sex was to meet and take the prick thrown into her as hard as it could be thrown, now that she was excited; but there was a weird wildness, a wild freedom, like children cavorting, uncontrolled, set free, but not hysterical merely without restraint; the odd, thickened, knobbed pole springing back and forth as if mounted on a web of wide rubber bands; it was a naïve and a complete release. I whomped it in and she went, "UHNNN!" and a half-iota of a second later, I was seated all the way in her, I jerked a minim of an inch deeper in her, and went "UHNNN!" too. Her whole body shook. She would go, "UHN!" And I would go, "UHN!"

Then when it see.ned from her strengthening noises and her more rapid and jerkier movements that she was near the edge of coming, I'd start to place whomps, in neater and firmer arrangements, more obviously in a rhythm, more businesslike, more teasing with pauses at each end of a thrust; and that would excite her up to a point; but then her excitement would level off, and not go over the brink. So I would speed up: I'd thrust harder, then harder yet, then harder and faster; she made her noises and half-thrust back. She bit her lower lip; she set her teeth in her lower lip; blood appeared. I fucked still faster, but on a shorter stroke, almost thrumming on her, and angling my abdomen hopefully to drum on her clitoris; sometimes her body would go limp; but her cries would speed up, bird after bird flew out of her mouth while she lay limp as if I were a boxer and had destroyed her ability to

move; then when the cries did not go past a certain point, when
she didn't come, I'd slow and start again. I wished I'd been a
great athlete, a master of movement, a woman, a lesbian, a man
with a gigantic prick that would explode her into coming. I
moved my hands to the corners of the mattress; and spread my
legs; I braced myself with my hands and feet; and braced like
that, free-handed in a way, drove into her; and the new posture,
the feeling she must have had of being covered; and perhaps the
difference in the thrust got to her; but Orra's body began to set
up a babble, a babble of response then—I think the posture
played on her mind.

But she did not come.

I moved my hands and held the dish of her hips so that she
couldn't wiggle or deflect the thrust or pull away: she began to
"Uhn" again but interspersed with small screams: we were like
kids playing catch (her poor brutalized clitoris), playing hard
hand: this was what she thought sex was; it was sexual, as throwing a ball hard is sexual; in a way, too, we were like acrobats
hurling ourselves at each other, to meet in mid-air, and fall entangled to the net. It was like that.

Her mouth came open, her eyes had rolled to one side and
stayed there—it felt like twilight to me—I knew where she was
sexually, or thought I did. She pushed, she egged us on. She
wasn't breakable this way. Orra. I wondered if she knew, it made
me like her how naïve this was, this American fuck, this kids-
playing-at-twilight-on-the-neighborhood-street fuck. After I seated it and wriggled a bit in her and moozed on her clitoris with
my abdomen, I would draw it out not in a straight line but at
some curve so that it would press against the walls of her cunt
and she could keep track of where it was; and I would pause
fractionally just before starting to thrust, so she could brace herself and expect it; I whomped it in and understood her with an
absurd and probably unfounded sense of my sexual virtuosity;
and she became silent suddenly, then she began to breathe loudly,
then something in her toppled; or broke, then all once she shuddered in a different way. It really was as if she lay on a bed of
wings, as if she had a half-dozen wings folded under her, six huge
wings, large, veined, throbbing, alive wings, real ones, with fleshy
edges from which glittering feathers spring backwards; and they
all stirred under her.

She half-rose; and I'd hold her so she didn't fling herself around and lose her footing, or her airborneness, on the uneasy glass mountain she'd begun to ascend, the frail transparency beneath her, that was forming and growing beneath her, that seemed to me to foam with light and darkness, as if we were rising above a landscape of hedges and moonlight and shadows: a mountain, a sea that formed and grew; it grew and grew; and she said "OH!" and "OIIIIIIH!" almost with vertigo, as if she was airborne but unsteady on the vans of her wings, and as if I was there without wings but by some magic dispensation and by some grace of familiarity; I thunked on and on, and she looked down and was frightened; the tension in her body grew vast; and suddenly a great, a really massive violence ran through her but now it was as if, in fear at her height or out of some automatism, the first of her three pairs of wings began to beat, great fans winnowingly, great wings of flesh out of which feathers grew, catching at the air, stabilizing and yet lifting her: she whistled and rustled so; she was at once so still and so violent; the great wings engendered, their movement engendered in her, patterns of flexed and crossed muscles: her arms and legs and breasts echoed or carried out the strain, or strained to move the weight of those winnowing, moving wings. Her breaths were wild but not loud and slanted every which way, irregular and new to this particular dream, and very much as if she looked down on great spaces of air; she grabbed at me, at my shoulders, but she had forgotten how to work her hands, her hands just made the gestures of grabbing, the gestures of a well-meaning, dark but beginning to be luminous, mad, amnesiac angel. She called out, "Wiley, Wiley!" but she called it out in a *whisper,* the whisper of someone floating across a night sky, of someone crazily ascending, someone who was going crazy, who was taking on the mad purity and temper of angels, someone who was tormented unendurably by this, who was unendurably frightened, whose pleasure was enormous, half-human, mad. Then she screamed in rebuke, "Wiley!" She screamed my name: "*Wiley!*"—she did it hoarsely and insanely, asking for help, but blaming me, and merely as exclamation; it was a gutter sound in part, and ugly; the ugliness, when it destroyed nothing, or maybe it had an impetus of its own, but it whisked away another covering, a membrane of ordinariness—I don't know—and her second pair of wings began to beat; her whole body was aflutter on the bed. I

was as wet as—as some fish, thonking away, sweatily. Grinding
away. I said, "It's OK, Orra. It's OK." And poked on. In mid-air.
She shouted, "*What is this!*" She shouted it in the way a tremen-
dously large person who can defend herself might shout at someone who was unwisely beating her up. She shouted—angrily, as
an announcement of anger, it seemed—"*Oh my God!*" Like:
Who broke this cup? I plugged on. She raised her torso, her head,
she looked me clearly in the eye, her eyes were enormous, were
bulging, and she said "*Wiley, it's happening!*" Then she lay
down again and screamed for a couple of seconds. I said a little
dully, grinding on, "It's OK, Orra, It's OK," I didn't want to say
Let go or to say anything lucid because I didn't know a damn
thing about female orgasm after all, and I didn't want to give her
any advice and wreck things; and also I didn't want to commit
myself in case this turned out to be a false alarm; and we had to
go on. I pushed in, lingered, pulled back, went in, only half on
beat, one-thonk-one-thonk, then one-one-one, saying, "This is
sexy, this is good for me, Orra, this is very good for me," and
then, "Good Orra," and she trembled in a new way at that,
"*Good* Orra," I said, "*Good . . . Orra*," and then all at once, it
happened. Something pulled her over; and something gave in;
and all three pairs of wings began to beat: she was the center and
the source and the victim of a storm of wing beats; we were at
the top of the world; the huge bird of God's body in us hovered;
the great miracle pounded on her back, pounded around us; she
was straining and agonized and distraught, estranged within this
corporeal-incorporeal thing, this angelic other avatar, this other
substance of herself: the wings were outspread; they thundered
and gaspily galloped with her; they half broke her; and she
screamed, "*Wiley!*" and "*Mygodmygod*" and "*IT'S NOT STOP-
PING, WILEY, IT'S NOT STOPPING!*" She was pale *and* red;
her hair was everywhere; her body was wet, and thrashing. It was
as if something unbelievably strange and fierce—like the holy
temper—lifted her to where she could not breathe or walk: she
choked in the ether, a scrambling seraph, tumbling, and aflame
and alien, powerful beyond belief, hideous and frightening and
beautiful beyond the reach of the human. A screaming child, an
angel howling in the Godly sphere: she churned without delicacy,
as wild as an angel bearing threats; her body lifted from the
sheets, fell back, lifted again; her hands beat on the bed; she

made very loud hoarse tearing noises—I was frightened for her: this was her first time after six years of playing around with her body. It hurt her; her face looked like something made of stone, a monstrous carving; only her body was alive; her arms and legs were outspread and tensed and they beat or they were weak and fluttering. She was an angel as brilliant as a beautiful insect infinitely enlarged and irrevocably foreign: she was unlike me: she was a girl making rattling, astonished, uncontrolled, unhappy noises, a girl looking shocked and intent and harassed by the variety and viciousness of the sensations, including relief, that attacked her. I sat up on my knees and moved a little in her and stroked her breasts, with smooth sideways, winglike strokes. And she screamed, *"Wiley, I'm coming!"* and with a certain idiocy entered on her second orgasm or perhaps her third since she'd started to come a few minutes before; and we should have gone on for hours but she said, "It hurts, Wiley, I hurt, make it stop . . ." So I didn't move; I just held her thighs with my hands; and her things began to trail off, to trickle down, into little shiverings; the stoniness left her face; she calmed into moderated shudders, and then she said, she started to speak with wonder but then it became an exclamation and ended on a kind of a hollow note, the prelude to a small scream: she said "I *came* . . ." Or "I ca-a-a-ammmmmmmme . . ." What happened was that she had another orgasm at the thought that she'd had her first.

That one was more like three little ones, diminishing in strength. When she was quieter, she was gasping, she said, "Oh you *love* me . . ."

That too excited her. When that died down, she said—angrily—"I always knew they were doing it wrong, I always knew there was nothing wrong with me . . ." And that triggered a little set of ripples. Some time earlier, without knowing it, I'd begun to cry. My tears fell on her thighs, her belly, her breasts, as I moved up, along her body, above her, to lie atop her. I wanted to hold her, my face next to hers; I wanted to hold her. I slid my arms in and under her, and she said, "Oh, Wiley," and she tried to lift her arms, but she started to shake again; then trembling anyway, she lifted her arms and hugged me with a shuddering sternness that was unmistakable; then she began to cry too.

The Moon in Its Flight

GILBERT SORRENTINO

THIS WAS IN 1948. A group of young people sitting on the darkened porch of a New Jersey summer cottage in a lake resort community. The host some Bernie wearing an Upsala College sweat shirt. The late June night so soft one can, in retrospect, forgive America for everything. There were perhaps eight or nine people there, two of them the people that this story sketches.

Bernie was talking about Sonny Stitt's alto on "That's Earl, Brother." As good as Bird, he said. Arnie said, bullshit: he was a very hip young man from Washington Heights, wore mirrored sunglasses. A bop drummer in his senior year at the High School of Performing Arts. Our young man, nineteen at this time, listened only to Rebecca, a girl of fifteen, remarkable in her New Look clothes. A long full skirt, black, snug tailored shirt of blue and white stripes with a high white collar and black velvet string tie, black kid Capezios. It is no wonder that lesbians like women.

At some point during the evening he walked Rebecca home. She lived on Lake Shore Drive, a wide road that skirted the beach and ran parallel to the small river that flowed into Lake Minnehaha. Lake Ramapo? Lake Tomahawk. Lake O-shi-wa-noh? Lake Sunburst. Leaning against her father's powder-blue Buick convertible, lost, in the indigo night, the creamy stars, sound of crickets, they kissed. They fell in love.

One of the songs that summer was "For Heaven's Sake." Another, "It's Magic." Who remembers the clarity of Claude Thornhill and Sarah Vaughan, their exquisite irrelevance? They are gone where the useless chrome doughnuts on the Buick's hood

34

have gone. That Valhalla of Amos 'n' Andy and guinea fruit peddlers with golden earings. "Pleasa No Squeeza Da Banana." In 1948, the whole world seemed beautiful to young people of a certain milieu, or let me say, possible. Yes, it seemed a possible world. This idea persisted until 1950, at which time it died, along with many of the young people who had held it. In Korea, the Chinese played "Scrapple from the Apple" over loudspeakers pointed at the American lines. That savage and virile alto blueclear on the sub-zero night. This is, of course, old news.

Rebecca was fair. She was fair. Lovely Jewish girl from the remote and exotic Bronx. To him that vast borough seemed a Cythera—that it could house such fantastic creatures as she! He wanted to be Jewish. He was, instead, a Roman Catholic, awash in sin and redemption. What loathing he had for the Irish girls who went to eleven o'clock Mass, legions of blushing pink and lavender spring coats, flat white straw hats, the crinkly veils over their open faces. Church clothes, under which their inviolate crotches sweetly nestled in soft hair.

She had white and perfect teeth. Wide mouth. Creamy stars, pale nights. Dusty black roads out past the beach. The sunlight on the raft, moonlight on the lake. Sprinkle of freckles on her shoulders. Aromatic breeze.

Of course this was a summer romance, but bear with me and see with what banal literary irony it all turns out—or does not turn out at all. The country bowled and spoke of Truman's grit and spunk. How softly we had slid off the edge of civilization.

The liquid moonlight filling the small parking area outside the gates to the beach. Bass flopping softly in dark waters. What was the scent of the perfume she wore? The sound of a car radio in the cool nights, collective American memory. Her browned body, delicate hair bleached golden on her thighs. In the beach pavilion they danced and drank Cokes. Mel Tormé and the Mell-Tones. Dizzy Gillespie. "Too Soon To Know." In the mornings, the sun so crystal and lucent it seemed the very exhalation of the sky, he would swim alone to the raft and lie there, the beach empty, music from the pavilion attendant's radio coming to him in splinters. At such times he would thrill himself by pretending that he had not yet met Rebecca and that he would see her that afternoon for the first time.

The first time he touched her breasts he cried in his shame and delight. Can all this really have taken place in America? The trees rustled for him, as the rain did rain. One day, in New York, he bought her a silver friendship ring, tiny perfect hearts in bas-relief running around it so that the point of one heart nestled in the cleft of another. Innocent symbol that tortured his blood. She stood before him in the pale light in white bra and panties, her shorts and blouse hung on the hurricane fence of the abandoned and weed-grown tennis court and he held her, stroking her flanks and buttocks and kissing her shoulders. The smell of her flesh, vague sweat and perfume. Of course he was insane. She caressed him so far as she understood how through his faded denim shorts. Thus did they flay themselves, burning. What were they to do? Where were they to go? The very thought of the condom in his pocket made his heart careen in despair. Nothing was like any-thing said it was after all. He adored her.

She was entering her second year at Evander Childs that com-ing fall. He hated this school he had never seen, and hated all her fellow students. He longed to be Jewish, dark and mysterious and devoid of sin. He stroked her hair and fingered her nipples, mas-turbated fiercely on the dark roads after he had seen her home. Why didn't he at lease *live* in the Bronx?

Any fool can see that with the slightest twist one way or anoth-er all of this is fit material for a sophisticated comic's routine. David Steinberg, say. One can hear his precise voice recording these picayune disasters as jokes. Yet all that moonlight was real. He kissed her luminous fingernails and died over and over again. The maimings of love are endlessly funny, as are the tiny figures of talking animals being blown to pieces in cartoons.

It was this same youth who, three years later, ravished the whores of Mexican border towns in a kind of drunken hilarity, falling down in the dusty streets of Nuevo Laredo, Villa Acuña, and Piedras Negras, the pungency of the overpowering perfume wedded to his rumpled khakis, his flowered shirt, his scuffed and beer-spattered low quarters scraping across the thresholds of the Blue Room, Ofelia's, The 1-2-3 Club, Felicia's, the Cadillac, Tres Hermanas. It would be a great pleasure for me to allow him to meet her there, in a yellow chiffon cocktail dress and spike heels, lost in prostitution.

One night, a huge smiling Indian whore bathed his member in gin as a testament to the strict hygiene she claimed to practice and he absurdly thought of Rebecca, that he had never seen her naked, nor she him, as he was now in the Hollywood pink light of the whore's room, Jesus hanging in his perpetual torture from the wall above the little bed. The woman was gentle, the light glinting off her gold incisor and the tiny cross at her throat. You good fuck, Jack, she smiled in her lying whore way. He felt her flesh again warm in that long-dead New Jersey sunlight. Turn that into a joke.

They were at the amusement park at Lake Hopatcong with two other couples. A hot and breathless night toward the end of August, the patriotic smell of hot dogs and french fries in the still air. Thin and cranky music from the carrousel easing through the sparsely planted trees down toward the shore. She was pale and sweating, sick, and he took her back to the car and they smoked. They walked to the edge of the black lake stretching out before them, the red and blue neon on the far shore clear in the hot dark.

He wiped her forehead and stroked her shoulders, worshiping her pain. He went to get a Coke and brought it back to her, but she only sipped at it, then said O God! and bent over to throw up. He held her waist while she vomited, loving the waste and odor of her. She lay down on the ground and he lay next to her, stroking her breasts until the nipples were erect under her cotton blouse. My period, she said. God, it just ruins me at the beginning. You bleeding, vomiting, incredible thing, he thought. You should have stayed in, he said. The moonlight of her teeth. I didn't want to miss a night with you, she said. It's August. Stars, my friend, great flashing stars fell on Alabama.

They stood in the dark in the driving rain underneath her umbrella. Where could it have been? Nokomis Road? Bliss Lane? Kissing with that trapped yet wholly innocent frenzy peculiar to American youth of that era. Her family was going back to the city early the next morning and his family would be leaving toward the end of the week. They kissed, they kissed. The angels sang. Where could they go, out of this driving rain?

Isn't there anyone, any magazine writer or avant-garde film-

maker, any lover of life or dedicated optimist out there who will
move them toward a cottage, already closed for the season, in
whose split log exterior they will find an unlocked door? Inside
there will be a bed, whiskey, an electric heater. Or better, a fireplace. White lamps, soft lights. Sweet music. A radio on which
they will get Cooky's Caravan or Symphony Sid. Billy Eckstine
will sing "My Deep Blue Dream." Who can bring them to each
other and allow him to enter her? Tears of gratitude and release,
the sublime and elegantly shadowed configuration their tanned
legs will make lying together. This was in America, in 1948. Not
even fake art or the wearisome tricks of movies can assist them.

She tottered, holding the umbrella crookedly while he went to
his knees and clasped her, the rain soaking him through, put his
head under her skirt and kissed her belly, licked at her crazily
through her underclothes.

All you modern lovers, freed by Mick Jagger and the orgasm,
give them, for Christ's sake, for an hour, the use of your really
terrific little apartment. They won't smoke your marijuana nor
disturb your Indiana graphics. They won't borrow your Fanon or
Cleaver or Barthelme or Vonnegut. They'll make the bed before
they leave. They whisper good night and dance in the dark.

She was crying and stroking his hair. Ah God, the leaves of
brown came tumbling down, remember? He watched her go into
the house and saw the door close. Some of his life washed away in
the rain dripping from his chin.

A girl named Sheila whose father owned a fleet of taxis gave a
reunion party in her parents' apartment in Forest Hills. Where
else would it be? I will insist on purchased elegance or nothing.
None of your warm and cluttered apartments in this story, cats on
the stacks of books, and so on. It was the first time he had ever
seen a sunken living room and it fixed his idea of the good life
forever after. Rebecca was talking to Marv and Robin, who were
to be married in a month. They were Jewish, incredibly and won-
drously Jewish, their parents smiled upon them and loaned them
money and cars. He skulked in his loud Brooklyn clothes.

I'll put her virgin flesh into a black linen suit, a single strand of
pearls around her throat. Did I say that she had honey-colored
hair? Believe me when I say he wanted to kiss her shoes.

Everybody was drinking Cutty Sark. This gives you an idea,

not of who they were, but of what they thought they were. They
worked desperately at it being August, but under the sharkskin
and nylons those sunny limbs were hidden. Sheila put on "In the
Still of the Night" and all six couples got up to dance. When he
held her he thought he would weep.

He didn't want to hear about Evander Childs or Gun Hill Road
or the 92nd Street Y. He didn't want to know what the pre-med
student she was dating said. Whose hand had touched her secret
thighs. It was most unbearable since this phantom knew them in a
specifically erotic way that he did not. He had touched them
decorated with garters and stockings. Different thighs. She had
been to the Copa, to the Royal Roost, to Lewisohn Stadium to
hear the Gershwin concert. She talked about *The New Yorker* and
Vogue, e.e. cummings. She flew before him, floating in her black
patent I. Miller heels.

Sitting together on the bed in Sheila's parents' room, she told
him that she still loved him, she would always love him, but it
was so hard not to go out with a lot of other boys, she had to keep
her parents happy. They were concerned about him. They didn't
really know him. He wasn't Jewish. All right. All right. But did
she have to let Shelley? Did she have to go to the Museum of
Modern Art? The Met? Where were these places? What is the
University of Miami? Who is Brooklyn Law? What sort of god
borrows a Chrysler and goes to the Latin Quarter? What is a
supper club? What does Benedictine cost? Her epic acts, his
Flagg Brothers shoes.

There was one boy who had almost made her. She had allowed
him to take off her blouse and skirt, nothing else! at a CCNY
sophomore party. She was a little high and he—messed—all over
her slip. It was wicked and she was ashamed. Battering his heart
in her candor. Well, I almost slipped too, he lied, and was terrified that she seemed relieved. He got up and closed the door,
then lay down on the bed with her and took off her jacket and
brassiere. She zipped open his trousers. Long enough! Sheila said,
knocking on the door, then opening it to see him with his head on
her breasts. Oh, oh, she said, and closed the door. Of course, it
was all ruined. We got rid of a lot of these repressed people in the
next decade, and now we all are happy and free.

At three o'clock, he kissed her good night on Yellowstone Boulevard in a thin drizzle. Call me, he said, and I'll call you. She

went into her glossy Jewish life, toward mambos and the Blue Angel.

Let me come and sleep with you. Let me lie in your bed and look at you in your beautiful pajamas. I'll do anything you say. I'll honor the beautiful father and mother. I'll hide in the closet and be no trouble. I'll work as a stock boy in your father's beautiful sweater factory. It's not my fault I'm not Marvin or Shelley. I don't even know where CCNY is! Who is Conrad Aiken? What is Bronx Science? Who is Berlioz? What is a Stravinsky? How do you play Mah-Jongg? What is schmooz, schlepp, Purim, Moo Goo Gai Pan? Help me.

When he got off the train in Brooklyn an hour later, he saw his friends through the window of the all-night diner, pouring coffee into the great pit of their beer drunks. He despised them as he despised himself and the neighborhood. He fought against the thought of her so that he would not have to place her subtle finesse in these streets of vulgar hells, benedictions, and incense.

On Christmas Eve, he left the office party at two, even though one of the file girls, her Catholicism temporarily displaced by Four Roses and ginger, stuck her tongue into his mouth in the stock room.

Rebecca was outside, waiting on the corner of 46th and Broadway, and they clasped hands, oh briefly, briefly. They walked aimlessly around in the gray bitter cold, standing for a while at the Rockefeller Center rink, watching the people who owned Manhattan. When it got too cold, they walked some more, ending up at the Automat across the street from Bryant Park. When she slipped her coat off her breasts moved under the crocheted sweater she wore. They had coffee and doughnuts, surrounded by office party drunks sobering up for the trip home.

Then it went this way: We can go to Maryland and get married, she said. You know I was sixteen a month ago. I want to marry you, I can't stand it. He was excited and frightened, and got an erection. How could he bear this image? Her breasts, her familiar perfume, enormous figures of movie queens resplendent in silk and lace in the snug bedrooms of Vermont inns—shutters banging, the rain pouring down, all entangled, married! How do we get to *Maryland?* he said.

Against the table top her hand, its long and delicate fingers, the perfect moons, Carolina moons, of her nails. I'll give her every marvel: push gently the scent of magnolia and jasmine between her legs and permit her to piss champagne.

Against the table top her hand, glowing crescent moons over lakes of Prussian blue in evergreen twilights. Her eyes gray, flecked with bronze. In her fingers a golden chain and on the chain a car key. My father's car, she said. We can take it and be there tonight. We can be married Christmas then, he said, but you're Jewish. He saw a drunk going out onto Sixth Avenue carrying their lives along in a paper bag. I mean it, she said. I can't stand it, I love you. I love *you*, he said, but I can't drive. He smiled. I *mean* it, she said. She put the key in his hand. The car is in midtown here, over by Ninth Avenue. I really *can't* drive, he said. He could shoot pool and drink boilermakers, keep score at baseball games and handicap horses, but he couldn't drive.

The key in his hand, fascinating wrinkle of sweater at her waist. Of course, life is a conspiracy of defeat, a sophisticated joke, endless, endless. I'll get some money and we'll go the holiday week, he said, we'll take a train, O.K.? O.K., she said. She smiled and asked for another coffee, taking the key and dropping it into her bag. It was a joke after all. They walked to the subway and he said I'll give you a call right after Christmas. Gray bitter sky. What he remembered was her gray cashmere coat swirling around her calves as she turned at the foot of the stairs to smile at him, making the gesture of dialing a phone and pointing at him and then at herself.

Give these children a Silver Phantom and a chauffeur. A black chauffeur, to complete the America that owned them.

Now I come to the literary part of this story, and the reader may prefer to let it go and watch her profile against the slick tiles of the IRT stairwell, since she has gone out of the reality of narrative, however splintered. This postscript offers something different, something finely artificial and discrete, one of the designers sweaters her father makes now, white and stylish as a sailor's summer bells. I grant you it will be unbelievable.

I put the young man into 1958. He has served in the army, and once told the Automat story to a group of friends as proof of his sexual prowess. They believed him: what else was there for them to believe? This shabby use of a fragile occurrence was occasioned by the smell of honeysuckle and magnolia in the tobacco country outside Winston-Salem. It brought her to him so that he was possessed. He felt the magic key in his hand again. To master this overpowering wave of nostalgia he cheapened it. Certainly the reader will recall such shoddy incidents in his own life.

After his discharge he married some girl and had three children by her. He allowed her her diverse interests and she tolerated his few stupid infidelities. He had a good job in advertising and they lived in Kew Gardens in a brick semi-detached house. Let me give them a sunken living room to give this the appearance of realism. His mother died in 1958 and left the lake house to him. Since he had not been there for ten years he decided to sell it, against his wife's wishes. The community was growing and the property was worth twice the original price.

This is a ruse to get him up there one soft spring day in May. He drives up in a year-old Pontiac. The realtor's office, the papers, etc. Certainly, a shimmer of nostalgia about it all, although he felt a total stranger. He left the car on the main road, deciding to walk down to the lake, partly visible through the new-leaved trees. All right, now here we go. A Cadillac station wagon passed and then stopped about fifteen yards ahead of him and she got out. She was wearing white shorts and sneakers and a blue sweat shirt. Her hair was the same, shorter perhaps, tied with a ribbon of navy velour.

It's too impossible to invent conversation for them. He got in her car. Her perfume was not the same. They drove to her parents' house for a cup of coffee—for old times' sake. How else would they get themselves together and alone? She had come up to open the house for the season. Her husband was a college traveler for a publishing house and was on the road, her son and daughter were staying at their grandparents' for the day. Popular songs, the lyrics half-remembered. You will do well if you think of the ambience of the whole scene as akin to the one in detective novels where the private investigator goes to the murdered man's summer house. This is always in off-season because it is magical then, one sees oneself as a being somehow existing outside time, the year-round residents are drawings in flat space.

When they walked into the chilly house she reached past him to latch the door and he touched her hand on the lock, then her forearm, her shoulder. Take your clothes off, he said, gently. Oh gently. Please. Take your clothes off? He opened the button of her shorts. You see that they now have the retreat I begged for them a decade ago. If one has faith all things will come. Her flesh was cool.

In the bedroom, she turned down the spread and fluffed the pillows, then sat and undressed. As she unlaced her sneakers, he put the last of his clothes on a chair. She got up, her breasts quivering slightly, and he saw faint stretch marks running into the shadowy symmetry of her pubic hair. She plugged in a small electric heater, bending before him, and he put his hands under her buttocks and held her there. She sighed and trembled and straightened up, turning toward him. Let me have a mist of tears in her eyes, of acrid joy and shame, of despair. She lay on the bed and opened her thighs and they made love without elaboration.

In the evening, he followed her car back into the city. They had promised to meet again the following week. Of course it wouldn't be sordid. What, then, would it be? He had perhaps wept bitterly that afternoon as she kissed his knees. She would call him, he would call her. They could find a place to go. Was she happy? Really happy? God knows, he wasn't *happy!* In the city they stopped for a drink in a Village bar and sat facing each other in the booth, their knees touching, holding hands. They carefully avoided speaking of the past, they made no jokes. He felt his heart rattling around in his chest in large jagged pieces. It was rotten for everybody, it was rotten but they would see each other, they were somehow owed it. They would find a place with clean sheets, a radio, whiskey, they would just—continue. Why not?

These destructive and bittersweet accidents do not happen every day. He put her number in his address book, but he wouldn't call her. Perhaps she would call him, and if she did, well, they'd see, they'd see. But he would *not* call her. He wasn't that crazy. On the way out to Queens he felt himself in her again and the car swerved erratically. When he got home he was exhausted.

You are perfectly justified in scoffing at the outrageous transparency of it if I tell you that his wife said that he was so pale that he looked as if he had seen a ghost, but that is, indeed, what she said. Art cannot rescue anybody from anything.

Some of the Rewards
and Pleasures of Love

DINAH BROOKE

EXQUISITE CREATURE. Exquisite, charming, adorable blonde—as long, that is, as she stays at the other end of the room. Not many men would say that about her. In fact I hear them saying quite otherwise night after night when she comes back from the pictures or the pub. The walls are very thin, and I can hear just about everything that goes on. She likes to hold out and play coy, but she doesn't have the sort of resistance that lasts very long, if you see what I mean. Sometimes I'm tempted to interrupt them in the middle—shout and scream so that she has to come to me. She'd be as mad as hell at the time, but she might even thank me for it in the long run, the way she looks so sick and fed up in the mornings.

She gets me out of bed and up to the table for breakfast with her wrapper half open so that I can see her tits and her belly too sometimes, and she stinks of sweat and sex; that's before she's had her wash. Her cheeks are sallow and shiny then, and sometimes a bit spotty, and there are dark wrinkles under her eyes. As she gets me up and washes and dresses me (not much more than a lick and a promise unless I scream at her) she complains all the time: "I don't know why I go on like this; I'd like a different sort of life—something with a bit of order to it. Men, men, men; I get so sick of them. But what else is there to do in the evenings in this dump? I'd turn pro if I had any sense, and make a bit of money. You don't hardly bring me in enough to pay for your keep, let alone the trouble."

I've never had her myself; I used to go on at her once, but she

44

never let me. I suppose she knew that if she did she'd never get any peace. Anyway I'm not sure that I want to. She's here to look after me; to feed me and keep me clean, and comb my moustache. She shaves me, too, not badly for a woman. Getting up is the part of the day that I enjoy most; it's a pity she's so bad-tempered, and smells. But still, it gives me pleasure to sit up in front of the mirror and watch her lather my face carefully with the old-fashioned beaver-hair shaving brush, and then make slow, careful strokes down the side of my cheek with the razor. I like to see the way the texture of the smooth skin appears suddenly in the wake of the razor, contrasted against the foamy blue white-ness of the lather. If I tilt my head at a bit of an angle, so that I can see my face three-quarter view in the mirror, I look like a man in a painting that I saw a picture of once, in a magazine. Especially my moustache. My moustache is thick and soft, and grows in a big wave on either side of my upper lip. I make her cut it off straight at the bottom, and leave an extra little curl at each corner. I enjoy running my tongue along its rough, silky texture, and playing with the two curls; but I don't do it when she's in the room.

How she makes her living is that she has this little shop her husband left her. He died four or five years ago. It's a grocer's shop, though she thought of changing over to sweets and ciga-rettes; someone told her that you couldn't lose on sweets and ciga-rettes, but Dylis could lose money on anything. Every time some-one comes in asking for something she doesn't have she'll say, "Oh, I'm ever so sorry, I don't stock it any more, but I'll get it in for you." Once she ordered five pounds of stuffed derma, and of course the woman never came back again.

"Whoever eats stuffed derma round here?" I told her. "I did hear there were some Jews living in Marshall Street, but they're not going to come over here to do their shopping."

"The lady came over once, she'll come again," the poor stupid cow would say, and try to feed me the filthy stuff.

"She was just passing by. Maybe she had to go to the hospital to see her daughter who was having a baby."

"Oh, shut up, you don't know anything about business," said Dilys, and went off to do her shopping, leaving me still strapped in the high chair after dinner, instead of in front of the fire with the wireless on, as I usually like to be.

One advantage from her point of view about having so few customers is that she can go off when she likes to look at the shops and talk to her friends. It's not so nice for me, though. I don't like having to shout to people who come in (she always takes the money with her), "She'll be back in just a few minutes."

I don't like the idea of people in the next room who don't know me. I prefer it when Dilys has her friends in in the afternoon, and they all sit nattering over cups of tea, their voices rising with excitement, and falling with an acid drag. When they go in the late afternoon, just before their husbands get home from work, their faces are flushed from sitting over the fire, and their eyes are smug and bright, as if they've been taking part in great events.

It was during one of these afternoons that I heard about Kim. Mrs. Pryor was telling them about her nephew. She was leaning forward talking in a low voice, and they would all glance at me from time to time, as if I might be embarrassed. I have sharp ears and could hear everything she said, so she needn't have bothered to lower her voice, and, anyway, I don't mind. I'm a realist; I know what sort of a man I am, and what sort of life I can expect, and I'm fairly content. Her nephew, he was about fourteen then, has got water on the brain. His head's all swollen up so that he looks like a balloon boy, as if he should float up and bounce gently against the ceiling if someone didn't hold onto his legs. It seems his mother had put him in an institution because she couldn't bear the sight of him, and she wouldn't come and visit him either, so he was lonely. She'd go herself once a week, Mrs. Pryor said, but she couldn't spare the time.

"I'll go," I said, and they all looked round in surprise, as if they'd forgotten I was there. Though by the way they'd been lowering their voices and looking over their shoulders they certainly hadn't forgotten me when they were describing what Kim and the other boys in the institution looked like. I knew that better than they did, of course, because I've spent most of my life in the same sort of place. Not so nice as Kim's, because it was ten years ago that I came to live with Dilys and her husband, and things were worse in those days. I used to spend most of my time just lying on my back in the cold dormitory, though in the summer I was allowed to roll around on the grass (I've got no arms or legs) in the sunshine. People would talk to me sometimes, and when I could persuade them, read to me. I never learned to read myself, although I did go to school for a bit, but I never got enough practice, what with finding someone to prop the book up for me, and turn the pages. It was the wireless that occupied most of my time. You could say that I've lived my life to the B.B.C. Home Service. How I came to live with Dilys was like this.

One day at the hospital my grandmother came to see me. I suppose my mother couldn't bear the sight of me, like Kim's mother. Anyway, my grandmother was a nice old lady with a fur coat, and a swaying double chin, and a feather hat. She leaned very close to me when she spoke, as if she was afraid I wouldn't understand. Not to kiss me, as I thought with a sort of excitement at first. I could smell her musky smell, and see the wrinkled beginnings of her breasts, and the thin straps of her underwear. She only came once, and asked me if there was anything I wanted. I said that I would like to live in a house, and a few weeks later I was brought here to Dilys. My grandmother paid her five pounds a week to look after me, and left it to me in her will when she died.

"I suppose you could at that, Mr. Gregory," said Mrs. Pryor, staring at me dubiously, with her head cocked awkwardly over her shoulder. She shifted her chair round, making the legs squeak on the old red lino, and Dilys got up to turn on the light so they could all see me better. I was propped up comfortably against my cushions, and I looked back steadily at each one in turn, straight in the eye. Dilys settled her elbows on the table again, and said, "It'd make an outing for you."

So once a week after that, I went to see Kim. Mrs. Pryor would take me in on her way to the shops or the cinema, and she or Dilys would fetch me away in the evening. They trundled me through the streets in an old pram, propped up against the dirty washing on its way to the launderette, or the sharp corners of packets of Tide and cornflakes, and tins of Heinz baked beans. Dilys tries to use up whatever won't sell in the shop, so everything we eat is either stale or rancid. Her husband never complained, but I did, and when he died I made her try some of those new tins. They're getting better all the time. Everything's getting better all the time—I see it when I ride through the streets. The shops are brighter and full of things, the advertisements are bright and gay, and people look better, and wear brighter-colored clothes.

I tried to work out once how much I cost her, since she's always complaining. I certainly don't eat five pounds worth of bread and bacon a week, and I don't take up much room, I sleep in a sort of box in a corner of the kitchen. Her husband made it for me, and he made my chair too—the pram was given to her by a woman down the road. There's the washing and ironing, of course. I have three shirts, and a waistcoat, and several ties, and a jacket for winter. Mr. Peake sometimes brings me a tie when he comes to see me. I like bow ties best—last year he brought me a nice one in red brocade, and the waistcoat. He is my grandmother's solicitor, and comes to see if I have everything I need, and if Dilys is treating me right. As a matter of fact, I think he gave her something extra the last time he came, because she took him into the shop, and I heard her hissing about "baby," and "mess." If I could clean myself up I would. Anyway, that week she got herself a new dress, and a coat with a fur collar on it.

The institution that Kim was in is really beautiful. All new buildings, with white paint, and lawns of green grass, and trees, and even a swimming pool. In the summer they're all taken out and allowed to lie in the grass, in the sun. The place I was, I could remember every one of the times I'd been outside, in my whole life. I told you, things are really getting better.

Kim had a room on the ground floor, which he shares with just one other balloon boy. There are big windows which open up onto the garden, like doors. Sometimes I come straight in through the windows from the greenness and brightness outside, to the shadowy room where everything is blue and gray and white; steel bedposts and chairs, polished floors, white sheets, and Kim and his friend sitting opposite each other in their pale shining eyes, and delicate huge domes balanced above their eyes. It's not only because of their heads that I call them balloon boys, but also because that's one of the games they like to play. I bring a few whenever I can persuade Dilys to buy them for me, and one of the nurses blows them up, and they pat them gently from bed to bed with their spindly fingers, laughing with shrill, fragile cries, and panting with excitement, like birds.

When it's cold they wheel me in through the long corridor, empty and bare, but also shining and clean, with a reddish floor that makes no noise. I don't know why, but as soon as they get inside the gates of the institution both Dilys and Mrs. Pryor start to whisper if they talk to me. If they pass a nurse or doctor who says "hello," they giggle and blush like little girls. They're always very apologetic: "Ooh, I am sorry to bother you, I hope we're not dirtying up your nice clean floor," but if anyone offers to wheel my pram through to Kim's room they give it up like a shot, and are off back outside, to their cinemas and their shopping.

The nurses and doctors are all very nice to me, and thank me for coming to see Kim. They say it cheers him up, because he misses his mum and the rest of his family. I tell him he's lucky to have lived with his own family at all; I only had that one glimpse of my grandma. He told me about his sister Karen, who was much cleverer than he was although she was two years younger, and used to laugh at him. She did her hair differently every day, and liked to wear party dresses. Their mum was always knitting or crocheting a new dress for her, and once the teacher sent her back from school, saying she should come in something plainer. Neither Karen nor her mum liked boys very much, especially funny looking boys like Kim.

"I imagine I'm flying," said Kim. "That's what I do all day now. And I can fly everywhere, not only in the air, but through the wall and into the floor and back to my mum's house if I want to. I can fly in the sea, too, and I swallow the water instead of breathing. I drink it in, in great gollops, and it flows through my arms and legs."

"You swim in the sea, you don't fly in it," said the other boy. He had a thick, harsh accent, though his voice was thin and watery.

"Kim can fly in the sea because he has imagination," I said. "You have no imagination."

"I've never seen the sea," said Kim, "but I know what it tastes like. It tastes like tears; my mum told me that once." His head swayed from side to side, and the tendons on his neck stood out delicately.

"I live in a silver tent. Sometimes it turns into a balloon, and we float up into the sky; the clouds press round and rub against us, and the walls start to billow in, like when I push my head into the pillow, and it begins to rain, and water streams down outside, and the tent gets wet and clings to my body like a cloak; it's like falling in the bath with all your clothes on, and the water beats and presses against me till I'm all small and thin, and then I float down to earth again."

By the time it was summer again Kim didn't go out at all, and he couldn't play the balloon game any longer. He couldn't talk for very long either without getting tired. He sat in bed wearing blue pajamas; his head was growing bigger all the time, and strained toward the ceiling.

"I see interesting shapes sometimes. I don't even have to close my eyes. They're grayish and blue, and made up of lots of little tiny dots; they're usually round, but shaped like battlements at the edges. Soft battlements that sway in the wind, with no soldiers in them."

After I'd talked to Kim for a bit, if it was sunny, one of the nurses would take me out of the pram and put me on the grass outside his window. I had one special friend, a South African physiotherapy lady who used to say that one day she might put me into the swimming pool, with a life jacket on. I don't know if I liked the idea or not. But lying on the grass, or sitting propped up against a cushion, was lovely. There was a gently sloping bank of grass outside Kim's window, and six or seven rooms opened onto it. They all had children in them, mostly younger than Kim.

There was one little girl, she couldn't have been more than three, who used to lie out there every day, in a nest of nappies, either in her pram or on the grass. There was something wrong with her bottom—it was round the wrong way. Anyway, she used to lie there, buried in all these cloths, peering up with bright dark eyes, like a little bird. No, they weren't like a bird, her eyes, they were hot and deep; she stared and stared, and you couldn't stop looking back at her. Her name was Marjie. She didn't speak very much, just a few sounds that were more gurgles than words. She lay there, her little bottom bare to the sun, with a nasty red rash on it, and her feet curled up underneath her, and sucked at a piece of blanket, or her thumb, or stroked her cheek with her hand. Her cheeks were red, too, and her hair was brown and damp, and waved a bit. I rolled over closer and smiled at her, and she wriggled in her blankets. She was sucking her finger and staring at me and smiling—she couldn't have been smiling, but her eyes were, her eyes were inviting me and laughing at me. She looked like a jewel in a silver ring, surrounded by all those curves and swirls of drapery. She took her finger out of her mouth, and I felt my stomach shrink.

"She's a baby, she's only a little girl," I whispered to myself, and wriggled nearer. Her lips were red and damp, and the under-side of her tongue was red, too, and I could see a little pool of saliva between her white, pointed teeth. She stuck out her finger and put it into my mouth. It was still wet with her saliva. The skin was very soft, and I could feel with my tongue the delicate ridges of her knuckles, and the sharp curve of her nail, still a little soft, a baby nail, but scratchy. I stared into her eyes and caressed that soft magical finger with my tongue. She curled it round, and rubbed her head from side to side, and stretched her legs. An ecstatic sickness rose into my throat and made my stomach melt.

I felt a chill on my face, and Marjie's finger slipped out from between my lips. I opened my eyes. A nurse was standing be-tween me and the sun, straightening Marjie's blankets.

"Oh, that Marjie, she's such a tease. What have you been doing to poor Mr. Gregory?" She pinned a nappy on Marjie with expert speed, and picked her up, tucking her under one arm.

"Time to go in for tea now; and here's Mrs. Pryor come for you, Mr. Gregory."

As she turned round I saw Marjie's face again. She twisted her head to stare at me with that same secret smile, and held out her little hand toward me. Her finger was still red and damp from my mouth.

Mrs. Pryor and Dilys heaved me into my pram with much groaning and complaining.

"Oh, my poor back."

"They have an easy life here and no mistake."

"I do like Cliff Richard though, don't you?"

We looked in to say good-bye to Kim, but he was asleep. I don't suppose I'll ever go to the institution again, because the next week Dilys told me that Kim had died. They had made a little hole in his head and tapped off some of the water, but it didn't make any difference.

"You can't expect to live long in that condition," she said. "It's a merciful release, really."

I'd like to have asked to go and visit Marjie, but they wouldn't see much point in it when she can't talk yet. Maybe I will in a year or so.

A Very Old Man with Enormous Wings

A *Tale for Children*

GABRIEL GARCÍA MÁRQUEZ

ON THE THIRD DAY of rain they had killed so many crabs inside the house that Pelayo had to cross his drenched courtyard and throw them into the sea, because the newborn child had a temperature all night and they thought it was due to the stench. The world had been sad since Tuesday. Sea and sky were a single ash-gray thing and the sands of the beach, which on March nights glimmered like powdered light, had become a stew of mud and rotten shellfish. The light was so weak at noon that when Pelayo was coming back to the house after throwing away the crabs, it was hard for him to see what it was that was moving and groaning in the rear of the courtyard. He had to go very close to see that it was an old man, a very old man, lying face down in the mud, who, in spite of his tremendous efforts, couldn't get up, impeded by his enormous wings.

Frightened by that nightmare, Pelayo ran to get Elisenda, his wife, who was putting compresses on the sick child, and he took her to the rear of the courtyard. They both looked at the fallen body with mute stupor. He was dressed like a ragpicker. There were only a few faded threads left on his bald skull and very few teeth in his mouth, and his pitiful condition of a drenched great-grandfather had taken away any sense of grandeur he might have had. His huge buzzard wings, dirty and half-plucked, were forever entangled in the mud. They looked at him so long and so closely that Pelayo and Elisenda very soon overcame their surprise and in the end found him familiar. Then they dared speak to him, and he answered in an incomprehensible dialect with a strong

52

sailor's voice. That was how they skipped over the inconvenience of the wings and quite intelligently concluded that he was a lonely castaway from some foreign ship wrecked by the storm. And yet, they called in a neighbor woman who knew everything about life and death to see him, and all she needed was one look to show them their mistake.

"He's an angel," she told them. "He must have been coming for the child, but the poor fellow is so old that the rain knocked him down."

On the following day everyone knew that a flesh-and-blood angel was held captive in Pelayo's house. Against the judgment of the wise neighbor woman, for whom angels in those times were the fugitive survivors of a celestial conspiracy, they did not have the heart to club him to death. Pelayo watched over him all afternoon from the kitchen, armed with his bailiff's club, and before going to bed he dragged him out of the mud and locked him up with the hens in the wire chicken coop. In the middle of the night, when the rain stopped, Pelayo and Elisenda were still killing crabs. A short time afterwards the child woke up without a fever and with a desire to eat. Then they felt magnanimous and decided to put the angel on a raft with fresh water and provisions for three days and leave him to his fate on the high seas. But when they went out into the courtyard with the first light of dawn, they found the whole neighborhood in front of the chicken coop having fun with the angel, without the slightest devotion, tossing him things to eat through the openings in the wire as if he weren't a supernatural creature but a circus animal.

Father Gonzaga arrived before seven o'clock, alarmed at the strange news. By that time onlookers less frivolous than those at dawn had already arrived and they were making all kinds of conjectures concerning the captive's future. The simplest among them thought that he should be named mayor of the world. Others of sterner mind felt that he should be promoted to the rank of five-star general in order to win all wars. Some visionaries hoped that he could be put to stud in order to implant on earth a race of winged wise men who could take charge of the universe. But Father Gonzaga, before becoming a priest, had been a robust woodcutter. Standing by the wire he reviewed his catechism in an instant and asked them to open the door so that he could take a close look at that pitiful man who looked more like a huge decrepit hen among the fascinated chickens. He was lying in a corner drying his open wings in the sunlight among the fruit peels and breakfast leftovers that the early-risers had thrown him. Alien to the impertinences of the world, he only lifted his antiquarian eyes and murmured something in his dialect when Father Gonzaga went into the chicken coop and said good morning to him in Latin. The parish priest had has first suspicion of an impostor when he saw that he did not understand the language of God or know how to greet His ministers. Then he noticed that seen close up he was much too human: he had an unbearable smell of the outdoors, the back side of his wings was strewn with parasites, and his main feathers had been mistreated by terrestrial winds, and nothing about him measured up to the proud dignity of angels. Then he came out of the chicken coop and in a brief sermon warned the curious against the risks of being ingenuous. He reminded them that the devil had the bad habit of making use of carnival tricks in order to confuse the unwary. He argued that if wings were not the essential element in determining the difference between a hawk and an airplane, they were even less so in the recognition of angels. Nevertheless, he promised to write a letter to his bishop so that the latter would write to his primate so that the latter would write to the Supreme Pontiff in order to get the final verdict from the highest courts.

His prudence fell on sterile hearts. The news of the captive angel spread with such rapidity that after a few hours the courtyard had the bustle of a marketplace and they had to call in troops with fixed bayonets to disperse the mob that was about to knock the house down. Elisenda, her spine all twisted from sweeping up so much marketplace trash, then got the idea of fencing in the yard and charging five cents admission to see the angel.

The curious came from far away. A traveling carnival arrived with a flying acrobat who buzzed over the crowd several times, but no one paid any attention to him because his wings were not those of an angel but, rather, those of a sidereal bat. The most unfortunate invalids on earth came in search of health: a poor woman who since childhood had been counting her heartbeats and had run out of numbers; a Portuguese man who couldn't sleep because the noise of the stars disturbed him; a sleepwalker who got up at night to undo the things he had done while awake;

and many others with less serious ailments. In the midst of that shipwreck disorder that made the earth tremble, Pelayo and Elisenda were happy with fatigue, for in less than a week they had crammed their rooms with money and the line of pilgrims waiting their turn to enter still reached beyond the horizon.

The angel was the only one who took no part in his own act. He spent his time trying to get comfortable in his borrowed nest, befuddled by the hellish heat of the oil lamps and sacramental candles that had been placed along the wire. At first they tried to make him eat some mothballs, which, according to the wisdom of the wise neighbor woman, were the food prescribed for angels. But he turned them down, just as he turned down the papal lunches that the penitents brought him, and they never found out whether it was because he was an angel or because he was an old man that in the end he ate nothing but eggplant mush. His only supernatural virtue seemed to be patience. Especially during the first days, when the hens pecked at him, searching for the stellar parasites that proliferated in his wing, and the cripples pulled out feathers to touch their defective parts with, and even the most merciful threw stones at him, trying to get him to rise so they could see him standing. The only time they succeeded in arousing him was when they burned his side with an iron for branding steers, for he had been motionless for so many hours that they thought he was dead. He awoke with a start, ranting in his hermetic language and with tears in his eyes, and he flapped his wings a couple of times, which brought on a whirlwind of chicken dung and lunar dust and a gale of panic that did not seem to be of this world. Although many thought that his reaction had not been one of rage but of pain, from then on they were careful not to annoy him, because the majority understood that his passivity was not that of a hero taking his ease but that of a cataclysm in repose.

Father Gonzaga held back the crowd's frivolity with formulas of maidservant inspiration while awaiting the arrival of a final judgment on the nature of the captive. But the mail from Rome showed no sense of urgency. They spent their time finding out if the prisoner had a navel, if his dialect had any connection with Aramaic, how many times he could fit on the head of a pin, or whether he wasn't just a Norwegian with wings. Those meager letters might have come and gone until the end of time if a providential event had not put an end to the priest's tribulations.

It so happened that during those days, among so many other carnival attractions, there arrived in town the traveling show of the woman who had been changed into a spider for having disobeyed her parents. The admission to see her was not only less than the admission to see the angel, but people were permitted to ask her all manner of questions about her absurd state and to examine her up and down so that no one would ever doubt the truth of her horror. She was a frightful tarantula the size of a ram and with the head of a sad maiden. What was most heartrending, however, was not her outlandish shape but the sincere affliction with which she recounted the details of her misfortune. While still practically a child she had sneaked out of her parents' house to go to a dance, and while she was coming back through the woods after having danced all night without permission, a fearful thunder clap rent the sky in two and through the crack came the lightning bolt of brimstone that changed her into a spider. Her only nourishment came from the meatballs that charitable souls chose to toss into her mouth. A spectacle like that, full of so much human truth and with such a fearful lesson, was bound to defeat without even trying that of a haughty angel who scarcely deigned to look at mortals. Besides, the few miracles attributed to the angel showed a certain mental disorder, like the blind man who didn't recover his sight but grew three new teeth, or the paralytic who didn't get to walk but almost won the lottery, and the leper whose sores sprouted sunflowers. Those consolation miracles, which were more like mocking fun, had already ruined the angel's reputation when the woman who had been changed into a spider finally crushed him completely. That was how Father Gonzaga was cured forever of his insomnia and Pelayo's courtyard went back to being as empty as during the time it had rained for three days and crabs walked through the bedrooms.

The owners of the house had no reason to lament. With the money they saved they built a two-story mansion with balconies and gardens and high netting so that crabs wouldn't get in during the winter, and with iron bars on the windows so that angels wouldn't get in. Pelayo also set up a rabbit warren close to town and gave up his job as bailiff for good, and Elisenda bought some satin pumps with high heels and many dresses of iridescent silk, the kind worn on Sunday by the most desirable women in those times. The chicken coop was the only thing that didn't receive any attention. If they washed it down with creoline and burned tears of myrrh inside of it every so often, if was not in homage to the angel but to drive away the dungheap stench that still hung everywhere like a ghost and was turning the new house into an old one. At first, when the child learned to walk, they were careful that he not get too close to the chicken coop. But then they began to lose their fears and got used to the smell, and before the child got his second teeth he'd gone inside the chicken coop to play, where the wires were falling apart. The angel was no less standoffish with him than with other mortals, but he tolerated the most ingenious infamies with the patience of a dog who had no illusions. They both came down with chicken pox at the same time. The doctor who took care of the child couldn't resist the temptation to listen to the angel's heart, and he found so much whistling in the heart and so many sounds in his kidneys that it seemed impossible for him to be alive. What surprised him most, however, was the logic of his wings. They seemed so natural on that completely human organism that he couldn't understand why other men didn't have them too.

When the child began school it had been some time since the sun and rain had caused the collapse of the chicken coop. The angel went dragging himself about here and there like a stray dying man. They would drive him out of the bedroom with a broom and a moment later find him in the kitchen. He seemed to be in so many places at the same time that they grew to think that he'd been duplicated, that he was reproducing himself all through the house, and the exasperated and unhinged Elisenda shouted that it was awful living in that hell full of angels. He could scarcely eat and his antiquarian eyes had also become so foggy that he went about bumping into posts. All he had left were the bare cannulas of his last feathers. Pelayo threw a blanket over him and extended him the charity of letting him sleep in the shed, and only then did they notice that he had a temperature at night, delirious with the tongue-twisters of an old Norwegian. That was one of the few times they became alarmed, for they thought he was going to die and not even the wise neighbor woman had been able to tell them what to do with dead angels.

And yet, he not only survived his worst winter, but seemed improved with the first sunny days. He remained motionless for several days in the farthest corner of the courtyard, where no one would see him, and at the beginning of December some large, stiff feathers began to grow on his wings, the feathers of a scarecrow, which looked more like another misfortune of decrepitude. But he must have known the reason for those changes, for he was quite careful that no one should notice them, that no one should hear the sea chanties that he sometimes sang under the stars. One morning Elisenda was cutting some bunches of onions for lunch when a wind that seemed to come from the high seas blew into the kitchen. Then she went to the window and caught the angel in his first attempts at flight. They were so clumsy that his fingernails opened a furrow in the vegetable patch and he was on the point of knocking the shed down with the ungainly flapping that slipped on the light and couldn't get a grip on the air. But he did manage to gain altitude. Elisenda let out a sigh of relief, for herself and for him, when she saw him pass over the last houses, holding himself up in some way with the risky flapping of a senile vulture. She kept watching him even when she was through cutting the onions and she kept on watching until it was no longer possible for her to see him, because then he was no longer an annoyance in her life but an imaginary dot on the horizon of the sea.

Translated from the Spanish by Gregory Rabassa

To Byzantium

ANDREW FETLER

AMONG MY BROTHER'S EFFECTS in the cardboard box I brought
home from the state hospital at Newhall, California, was a photo
of my mother—her last formal portrait at 71—and, stuck in the
frame, a snapshot of himself. The snapshot shows him standing on
the steps of our church in the Los Feliz hills overlooking Los
Angeles. Feet apart, arms folded over his chest, head high in half
profile. So he had treasured this snapshot. I had taken it eight
years ago, the day after we buried our father. My brother had
marked an X in the gravel before the church, the spot where I
was to stand with his camera, and I had watched him through the
viewfinder as he struck his pose and gave me the word to snap
the picture.

He loved being photographed, to record important moments in
his life. I had taken pictures of him in the cemetery, where he
had stood meditating at our father's grave. And next morning he
got the flash attachment and had me photograph him sitting at
our father's desk, pen in hand and an expression of deep thought
on his face. After lunch he dragged me out again, and there we
were, before our father's church.

"That's wrong," he said, before I could snap the picture. "I
should be facing the door." He faced the church door and struck
his pose again, head high and arms folded. "How's this?"

"Great."

"Are you getting the cross on the door?"

I hadn't noticed. "I'm getting it," I said. "Are you ready?"

He drew a deep breath and pushed out his chest. "Go ahead."

59

The doctor at Newhall said my brother had swallowed enough pills to kill a horse.

He never showed me this picture, and now that I have it I feel mildly surprised at seeing the resemblance between my father and my brother. In life, the only resemblance I saw was that between the real thing and a distorted copy. In my mind I had never admitted my brother to my father's company.

But I had not known my father when he was as young as my brother. In my earliest family album is a yellowed snapshot of my father on those same church steps in 1921, when he broke with his American patriarch. Except for his beard and priestly robes, he looks like my brother's double—feet pugnaciously apart, the points of his shoes sticking out from under the hem of his cassock, head high in half profile, and arms folded inappropriately over the cross on his chest, as if he had forgotten this burden hanging by a chain from his neck. The same stance of defiance as my brother's, the same self-conscious air of nobility and Old World earnestness and innocence of irony. Father and son.

My father was one of those rare émigrés who came out intact one step ahead of the Revolution. With nobody but God to guide him, he sank his entire fortune into the church and the hilltop it stood on, which he christened Old Russia, only to see his inspiration frowned upon by his new ecclesiastical superiors, whom he had thought to surprise and delight with his monument to Holy Russia.

What the difficulty was, exactly, I don't know. Unlike my brother, I could never appreciate theological niceties. I suspect that my father's quarrel with his superiors in 1921 was less a matter of theology than taste. These beardless American priests with their cars and radios could be expected to look doubtfully at a church that seemed made of Christmas cookies and peppermint sticks, and wonder at its builder. His eventual excommunication, which he lived to regret, made him no less Orthodox in his own eyes. He revived liturgical variants heard since the seventeenth century only in the Monastery of the Grottoes in Kiev. He dedicated an arbor in our garden to the memory of an ancient abbot, and hung an image of St. Vladimir in the church beside the Holy Mother of Kazan.

I have a funny friend in Boston, an Irishman, who bangs the table with his fist when he talks, and having yelled himself out

asks with a timid smile, "Isn't it?" or, "Am I not right?" He likes
to hear about Old Russia. His father was a boozing Irish Catholic,
a Boston patriot who bounced through the streets on a fat beer
horse, at the head of his precinct on the Fourth. And although his
father's memory embarrasses him, he will arise and go to Galway
and Galway Bay, and parade through town with hat and cane
and two fine setters in leash, some day. Yet his irreligion is loud
and emphatic. When he talks about religion he seems to be talking about sexual repression, and his voice loses the resonance I
hear in his Irish jokes.

His example cautions me. As a child I must have been exposed
to a good deal of resonance. I had an edifying hallucination, for
example. I saw the great Los Angeles fire when I was six, which
engulfed the houses and temples and plazas from Hollywood to
Santa Monica. I stood by the gates of our Old Russia in the Los
Feliz hills, between the Swiss chalet and the Taj on adjoining
hills, and watched the smoke roiling over the rooftops far below.
The merchandise of gold and silver, and precious stones, and of
pearls, and fine linen, and purple, and silk, and scarlet, and all
thyine wood, and all manner vessels of ivory, and all manner vessels of most precious wood, and of brass, and iron, and marble,
and cinnamon, and odors, and ointments, and wine, and oil, and
fine flour, and wheat, and beasts, and sheep, and horses, and bodies—all up in smoke in that city, wherein were made rich all that
had ships in the sea by reason of her costliness. My father's incantations at the table lulled me to sleep in those days. I may have
seen a movie of a city burning. I asked my brother, my senior by
seven years, and of course Los Angeles had enjoyed no such con-
flagration. But I know the revulsion Los Angeles arouses in travelers. One fine morning those miles of glitter will be gone and the
desert stretch to the horizon where the city had stood.

Our own forty acres of poplars and silver birches, like the Taj
on the next hill, were rented to film companies. Nothing was native to the place—neither plants nor people, nor religion. My father built Old Russia because he could not go back to his century.
We did not read Soviet writers there, but the old romantics. You
left your car by the wooden gates and walked up an avenue of
poplars to the priest's house. I must have been thirteen or fourteen when I realized that we had become professional ethnics.
You might see my parents slouching in rattan chairs on the veran-

da, the samovar steaming between them. My brother would be playing old liturgical music on the upright in the parlor within, cluttering the music with expansive ornaments all his own, trills and gorgeous arabesques, giving expression to his sense of well-being.

There would be a reason for my brother's musical inventions. He was tormented by the imperatives of moral purity in the morning, crushing boredom and drowsiness at noon, and lust at night. He had a passion for logic and could spot inconsistencies, and picked fights, interrogated, quarreled. I don't know if he ever changed anybody's mind, but he claimed victories in the meeting halls he frequented in his exhausting search for God and women, among the sects and societies that litter California's coast. He could not sin deliberately, with a will, but only on the sly, behind his own back. Then he confessed his sins to his own heart, damned himself, and read poetry about the night of the soul. In this manner he purified himself, and at the piano added grace notes in transports of redeemed innocence.

I sat on the couch doing my homework. He played the piano with his head thrown back and eyes closed. Communing. A strong scent of lilac drifted in through the open window. Then the vacuum cleaner began to whine upstairs, and the music stopped. Above the noise of the vacuum cleaner we could hear our mother singing to herself.

"What is she doing?" he said, glaring at the ceiling.

"She's vacuuming your bedroom."

He turned on the piano stool. Whenever he bothered to look at me I had to brace myself. "Why," he said, folding his arms, "are you sitting there? I'm really interested."

"I'm doing my homework," I said piously.

"What homework?"

"Math, if you must know."

"What will you do with math? What will you measure? This house? I mean, how is it with people like you? Do you ever stop to think *why* you do anything? Or do you just do your homework, as you say?"

"I don't know," I said, to irritate him, and gave him my stupid look.

"Fascinating. You eat, you sleep, you run about like a dog. Doesn't it hurt you to live like a dog?"

At that moment our mother appeared on the stairs with a red kerchief on her head and a rag in her hand. "Did you throw a razor blade in the sink?" she asked him.

"I have more."

My father, too, found it painful to live with one foot on earth. Nothing consoled him for his expulsion from Russia, and in the wild hills above Los Angeles he fought off barbaric America to preserve a quality, a tone, a style. In his defiant days he had built Old Russia to the glory of God with materials scarcely more convincing than those of Disneyland. Old Russia transported him to Byzantium. He could not turn from that dream, and sought to restore his losses with plaster and paint.

Our wooden church walls were made to look like stone three feet thick, but they housed a real church. My father was an actor, yet a priest. The rituals were charades, yet redemptive. Everything was faked except the corpses in our cemetery behind the church. The corpses were real. The years had decimated Old Russia. The resourceful in my father's congregation, the born criminals, caught on to insurance in Toledo, Ohio, or the stock market in Chicago. The old were dumped by their children in commercial nursing homes. A nervous poet who used to walk our paths with a book under his arm tried Mexico and cut his wrists. "In this life to die is nothing new—but to live, of course, is not new, either." And the second-generation children roared up the hill in blue and red sports cars of a Sunday morning, to see the religious antics their folks had been up to a million years ago. When they slammed out to the beaches, the dust they kicked up drifted in the sun past the veranda with its rattan chairs and samovar stand.

Two old babas lived forever, it seemed. Long black skirts, white kerchiefs, chattering up the path, taking Easter cakes to the church. Inside, they kissed the stone floor which I was supposed to have mopped. Down on all fours like two wolves, pressing their mouths to the stone, drinking the spirit. They kissed holy pictures, walls under pictures, each other, and my father's hand when he approached in his priestly robes. He suffered them, but sought refuge at the altar, turning his back on the thirty unbelievers who had been herded in from a sightseeing bus parked by the gates.

Small-town librarians and schoolteachers, in respectful attitudes, hands folded, their faces stiff and reserved, noses sniffing the incense in the artificial darkness, eyes staring at the flame before the Holy Mother, and feet edging toward a wall or pillar as the service dragged on. He refused to install chairs or even benches, as in the valley the Greek Orthodox had done, and would not cut a minute of his interminable ritual. Two sightseeing companies in Hollywood struck him from their itineraries, and Pleasure Tours complained they were stopping too long between the Taj and Homes Of The Stars. But the priest worked the altar as if God's clemency depended upon it. The church choir had long since disappeared, to be replaced by my brother at the organ in the balcony, where he played his responses to my father's exclamations at the altar, yanked the rope that rang the bell, and squinted down at girls like a prisoner from his cage.

We rotted on that hilltop as if cut off from the Body of Christ, not serving but catering, tourists having replaced believers. From time to time, when threatened by bankruptcy, we sold bits and pieces of Old Russia to subdividers. Pretentious houses crawled up the hillside, with billboards advertising "Paradise Now!" and "Heavenly View!" The sick old man, cornered by Los Angeles, clutched his stomach with one hand and dragged himself up and down our paths, around the church, to the cemetery and back, lashed by the far din of construction gangs.

No continuing city. He grew small and bent, and forgot to comb his beard, but remembered to greet my mother in the kitchen, on the morning of Easter Sunday: "Christ is risen!" And she answered, "Verily, He is risen!" He delayed going to church as long as possible, cooling his tea in the saucer and playing with a vest-button hanging by a thread. I sat watching him. A boy of fifteen can hurt to see his father reduced to a caterer.

"Dad?" I said. "Why do the tourists have to come on Easter Sunday?"

"Don't bother him now," my mother said. "Go find your brother. It's time we started for church."

"I can't tell them to go away," my father said to her.

"Of course not."

"Jesus died for them, too. What would He think of me?" And he gave me an astonished look.

From the gates the Pleasure Tours bus honked twice to announce its arrival, on Easter Sunday as on any morning, starting him to his feet. Then my brother, twenty-two at the time, whom I once caught in the vestry trying on our father's priestly robes, stuck his head in at the door and yelled, "We're late!"—and ran.

My father hobbled out the back way. I followed him the length of our garden and out over a turnstile beyond the church grounds proper, the long way around, past construction lumber and foundation pits gouged in the hillside, over land no longer ours, to avoid visitors with cameras. In the old days he used to like being photographed. No more. Now, he stole into the vestry by the back door, and we did not speak as I attended him and he dressed for the show that was not a show. He took the amethyst from the jewel box I held for him, and put it on his finger. He took the chain and kissed the cross and hung it round his neck. When he was ready, when it was time to show himself to the people, he turned instead to the mirror beside the alcove.

I saw a flicker of curiosity in his eyes. In the balcony my brother had started the music for his cue, but here the priest stood, absorbed by his image in the dark glass, seeming not to know himself, forgetting his vocation. Then he caught my eye in the mirror. "After all is said and done—" he began, but did not finish. We stood looking at each other, father and son, and when his cue came and went and he did not move, I knew something awful was happening.

Priest and father in his splendid robes, he stood looking at me with a petrified expression in his eyes. He had dressed gorgeously for his Beloved's body and blood: his vestment glittered with glass and foil on silver brocade, and was garlanded with flowers embroidered in gold thread, spangles, and blue chenille; and his cope—gold cut velvet glowing with sweetbrier buds and carnations on pale silk—bore an inscription in Church Slavonic from shoulder to shoulder, underlined by a row of pearls. Thus he swayed before my alarmed wonder, fathoms deep in a golden twilight. His lip gave a twitch, and all at once he sank to one knee and embraced me. Pulled me into his arms and held. My confusion cut loose from my lungs a short, choppy, derisive laugh, like a bark, and he leaned away, his body wobbling on one knee as if I had plunged a dagger into his chest.

"Tell them to go away, Dad. *Please?*"

Then he understood, and he wrung my name from his throat as if I had been weeping all along. I fled. I ran the length of Old Russia in the fragrant morning, and hiding in a pile of lumber heard the bell strike, and burst into tears.

We never drew so close again. At fifteen I did not know how, and he denied himself his last vanity—a son's love.

About that time my brother discovered his mission: to stop the religious freak show in Old Russia and turn the church to a true worship of the Divine Spirit. My brother felt more comfortable with the Divine Spirit than with God and Jesus Christ. But he could not speak of such reforms to our father, and bided his time running after girls in the I-Thou Temple in Hollywood.

He sat on the veranda after dinner, reading the paper and burping. He had always been too old to play with me, absorbed in matters too elevated for my understanding, but he liked to instruct. If I wanted to sit with him, I had to be instructed.

"Where's Dad?" he said, as I sat down beside him.

"In his room."

My brother put down the paper. "He doesn't know what he's talking about. He's never been to the I-Thou Temple. It's not at all like the Church of the Open Door. At the I-Thou it's all inter-personal. Do you know what that means?"

"No."

"That means your fellow man is not an It, he's a Thou. If you treat a person as a thing—as Dad treats me, for example—you only isolate yourself. We call it alienation. That's what Dad suffers from—alienation. He's finished."

It would have seemed so, at first glance. From my brother too the old man averted his face. He subsided and sank from us, deaf to us, locked up in himself. One thing remained for him to do, to unburden himself of a last burden, without debate, without seeking my mother's counsel. Clutching his stomach, he had my brother drive him down the hill to the District Court to have his name changed from Viliki to Krotki. To the judge who granted his prayer neither name meant anything. Viliki means great, and Krotki means gentle.

I could not make a fuss about the new name devolving upon me as a minor. With a different breakfast in his stomach, my father might have chosen a name like Unknown, or Clean Spit. But my brother stormed, wanting his father's true name. And he kept his father's true name, having attained his majority when our father humbled himself.

I went away to college, and to war. And when I came home

from the war, when I myself felt like a tourist in Old Russia, I saw my father sitting in his rattan chair on the veranda. He blinked his watery eyes at me and pulled from his pocket a caramel coated with dust and a curling white hair. "For your sweet tooth." He had the quiet insanity of a well-behaved child. He made a joke about his new name which he repeated at odd moments at the table, diverting him more than us. "Yes, it's true," he would say, apropos of nothing. "I went out great, and the Lord has brought me home again gentle."

In my mind I have a heaven for him, and a chair to sit in, by reason of that same disastrous Sunday morning, when after all was said and done he wished to abide if he could in Jesus Christ, that he might have confidence and not be ashamed before Him at His coming.

So he died. And my brother felt born again. He played with his father's jewels, wore his father's tattered bathrobe, slammed doors, and ignored the dinner bell as his father had ignored it before him.

Having heard the icy call of the Lord, my brother assumed that he was chosen. He believed every spirit that came to plead with him from every corner of his possessed soul. My brother and inheritor stretched his arms as if waking from a long sleep, yawned, smiled, spat. Alive to himself, not doubting himself, not puzzling himself. And went out to look at Old Russia, to see what all needed to be done, and had me photograph him on the church steps for an historical record, his feet apart and arms folded over his chest, not having been shot dead to himself by the Implacable Hunter.

He still ran after girls at the I-Thou Temple in Hollywood, and came home to argue that nothing could revive Old Russia except an ecumenical spirit. He spent an afternoon framing a photo of our mother for his nightstand. "We have a date Saturday, you and I," he joked with her.

No joke. He took her out to rich dinners she could not eat and movies that put her to sleep. He brought her home exhausted and confused, and at midnight shook her from her snooze in her rocker, and dragged her to his bedroom for prayers, to pray with him as she had prayed with our father. "Yes, yes," she would say, staring about at the charts and religious posters and mystical symbols on his walls. "Yes, dearest, let us pray. God will forgive everything." He kept her on her knees for thirty minutes, as he read from some greasy pamphlet or other, and sent her to bed with a reminder that they had a date Saturday. Then he sulked for days and ignored her, and prayed and fasted alone by her photo in his bedroom.

In our climate every conceivable religious plant creeps, slithers, entwines, snaps, exhales, twists, breeds in the sun. My brother felt at home in this jungle. He knew what to do and how to go about it. Not to repeat his father's mistakes, he did not have himself ordained, but took care to be licensed by the I-Thou Temple. He sat at his father's desk, stuffing his head with catalogues of metaphysical distinctions and occult fads. Late at night he pored over geometric figures, circles detached and overlapping, and triangles with an eye at the apex, and crosses formed by the asymptotes of hyperbolas, and psychospiritual organizational tables that would have impressed General Motors, and calendars of duties, and charts tracing his personal oscillations through the darkness and the light. During my visits, I might have learned something about him if he had expressed a preference for chocolate ice cream over vanilla. But he had become a Deep Thinker and was not accessible.

When next I visited, a small billboard had been erected over the gates. "Welcome To The I-Thou Russian Church." The parent Temple in Hollywood encouraged him to keep what he liked of the old rituals and wardrobe. For two years our scandalized Orthodox remnant probed the thickets of a lawsuit against my brother, and settled out of court for the best slice of the land, where they proposed building a modern Orthodox church with indirect lighting. Old Russia was reduced to the priest's house, the church, and the cemetery.

"How I pray he marries!" my mother said to me in the kitchen, cutting away the rot from potatoes. She had grown old and had begun to forget English and sometimes sprinkled sugar on her stew. "You must know some good girls. Can't you take him away from here, to meet your friends?"

"My friends are trivial. He's too deep for them."

"Why are you nasty? You know nothing about him."

"Don't you care what he did to the church?" I asked.

"Did what! Now we have a fire insurance! If it burns down we can build again."

My brother never found the wife he thought he wanted, the

young girl his fancy installed at the organ in the church balcony while he celebrated the I-Thou mysteries at the altar. The balcony spot went to a paid organist from a Fundamentalist radio station that advertised professional anti-Communists, itinerant faithhealers, and blest handkerchiefs. With the help of this musicologist he put together a service from the more dramatic parts of the Orthodox ritual and Fundamentalist clatter. The tourist clientele fell off, the Orthodox ceased altogether, but varieties of existentialists got wind of the new thing in Old Russia and flocked up the hill.

His success should not have astonished me, I realize now. He was a compulsive talker, loved to preach, and during a Latin collect he moved our father's Bible from the gospel side of the altar to the epistle side without rhyme or reason. In the vestry after the service he asked me to help him with his robes. "How was I?" I had never seen him so elated. He offered me the job of sacristan—room, board, and pocket money. Well, how was he? When you stripped his sermon of fashionable words like *existential* and *ambience,* and mystical pretensions, and a love of spectacle, you saw a simple commitment to the old verities. Seeing him there in our father's priestly robes, pulling in the new breed of celebrants who lounged about in comfortable Balaban & Katz chairs—"No Smoking!"—I thought the church felt as secure from disintegration as it had felt in the old days, before Pleasure Tours and subdividers had sniffed its carcass.

Tea on the veranda as in the old days, and the lilac bloomed. My brother ran into the house to fetch his Plato, and came out turning the pages of the book nearsightedly, impatient to enlighten my dark mind with Plato's delightful passage about the heavenly pattern. He coupled his rhetorical questions with other questions and other premises, breeding monsters of logic with several heads and tails, but I understood him to mean that we lived in a finite universe, and the earth stood fixed at the center of the spheres of sun and moon, the stars and all the planets. He did not say these antiquated things, but with the lilac's thick fragrance in the air he made me feel them, and I thought him beautiful as he read, holding the book close to his nose: "'In heaven,'" I replied, 'there is laid up a pattern of it, methinks, which he who desires may behold, and beholding, may set his own house in order. But whether such a one exists, or ever will exist in fact, is no matter;

for he will live after the manner of that city, having nothing to do with any other.'"

"That's good," I said.

"How can you say that's good," my brother cried, "and not believe? If you don't believe, then you are not moved. If you are moved, then you must believe."

"All right, I believe."

"But you don't! Why are you lying?"

In those last days, before my mother's death and my brother's commitment to the state hospital at Newhall, if you happened to come by on a quiet afternoon, left your car by the white gates and walked up the avenue of poplars to the priest's house, you might have seen the old woman sweeping the veranda, and heard the piano tinkling in the dark house within. She would have been anxious to please you, and might have taken it into her head to show you the church. Descending sideways down the steps, favoring her stiff leg, she would have approached you with her hands clasped in an expression of pleasure. A new face!

What part of Russia did you come from? Had you known her husband? *This way, this way!* she would gesture, her English fading. She might tug at your sleeve and step back to have a better look at you, working her gums, smiling and pointing to the church. Did you come to see the church? You would look into the trees where she pointed and see something golden and white behind the green foliage. *So nice, so nice!* she would seem to say, laughing soundlessly, and start up the path. *That's right, come along. I'll show you everything!* You would follow past neglected flowerbeds and unpruned bushes, past a dilapidated arbor and a rain-warped orange crate standing in the high grass and nettles. At a turn in the path by a dead lemon tree she would suddenly stop and stretch her neck forward like a buzzard, to see if the church was still there. Yes, her old eyes could see it still, and she would give you a look of infinite gaiety. Could you see it? Could you see what she saw?

You might, if you happened to be in Plato's mood.

If not, you would see that the church in Old Russia was not a bad tourist stop, as such attractions go, the blue doors and windows decorated like Christmas cookies, the pillars twisted into candy sticks, and the large golden onion at the top sprinkled with blue stars. This dome, you would see, pleased the artist enough to add two small domes as an afterthought, asymmetrically, one near the main door and the other half sunk behind the vestry gable. Something to photograph, if you photograph such things.

But if you did not calculate the uses of such a place and were in no hurry to see the Taj, if for once you were neither rich nor poor, felt neither trapped nor abandoned by life, and sensed a momentary order in your soul, you might have stopped beside the old woman and stood still with a small intake of breath, and heard the wind in the grass and seen the church floating in the sky.

The old woman who had blossomed there, and was soon to die like her lemon tree, would not trouble her mad son for the keys. Giving the church door a shake to show that it was really locked, she would pull you round to a smaller path grown over with weeds, where the thick bushes darkened the earth and the damp air would chill your feet.

This way, this way!—and you follow her to the very spot where Emil Richter filmed the closing scene for his *Fathers and Sons*. The willow he planted grows aslant the stagnant pond to this day, hanging its unkempt head over rockweed, skunk cabbage, pond scums, stoneworts. As you approached you might hear the splash of a toad, and lifting your eyes see the luminous algae glowing darkly with emanations from the dead. Mr. Richter was fond of a melancholy little bench, where Bazarov's old father sat watching as his wife touched up their son's grave. For years that bench lay overturned in the grass behind the compost heap, but when my father died my mother dragged the bench to his grave.

"My husband," she would tell you, smiling gaily and inviting you to sit and look at death.

A Tale of Pierrot

THERE IS A TOWN in the south of France with steep cobblestone streets, a hilltop château that is a vintnery, an old square shaded by enormous trees. Under the trees (it is night) a canvas canopy glows enticingly in stripes of orange and white. Townsfolk have gathered here. Some are chatting in little groups, but most are standing at long tables shaping mounds of clay, or pressing strips of paper over images already formed, or daubing colors on finished masks of papier mâché.

The canopy is open both to the promenade and the park. On the one side, waiters hurry back and forth, while on the other masked children chase each other and leap from behind trees with their hands in the air. One hears the discreet, yet insistent, dense clicking of the steel balls of *la petanque*.

Let us imagine that among these crowds is a man who belongs rather to legend, or dream, than to towns and squares, even imaginary ones. Yet he possesses a local history and human fate.

For more than a week now, while he has played *la pentanque*, or has chatted with acquaintances under the canopy, he has been followed by the shy, adoring eyes of a young woman who is a dancer and mime.

His story is told by his nephew, Jacques.

1. Minot's Mask

Minot Larbaud was my mother's younger brother. At the time of our carnival he was 32 and I was 20. We were devotees of *la petanque* and played almost every evening, often with his fiancée Estelle and her youngest sister; and then we'd go to the workshop under the canopy, where for several weeks a company of actors had been instructing the town in the making of masks.

One of this company, a slender young woman who was a dancer and mime, became enamored of Minot. After many days, she spoke with him. She blinked and winced. She was shy beyond belief. One could imagine that her true speech consisted entirely of ecstacy and despair, and that she had become a mime for sheer lack of ordinary words. A few days later, we noticed that she had begun to imitate the intonations of his voice.

Such things were frequent with Minot. People stared when he passed; they turned and stood there gazing. Nature had grown boastful in producing him. He was not tall, but was like a mighty Percheron, broad, immensely powerful, yet light and natural in his bearing. His eyes and close-cropped hair were glossy black. His skull was massive, his face broad at the cheekbones and chin.

Minot's power was magnetic, but the wondrous thing about him was his kindness. It was not a kindness of duty, but of pleasure. It made him glad. Nor was there any burden of gratitude in its wake, but a response of pride, for we understood that kindness like Minot's was quite without fear. Men, especially, were proud of him. They greeted him in tones that made the ordinary formulas of civil life ring like shouts of praise. Yet all else about Minot—his courtesy and rectitude, his conservative style of dress—was the very image of ordinary civil life. He was a businessman, a superbly brilliant one. For five years he had been the virtual manager of the entire operation of our family's vintnery in the old château.

This, then, was the man our young mime had come to adore. As for Minot—he softened his voice when he spoke to her. She was a convalescent in the world.

She asked him one night if he would allow her to make a casting of his face.

He sat in a chair and she put a sheet around him. She dipped into a jar of vaseline and slicked his eyebrows with it, and the line of his hair. A little crowd stood by. Even the waiters paused, some with full trays balanced shoulder high.

Minot in repose was compelling. The kindly élan one found so attractive resided chiefly in his eyes. When his eyes were closed, onc saw the massiveness of his features, and their calm, indifferent power.

He climbed onto a table she had prepared for him, and lay flat. She placed straws in his nostrils and wedged them with bits of cotton. She stretched a towel over his hair and pinned it under his chin. And then, pat by pat, she covered his face with plaster. She stepped back. Minot lay still. He looked like some chalky effigy dug from the ground.

Several nights later, he and I were playing *boules*. As we finished our game we looked up and saw that three monsters had been observing us. One of them cried gruffly, "Good throw, Larbaud!" A moment later we heard the voice of the mime. "Monsieur Larbaud!" She came running, holding a cardboard box before her. She opened it and took out a casting of his face. The monsters lifted their masks and crowded beside us.

The casting was fine. One could see even the lashes of his closed eyes. She held it so that it caught the light.

"It's excellent work," he said.

She was glowing. "I'll make you one," she said. She put the casting in the box almost anxiously, and lifted out a papier mâché duplicate. "I thought you might like this . . ."

Minot held it at arm's length. He smiled and nodded . . . but there was something about these masks that he didn't like.

2. Carnival

After two centuries without it, we were reviving our ancient carnival, though in a secular form, and at the harvest of the grapes rather than at Lent.

Cars had been banned from the old city. Strings of paper lanterns swayed like necklaces over the darkened streets.

At dusk our doorbell rang. There was a knock at the inner door, and a massive Pierrot strode in.

My mother laughed, "How *odd*, Minot!"

He was wearing the mask of his own face. He had cut holes in the eyes and had painted the eyebrows black.

"But you look fine," she said. "Let me see you."

He posed for her, turning slowly to show off the multicolored lozenges of his costume and the collar of paper lace. He bowed to her, sweeping the floor with his large cocked hat.

I was dressed in a turban and cape. We could hear singing and shouting. My mother pushed us toward the door. She promised to meet us in the park.

Torches seemed to float in the darkness. They bobbed steeply down our hillside streets. Tiny goblins and princesses darted this way and that, and hastened back to striding groups to clutch the hands of kings and witches, houris, bandits. Trumpets sounded below us in the square, while just above our heads our neighbors called to us good-naturedly. One saw that the darkness was night, and that night was continuous, it mounted to the sky, pitch black and starry.

Minot and I joined our committee at the ancient town hall. The courtyard was noisy. Wineskins were thrust toward us. Several bears, holding wrenches and screwdrivers, seemed to be tightening the slats of a four-wheeled cart. A stout monk stood on a chair and addressed the gathering in the voice of our socialist mayor. And then spoke a bear who sounded much like our fire chief. The musicians boarded their cart. We handed up flutes and trumpets, a violin, wineskin. We had arranged for a horse to pull this bulky contraption, and our monk emerged from the shadows leading it, but before he could reach the cart a startling laugh issued from the mask of Minot. He leaped between the shafts and seized them with his hands. Someone called "Pierrot!" There was a roar of approval. Minot strained. The cart began to roll. Several of us ducked between the shafts and got behind him. Our mayor abandoned the horse and scampered out front with his big bass drum. We emerged into the square and were met by a vast *hurrah*. The musicians struck up heartily. Our carnival was under way.

Of the many events of that pleasurable night, now far, far in the past, I would like to describe one, not only for its charm, but because it affected Minot and contributed to his own fateful performance.

We had stopped our cart at a corner near the square, where a fire truck awaited us, clanging its bell. Our horde of followers fanned out. Searchlights played over a building and then settled on a window two stories up, at which a lovelorn maiden appeared. She held a papier mâché rose, and she sighed to the heavens, opening and closing her arms while our musicians played lovelorn music. Suddenly a handsome prince ascended miraculously into the air, almost to a level with the maiden. She was overjoyed. So was the crowd. The acrobatic prince dropped out of sight, but soon hurtled skyward again, propelled by at least 20 bears heaving a canvas rescue net in the darkness below. He clapped his hands to his heart, pedaling in the air to keep his balance. He opened his arms wide, and she handed him the rose. He descended into the dark. A moment later he returned, and they plighted their troth with outstretched arms. But now another searchlight played upon the window just above our maiden's, and alas! a second maiden appeared there, a very beautiful one. A strained whisper could be heard among the firemen down below: *one . . . two . . . THREE!* The prince shot upward. He passed the first maiden, who clutched her head. He ascended to the window of the beautiful newcomer and, treacherous man! handed her the rose. He kissed his fingers and dropped into the darkness. Once again we heard the whispers of the bears . . . and our ambitious prince was transformed into a clown, for his heavenward flight was interrupted by the descent of an enormous skillet, like the rose, made of papier mâché. Holding his ears and thrusting out his tongue, he dropped into the net. The lights went out. The music soared and the fire bell clanged. There was light again, and amidst laughter and cheering the prince shot aloft one more time and sketched a bow in the air, while the two maidens bowed at their windows.

Late that night, or rather early in the morning, after other entertainments and the consumption of surely several tons of pastries, our town was contentedly falling asleep—except that 50 or 60 couples were still dancing under the strings of paper lanterns in front of the band pavilion in the park.

Estelle and Minot had quarreled. That is, Minot was acting strangely and Estelle had quarreled with him. I had escorted the women home and had returned to the park. The musicians were playing a waltz. I found Minot gliding and pirouetting among the dancers by himself. Estelle had said that he was drunk, that she had never seen him this way, that he had refused to listen to her, etc.

He still wore his mask. His movements were so graceful, so extraordinarily balanced that I could not believe he was intoxicated. He seemed to float. His eyes were visible at the cut-out eyes of the mask, and I could see that from time to time, and for long moments at a time, his eyes were closed. The other dancers had

removed their masks, as had I. We had removed them all together, hours ago, under the striped canopy where the refreshments
had been served. Not that we meant to return yet to our lives of
calendars and clocks! The musicians gave no sign of wanting to
stop. There were bottles, cups, and glasses on the bandstand at
their feet, and a cluster of paper in which pastries and sandwiches
had been wrapped.

I spoke with Minot. The dark eyes that peered from his mask
looked directly into mine, but without reciprocity.

I said, "I took them home," and he echoed my last word:
"Home."

I was disconcerted and said, "Well, our carnival has been a
great success." The massive head nodded, and the voice said,
"Success."

I said, "Do you suppose there's more wine?"

Pierrot nodded again and said, "More wine." And then he
laughed, laughed so winningly and deliciously, and with such
prolonged abandon, that I too began to laugh, as did several couples nearby, who picked up his echo: "More wine! More wine!"

Hands thrust a wineskin toward me. Dancing couples stopped
to chat, and little groups of talkers danced as they talked, trios
and quartets gliding this way and that with their arms round each
others' waists. We made up names of songs and requested them,
and the musicians invented songs and filled our requests. The
night air was as tasty as the wine. Above the gaily colored lanterns and the shadowy, massed leaves of our trees, a pointed
moon could be seen. I heard laughter. Someone cried, "Larbaud!"
I turned to see who was calling, but could not tell and could not
see Minot. Then with comic abruptness the cocked hat and
masked face of Pierrot rose above the dancers. He held a wineglass. Several voices cried, "Larbaud!" He dropped out of sight. A
moment later he emerged again, and there was laughter and a
flourish of trumpets. Many voices called, "Larbaud!" He pretended to sip from his glass. This gesture, and his elevation in the air,
made the grave face of his mask seem hilarious. He soared upward again—to a surprising height. The band greeted him with a
crescendo, and we dancers, all of us, without ceasing to dance,
cried, "Larbaud!" We were no longer a mere social group. We
were the dancers of the dance called The Leaps of Pierrot. We
whirled and laughed and shouted, "Larbaud!" And our glee

brimmed over into joy, confused, disoriented joy, for he performed what one would have thought to be impossible.

The nearest strings of lanterns were not high, but they were higher than our heads. He rose into the air. He seemed to move like a seal in water. His head and shoulders reached the height of the lanterns. He raised one arm and turned his back to them, as if baring his belly to the stars. He passed over the lanterns and came to earth lightly on the other side.

We could not believe what we had seen. Rather, some believed and some did not. What a hubbub there was! The band was simply blaring. We were shouting all kinds of things. Perhaps we were singing. Pierrot threw up his arms and ran off into the night.

I went after him, calling first, "Larbaud!" and then, "Minot!"

He was trotting up the hill. He stopped and waited for me. We went through the narrow streets and came out on the hilltop, where there were trees. He was singing and reciting verses. I was laughing and talking volubly. I kept falling behind and then running to catch up. I was talking about some exploit, some marvelous event that made me laugh. Was it only a leap? The framework of the universe—that is to say, the structure of my thought—kept coming apart. One moment I was anxious, the next moment giddy and free. What song was he singing? I overtook him and began singing too, at the top of my voice. And then I shouted, "Minot! What have you done? It's absurd, Minot!"— and I laughed and fell behind, and felt the universe hammer frighteningly at the framework of my thought. What was he shouting? That bulky Pierrot was striding away. I had to run to catch up. He had lost his hat. His mask rode the top of his head, observing the stars. He was singing again, was quite drunk, actually, yet looked like an ecstatic choirboy. I felt that I should reason with him—that is, I kept reasoning with him, but always ended by joining his song.

3. Games

There are men whose gifts surpass the ordinary more spectacularly than did Minot's, gifts of spirit, intellect, language, imagination. We are accustomed to the almost godlike superiority of a handful of men. And certainly there was superiority in Minot's gift. But there was also something primitive. Even his admirers, seeing him leap, could not suppress their smiles. Minot himself would shrug with amusement. On the other hand, he could not resist leaping. He was possessed. And his demon, alas, was a giddy little boy . . . or something worse.

As for me . . . I was elated by this power. I wanted to be close to it. And truly, there were times when it was not ludicrous at all, but sublime. I would say this especially of the international competition that established his fame.

I carried a card that identified me as his trainer and gave me access to the grassy field bounded by the running track. I held his sweatsuit while he leaped. I carried his extra shoes and a hamper for food. Otherwise I lay on the grass and watched the games, indulging the sweet fancy that the long evenings of my boyhood had come again, our wrestling matches and games of soccer, but heightened in a public form and brought to the very edge of human capacity. The games are decorative. Here in this great arena was the physical splendor of the human race. And here were we others who admired and shouted praise. The athletes were our ornaments and we were theirs.

The air was clear and brisk. The national flags that crowned the ring of steep bleachers trembled continually and were occasionally lifted into full display. Beyond the flags one could see the tops of mountains, and above the mountains a pale bright sky with vivid clouds.

Early in the day Minot attracted attention. His massy, powerful body was matched by two or three others, but his bearing was unique. He could not divest himself of authority. It was in his posture, his level gaze, his composure, his courteous attention to everything around him. Young competitors attempted to cow each other. They made displays of confidence, or of contempt. Minot was benign, encouraging, personally indifferent. But then came the moment of leaping, and I myself, who loved him, felt a twinge of embarrassment. Where the other jumpers loped toward the bar and sprang into the air from one foot, Minot simply stood before the bar and looked up at it. His patriarchal grace would vanish. Here was a stout little boy bending his knees and swinging his arms, as if preparing to jump down from a chair, or the step of a porch, except that his eyes were raised. The other jumpers would gather by the pit, for the word had gone round, "Larbaud is up!" He would bend his knees deeply several times, and then with a great swing of both arms would launch himself upward, headfirst. His leaps were greeted by laughter, rather admiring than derisive, and by shouts of candid delight. "*Olé* Larbaud!" "*Viva* Larbaud!" "*Jawohl* Larbaud!" He would emerge from the sawdust pit with a smile and a massive shrug, as much as to say, "It can't be helped."

Later in the day the cheering ceased. Still later there were glances of hostility. But by now the crowd in the stands had discovered him. They called his name before he leaped, and cheered and stamped their feet after he had cleared the bar. They saw him, certainly, as an underdog, an outsider who nevertheless might win.

We ate on the field and rested.

All through the day there had been sprints and relays, javelin and discus. The slow mountain twilight deepened in the grass and drifted upward like a dye in clear water. The leisurely high jump entered its final rounds.

The stands were crowded at our end of the field. French athletes gathered at the jumping pit and feasted their eyes on this remarkable teammate, of whom they knew nothing but rumor. When Minot leaped now our cheers expressed more than mere enthusiasm. Some deeply lodged hope, if hope is the right word, had been stirred into wakefulness.

A blaze of light, shocking in its suddenness, closed off the sky and drained the color from the grass.

Only three competitors were left: the tall black American, the muscular Russian, and Minot. A booming electrical voice announced that all three had surpassed the former record. Another voice succeeded the first, and then another, in the languages of the nations. The bar was set higher.

Minot won. There was prolonged, delighted cheering, and the French members of the combined international band released a salvo of the "Marseillaise."

The crackling voices spoke again, but in less official, more human tones, for they were obliged to inform us not only that Monsieur Minot Larbaud of France had established a new record of seven feet six inches, but also that he would attempt the unprecedented height of eight feet. In this event, as in the sprints, such an increment is vast; it represents the accumulated prowess of many decades. The other athletes understood this. They pressed together in great numbers round the jumping pit, but they were silent, or looked into each others' faces and spoke in consternated whispers. The shadowy thousands in the stands, however—or a great many of them—seemed released into glee. They stood on tiptoe and waved. They clambered on seats and called ecstatically, "Larbaud! Larbaud!" Photographers forced their way to the pit and knelt or threw themselves beside it.

Minot was bending his knees and swinging his arms. This style, which had seemed so comical earlier in the day, evoked a concentrated hush. His final gathering of force was accompanied by the assisting gasps of thousands, and he soared upward, reaching with both arms. At the peak of his rise he curled into a ball and rolled over the bar.

A sibilant great breath passed over the amphitheater, many-throated, yet soft and high. It was followed by silence. A young athlete beside me was sobbing violently. A few cursed, and I heard moans that were like moans of despair. Now came an explosion of voices that was positively frightening. The crowd was roaring.

Minot stood beside me, his blue cotton jersey draped across his back. His face was radiant. His eyes were opened wide and were shining and unfocused. Officials measured the bar. They measured the measuring tape itself; and each little group gave way to another which repeated the procedure. They conferred with Minot, who said he would jump ". . . one last time." This was accepted, although the tradition is to perform to the point of failure. He asked them to set the bar at nine feet. They stared at him uncomprehendingly, and said. "Of course. Yes." With the aid of boxes, the bar was set.

The roaring in the stands abated to a rumbling. The first crackling of the loudspeakers brought silence. A faltering voice announced that Monsieur Minot Larbaud of France—and this name, now, had become a universal property, it was no longer the name of a competitor, it was Monsieur Minot Larbaud of France—would jump "one last time." The announcer omitted to state the height. He could not bring himself to speak it. Nor could those who followed him. The silence that now fell endured for many minutes. A subterranean, a secret information sped outward from the jumping pit in whispers: *the bar is set at nine.*

Minot stood before the bar and gazed at it. If an unreasoning hope had been released among us—if, to put it fancifully, invisible doves in thousands fluttered above our heads, this image of Minot gazing upward to that impossible height stopped our throats with pathos: we stood in the darkness of the cosmos in a tiny point of light; how small man is! how limited! The stadium was silent and was utterly without motion. Even when he bent his knees in his final burst of force, there was no responding gasp.

His body arched upward in the glare of light, an arc like a motion of the mind, so pure it was, and so free of the restraints of our heavy earth. To the purity of this arc he added, as he soared outstretched across the bar, a gesture of grace, or joy, that swept us all into a delirium of pride: he lifted his head and spread his arms like wings.

We many thousands stood there singing—or so it seemed. There were, in actuality, complex emotions scattered through the mass. A voice cried, *"Mein Gott!"* Another: "He didn't do it!" There were shouts of rage and indignation. But the torrential jubilation swept everything away. The stands were a waterfall of human bodies pouring toward Minot. He was lifted on shoulders and hands, was carried about the field like a banner, was placed alone on the platform on which other victors had received their prizes. The band was playing 30 songs at once. The loudspeakers were mute. Minot stood there smiling, one arm raised. Someone handed him a glass of wine. He held it aloft and turned in all directions. The cheering never ceased. Fragments of the "Marseillaise" could be heard. Minot turned toward the music and, heels together, tossed off the wine. The cheering voices rose still higher. Hands and shoulders claimed him again, he was whirled about the field, and finally—followed by a capering, crazily shouting throng—was carried through the gates outward into the night, outward, that is to say, toward the lights of the nearby town.

The newspapers of the world were filled next day with images of Minot Larbaud. Larbaud crouched at the jumping pit. Larbaud in the air, arms outstretched like wings. Larbaud on the platform saluting his admirers with a glass of wine.

4. Fame/Dejection/The Everyday Surreal

In the months after Minot's victory, no newspaper or magazine could go to press without his photograph, his quoted words, or words about him. One could not listen to the radio but one would hear Minot himself, or doctors, psychologists, politicians, film stars offering praises—and interpretations—of his extraordinary powers. The effect on our vintnery's sales was breath-taking. But Minot himself was vanishing. He was bewitched, vacant, elated—and apparently was unaware of the isolation that pursued him in the very thick of his public life. The world was ringing in his ears.

A well-known impresario organized a tour of exhibitions. I could not forego taking part, though I came to dread the sight of Minot in short pants, barelegged, the number 9 displayed on chest and back, saluting his audience with a glass of our vintnery's wine. Yet the leap itself—"the prodigious leap," as it had come to be called—was as dazzling as ever. We performed in every city of Western Europe and made two trips to England. Within five short months Minot was wealthy. An American tour was arranged.

But now a number of things happened, the first and most important of which was the dejection of Minot.

The spell was wearing off. Rather, it was intermitted by periods of clear-eyed restlessness and by moments of what seemed almost to be despair. His long romance with Estelle had ended, but it was not this that was troubling him.

One night, in a taxi carrying us back to the hotel from what had seemed to be a triumph (and he had been elated, but now was sitting in the corner with his head bowed and his arms folded on his chest), I urged him to put an end to this career. For I had come to believe that his talent was a meager thing compared to the rare intelligence he possessed; compared, too, to his character, which was perhaps the rarest thing of all. The words I spoke to him were these (I remember them clearly, for they rang very foolishly in my ears): "Take up your old life again. You were happy."

He was silent. I realized how dreadful those words must have sounded. "Take up your old life." As if anyone can do that

At length he said—to my surprise—"I look forward to leaping."

The newspapers that week reported the proceedings of an international athletic conference. Minot's leap had had a devastating effect on the champions of other countries. There was talk of removing the high jump from future competitions. But this too had proved depressing. Nothing had been resolved.

The very same issues of the Paris papers carried an advertisement for a circus, the star of which was a clown who called himself *M. Aussi-Larbaud* . . . and there he was, in baggy pants and painted face, sailing through the air "ten feet high," a bottle of beer in one hand. Minot was delighted. He laughed with a gaiety I had not heard in many months. "Ah!" he said. "We must go!"

We did, and the clown was marvelous. He wore enormous springs on his feet, concealed by his trousers. He stood at least eight feet high and before jumping paraded around the arena with a gait that reduced us all to helpless laughter. He leaped a ten-foot bar with ease, swigging from his bottle as he crossed it. He would not stop leaping. He leaped over the ringmaster, who began to pursue him. He leaped over an elephant, over a horse, over a painted wagon. Soon dozens were pursuing him, and he eluded them all with great bounds, swigging from his bottle. But now five other clowns burst into the arena, all eight feet tall, all equipped with springs. They too chased him, and the whole procession bounded exuberantly out the exit.

Even after the lights came on, people remained at their seats chattering and laughing. We heard the following conversation:

"You see, my friend, there is nothing much to it."

"Eh? What? He's wearing springs!"

"Precisely."

"Larbaud jumps without springs. He jumps barelegged. Everyone can see."

"Exactly the ruse of a clever charlatan."

Minot was listening intently. He glanced at me . . . and seeing the look on my face, shrugged calmly.

He was subjected, in the next few weeks, to a perfect plague of comedians, the most noteworthy of whom was a nightclub entertainer who began appearing everywhere with an absurd explanation of the famous leap. Speaking in grandiose intellectual tones, he presented himself as an *ologist*, the world's leading *ologist;* and praised *ology* as the purest form of knowledge, much superior to the corrupted lesser *ologies:* soci, psych, physi, anthrop . . . and suchlike rant for five or ten minutes, coming at last to The Integral Theory of The Prodigious Leap, which was nothing but the bare assertion that there were in reality four Larbauds, each of whom jumped two and a quarter feet, adding up to nine.

The disturbing thing about this absurd performer was the hilarity he induced in his listeners. One did not know what to make of it. Minot, too, was taken aback. The worst, however, was yet to come.

The estimable magazine *European Sports* published the resolutions of a multinational committee of athletes, trainers, and athletic directors. With distressing unanimity they agreed that the high jump should be rigorously defined, and that such styles as Minot's (which was referred to by a variety of disparaging names: Kangaroo Hopping, Cannonballing, etc.) be absolutely forbidden. Many suggested that his performance be stricken from the records. This was not agreed upon, although that memorable night was indeed reduced to a footnote.

There now appeared in one of our scandal-mongering newspapers an article by a pseudo-scientific oddity-hawker, who speculated that Minot Larbaud—whom he called The Cat Man—was a mutant, a freak of nature whose prowess could be explained by the fact that he possessed the striated muscles of the cat family. The article was replete with charts and diagrams, and ended with the observation that were Larbaud actually a cat, his leap would not be prodigious at all, but mediocre.

Minot's last performance was a disaster. It was in the south of France, in an indoor arena. The preliminary entertainments passed without incident. He made his entrance and saluted the audience. I stood near the improvised jumping pit. The house lights were darkened and a spot of light followed Minot. He removed his sweatsuit and handed it to me. He stood before the pit and gazed at the bar, and then began the rhythmic crouching that would end in the explosive leap. At the very moment of his deepest crouch a chorus of catcalls split the silence. Minot stood erect, listening. The greater part of the audience was loyal to him and shouted their indignation, but the catcalls broke out anew, louder than before. Minot came to me and took the sweatsuit from my hands, calmly donned it, and walked in measured strides from the arena. He never leaped again.

The local newspapers carried headlines: CAT MAN WALKS OUT. Even the Paris papers questioned the authenticity of the prodigious leap.

The final blow was a radio symposium devoted to this very question. Among the disputants was an undersecretary of educa-

tion. He seized attention by saying that he had been present that
night at the international competition. And then with devastating
bland assurance, he remarked that a trampoline had been concealed at the jumping pit. It was evident that no one believed
him. On the other hand, no one called his lie. The moderator
said, "The allegation is serious. Are you quite certain?" And the
secretary replied, "My dear fellow, I bounced on it."

What Minot felt at this time, I am unable to say. I tried to
reach him that very night. He was not at home. Worse, he did not
return.

5. Away

My mother was distraught. It was unlike Minot to retreat like
this, unlike him to reject us in his time of need. Yet because of
this rejection in the face of love, I came to see that when a man is
struggling with his world, even love is of the world.

For three months we waited anxiously. There came at last a
letter from one M. Blanchard requesting that we meet him in
Paris.

At the appointed time and place, Blanchard appeared; that is,
Minot appeared.

He had gained a great deal of weight. He wore a beard. His
hair was long and full. Both hair and beard were dyed a chestnut
brown.

We were so glad to see him that I did not at first fully notice
the quiet that had come into his speech and manner. He had
digested a melancholy that must have been severe. I thought that
I understood him. He had suffered injustice and a massive insult;
his notoriety was painful. The events of later years taught me that
I understood him very little, if at all.

He begged us to protect his new identity. He said that he wanted peace, and longed for obscurity. We ate and talked. He had
made elaborate plans for a new life. We strolled by the Seine
listening to his words of hope while our hearts sank.

My own life, and my mother's life, were much changed by the
change in Minot's. I will not say that our lives became drab, for
they did not . . . but they were grievously diminished.

I married the sweetheart of my youth. Four children were born to us. I did not leave the vintnery, although I often longed to do so.

Minot, too, eventually married. We visited him frequently, but visits are a poor substitute for daily life in common.

He had settled expensively, near Paris, and had established a factory of electronic equipment. He prospered, raised three sons, erected an extraordinary greenhouse in his garden, and divided his evenings and weekends between horticulture and literature. Novels, plays, books of poems filled the shelves of his study. There came a time when his letters slacked off. For several months they ceased altogether. Our telephone rang one night and my mother answered. I heard her greet Mathilde, Minot's wife . . . and then she cried out in alarm.

Minot had been taken to a psychiatric hospital. Mathilde could not say what the trouble was. He had become melancholy, had refused to leave his room, had refused to speak, and finally had lost so much weight that she had become terrified.

Late that night we were put through to his doctor, a young psychiatrist, who added nothing to Mathilde's description, yet managed somehow to calm us while at the same time imparting the information that we would not, as yet, be allowed to visit.

We met this young man several weeks later in the lobby of the hospital. He was tall and austere. He cautioned us not to demand a response from Minot, and he requested that we visit him singly. My mother went first.

I questioned him. No, he said, Minot was not deranged. Nor was it quite correct to say that his extreme withdrawal was self-destructive, though certainly it was dangerous.

"My impression," he said, "is not that he has attacked the self, but that he has withdrawn volition from it. One might say that temporarily he is without self. He does not know what to do."

His face came alight. "He is vital," he said. "He is extraordinary. He is like a baffled animal who gathers himself within his fur and waits. My treatment . . ."—here he smiled in such a way as made me want to take his hands. It was a smile that told me much. It lit his face with an expression that men inherit from their mothers; and I understood that this austere young aristocrat had come from a working-class home; I even fancied that I could see his mother bending at her work, harassed, overburdened, vehement in opinion . . . and intellectually free.

" . . . my treatment," he said, "is to keep away. No drugs. No talk. He is curing himself. I know he is."

He nodded—it amounted to a bow—and went away.

The blank face of the elevator opened and my mother emerged. Her plump cheeks were wet and she was wiping her eyes.

"I cannot understand it," she said.

"Did you speak with him?"

"No . . . and yet I think he is all right. Ah . . ."

Minot lay motionless in bed, his arms at his sides on the unwrinkled blanket. His head was raised by a pillow. He had aged appallingly. For a moment his eyes touched mine, and I fancied that they greeted me. I was so swept by emotion that perhaps I did not act wisely. I wanted to embrace him and could not hold back, but before I reached the bed he had closed his eyes. I kissed his brow.

It was hard to believe that he had glanced at me a moment past. His breathing was so regular and calm, his eyelids and temples so relaxed in closure that he seemed to be asleep, more deeply asleep than sleep.

I sat in a chair by the bed.

His thick hair and beard were gray. It was this, chiefly, that had shocked me. And then I realized that he must have stopped dying them. Perhaps they had been gray for years. He was gaunt. Nevertheless, this massive skull, these broad cheekbones and wide, nervously modeled brow seemed more than ever awesome. I was struck most of all by the play of thought upon this motionless face. His face was alive with thought, not such thoughts as begin in words, but the deep thoughts of the organs and limbs.

I sat there for 30 minutes. We spoke not a word, nor did he open his eyes. I listened to his breathing. Perhaps he listened to mine. And I felt that—as happens at Quaker meetings when complex decisions evolve in communal silence—our silence was fertile and achieved a meaning.

My next two visits, a week apart, were the same. We communed in silence.

And then I found him sitting up in bed. He nodded to me when I came in. And while I stood there soaking up the past that once again appeared familiarly in his eyes, he said gravely, "Thank you, Jacques."

Words came tumbling out of me. I wanted him to be well. I wanted to cancel out the interlude of sickness.

He shook his head. "Jacques," he said, "I've been resting from making sense."

Yet we did talk, and the following week talked more, and more still the week after that. At the conclusion of which visit he handed me a piece of paper bearing the title of a book, and asked me to buy it for him and send it at once by messenger.

It was a book on birds, large and handsomely illustrated. The following evening I was at home. The telephone rang. It was Minot.

"Where are you?" I cried.

"At the hospital," he said.

"Jacques," he went on, "I have finished the book. It was delightful. Will you do something?"

I was astonished. The book contained more than 600 pages. Past events came back to me: prizes Minot had won at school, his brilliance in business, his phenomenal memory.

He dictated the titles of several books and asked that I bring them when I came.

All were on birds, their anatomy, the mechanics of flight, social organization, evolution.

I found him sprawled comfortably on the bed in a welter of books. He was cheerful. When I asked why he so admired birds, he laughed and said, "I don't. They are dreadfully bourgeois: territory, status, duties of the home. I except the very young. Best of all is the egg."

I too laughed. But I repeated my question. He shrugged it away and held out his hand for the new books.

A few days later I received the following letter:

Dear brother,

I shall be going home tomorrow.

You and Berthe have been so patient! I have seen how often you have wanted to understand and yet refrained from plying me with questions. I would like to explain to you now as much as I can, and then, if you will agree, never speak of these things again.

You know how painful it was for me to leave you and Berthe. I

won't dwell on this. But I doubt that you have guessed how painful-
ly I have suffered the loss of the town itself. Apparently I was happy there. I mean that I must have experienced the one true happiness of life, the happiness one can possess only if one is unaware of
it. Yet there is some solace in acknowledging that a wound of this
kind never heals. I don't mean that I regret the past. It could not
have been otherwise. I am not sure that you have understood this. I
know that you thought me somewhat ridiculous in my exhibitionis-
tic career. Well, Jacques, I did too. But I must tell you this: it was a
joy to leap, a joy to give way utterly to my powers. I was glad to
throw myself away. What is self compared to joy?

Yet everything was wrong. I would have preferred that such
powers as mine were ordinary, as ordinary as dancing or skating; I
should have had company, and might have shared my happiness
and have partaken of the happiness of others, just as the brothers at
the abbey routinely share their matins and vespers. As it was, I
suffered isolation without the relief of solitude; and then insult
without any hope of correction.

Well, I am strong-willed, I willed away the past. In material
ways, as you know, I prospered. My deliberate forgetting became a
habit, as familiar as the habit of unhappiness. I am describing the
formula for the passing of time: it flows right by; one can almost
see it go.

But then something happened that I was powerless to control. All
that I had banished from my waking life erupted in my dreams. I
doubt that I can describe them to you. They were intolerably beautiful. I dreamed of leaping—not as I leaped at the international
games, or later, but as I leaped that splendid night of our carnival.
Except that my leaps became flight, sustained, effortless flight.
Night after night I took to the sky, the sky of noon, always,
drenched in sunlight. The settings of these flights were not exotic—
nor were they the environs of the suburb in which I now live, but
our town, Jacques, and my own home. Think of the things you
know well . . . the olive trees in the garden (the one we mended so
many years ago was thriving!), the chestnuts, the asparagus bed, the
stone fountain. But imagine that when you look at them they respond, they receive. I cannot describe it. They were so dear to me.
And there were the cobblestone streets of our hill, and the iron
railings, and the houses. There was never a soul in sight, and yet I
wasn't saddened or confused, rather I awaited their return, almost
deliciously, as one awaits the resolution of a movement in music.
How much green there is from the sky! How many shades! How
well they go with the ochers of our bare earth, and our terracotta
roofs!

One aspect of these flights I dare not dwell on even now. I saw things I had never seen before and could not have guessed existed. There is a bird's nest in Popil's English chimney. It is braced against the bricks where the lining is broken. Near the peak of Tabard's terracotta roof there is a whole line of glazed tile, deep blue. And do you know that the servants of our wealthy recluse, Boudaille, live in a wretched hut of galvanized metal at the end of the garden? I had thought it was a potting shed, but there is a television antenna on the roof. One of the metal sheets of that roof was formerly a sign of some sort. I could make out faded orange letters . . . AUD . . . FILS.

Do these things exist? God help me, perhaps they do! I would rather not know.

How much I could tell you about flight! We associate colors with sounds, though certainly we cannot see them. The currents of the air have a similar effect. The updrafts are like the sun; the downdrafts are cool and silvery, they are like waterfalls, but gentler. Can you imagine birds diving away beneath you? I could not identify them.

I am told that dreams are brief. These seemed to last entire nights. I would awaken with images of clouds in the corners of my eyes, and my lips still tingling from the wind. And alas! here was my heavy body. Here was my motionless bed. Here was my heavy clothing, my stonelike shoes, my heavy, heavy life. I could not bear the thought of *responding* to anyone. And then I could not bear the thought of speaking at all. And finally I did not even wish to move.

I know that you believe my collapse was due to unhappiness. But it was not that, Jacques. It was joy. Joy attacked me every night and beat me down.

Yet there was something providential in those dreams. My memories have been tamed, the real past subdued.

The books you searched for so patiently, and so kindly brought to me, were suggested by Henri, for whose presence here I thank my stars. He is a brilliant and compassionate man.

Perhaps, to anyone but me, his suggestion was obvious. I did not think of it, and would not have. Nor could I have said to myself, as he said to me, that my collapse was not the first stage of illness, but the second stage of a recovery that began in dream.

Some aura of those dreams does indeed seem to flicker through these pages. And the imagined space of my flights has become the real space through which these highly organized creatures make their way. I have seen, too, that the more specialized these texts become, the more general they really are. Which is only to say that nature is continuous. "From the evolutionary point of view, the bird is simply the method by which the egg perpetuates itself." I read this sentence with something like joy. And I experienced my only intuition of eternity . . . which, so it seems, has nothing to do with time, but with the imperishability of the boundary at which consciousness becomes aware of itself gazing at the inexplicable. To glimpse this boundary, or better (should one be so blessed) to stand at it, must be, surely, to attach oneself to the spirit that endures long after life has passed.

But I will call you soon and we can talk of this at length.

6. Minot Blanchard

For years Minot had preserved a Mediterranean presence in the large garden of his home near Paris. That is to say, he had nurtured through all weathers two trees, an olive and a fig. They represented the south to him; I should say, rather, they were an actual piece of it. The large greenhouse turned an "L" in the garden and was constructed so that a sheltering dome, in the arms of the "L," could be placed over the trees in winter.

It had always been a pleasure to step into this leaf and flower-crowded space. The light of day was rich and variegated, and at night the recessed shadows of indented leaves were enticing. When Minot returned from the hospital, this domesticated wilderness became his true home. He equipped the far end of the greenhouse with bookcases, worktables, and a leather sofa. He retired from business, and spent his waking hours in the softened light of this retreat.

Minot's three sons grew to strapping young manhood. The large house was their domain, and their mother's. All were vigorous, endlessly active; yet when Minot emerged into the dining room for the evening meal, the house grew quiet. It was not that they feared him—on the contrary, he was kindly, and they seemed to adore him—but that an aura of solitude surrounded him, I would say *attended* him, like the retinue of a monarch.

He had grown stout. He seemed enormous. His steel-gray hair had become a mane, his beard a luxuriant patriarchal emblem. He would pause in the doorway and remove his spectacles and rub his eyes while his vision adjusted to the indoor light. He was so centered, so gathered within himself, that one watched his simplest movements with fascination. When he peered through his glasses again, stepping with weighty ease into the room, his eyes were warm and his smile openly affectionate.

Costly equipment appeared in the greenhouse: a microscope, a cabinet for slides, dissecting tools, a balance scale. Pages of manuscript accumulated on the desk.

I did not know what to make of this work. But there was much that I did not know at this time. I did not know, for instance, that Minot had established a correspondence with scholars in several fields.

By custom, during our visits, it was I who went to fetch him for dinner. I would take him an aperitif, and we would sit and talk for a few minutes before going in. Often he would turn aside, suspending a phrase he had just begun, and would jot down a note or two, or a paragraph, or a whole page. And I would sit there and watch him write, knowing that even if I had wished to disturb him I would not have been able to. Green leaves cascaded around us. On a shelf near his bent head, the skeletons of three small birds were mounted as if in flight, one behind the other, like generations of the dead, or the unborn. Below them, on the same shelf, lay a single, somewhat dusty egg. Minot finished his notes, reached for his aperitif, and resumed the conversation.

If he never spoke of the papers that grew so numerous on his desk, he spoke enchantingly of the lives of birds; and of problems of evolution and genetics; and of the ecology of the small islands on which some few species had become wingless; and of oddities of creaturely perception, the cameralike vision of the bird, with its uniform focus and narrow band of binocular vision straight ahead. He had enticed many birds to nest and feed in the garden, and had become fascinated by the question of individual differences within a species.

The publication of Minot's first book was an occasion of delight. More than five years had passed since he had become a monk of study. We arrived one weekend and were greeted with suppressed excitement by Mathilde, who said only, "Go to the garden!"

Minot was striding up and down with his hands behind his back. He raised one arm in an exuberant greeting.

"You seem pleased," I said, and I inquired *why* with a shrug.

"Yes," he said softly, "I am pleased . . ." and he held up beside him, on a level with his face, as if it were a companion he might throw one arm around, a large thick book with a glossy cover. Its title, now, is well known. A moment went by before we registered that beneath the title was printed the name Minot Blanchard.

His three strapping lads came running to join us. It was a delightful moment. His pleasure was so open that we were able to embrace him, pat his back, shake his hand, and fuss about him to our heart's content. The book went from hand to hand.

Later, over pastries and champagne in the garden (and still following the book with his eyes when it passed from one lap to another), he said, "We take our books for granted, but you know, they really are magic. I don't mean their replication, though that's quite wonderful, and it's certainly true that my existence has been multiplied. No, I mean that spirit becomes matter, and matter again becomes spirit. Any primitive could tell you that an object capable of such a thing is magical."

Intellectuals who were not scientists admired the structure of Minot's book, and its style, but said that he had not added anything to existing knowledge. Scientists, however, who knew better the immensity of human ignorance, praised the book warmly. He was such a pupil as masters long for. But more than that, he had brought several fields together not by stressing their common knowledge, but their common mysteries, which he had made visible not solely as intellectual questions, but as the delight and solitude of the questioner, and the social bond that makes him spell it out. It was a radiant book.

Paris was clamoring to see him. He never stirred from the study in the garden. It was at this time that I realized—though I had known it all along—that for five years he had not ventured from the house. Our two families, and the young doctor who had remained his friend, were his entire acquaintance.

I believe that certain men know intuitively the master rhythms of their lives; they know the time of death quite accurately. Minot was husbanding time.

His second book was printed three years later. It too caused quite a stir, but in other quarters, for it was speculative and difficult. Its merits are debated in learned journals. I have not followed its fortunes and am not competent to do so. Perhaps (how can one know?) I have deferred this study. I have little motive at present. Within three months of the publication of the book, Minot was dead of a cerebral hemorrhage. He had entered his 61st year.

I was named executor of his literary remains. For three months I went daily to the desk in the greenhouse and studied and sorted his papers. His correspondence was large. There were letters from amateurs and scientists, and later, after his own book had become known, from poets and writers and members of the general public. We must track down his replies, as he did not make copies. But there will be a volume of selected correspondence, and then perhaps (it is not in my hands) a volume of studies and notes. I would like for any forthcoming books, or new editions of the old ones, to display somewhere, perhaps on the title page, a drawing of the three small skeletons in flight above his desk, and the single egg that lies beneath them. I looked at them often during my days in the greenhouse; and I came to believe that they were not—at least in the narrow sense—exhibits of science, but a work of art he had created to be an emblem. Perhaps, actually, there is no distinction.

In his will, Minot requested cremation. The words were addressed to me, and I will quote them:

> I entrust this to you more than to the others, as I know you will not be turned aside by sentiment or convention. I do wish earnestly for my body to be cremated, and I do not wish for my ashes to be buried, or for any stone or memorial to be erected. Scatter my ashes in the garden, or for that matter anywhere. I mean that I am at home, Jacques. I know that you understand.

7. *Four Memories*

I. During my 16th year I was ill for three weeks. A celebrated theater company was touring *Tartuffe*, but I was confined to my bed the night they played in our town, and I was obliged to content myself with reading the text. Late that evening, I heard Minot's voice downstairs, and the voice of a woman I knew to be Estelle Drolet. A moment later they entered my room, followed by my mother.

The sight of them was almost tormenting. Their faces were glowing. Minot was dressed in black, with a dazzling white shirt and black tie. His close-cropped hair was black, his eyebrows black, his eyes black and brilliant. Estelle, though somewhat taller than he, gave the impression of looking up into his face. After every glance she seemed alight with gaiety. She wore long black gloves and a black dress that left her arms and throat bare. I had seen her often; why was I so bewildered? There was something mysterious in the way her hips curved into a waist as slender as a young girl's, and in how that waist passed so smoothly into her lower ribs. She wore a delicate silver necklace that glinted dully as she breathed.

Minot was talking volubly, something rare with him. His voice was not loud, but its timbre was very dense, compacted in that mighty chest. My mother brought chairs.

"Was it good?" I said. "I mean the actors. I mean was the production good? I mean did you enjoy yourselves?"

"It was excellent," said Minot. He threw up one arm and recited several lines, apparently in the accents of the leading actor. My mother laughed delightedly, and Estelle lowered her head and smiled at him. She turned to me and said, "Oh, it was crowded!"

I knew where they had sat: in a loge at one side, reserved in perpetuity for our family; for the theater itself had been given to the town by a later generation of the same ancestors—my father's side—whose château is now the vintnery. My mother's side goes back just as far: she and Minot are descended from the broad-backed laborers who had hauled the château's stones.

"A great lot of your chums were there," said Minot.

"Well, what . . . what . . . "—I ended by saying, "Were the sets very fine?"

Minot was smiling at me. "When the curtain opened," he said—and drew apart his powerful, short-fingered hands . . .

He described the set. He described the entrances of the actors, and spoke their lines. He began to pace and to gesticulate and change his voice. Our smiles faded as we listened. He no longer glanced at us. His face was ablaze with energy, and yet was somnambulistic. I had never seen him look so happy.

"Good heavens!" whispered Estelle, as he rounded a couplet, "Exactly so!"

My mother was biting her lower lip. Minot moved about the room.

My mother came to the bed and sat beside me. "The book," she whispered, and pointed to the end table.

We opened the book and found our place. The text read:

"... *Les hommes la plupart sont étrangement faits!*
Dans la juste nature on ne les voit jamais;

> *La raison a pour eux des bornes trop petites;*
> *En chaque caractère ils passent ses limites . . ."*

Minot raised one hand and shook his head. *"Les hommes la plupart sont étrangement faits!"* he said. *"Dans la juste nature on ne les voit jamais; la raison a pour eux des bornes trop petites; en chaque caractère ils passent ses limites . . ."*

At the end of Act One he emerged from his revery and smiled. "Intermission," he said.

"Minot," said my mother, "you are incredible!"

"How did you do it?" I cried. "How can you *remember* all that?"

He came over and sat on the bed. His great weight tilted the mattress so that my mother and I had to adjust our positions.

I thought that he was trying to phrase an answer to my question. But he smiled and pointed to the book and said, "Did I do it right?"

My mother nodded and said, "Perfectly, Minot."

"Good," he said, and stood up.

"Perhaps if you just started playing soccer," he said, "your body would decide to get well."

"Please, Minot," said my mother.

Before I fell asleep that night, I thought long about the differences between men. And something I had noticed but had not understood persisted in my mind as a question. This was the face of Estelle—for when Minot had finished his performance she had glanced at him almost with fear. Fear is too strong a word. Yet a serious disquiet had sped across her face.

II. By the time I was 12 years old I had come to savor the prestige of having Minot for an uncle. He seemed to know everyone. His local fame was greater and more enduring than that of our mayors, though—as far as I could tell then—it was based on nothing more than the pleasure of greeting him as he passed. He traveled everywhere on his bicycle. One would see him flitting among the cars of the morning and evening rush, waving almost continually, his briefcase flapping from the handlebars.

Late one afternoon my young chums and I were sprawled on the grass of our soccer field. We saw him speeding down the precipitous street above us. I leaped up and waved. I did not know that he was coming to our house for dinner, and I was not sure that he could see me. He jumped his bike over the gutter, glided down the grassy slope, and pulled up short in our very midst. My chums greeted him gleefully. He motioned for me to hop on the crossbar, which I did. We circled deep into the field, and then turned back toward the slope. He pedaled mightily, leaning as far as he could over my crouching figure. Our speed carried us to the top. He jumped the gutter and entered traffic. I glanced back at my chums. The looks on their faces filled me with joy.

III. He stands in the doorway of our house, both arms above his head, a bottle of wine in each hand. It is his sister's—my mother's—birthday. I hear my own voice crying shrilly, "Minot is here! Minot is here!" And then I run to fetch my mother.

I am nine years old. Minot is 21.

IV. Early in my fourth year, and not long after my father's death, Minot and my mother and I spent a week at the beach in St. Tropez. We preferred the little cove on the outskirts of the town. My mother read under an umbrella. Minot held me in the shallow water and showed me how to paddle with my arms and legs. I played near my mother then, and he searched the little tide pools for whatever might be found. His massive body had not yet grown hard. He was a patient, quiet boy. All afternoon he studied the sea moss and tiny life forms in a few feet of sand, rock, and water. From time to time, he came to us to show what he had found. He came once walking carefully, holding his hands before him like a bowl.

Kneeling in the sand, our heads bowed over his cupped hands, we saw a pool of water, slightly shaded, clear and cool, such as one might find in a cavern, near the entrance; and in the pool a tiny, almost transparent fish, the body of which, when it was still, drifted outward like a ghostly pennon from the anchor of its round black eye. It darted to and fro so unpredictably that one might think it bodiless, a mere neural impulse in some larger other body; and then it would be still, and the black speck of its eye would accumulate presence and begin to seem like a gathered intelligence.

Wash Far Away

JOHN BERRYMAN

LONG AFTER THE PROFESSOR had come to doubt whether lives
held crucial points as often as the men conducting or undergoing
them imagined, he still considered that one day in early spring
had made a difference for him. The day began his deeper—deepest—acquaintance with "Lycidas," now for him the chief poem
of the world, to which he owed, he thought, as much as anything
else, his survival of his wife's death. The day had humbled him
and tossed him confidence. One decision had come out of it—to
give up research. He had gone back, of course, two or three
times, but briefly, guiltily, without commitment and without result, abandoning it again each time more firmly; now he had not
touched it for years. He knew that his appointment with tenure,
four years later, must have been opposed on this ground, and
barely managed through by his department chairman. The sense
of stepping up on Alice's body came bitterly back—she had just
died, and he had even at the time seen clearly what silenced the
opposition. Not that he had cared for promotion, for anything,
then. And that day seemed to him the last day of his youth,
though he was already a year over 30 and had not for a long time
thought of himself as young.

He sighed and smiled awry: he *had* been young. He closed his
eyes.

This is not exactly what he remembered.

He stepped down into the brilliant light, blinked, sweating, and
set out. My god, away. The small leaves of the maple on the

corner shook smartly as he passed. Alice's fierce voice echoed.
Sunlight plunged to the pavement and ran everywhere like water,
vivid, palpable. I am a Professor, he reflected, moving rapidly, or
a sort of professor; there is a breeze, a wild sun. As he leveled his
palm sailing along the even hedge, it tingled. He felt his toes in
his shoes. The hedge danced faintly.

My life is in ruins, he thought. She begins the quarrels, but they
are my fault. Here is this weather and we are desperate. Hugh
and Penny never quarreled. I'm no further on than when we
started—*I* started.

He groped back seven years to the brimming fear that had
choked him while he waited in the hallway before entering his
very first class. He had handled it, empty, irrecoverable. But the
students had been friendly. What passion that year called out!
Hugh and he had been worked like Percherons, and they had
stood it and done more than anyone wanted, half the night up
with papers, all day with students, planning coups in class, coax-
ing, worrying, praising, ransacking like a bookshop the formless
minds in front of them for something to be used for understanding, levering rich in alternatives, roaming the real world for anal-
ogies to cram into the boys' world for truth. He saw the faces
strained, awed, full, at the hour's end. I must do it again.

He had been teaching for seven years and he felt quietly that
he had been dead for the last five. The Dostals' garden, anemo-
nes, snapdragons, crimson, yellow, rose-pink; colors swimming,
the air sweetened, he went by. He thought: I enjoy myself, I
quarrel, but I am really dead.

What could change? Hugh, it seemed to him with the first resentment he had ever felt for his friend, kept steadily with him
like a deadweight he could never live up to. He had once thought
of himself as going-to-be-a-writer; but he had never actually written anything except his dissertation, some unfinished stories, three
articles. Hugh *had* been a writer. They had been going to revolu-
tionize scholarship too. The Professor acknowledged that he had
no such wish now. He was just a teacher (word he didn't like—
assistant professor was better); not a very good one, and stale.

Of the class that was meeting this afternoon, he really knew—
what? Nelen was dark, from Philadelphia, lazy. Warner was articulate and disconcerting; the blond fashion plate who sat by the
door, Stone, was not so dull as he looked; Landes, who was always

carefully prepared, always grinned; Holson twitched and could not keep to the issue; Rush was a wit. The others were dimmer, except Smith, who took in every point made, a likable boy. He liked them all, and he was aware that they liked him (he wondered why), but he didn't know them. Yet he could still write out, he supposed, half the troubles and strengths of his students of that first year of teaching.

He was doomed to the past or an unalterable present. What could change his hopeless relation with Alice?—quarrel and reconciliation; quarrel and reconciliation. Another emotion mounted new to the history of his memory of Hugh: he felt that Hugh was lucky—if he had lived, he and Penny might have quarreled. They had had two years only; that was lucky.

The bell rang slowly down from the campus.

He could determine to teach today as he hadn't for a long time, to swing the whole class to a fresh, active relation, an insight grave and light. Well, he did determine. What must it come to, under the inescapable routine? Since the first year, the boys repeated each other. He repeated himself. Teaching was worthy, and indispensable; but it was dull. No riskiness lived in it—not after the beginning. Perhaps when one came to organize one's own courses; but he doubted that. It was no use pretending: what had truly counted—the reciprocal learning—who older could set up again? He thought he was a man modest enough, but greater modesty than his was wanted to hope to learn from Landes or Stone.

Yet he was glad of his resolution. It seemed to bring forward for possible settlement some issue that he could hardly define but knew should be at stake. He glowed, unsmiling, and strode faster, confident.

The Professor paused for traffic and experienced a disappointment. "Lycidas." He was teaching "Lycidas." He crawled across the street.

There was no poem he liked better. In his junior year he had written a defense of Dr. Johnson's supercilious remarks about it, then had his position swept away by his experience of the poem when reading it next. But he knew the boys would find it formidable, egotistical, frozen, their hatred of Milton developed to a fine pitch in the schools. A burden fell on him—that unpleasant majesty, cold grandeur of Milton. And the poem was about Death and Poetry; what did they care for either? He could substitute some attractive poem of the period in their anthology. The boys not having been assigned any other, time would be wasted; he cast about all the same, dawdling, magnolias gleaming on the wall ahead. He would have to do "Lycidas."

If he shirked the greatest poem in English—he turned into the gate—what could his resolution be worth, or his teaching? Nothing, and his confidence returned in the sunlight. "A dreamy and passionate flux," he remembered Robert Bridges's phrase, though none from his own essay, and entering the high doorway of his building smiled at himself for the comparison, half-pleased nevertheless with himself and remembering that at any rate Bridges hadn't known Milton borrowed his river-god Camus from Fletcher, not made him up. Except for one student and a committee meeting—no, called off—he would have the whole morning for preparation. Which Fletcher? He had forgotten (not John, anyway); and he found two students waiting to see him.

One rose and stood forward, diffidently holding a paper while he unlocked the door of his office. Sperry, dull and willing. Don't know the other, do I? "Good morning, come in."

The Professor was no scholar, though he had wearied through several Elizabethan authors to find a degree; but he had once noticed Camus, he had a memory, and it vexed him to forget. Settled at his desk in the low bright room, he answered questions and helped the boy normalize a small bibliography, feeling attentive, virtuous, competent. Phineas, I expect, but where? " . . . and remember that the authors' names are *not* inverted in the footnotes; only for alphabetizing. Good luck with it."

Sperry closed the door. In a moment there would be a knock. The sun lay level across his blotter, photographing the dust on a dust jacket. Abruptly he saw it in a line-end, "old *Chamus* from his cell," guarded by a hundred nymphs or something—some short piece of Phineas's. "Come in!" he called, radiant.

This was a young man with a high forehead and a nervous smile who wanted advice about majoring in English, his adviser having given him less than satisfaction. He explained that the Professor had had his brother several years before, so that he—Oh yes: what was his brother doing now? His brother was lost in Italy.

The Professor's mind as well as his brow clouded.

He remembered Sutton: a broad brow like this boy's and large eyes, a yellow sweater, smoking. Once they had had an argument about *Volpone* in conference, and he had an impression later that Sutton was right. He remembered it all. Indeed—he thought with a vacant grin—do I do anything ever but remember? Does anything *happen?* Why yes . . . yes . . . students in yellow sweaters die. "Camus, reverend sire, came footing slow." As the line sounded heavily in his ear, its movement was terrifying, as if Camus were Death. It would be good to say "Sutton, you were quite right about *Volpone,* I hadn't considered it deeply enough." A ranging mind, original. "Sutton, Wade" on a course- or casualty-list, the name forever reversed. With the most serious effort he had required for some time, the Professor wrenched himself to expectancy, muttering, "I'm sorry. . . ."

Sutton's brother kept him nearly half an hour. After the first ten minutes, urgent for the afternoon, he itched to come at "Lycidas," but he couldn't bring himself to hurry the boy, and the record, the possibilities, dragged on. The portrait of Hugh, with its living depthless eyes and indefinable unease, watched them from the low shelf over the books at the back of the desk. The sunlight died, returned, died. He spun an ashtray, talking. At last the boy stood up, effusively grateful, knocking a book on the floor, effusively contrite, and, undecided, departed.

Instead of plunging into Milton, the Professsor went to his window with a fresh cigarette and looked down a little into the bright, sunless lawn. The rememberer. Teaching is memory. If it came to that, he could remember enough. How proudly he had begun at some point to say, "I haven't read that for ten years." Hugh's golden stories the summer in Canada. Tunes that summer. This was the superiority of aging one waited for: just to remember. True or false, evil or gay, never mind. The Nobel Prize for Memory. Recipient a suicide en route to Stockholm, having remembered all his sins at once, sitting in a deck chair, sharpening a pencil.

Now the sun moved out from a cloud, and forsythia blazed by the walk. " . . . think to burst out into sudden . . ." Hugh lay on a couch in the August sun, his short beard glinting, saying, "It's just as well. I could never have got done what I wanted to." Later, when he had got very weak and was chiefly teeth and eyes, his wandering mind wanted pathetically to live, certain he would. But the Professor clung still to the resignation, the judgment on the couch; he himself had done nothing he wanted, and he had come to believe that Hugh was right. He had come to believe this after his grief had dimmed. When he took over Hugh's classes he had felt, perhaps, as a tree would, growing into a dry riverbed grieving still for water—good, but unexpected, trembling, and wholly inadequate. He stared at the forsythia beyond the flat green. "Came footing slow . . ." Came footing fast. But it was "*went* footing slow," and recalling this he exorcised suddenly the ominous in the line. He felt unaccountably relieved, normal; he enjoyed an instant the luminous scene, and turned back to his desk under the torn beloved print of the "Anatomy Lesson."

The Professor was a systematic man. He opened his Milton and read the poem thoughtfully, twice, before he laid out side by side two other Miltons got from the library early in the week and began to work his way through the editors' notes. The Professor was also honest. Though he'd not looked at the poem for months, he felt very little as he read, except admiration for the poet's language and minute flirts of emotions he had probably experienced in previous readings, and he did not pretend to feel more. Consistently Lycidas was Hugh—even was Sutton—but without pressure. What were teachers if not shepherds? "Henceforth thou art the Genius of the shore," he whispered reverently to the brown portrait, thinking of his class, ". . . and shalt be good To all that wander in that perilous flood." The second time through he was uncomfortable with the sterile complaint, "What boots it with uncessant care To tend the homely slighted Shepherd's trade?" Both times he was gently moved by the exquisite melancholy of a semi-couplet at the end of the flower-passage:

> For so to interpose a little ease,
> Let our frail thoughts dally with false surmise;

He wrote "exquisite melancholy" in the margin the second time.

The editors he read closely, he read long, and he was astonished when he learnt that "flashy" meant insipid. What were the "songs"? Preaching . . . teaching. Insipid teaching, like his. Was all this preparation a mistake? His teaching during the first years had been very disorderly, quick, dialectical, free. He and Hugh had hated elaborate plans—sometimes too they hadn't a moment to prepare but for reading the assignment—but they had learnt and worked things out *with* the students, and that made the difference. Today he would be as free as he could. He wanted still to learn, he didn't feel superior to the students (Smith, Sutton) more now than then. But his experience was what it was. Who would know "flashy" unless he told them? He went eagerly on.

A student knocked, went off with a book.

As Milton's imitations and telescopings multiplied, he commenced to feel restless, distant, smaller. What one editor neglected, another observed, and he began to have a sense of the great mind like a whirring, sleepless refinery—its windows glittering far out across the landscape of night—through which poured and was transformed the whole elegiac poetry of Greece and Italy and England, receiving an impress new and absolute. *Mine!* it seemed to call, seizing one brightness, another, another, locking them in place, while their features took on the rigidity and beauty of masks. Through the echoing halls they posed at intervals, large, impassive, splendid; a special light moved on their helms, far up, and shadows fell deep between them. The Professor collected himself and glanced at the time.

Naturally he wouldn't finish. It would take fortnights to weigh all the notes. And questions marked for further study would have to go—not that they were likely to come up. Making a late lunch, he ought to be able to do everything else. He stretched, luxurious, warm. When had he felt so thoroughly and profitably occupied? Throwing the window wider, he went rapidly, speculationless, through the notes to the end of the poem. This done, he closed the books except one, put them aside, pulled his ear, and stared at "Lycidas."

Now came the part he called "penetration." Although he knew very well what the subject of the poem was, he pretended he didn't, and pondered it pencil in hand, to find out. Elegy by an ambitious, powerful, obscure man of 28 for a successful junior of 25, drowned. Academic status: Non-Fellow (grand poet) for Fellow (little poet). Probably commissioned or at least requested.

Invocation, or *complaint*
Elegy proper: another invocation
    (his own death)
    their friendship
    Nature's lament
    Nymphs, where?
    (Fame: Apollo)
    the cause? Triton, Aeolus
    University mourns: Camus
    (Clergy: St. Peter)
    flowers for hearse
    where now? Nature godless
Consolation by metamorphosis (Christian, pagan)
Ottava rima "Thus sang . . ." & so an end.

Four sections, with three personal digressions. And the opening
was really another personal digression, this unpleasing insistence
on his being compelled to write. No one *made* you, after all. The
Milton-passages came to less than a third of the poem—but where
the power was. Reasonable enough; Milton may never have spoken to Edward King, except to ask for the salt. The Professor
studied the text and his notes, waving his pencil slowly by his ear.
Cunning. He saw that. The testimony of Triton and Aeolus, and
the speeches of Camus and Peter, actually made up a sort of
trail—so that the poet's diverse materials would be given an air of
unity. What on earth made Milton think of a trial? . . . *Oh.* His
own inquisition of the nymphs above! They had deserted Lycidas,
when he needed them: who then *had* been with him, for evil? Let
a court find out.

The Professor leaned back in his chair with surprise. All this
revealed only in the word "plea" and the sense of the passages.
And one meaning of "felon." His vision of the refining plant re-
curred to him, but he grimaced impatiently at it. Better say Vatican. Only the "privy paw." A Puritan Vatican then, with cata-
combs.

Bending to the poem again, after a new cigarette and a dozen
notes made compactly on a small yellow pad, he approached almost warily, as if toward an animal long familiar suddenly dis-
playing resources unsuspected, even dangerous. But in the first
moment he saw that his discovery made the Fame passage more

obviously than ever an excrescence, and with a touch of indignation he relaxed. It split the trial. Milton's mounting sense must
have worked strongly indeed if he was willing to do this; and then
that fantasy of arrogance wherein Phoebus singles him out by
touching his ears! The Professor, no poet, pulled his own ear.

He drew up a schedule for the discussion. How many hours, he
wondered, would it take to teach "Lycidas" properly? I might
give a course (first semester) English 193: "Lycidas" 1–84. He
stretched again, smiling, crinkling his eyes toward the light-
stream.

And finally—it was very late—the "lesson." He wouldn't have
admitted to anyone, of course, that this was what he called it, but
call it this he did, had for years. He remembered a time when he
hadn't used the "lesson," when in fact he had detested above all
things a "message" (his derisive tone he heard still) of any sort. So
had Hugh. His face shadowed, and he shifted his eyes to the portrait, which the sun reached. Have I betrayed you? Here in the
sun? Feeling melodramatic, he set his mind uneasily to the "lesson."

Then all at once he felt hopeless. What could a one-hour class
do to change what he had become? He had been a fool. One
class, he raged, and the new man leaps from the old skin. With
his schedule and his "penetration" and his "lesson." He stops catering to the boys' shiftlessness, he develops tongues of fire. A
marriage like a tiger lies down and purrs. Dark in his office at
one-thirty, he sat clamped in despair. And the despair threw him
onward. No, he *had* been a fool, but he was a fool still, a worse
one. You have to start. You have nothing to lose. Jump overboard
now, you might as well try. At least you can become serious, and
let the rhetoric take care of itself. If you fail, you fail anyway. He
would finish his preparation and do everything he could do this
afternoon, and see. Even the "lesson." Why not? It was only a
joke with himself. Hating "teacher," he pretended to submit to
"lesson"—merely the general moral truth, or some general moral
truth (God knows he wasn't dogmatic) arising out of whatever
they were doing. Nothing pretentious, nor original, but if you
didn't make a form for it you might pass it by altogether. Hastily
he wrote at the bottom of the schedule, cramping his hand, his
"lesson" for today, and as he wrote an image sprang up of Milton
rapt forward unconscious at a window-table in the twilight, his

drastic mind and dull eyes on the shade of King, his pen and the swirling threshold-forces on himself: "Whatever we do and think we are doing, however objective or selfless our design, our souls each instant are enacting *our own* destinies." Moral enough! Did the boys even believe in souls?—they didn't give a hoot for immortality. But this was the point of teaching.

He arranged his notes and ideas with returning satisfaction. Hat, window. But after these hours he was tired, very tired, and the breeze and the blaze brightened him less than he would have liked as he hurried toward the Club, deciding to have—how rare for him, how usual for others—a cocktail before lunch.

The bar was nearly empty, the Martini firm and immediate.

Through lunch he resisted the silly recurring desire to say aloud what he heard again and again in his head, "Nor yet where Deva spreads her wizard stream," a line that gave him intense pleasure; for example to his speechless neighbor at the round table, a dry short man, very hungry, evidently, in Classics. The verb seemed as brilliant as the epithet. King sailed from Chester-on-Dee. Deva, the Dee, like Wordsworth's Winander. Charles Diodati lived on the Dee; maybe he and Milton (Milton the diva of Christ's—beaten, disappointed genius) had sat on the bank the summer before and traded legends of the sacred stream . . . "youthful poets dream on summer eves by haunted stream." "What do you think of Edward King?" a soft voice. "I doubt he deserves a Fellowship," a stern one from the incredibly youthful face, "and it came to him too soon." Behind the slight body, clenched grass. "Your luck, John, wait, will change." The late afternoon airs, the dappled water. There was more in that line than the fatal sailing. He didn't even mention King in his letters to Diodati between the death and "Lycidas." However. Had he written to anyone of Hugh? None ever: how? Diodati had a year to live. Who did Milton write to then? God-given, God-withdrawn. The Dio stoops to the Dee; twice. And stoops no more.

He drank his coffee slowly. He hoped the boys had prepared well; he had told them to use the stacks. The dining room had emptied, a waiter hovered, still he lingered. He was remembering a lunch he and Hugh had had together once on a day as bright as this one—Friday too—in a restaurant neither could afford. Italian bread. Something had gone very wrong for him, and Hugh was consoling and sympathizing with him in the merriest, gentlest way imaginable. They had told jokes, and were free together as two old friends can be in a strange, agreeable setting. He was leaving the next day, he recalled; so that the occasion had urgency forward as well as back. But what was odd? He couldn't hear their voices. He could see the glints and sheen from the table, his own arms on the table, hand on a wineglass, he saw Hugh's face and the white wall, he saw the whole scene, but he heard nothing. It was completely silent. The Professor struck his palm on his table, and rose, his heart beating, and left.

The breeze had died away, leaving the campus placid, almost hot. Crossing, however, he looked forward eagerly like a defendant facing the last day of a suit that had so far gone well: anxious and confident, pacing out the final hour of his imputed, fantastic guilt. He went by his office for a book and notes, opened the window, touched the frame of the portrait, and arrived in his classroom just before the bell.

Where were the others? The high, dark-brown, sunfilled room, too large for a class of 14 anyway, seemed all but deserted, and he looked around it annoyed while the bell rang. Who were missing? Only Cotton, it appeared, in the infirmary ("A good place for Cotton," said somebody) and Fremd. He smiled, throwing his Milton on the table, and felt better, although where was Fremd?

"Well, gentlemen," he went over to the windows—well known for roaming and for picking up chairs, he knew, but he had long ceased trying to refrain, "how do you like it? I assume you acquired an unholy aversion to it in school, as also to *Macbeth* and some other works not perfectly uninteresting. But what do you think of it this time, Mr. Rush?"

"Marvelous," the young man said mildly.

"Your diction is rich, but your tone is slack," the Professor smiled, "as applied to the most celebrated poem in our language. What precisely is marvelous about it?"

Rush grinned above his olive tie and thought. "There is a marvelous lack of emotion."

"Oh?" Crossing for the book, he read the opening lines aloud. "Unemotional? Did the rest of you feel the same way?"

No, they didn't.

"I meant emotion about his friend," Rush amended.

"Well, what about these?" Refusing to be hurried into his thesis, he read aloud some other lines:

> But O the heavy change, now thou art gone,
> Now thou art gone, and never must return!

Their languid gloom oppressed him. "Those are about King straight enough."

"Well . . . all those nymphs and flowers and woodgods . . ."

"Such properties needn't be inconsistent with strong emotion, as we'll see presently. But let's find out what Milton's subject is. What's the poem *about*, gentlemen? What lay essentially in his mind as he set about it? We have a poem in the form of a pastoral elegy, heavy in certain parts with passion. What about?"

"It's about his friend's death, isn't it?" Wright duly said.

"No!" Landes's high confident voice broke out. "It's about Milton himself. In other words, it has a subject he felt very strongly about, and it's very emotional whenever it comes to him or things that interested him. King was just the occasion. If his cat had died instead, the poem might have been just as good."

"Hardly his cat," said the Professor, "though Gray did well enough. But I agree with you that the poem is not on the whole passionate about King . . ." He talked easily and warmly, striding about the room with restless sudden turns, his ideas thronging. As he sat down, lightly on the table edge, the sun streamed in afresh, glowing on the rim of Warner's glasses and white collar.

". . . In his crisis of discontent with hard long solitary study and protracted obscurity, *doubt* of the poetic priesthood he'd entered, *scorn* for the worthless pastors of the priesthood he had refused to enter," he caught Hale's eye back in the corner and realized with vexation that the tall, bland youth was engaged on some very different speculation of his own, "in this crisis all his passions and anxieties welled up at sight of a young man, dedicated as he was himself though hardly in the same degree, *cut off*. Ah! To what end, then: self-denial, labor, patience, wisdom even? King's had simply vanished, and so might his."

"I don't see why he was so worried about dying," said Nelen's good-natured, empty face.

A real young man's remark. "Two things. One I just indicated—a colleague five years younger suddenly being killed. The other is that there was some actual danger. The plague was fierce. People had died even in the little place where Milton was, Horton. And he planned to go to Italy the next year. As you sit here, a voyage from England to Italy seems safe enough, but travel was risky three hundred years ago. If King had drowned going just to Ireland, why couldn't he, going farther?"

"But there are only four lines about his own death," Smith drawled, in the voice that made everything he said sound like a man dreaming.

A hand moved, Nelen's again. "Sir, who *is* King?"

Ugh. "Edward King," the Professor explained with Oriental restraint, "was the *friend* of John Milton about whose death the poem we are discussing ostensibly is." Or rival.

"It seems to me the poem is about King," Stone said doubtfully, uncrossing his legs.

"Critics pretty much agree—Legouis and the rest—that Milton's feelings about himself are the real subject."

"Could they be wrong?"

Warner's simple, uninflected question somehow moved the Professor very much. The trust, the measureless respect both for them and for *his* judgment of them, entered him so deeply that he couldn't answer for a moment, but merely looked at the dark boy tilted back in his chair smoking. Perhaps it *was* after all an honor to be a critic, or even a teacher. But how deserve such confidence, this privilege?

"They certainly could. I've told you all year not to take anybody's word for anything if you feel competent to judge it yourself and can bring evidence forward. Sometimes, it's true, in matters of *feeling* there isn't much evidence. But here there is a good deal. Take the last line: 'To-morrow to fresh woods, and pastures new.' What do you make of that? Anybody."

Smith sat forward. "He doesn't want to be any more where his friend was with him, and all the things he sees will remind him of his loss."

Dumbfounded he looked down at the page. Smith's rapid intelligence working through the incantation of his voice had often affected the Professor, but this time he felt as if an oracle had spoken.

. . . Why not? "Yes, it seems possible. It's simpler . . . What I was going to say was that the line is usually taken as a reference to Milton's plans either for moving to London or traveling to Italy. Of course, there might be an allusion to this anyway. But your contemporary meaning is better—after all his readers knew nothing and cared less about Milton's plans."

"Sir? Did people like this poem when it came out?" asked Holson, crawling about on his seat.

Did they? "No, they didn't so far as we know. In fact, at least a century passed before any attention was paid to it at all, before any of his minor poems were recognized."

Curiously, from Rush, "Who recognized them?"

The Professor, puzzling still over Smith's point, felt cornered. He cast back. "I think Warton was the first important critic on their side, but Pope and Gray knew them well. It was really the beginnings of Romantic taste that rescued them." Or so I say.

"Classics don't like them?" Landes wondered.

"Well, Milton is a classical poet but he is also a Romantic. The word is difficult, as you probably know . . ."

He described its ambiguity, called Johnson's *Life of Milton* a model of respectful churlishness and vindictive merriment (he remembered his undergraduate phrases, after all), and glanced at the Pound-Eliot campaign against *Paradise Lost*, abbreviating, anxious to get on.

". . . But let me ask *you* some questions. Who are the 'rout'? In fact what does 'rout' mean? It's in line sixty-one."

"The Maenads," said Warner.

"No doubt. And who were they?"

Nobody knew, or nobody answered: he explained; and nobody knew that "rout" had any but its modern sense. Holson, indeed, thought the modern sense would be better. Briefly, and without expressing the asperity he felt, the Professor laid down precepts of submission to a poem and fidelity to an author's sense. He was aware of some resistance in the class. He should have been fuller. What was "welter"? Nobody knew exactly. He read a few lines aloud, farsing. For five minutes he probed their familiarity with the meaning of details.

"You've got to look these things up, gentlemen. It's not only the matter of intellectual responsibility" (who would ever have taught them that? the major thing?), "it's a matter of enjoyment. We miss quite enough anyway, inevitably. How many of you

know jessamine, crowtoe, woodbine—have visual images when
you see the words or hear them?"

One hand hesitated.

He went off to the windows. "I don't myself," he said looking
out. Forsythia, daffodils, snapdragons. "Now it's true the passage
has literary sources and a symbolic intention, but if the flowers
are nothing more than words for us, we miss a good deal.
Jammed in cities, we have to. The whole country experience is
disappearing. Not only the country. Do you know the old rhyme
about London bells? I can't remember it all, most of it though,
but each couplet rings the bells of some church, at first senseless-
ly, and then a frightening continuity commences to emerge.

> Brickbats and targets
> Say the Bells of St. Marg'rets,
> Brickbats and tiles—

It was '*Bulls'-eyes* and targets'—

> Say the Bells of St. Giles

and so on. It's violent and beautiful still, for a modern reader. It
sometimes stands my hair on end. But how dim must the effect
be, compared to its effect on its first hearers, accustomed all day
to hear the ringing of the peals, high and low, now here, now
there, from the hundreds of churches all over London, pealing
like friends and warnings across the otherwise more or less silent
city. No traffic or machinery, only the voice of the militant
Church, the bells. The poem must have been a nightmare of reality. From this point of view, in fact, our prolific, active cities,
with all their noise, have become in truth absolutely still—stiller
than that," he gestured to a print of the Roman Forum high on
the sidewall. "You lose out of literature some experience every
year, and you need all the knowledge you can get." Hugh would
have liked that. How quiet the room feels. Here comes Warner,
here comes a chopper.

"What's the knowledge *for?*" said Warner in a loud voice bris-
tling like his hair. "Poetry is supposed to be dreamy and vague,
like Keats. Why pick it apart? I'd like to know how a super-jet
works, that's useful knowledge, but I don't care how a poem

works. This poem makes me feel half-asleep. I like the feeling. I don't think a poem *does* work, I think it loafs, and teachers pretend to—no offense, Sir—pretend to know all sorts of things about it that don't really exist."

The Professor picked up his chair. A true feeling, though lazy enough; "dreamy and passionate flux"—and then all the claptrap.

"Tell me, Mr. Warner, would you admit that there are conventions in 'Lycidas'?"

"Sure," the boy stretched. "They're not real shepherds, they're Milton and his friend. The nymphs are fanciful, and so on. But that's all obvious."

"We might be more definite than that, and fuller. . . ." He elaborated a little, dangling his chair, on the artificial character of the properties. The poem seemed Watteau-*ish* as he talked—he did not like Watteau—and he felt abruptly that he was tired. Was he doing as well as he wanted to? What had happened to his excitement?

" . . . So. Now: who is the 'blind Fury,' Mr. Warner? Line seventy-five."

"What's-her-name. Atropos. The one who slices."

"Very accurate." (The yellow sweater smoked on, faceless.) "Except that she isn't a Fury."

"She's not? The fellow I read said she was."

"I doubt if he did. Atropos is a Fate. The poet in his rage against her *calls* her a Fury." He put the chair down.

Warner was decided, superior: "What's the difference?"

The Professor suffered a flick of rage. The cold self-assurance in the voice cambered as from endless metallic contempt for these subjects, these feathers.

> Thy age, like ours, O soul of Sir John Cheke,
> Hated not learning worse than toad or asp.

"The difference is between understanding a world-poet, Mr. Warner, and not. Or between cultivation, and Ignorance truculent." Warner sat straighter. (Fatuous, and then unjust?—as to Alice.) "Of course I don't mean yours, but the difference is frankly as great as if one of your friends referred to your mother as an aging woman—say she is one—and another called her a witch, an evil witch." Frank, indeed. "The point is that the anger and horror of the line will be wholly felt only by a reader who already knows that Atropos is not properly a Fury but a Fate. As most readers I suppose do, or did." He didn't look at Warner, then made his voice general, "Let me give you an analogy. Some time ago, a century and a quarter, say, an audience assembled to hear a new piano concerto in Vienna. Piano, orchestra, conductor, a large aristocratic uncomfortable room, ladies, gentlemen. Now there is nothing very striking about the concerto's opening phrase but, as the piano began it, every nerve in the audience tightened." He stopped.

Silence, curiosity.

Doubtfully, at last, from Holson, "Did you say the *piano* began . . . ?"

"Yes. Why not?"

"The piano played the introduction? But the orchestra always does," the boy said nervously.

"That's the point. It's the orchestra, gentlemen, in a piano concerto, that begins and prepares for the entrance of the piano, which is the star of the occasion. That night, for the first time in history, a piano concerto began *not* in the orchestra but with the piano. It was Beethoven's Fourth. What sort of position is a listener to it in who simply does not know that concerti begin in the orchestra? He won't even hear the most important thing about the opening phrase. This is an affair, isn't it, of pure knowledge? No quantity of attention or insight will assist your ignorance, if you happen to be ignorant."

Hale wanted something! "Yes?" That admirable courtesy.

"Is there a good recording of that, Sir?"

"What it comes to—just a minute—is that what the artist does is sometimes even more interesting in its negative aspect, that is, in the alternative or other-possibility that it displaces, than in what it is itself. So in 'Lycidas.' The fact that Milton couldn't keep to his subject, or his nominal subject, shows that he had powerfully other matter on his mind. The digressions are in a way the poem's best testimony to his complete seriousness. But the reader observes them precisely in the sudden disappointment of expectation; that is, the poem ceases to be about King. Mr. Hale, I think there is a recording by Schnabel, if not there is one by somebody else, and a question more remote from the drowning of King I haven't heard for fifteen minutes." He looked at his watch, "Sixteen minutes."

Several boys laughed.

The Professor had looked at his watch, however, to see what time it was, having lost during the Warner moment his usual sense of what piece of the 50 minutes had lapsed and what remained. More remained than he had feared, but it wasn't much.

"Sir," Smith spoke just before he hurried on, "what do you mean, that the poem ceases to be about King?"

Surprised, he explained: the two long, intense passages on Fame and the corruption of the clergy were obvious excrescences.

"But Milton qualifies their differences from the rest, doesn't he?"

"He does? Where?"

The slow-voiced, serious boy bent, scanning. Motes waltzed in a sunbeam across Hale.

"Here, eighty-six. He says *that strain* 'was of a higher mood.' From a god, that is. And one thirty-two, 'the dread voice is past.' At the end of each."

The professor studied the lines. He felt, uneasily, as if he had never seen them before.

"Maybe *'various* quills' at the very end is more of the same explanation," the boy went on.

"I don't quite see how these *explain* them. It would be easy to invent transitions at the ends after you had left your theme—or come to it, rather, nakedly, since Milton is his own theme."

"But they grow naturally out of the situation," Smith argued. "Each of King's masters gets a word in: Apollo, Cambridge, St. Peter. Orpheus perished horribly, like Lycidas; therefore why break your neck to be a poet? Then the Church mourns, right after the University—promising son lost. What's out of order about that?"

"It's not so much that they're out of order, as that they're about Milton, not King," the Professor repeated.

"Well, Milton felt them hard. It might be his own situation. It *is* King's though, isn't it? The only things I know about him are that he was a scholar and poet and was going to be a clergyman." The boy considered. The others were listening to him with interest. "It's King's life that got slit, and then Apollo consoles Milton by saying that his lost friend, after all, will be judged in Heaven, not here. So will Milton, but that doesn't keep it from being about King."

"But it's Milton Apollo singles out by touching his ear," exclaimed the Professor, resisting a weak sense that the discussion was getting—how?—past him, dragging him.

"Only to defend him," Stone said unexpectedly. The blond, handsome boy lifted his book. "My editor said if your ear trembles, you're being talked about, that is, "people would be saying Milton had his own fame in mind, so Apollo reproved them—for him. Fame is only Heaven's judgment, where King is.""

"But the genuine rage is in the other passage," drawled Smith. "It seems to me King's death is awful to Milton, especially, because the Church needed good men."

"Why didn't Milton go in then?" Rush asked.

"How do I know?" Smith tilted his chair to see past Holson. "You don't have to do something yourself to want other people to do it well. Milton was a damned serious man. Maybe he thought poetry was more important."

"He quit it for politics for years. He probably was too aggressive to be a clergyman," Stone said from his corner.

The Professor found his voice. The storm that had seemed to be gathering round him, from Smith, had somehow not descended. But was the boy right? What do I think? He wished the hour were over. Milton or King, he wondered wearily, what matter? He smiled at "aggressive" to raise his spirits; Stone it was who had remarked admiringly that Shakespeare's Cleopatra "had *id.*"

Pacing the front of the classroom again, he told them his discovery of the morning, the Trial that linked Triton-Aeolus-Camus-Peter. "What brought into Milton's imagination, do you suppose, the notion of a trial?" he asked, sitting on the warm sill and lighting a cigarette. "Mr. Nelen, any ideas?" Mr. Nelen had no ideas, he revealed. "Mr. Holson?"

While Holson was reflecting, the Professor made a short excursion. He climbed, dripping, under a blinding sun, up and up a sand dune, one of the vast dunes hanging over Lake Superior, panting. He was laughing and calling up. Once he looked back, fearful. Hugh helped him at the top, and as he stood up a wind caressed all his skin. The miles of blue lake gleamed. No other dune so white as this. The sky was full of the sun. He wanted to stay. But he knew Hugh was saying, "It's wonderful," running back toward the edge, "just step as far as you can with each foot," then disappeared over it. Now he had to? Yes. He shuddered, cold, came toward the edge, shrank. Feet moved by strong love on. Fought. He leaned erect off the world's edge, toppling, and stept! Through empty air straight down, terror of the first, the bounce and astonishment of the second. Pure joy the third, his eyes cleared. He rushed through the sunlight wild with delight in deep jumps, foot far to foot, touching the earth, down and down toward Hugh, bounding far below. Far off, another world.

"Himself," Holson said.

"I'm sorry?" said the Professor, getting up.

"Did he want to show what a trial it had been for himself?"

"Hardly. The trial, I think, gentlemen, continues the dramatic method of Milton's own inquisition of the nymphs, earlier. It's a way of clamping his material together, producing an illusion of unity."

"Why the inquisition in the first place?" Stone's voice, after the pause, was thoughtful.

"Why not?" he smiled.

"Well," the young man in the corner went on deliberately, "but if the unity or the meaning isn't real, is just an illusion, how can the poem be good or true?"

The Professor reached for his book, but a light came on in his brain. *Why!* He heard his voice sudden and tense: "Why the inquisition! What does a man think when a friend dies, what does he do? He *asks questions*—'not loud, but deep.' *Why? Where now? Why? Where?*" He saw the class again, and realized he was trembling. "But you can't just ask these questions over and over again in a poem, as you do in life. You have to have something to ask them about. What situation will let you ask the most questions? A trial. An inquiry, a trial. It doesn't matter what the questions pretend to be about. Where the nymphs were on Tuesday, which wind blew. What matters is that there *be* questions. Behind all the beauty we haven't had a chance to discuss, the versification, the imagery, behind the foliage, there is this urgency and reality."

His difficult, morning sense of the poem as a breathing, weird, great, incalculable animal was strong on him again. He returned to the table excited, constrained, for the book.

"That's like what I meant," Smith hastened his drawl, "he really asks the questions about King. They're his questions, but he kept himself out of the poem as much as he *could*."

His questions. Did he? The Professor as he opened the book felt

that all things were possible, and seeing the flower passage he
imagined a rustling, as if his metaphor were true, and under the
passage moved the animal, the massive insight of the grieving
poet.

"Yet the flowers are to satisfy himself, not King. Of course, the
whole elegy is in King's honor, but I mean their pathos is less than
their beauty. The melancholy is all Milton's. Listen.

> "Bid amaranthus all his beauty shed,
> And daffadillies fill their cups with tears,
> To strew the laureate hearse where Lycid lies.
> For so to interpose a little ease,
> Let our frail thoughts . . ."

At this point, an extraordinary thing happened. The Professor
saw the word "false" coming FALSE. He felt as if snatched up by
the throat and wrung. "False" threw its iron backward through
the poem. The room shook. Then the unutterable verse mastered
his voice and took it off like a tempest:

> "dally with false surmise;
> Ay me!"

The cry rang hopeless through his mind

> "whilst THEE the shores, and sounding seas
> Wash far away, where'er thy bones are hurled,
> Whether beyond the stormy Hebrides,
> Where THOU perhaps under the whelming tide
> Visit'st the bottom of the monstrous world—"

A bell sounded, and the Professor was able to dismiss the class a
moment later—remembering that he had forgotten after all the
"lesson." But whether he could have read a line more he wondered, as he closed the strange book and held it in both hands.
The students made for the door. The sun shone steadily in at the
windows. The class was over.

The Professor sat a long time in his office, not thinking of anything and perhaps not unhappy, before he went home. Once he
read over the transfiguration of Lycidas, and was troubled by the
trembling of light on the page; his eyes had filled with tears. He

heard the portrait's voice. At last he rose, closed the window and took his hat. Shutting the door as he left, in the still-bright hall he looked at the name engraved on his card on the door. He felt older than he had in the morning, but he had moved into the exacting conviction that he was . . . something . . . not dead.

In the Heart of the Heart
of the Country

WILLIAM H. GASS

a place

So I HAVE SAILED the seas and come . . .

                        to B . . .

                                  a small . . .

town fastened to a field in Indiana. Twice there have been twelve
hundred people here to answer to the census. The town is out-
standingly neat and shady, and always puts its best side to the
highway. On one lawn there's even a wood or plastic iron deer.

You can reach us by crossing a creek. In the spring the lawns
are green, the forsythia is singing, and even the railroad that guts
the town has straight bright rails which hum when the train is
coming, and the train itself has a welcome horning sound.

Down the back streets the asphalt crumbles into gravel. There's
Westbrook's, with the geraniums, Horsefall's, Mott's. The side-
walk shatters. Gravel dust rises like breath behind the wagons.
And I am in retirement from love.

weather

In the midwest, around the lower Lakes, the sky in the winter
is heavy and close, and it is a rare day, a day to remark on, when
the sky lifts and allows the heart up. I am keeping count, and as I
write this page, it is eleven days since I have seen the sun.

my house

There's a row of headless maples behind my house, cut to free
the passage of electric wires. High stumps, ten feet tall, remain,

121

and I climb these like a boy to watch the country sail away from me. They are ordinary fields, a little more uneven than they should be, since in the spring they puddle. The topsoil's thin, but only moderately stony. Corn is grown one year, soybeans another. At dusk starlings darken the single tree—a larch—which stands in the middle. When the sky moves, fields move under it. I feel, on my perch, that I've lost my year. It's as though I were living at last in my eyes, as I have always dreamed of doing, and I think then I know why I've come here: to see, and so to go out against new things—oh god how easily—like air in a breeze. It's true there are moments—foolish moments, ecstasy on a tree stump— when I'm all but gone, scattered I like to think like seed, for I'm the sort now in the fool's position of having love left over which I'd like to lose; what good is it now to me, candy ungiven after Halloween?

a person

There are vacant lots on either side of Billy Holsclaw's house. As the weather improves, they fill with hollyhocks. From spring through fall, Billy collects coal and wood and puts the lumps and pieces in piles near his door, for keeping warm is his one work. I see him most often on mild days sitting on his doorsill in the sun. I noticed he's squinting a little, which is perhaps the reason he doesn't cackle as I pass. His house is the size of a single garage, and very old. It shed its paint with its youth, and its boards are a warped and weathered gray. So is Billy. He wears a short lumpy faded black coat when it's cold, otherwise he always goes about in the same loose, grease-spotted shirt and trousers. I suspect his galluses were yellow once, when they were new.

wires

These wires offend me. Three trees were maimed on their account, and now these wires deface the sky. They cross like a fence in front of me, enclosing the crows with the clouds. I can't reach in, but like a stick, I throw my feelings over. What is it that offends me? I am on my stump, I've built a platform there and the wires prevent my going out. The cut trees, the black wires, all the beyond birds therefore anger me. When I've wormed through a fence to reach a meadow, do I ever feel the same about the field?

people

Their hair in curlers and their heads wrapped in loud scarves, young mothers, fattish in trousers, lounge about in the speedwash, smoking cigarettes, eating candy, drinking pop, thumbing magazines, and screaming at their children above the whirr and rumble of the machines.

At the bank a young man freshly pressed is letting himself in with a key. Along the street, delicately teetering, many grandfathers move in a dream. During the murderous heat of summer, they perch on window ledges, their feet dangling just inside the narrow shelf of shade the store has made, staring steadily into the street. Where their consciousness has gone I can't say. It's not in the eyes. Perhaps it's diffuse, all temperature and skin, like an infant's, though more mild. Near the corner there are several large overalled men employed in standing. A truck turns to be weighed at the Feed and Grain. Images drift on the drugstore window. The wind has blown the smell of cattle into town. Our eyes have been driven in like the eyes of the old men. And there's no one to have mercy on us.

vital data

There are two restaurants here and a tearoom. two bars. one bank. three barbers. one with a green shade with which he blinds his window. two groceries. a dealer in Fords. one drug, one hardware, and one appliance store. several that sell feed, grain, and farm equipment. an antique shop. a poolroom, a laundromat. three doctors. a dentist. a plumber. a vet. a funeral home in elegant repair the color of a buttercup. numerous beauty parlors which open and shut like night-blooming plants. a tiny dime and department store of no width but several floors. a hutch, homemade, where you can order, after lying down or squirming in, furniture that's been fashioned from bent lengths of stainless tubing, glowing plastic, metallic thread, and clear shellac. an American Legion Post and a root beer stand. little agencies for this and that: cosmetics, brushes, insurance, greeting cards and garden produce—anything—sample shoes—which do their business out of hats and satchels, over coffee cups and dissolving sugar. a factory for making paper sacks and pasteboard boxes that's lodged in an old brick building bearing the legend, OPERA HOUSE, still faintly golden, on its roof. a library given by Carnegie. a post office. a school. a railroad station, fire station. lumber yard. telephone company. welding shop. garage . . . and spotted through the town from one end to the other in a line along the highway—gas stations to the number five.

business

One side section of street is blocked off with sawhorses. Hard, thin, bitter men in blue jeans, cowboy boots and hats, untruck a dinky carnival. The merchants are promoting themselves. There will be free rides, raucous music, parades and coneys, pop, popcorn, candy, cones, awards and drawings, with all you can endure of pinch, push, bawl, shove, shout, scream, shriek, and bellow. Children pedal past on decorated bicycles, their wheels a blur of color, streaming crinkled paper and excited dogs. A little later there's a pet show for a prize—dogs, cats, birds, sheep, ponies, goats—none of which wins. The whirlabouts whirl about. The ferris wheel climbs dizzily into the sky as far as a tall man on tiptoe might be persuaded to reach, and the irritated operators measure with sour eyes the height and weight of every child to see if they are safe for the machines. An electrical megaphone repeatedly trumpets the names of the generous sponsors. The following day they do not allow the refuse to remain long in the street.

my house, this place and body

I have met with some mischance, wings withering, as Plato says obscurely, and across the breadth of Ohio, like heaven on a table, I've fallen as far as the poet, to the sixth sort of body, this house in B, in Indiana, with its blue and gray bewitching windows, holy magical insides. Great thick evergreens protect its entry. And I live *in*.

Lost in the corn rows, I remember feeling just another stalk, and thus this country takes me over in the way I occupy myself when I am well . . . completely—to the edge of both my house and body. No one notices, when they walk by, that I am brimming in the doorways. My house, this place and body, I've come in mourning to be born in. To anybody else it's pretty silly: love. Why should I feel a loss? How am I bereft? She was never mine; she was a fiction, always a golden tomgirl, barefoot, with an adolescent's slouch and a boy's taste for sports and fishing, a figure out of Twain, or worse, in Riley. Age cannot be kind.

There's little hand in hand here . . . not in B. No one touches except in rage. Occasionally girls will twine their arms around each other and lurch along, school out, toward home and play. I dreamed my lips would drift down your back like a skiff on a river. I'd follow a vein with the point of my finger, hold your bare feet in my naked hands.

the same person

Billy Holsclaw lives alone—how alone it is impossible to fathom. In the post office he talks greedily to me about the weather. His head bobs on a wild floor of words, and I take this violence to be a measure of his eagerness for speech. He badly needs a shave, coal dust has layered his face, he spits when he speaks, and his fingers pick at his tatters. He wobbles out in the wind when I leave him, a paper sack mashed in the fold of his arm, the leaves blowing past him, and our encounter drives me sadly home to poetry—where there's no answer. Billy closes his door and carries coal or wood to his fire and closes his eyes, and there's simply no way of knowing how lonely and empty he is or whether he's as vacant and barren and loveless as the rest of us are—here in the heart of the country.

weather

For we're always out of luck here. That's just how it is—for instance in the winter. The sides of the buildings, the roofs, the limbs of the trees are gray. Streets, sidewalks, faces, feelings—they are gray. Speech is gray, and the grass where it shows. Every flank and front, each top is gray. Everything is gray: hair, eyes, window glass, the hawkers' bills and touters' posters, lips, teeth, poles and metal signs—they're gray, quite gray. Cars are gray.

Boots, shoes, suits, hats, gloves are gray. Horses, sheep, and cows, cats killed in the road, squirrels in the same way, sparrows, doves, and pigeons, all are gray, everything is gray, and everyone is out of luck who lives here.

A similar haze turns the summer sky milky, and the air muffles your head and shoulders like a sweater you've got caught in. In the summer light, too, the sky darkens a moment when you open your eyes. The heat is pure distraction. Steeped in our fluids, miserable in the folds of our bodies, we can scarcely think of anything but our sticky parts. Hot cyclonic winds and storms of dust crisscross the country. In many places, given an indifferent push, the wind will still coast for miles, gathering resource and edge as it goes, cunning and force. According to the season, paper, leaves, field litter, seeds, snow fill up the fences. Sometimes I think the land is flat because the winds have leveled it, they blow so constantly. In any case, a gale can grow in a field of corn that's as hot as a draft from hell, and to receive it is one of the most dismaying experiences of this life, though the smart of the same wind in winter is more humiliating, and in that sense even worse. But in the spring it rains as well, and the trees fill with ice.

place

Many small Midwestern towns are nothing more than rural slums, and this community could easily become one. Principally during the first decade of the century, though there were many earlier instances, well-to-do farmers moved to town and built fine homes to contain them in their retirement. Others desired a more social life, and so lived in, driving to their fields like storekeepers to their businesses. These houses are now dying like the bereaved who inhabit them; they are slowly losing their senses . . . deafness, blindness, forgetfulness, mumbling, an insecure gait, an uncontrollable trembling has overcome them. Some kind of Northern Snopes will occupy them next: large-familied, Catholic, Democratic, scrambling, vigorous, poor; and since the parents will work in larger, nearby towns, the children will be loosed upon themselves and upon the hapless neighbors much as the fabulous Khan loosed his legendary horde. These Snopes will undertake makeshift repairs with materials that other people have thrown away;

paint halfway round their house, then quit; almost certainly maintain an ugly loud cantankerous dog and underfeed a pair of cats to keep the rodents down. They will collect piles of possibly useful junk in the backyard, park their cars in the front, live largely leaning over engines, give not a hoot for the land, the old community, the hallowed ways, the established clans. Weakening widow-ladies have already begun to hire large rude youths from families such as these to rake and mow and tidy the grounds they will inherit.

people

In the cinders at the station boys sit smoking steadily in darkened cars, their arms bent out the windows, white shirts glowing behind the glass. Nine o'clock is the best time. They sit in a line facing the highway—two or three or four of them—idling their engines. As you walk by a machine may growl at you or a pair of headlights flare up briefly. In a moment one will pull out, spinning cinders behind it, to stalk impatiently up and down the dark streets or roar half a mile into the country before returning to its place in line and pulling up.

my house, my cat, my company

I must organize myself. I must, as they say, pull myself together, dump this cat from my lap, stir—yes, resolve, move, do. But do what? My will is like the rosy dustlike light in this room: soft, diffuse, and gently comforting. It lets me do . . . anything . . . nothing. My ears hear what they happen to; I eat what's put before me; my eyes see what blunders into them; my thoughts are not thoughts, they are dreams. I'm empty or I'm full . . . depending; and I cannot choose. I sink my claws in Tick's fur and scratch the bones of his back until his rear rises amorously. Mr. Tick, I murmur, I must organize myself. I must pull myself together. Mr. Tick rolls over on his belly, all ooze.

I spill Mr. Tick when I've rubbed his stomach. Shoo. He steps away slowly, his long tail rhyming with his paws. How beautifully he moves, I think; how beautifully, like you, he commands his loving, how beautifully he accepts. So I rise and wander from room to room, up and down, gazing through most of my forty-one windows. How well this house receives its loving too. Let out like Mr. Tick, my eyes sink in the shrubbery. I am not here; I've passed the glass, passed second-story spaces, flown by branches, brilliant berries, to the ground, grass high in seed and leafage every season; and it is the same as when I passed above you in my aged, ardent body; it's, in short, a kind of love; and I am learning to restore myself, my house, my body, by paying court to gardens, cats, and running water, and with neighbors keeping company.

Mrs. Desmond is my right-hand friend; she's eighty-five. A thin white mist of hair, fine and tangled, manifests the climate of her mind. She is habitually suspicious, fretful, nervous. Burglars break in at noon. Children trespass. Even now they are shaking the pear tree, stealing rhubarb, denting lawn. Flies caught in the screens and numbed by frost awake in the heat to buzz and scrape the metal cloth and frighten her, though she is deaf to me, and consequently cannot hear them. Boards creak, the wind whistles across the chimney-mouth, drafts cruise like fish through the hollow rooms. It is herself she hears, her own flesh failing, for only death will preserve her from those daily chores she climbs like stairs, and all that anxious waiting. Is it now, she wonders? No? Then: is it now?

We do not converse. She visits me to talk. My task to murmur. She talks about her grandsons, her daughter who lives in Delphi, her sister or her husband—both gone—obscure friends—dead—obscurer aunts and uncles—lost—ancient neighbors, members of her church or of her clubs—passed or passing on; and in this way she brings the ends of her life together with a terrifying rush: she is a girl, a wife, a mother, widow, all at once. All at once—appalling—but I believe it; I wince in expectation of the clap. Her talk's a fence—a shade drawn, window fastened, door that's locked—for no one dies taking tea in a kitchen; and as her years compress and begin to jumble, I really believe in the brevity of life; I sweat in my wonder; death is the dog down the street, the angry gander, bedroom spider, goblin who's come to get her; and it occurs to me that in my listening posture I'm the boy who suffered the winds of my grandfather with an exactly similar politeness, that I am, right now, all my ages, out in elbows, as angular as badly stacked cards. Thus was I, when I loved you, every man I could

be, youth and child—far from enough—and you, so strangely
ambiguous a being, met me, heart for spade, play after play, the
whole run of our suits.

Mr. Tick, you do me honor. You not only lie in my lap, but you
remain alive there, coiled like a fetus. Through your deep nap, I
feel you hum. You are, and are not, a machine. You are alive,
alive exactly, and it means nothing to you—much to me. You are
a cat—you cannot understand—you are a cat so easily. Your nature is not something you must rise to. You, not I, live in: in
house, in skin, in shrubbery. Yes. I think I shall hat my head with
a steeple; turn church; devour people. Mr. Tick, though, has a tail
he can twitch, he need not fly his Fancy. Claws, not metrical
schema, poetry his paws; while smoothing . . . smoothing . . .
smoothing roughly, his tongue laps its neatness. O Mr. Tick, I
know you; you are an electrical penis. Go on now, shoo. Mrs.
Desmond doesn't like you. She thinks you will tangle yourself in
her legs and she will fall. You murder her birds, she knows, and
walk upon her roof with death in your jaws. I must gather myself
together for a bound. What age is it I'm at right now, I wonder.
The heart, don't they always say, keeps the true time. Mrs. Desmond is knocking. Faintly, you'd think, but she pounds. She's
brought me a cucumber. I believe she believes I'm a woman.
Come in, Mrs. Desmond, thank you, be my company, it looks
lovely, and have tea. I'll slice it, crisp, with cream, for luncheon,
each slice as thin as me.

more vital data

The town is exactly fifty houses, trailers, stores, and miscella-
neous buildings long, but in places no streets deep. It takes on
width as you drive south, always adding to the east. Most of the
dwellings are fairly spacious farmhouses in the customary white,
with wide wraparound porches and tall narrow windows, though
there are many of the grander kind—fretted, scalloped, turreted,
and decorated with clapboards set at angles or on end, with
stained glass windows at the stair landings and lots of wrought
iron full of fancy curls—and a few of these look like castles in
their rarer brick. Old stables serve as garages now, and the lots
are large to contain them and the vegetable and flower gardens
which, ultimately, widows plant and weed and then entirely dis-

appear in. The shade is ample, the grass is good, the sky a glorious fall violet; the apple trees are heavy and red, the roads are calm and empty; corn has sifted from the chains of tractored wagons to speckle the streets with gold and with the russet fragments of the cob, and a man would be a fool who wanted, blessed with this, to live anywhere else in the world.

education

Buses like great orange animals move through the early light to school. There the children will be taught to read and warned against Communism. By Miss Janet Jakes. That's not her name. Her name is Helen something—Scott or James. A teacher twenty years. She's now worn fine and smooth and has a face, Wilfred says, like a mail-order ax. Her voice is hoarse, and she has a cough. For she screams abuse. The children stare, their faces blank. This is the thirteenth week. They are used to it. You will all, she shouts, you will all draw pictures of me. No. She is a Mrs.—someone's missus. And in silence they set to work while Miss Jakes jabs hairpins in her hair. Wilfred says an ax, but she has those rimless tinted glasses, graying hair, an almost dimpled chin. I must concentrate. I must stop making up things. I must give myself to life; let it mold me: that's what they say in Wisdom's Monthly Digest every day. Enough, enough—you've been at it long enough; and the children rise formally a row at a time to present their work to her desk. No, she wears rims; it's her chin that's dimpleless. So she grimly shuffles their sheets, examines her reflection crayoned on them. I would not dare . . . allow a child . . . to put a line around me. Though now and then she smiles like a nick in the blade, in the end these drawings depress her. I could not bear it—how can she ask?—that anyone . . . draw me. Her anger's lit. That's why she does it: flame. There go her eyes; the pink in her glasses brightens, dims. She is a pumpkin, and her rage is breathing like the candle in. No, she shouts, no—the cartoon trembling—no, John Mauck, John Stewart Mauck, this will not do. The picture flutters from her fingers. You've made me too muscular.

I work on my poetry. I remember my friends, associates, my students, by their names. Their names are Maypop, Dormouse, Upsydaisy. Their names are Gladiolus, Callow Bladder, Prince

and Princess Oleo, Hieronymus, Cardinal Mummum, Mr. Fitch-
ew, The Silken Howdah, Spot. Sometimes you're Tom Sawyer,
Huckleberry Finn; it is perpetually summer; your buttocks are
my pillow; we are adrift on a raft; your back is our river. Sometimes you are Major Barbara, sometimes a goddess who kills men
in battle, sometimes you are soft like a shower of water; you are
bread in my mouth.

I do not work on my poetry. I forget my friends, associates, my
students, and their names: Gramophone, Blowgun, Pickle, Sere-
nade . . . Marge the Barge, Arena, Uberhaupt . . . Doctor Dildoe,
The Fog Machine. For I am now in B, in Indiana: out of job and
out of patience, out of love and time and money, out of bread
and out of body, in a temper, Mrs. Desmond, out of tea. So shut
your fist up, bitch, you bag of death; go bang another door; go
die, my dearie. Die, life-deaf old lady. Spill your breath. Fall over
like a frozen board. Gray hair grows from the nose of your mind.
You are a skull already—*memento mori*—the foreskin retracts
from your teeth. Will your plastic gums last longer than your
bones, and color their grinning? And is your twot still hazel-hairy,
or are you bald as a ditch? . . . bitch . . . bitch . . . .
bitch. I wanted to be famous, but you bring me age—my empti-
ness. Was it *that* which I thought would balloon me above the
rest? Love? where are you? . . . love me. I want to rise so high, I
said, that when I shit I won't miss anybody.

business

For most people, business is poor. Nearby cities have siphoned
off all but a neighborhood trade. Except for feed and grain and
farm supplies, you stand a chance to sell only what one runs out
to buy. Chevrolet has quit, and Frigidaire. A locker plant has left
its afterimage. The lumber yard has been, so far, six months
about its going. Gas stations change hands clumsily, a restaurant
becomes available, a grocery closes. One day they came and
knocked the cornices from the watch repair and pasted campaign
posters on the windows. Torn across, by now, by boys, they urge
you still to vote for half an orange beblazoned man who as a
whole one failed two years ago to win at his election. Everywhere, in this manner, the past sneaks, and it mostly speaks of
failure. The empty stores, the old signs and dusty fixtures, the

debris in alleys, the flaking paint and rusty gutters, the heavy locks and sagging boards: they say the same disagreeable things. What do the sightless windows see, I wonder, when the sun throws a passerby against them? Here a stair unfolds toward the street—dark, rickety, and treacherous—and I always feel, as I pass it, that if I just went carefully up and turned the corner at the landing, I would find myself out of the world. But I've never had the courage.

that same person

The weeds catch up with Billy. In pursuit of the hollyhocks, they rise in coarse clumps all around the front of his house. Billy has to stamp down a circle by his door like a dog or cat does turning round to nest up, they're so thick. What particularly troubles me is that winter will find the weeds still standing stiff and tindery to take the sparks which Billy's little mortarless chimney spouts. It's true that fires are fun here. The town whistle, which otherwise only blows for noon (and there's no noon on Sunday), signals the direction of the fire by the length and number of its blasts, the volunteer firemen rush past in their cars and trucks, houses empty their owners along the street every time like an illustration in a children's book. There are many bikes, too, and barking dogs, and sometimes—hallelujah—the fire's right here in town—a vacant lot of weeds and stubble flaming up. But I'd rather it weren't Billy or Billy's lot or house. Quite selfishly I want him to remain the way he is—counting his sticks and logs, sitting on his sill in the soft early sun—though I'm not sure what his presence means to me . . . or to anyone. Nevertheless, I keep wondering whether, given time, I might not someday find a figure in our language which would serve him faithfully, and furnish his poverty and loneliness richly out.

weather

I would rather it were the weather that was to blame for what I am and what my friends and neighbors are—we who live here in the heart of the country. Better the weather, the wind, the pale dying snow . . . the snow—why not the snow? There's never much really, not around the lower Lakes anyway, not enough to boast about, not enough to be useful. My father tells how the snow in the Dakotas would sweep to the roofs of the barns in the old days, and he and his friends could sled on the crust that would form because the snow was so fiercely driven. In Bemidji trees have been known to explode. That would be something—if the trees in Davenport or Francisville or Terre Haute were to go blam some winter—blam! blam! blam! all the way down the gray, cindery, snow-sick streets.

A cold fall rain is blackening the trees or the air is like lilac and full of parachuting seeds. Who cares to live in any season but his own? Still I suspect the secret's in this snow, the secret of our sickness, if we could only diagnose it, for we are all dying like the elms in Urbana. This snow—like our skin it covers the country. Later dust will do it. Right now—snow. Mud presently. But it is snow without any laughter in it, a pale gray pudding thinly spread on stiff toast, and if that seems a strange description, it's accurate all the same. Of course soot blackens everything, but apart from that, we are never sufficiently cold here. The flakes as they come, alive and burning, we cannot retain, for if our temperatures fall, they rise promptly again, just as in the summer, they bob about in the same feckless way. Suppose though . . . suppose they were to rise some August, climb and rise, and then hang in the hundreds like a hawk through December, what a desert we could make of ourselves—from Chicago to Cairo, from Gary to Columbus—what beautiful Death Valleys.

place

I would rather it were the weather. It drives us in upon ourselves—an unlucky fate. Of course there is enough to stir our wonder anywhere; there's enough to love, anywhere, if one is strong enough, if one is diligent enough, if one is perceptive, patient, kind enough—whatever it takes; and surely it's better to live in the country, to live on a prairie by a drawing of rivers, in Iowa or Illinois or Indiana, say, than in any city, in any stinking fog of human beings, in any blooming orchard of machines. It ought to be. The cities are swollen and poisonous with people. It ought to be better. Man has never been a fit environment for man—for rats, maybe, rats do nicely, or for dogs or cats and the household beetle.

A man in the city has no natural thing by which to measure himself. His parks are potted plants. Nothing can live and remain free where he resides but the pigeon, starling, sparrow, spider, cockroach, mouse, moth, fly, and weed, and he laments the existence of even these and makes his plans to poison them. The zoo? There *is* the zoo. Through its bars the city man stares at the great cats and coolly sucks his ice. Living, alas, among men and their marvels, the city man supposes that his happiness depends on establishing, somehow, a special kind of harmonious accord with others. The novelists of the city, of slums and crowds, they call it love—and break their pens.

Wordsworth feared the accumulation of men in cities. He foresaw their "degrading thirst after outrageous stimulation," and some of their hunger for love. Living in a city, among so many, dwelling in the heat and tumult of incessant movement, a man's affairs are touch and go—that's all. It's not surprising that the novelists of the slums, the cities, and the crowds, should find that sex is but a scratch to ease a tickle, that we're most human when we're sitting on the john, and that the justest image of our life is in full passage through the plumbing.

Come into the country, then. The air nimbly and sweetly recommends itself unto our gentle senses. Here, growling tractors tear the earth. Dust roils up behind them. Drivers sit jouncing under bright umbrellas. They wear refrigerated hats and steer by looking at the tracks they've cut behind them, their transistors blaring. Close to the land, are they? good companions to the soil? Tell me: do they live in harmony with the alternating seasons?

It's a lie of old poetry. The modern husbandman uses chemicals from cylinders and sacks, spike-ball-and-claw machines, metal sheds, and cost accounting. Nature in the old sense does not matter. It does not exist. Our farmer's only mystical attachment is to parity. And if he does not realize that cows and corn are simply different kinds of chemical engine, he cannot expect to make a go of it.

It isn't necessary to suppose our cows have feelings; our neighbor hasn't as many as he used to have either; but think of it this way a moment, you can correct for the human imputations later: how would it feel to nurse those strange tentacled calves with their rubber, glass, and metal lips, their stainless eyes?

people

Aunt Pet's still able to drive her car—a high square Ford—
even though she walks with difficulty and a stout stick. She has a
watery gaze, a smooth plump face despite her age, and jet black
hair in a bun. She has the slowest smile of anyone I ever saw, but
she hates dogs, and not very long ago cracked the back of one she
cornered in her garden. To prove her vigor she will tell you this,
her smile breaking gently while she raises the knob of her stick to
the level of your eyes.

house, my breath and window

My window is a grave, and all that lies within it's dead. No
snow is falling. There's no haze. It is not still, not silent. It's images are not an animal that waits, for movement is no demonstration. I have seen the sea slack, life bubble through a body without
a trace, its spheres impervious as soda's. Downwound, the whore
at wagtag clicks and clacks. Leaves wiggle. Grass sways. A bird
chirps, pecks the ground. An auto wheel in penning circles keeps
its rigid spokes. These images are stones; they are memorials. Beneath this sea lies sea: god rest it . . . rest the world beyond my
window, me in front of my reflection, above this page, my shade.
Death is not so still, so silent, since silence implies a falling quiet,
stillness a stopping, containing, holding in; for death is time in a
clock, like Mr. Tick, electric . . . like wind through a windup poet.
And my blear floats out to visible against the glass, befog its country and bespill myself. The mist lifts slowly from the fields in the
morning. No one now would say: the Earth throws back its covers; it is rising from sleep. Why is the feeling foolish? The image
is too Greek. I used to gaze at you so wantonly your body
blushed. Imagine: wonder: that my eyes could cause such flower-
ing. Ah, my friend, your face is pale, the weather cloudy; a street
has been felled through your chin, bare trees do nothing, houses
take root in their rectangles, a steeple stands up in your head. You
speak of loving; then give me a kiss. The pane is cold. On icy
mornings the fog rises to greet me (as you always did); the barns
and other buildings, rather than ghostly, seem all the more sub-
stantial for looming, as if they grew in themselves while I

watched (as you always did). Oh, my approach, I suppose, was
like breath in a rubber monkey. Nevertheless, on the road along
the Wabash in the morning, though the trees are sometimes obscured by fog, their reflection floats serenely on the river, reasoning the banks, the sycamores in French rows. Magically, the
world tips. I'm led to think that only those who grow down live
(which will scarcely win me twenty-five from Wisdom's Monthly
Digest), but I find I write that only those who live down grow;
and what I write, I hold, whatever I really know. My every
word's inverted, or reversed—or I am. I held you, too, that way.
You were so utterly provisional, subject to my change. I could
inflate your bosom with a kiss, disperse your skin with gentleness,
enter your vagina from within, and make my love emerge like a
fresh sex. The pane is cold. Honesty is cold, my inside lover. The
sun looks, through the mist, like a plum on the tree of heaven, or
a bruise on the slope of your belly. Which? The grass crawls with
frost. We meet on this window, the world and I, inelegantly,
swimmers of the glass; and swung wrong way round to one another, the world seems in. The world—how grand, how monumental,
grave and deadly, that word is: the world, my house and poetry.
All poets have their inside lovers. Wee penis does not belong to
me, or any of this foggery. It is *his* property which he's thrust
through what's womanly of me to set down this. These wooden
houses in their squares, gray streets and fallen sidewalks, standing
trees, your name I've written sentimentally across my breath into
the whitening air, pale birds: they exist in me now because of
him. I gazed with what intensity. . . . A bush in the excitement of
its roses would not have bloomed so beautifully as you did then. It
was a look I'd like to give this page. For that is poetry: to bring
within about, to change.

politics

Sports, politics, and religion are the three passions of the badly
educated. They are the Midwest's open sores. Ugly to see, a
source of constant discontent, they sap the body's strength. Appalling quantities of money, time, and energy are wasted on
them. The rural mind is narrow, passionate, and reckless on these
matters. Greed, however shortsighted and direct, will not alone
account for it. I have known men, for instance, who for years

have voted squarely against their interests. Nor have I ever noticed that their surly Christian views prevented them from urging
forward the smithereening, say, of Russia, China, Cuba, or Korea—Vietnam. And they tend to back their country like they
back their local team: they have a fanatical desire to win; yelling
is their forte; and if things go badly, they are inclined to sack the
coach. All in all, then, Birth is a good name. It stands for the
bigot's stick, the wild-child-tamer's cane.

final vital data

The Modern Homemakers' Demonstration Club. The Prairie
Home Demonstration Club. The Night-outers' Home Demonstra-
tion Club. The 100F, FFF, VFW, WCTU, WSCS, 4-H, 40 and 8,
Psi Iota Chi, and PTA. The Boy and Girl Scouts. Rainbows, Ma-
sons, Indians and Rebekah Lodge. Also the Past Noble Grand
Club of the Rebekah Lodge. Also the Past Noble Grand Club of
the Rebekah Lodge. As well as the Moose and the Ladies of the
Moose. The Elks, the Eagles, the Jaynettes, and the Eastern Star.
The Women's Literary Club, the Hobby Club, the Art Club, the
Sunshine Society, the Dorcas Society, the Pythian Sisters, the Pil-
grim Youth Fellowship, the American Legion, the American Le-
gion Auxiliary, the American Legion Junior Auxiliary, the Gardez
Club, the What-can-you-do? Club, the Get Together Club, the
Coterie Club, the Worthwhile Club, the No Name Club, the For-
get-me-not Club, the Merry-go-round Club. . . .

education

Has a quarter disappeared from Paula Frosty's pocketbook?
Imagine the landscape of that face: no crayon could engender it;
soft wax is wrong; thin wire in trifling snips might do the trick.
Paula Frosty and Christopher Roger accuse the pale and splotchy
Cheryl Pipes. But Miss Jakes, I *saw* her. Miss Jakes is so extremely
vexed she snaps her pencil. What else is missing? I appoint you a
detective, John: search her desk. Gum, candy, paper, pencils,
marble, round eraser—whose? A thief. I can't watch her all the
time, I'm here to teach. Poor pale fossetted Cheryl, it's determined, can't return the money because she took it home and
spent it. Cindy, Janice, John, and Pete—you four who sit around

her—you will be detectives this whole term to watch her. A thief. In all my time, Miss Jakes turns, unfists, and turns again. I'll handle you, she cries. To think. A thief. In all my years. Then she writes on the blackboard the name of Cheryl Pipes and beneath that the figure twenty-five with a large sign for cents. Now Cheryl, she says, this won't be taken off until you bring that money out of home, out of home straight up to here, Miss Jakes says, tapping her desk.

Which is three days.

another person

I was raking leaves when Uncle Halley introduced himself to me. He said his name came from the comet, and that his mother had borne him prematurely in her fright of it. I thought of Hobbes, whom fear of the Spanish Armada had hurried into birth, and so I believed Uncle Halley to honor the philosopher, though Uncle Halley is a liar, and neither the one hundred twenty-eight nor the fifty-three he ought to be. That fall the leaves had burned themselves out on the trees, the leaf-lobes had curled, and now they flocked noisily down the street and were broken in the wires of my rake. Uncle Halley was himself (like Mrs. Desmond and history generally) both deaf and implacable, and he shooed me down his basement stairs to a room set aside there for stacks of newspapers reaching to the ceiling, boxes of leaflets and letters and programs, racks of photo albums, scrapbooks, bundles of rolled up posters and maps, flags and pennants and slanting piles of dusty magazines devoted mostly to motoring and the Christian ethic. I saw a birdcage, a tray of butterflies, a bugle, a stiff straw boater, and all kinds of tassels tied to a coat tree. He still possessed and had on display the steering lever from his first car, a linen duster, driving gloves and goggles, photographs along the wall of himself, his friends, and his various machines, a shell from the first war, a record of Ramona nailed through its hole to a post, walking sticks and fanciful umbrellas, shoes of all sorts (his baby shoes, their counters broken, were held in sorrow beneath my nose—they had not been bronzed, but he might have them done someday before he died, he said), countless boxes of medals, pins, beads, trinkets, toys, and keys (I scarcely saw—they flowed like jewels from his palms), pictures of downtown when it was only a path by the railroad station, a brightly colored globe of the world with a dent in Poland, antique guns, belt buckles, buttons, souvenir plates and cups and saucers (I can't remember all of it— I won't), but I recall how shamefully, how rudely, how abruptly, I fled, a good story in my mouth but death in my nostrils; and how afterward I busily, righteously, burned my leaves as if I were purging the world of its years. I still wonder if this town—its life, and mine now—isn't really a record like the one of Ramona that I used to crank around on my grandmother's mahogany Victrola through lonely rainy days as a kid.

the first person

Billy's like the coal he's found: spilled, mislaid, discarded. The sky's no comfort. His house and his body are dying together. His windows are boarded. And now he's reduced to his hands. I suspect he has glaucoma. At any rate he can scarcely see, and weeds his yard of rubble on his hands and knees. Perhaps he's a surgeon cleansing a wound or an ardent and tactile lover. I watch, I must say, apprehensively. Like mine-war detectors, his hands graze in circles ahead of him. Your nipples were the color of your eyes. Pebble. Snarl of paper. Length of twine. He leans down closely, picks up something silvery, holds it near his nose. Foil? cap? coin? He has within him—what? I wonder. Does he know more now because he fingers everything and has to sniff to see? It would be romantic cruelty to think so. He bends the down on your arms like a breeze. You wrote me: something is strange when we don't understand. I write in return: I think when I loved you I fell to my death.

Billy, I could read to you from Beddoes; he's your man perhaps; he held with dying, freed his blood of its arteries; and he said that there were many wretched love-ill fools like me lying alongside the last bone of their former selves, as full of spirit and speech, nonetheless, as Mrs. Desmond, Uncle Halley and the ferris wheel. Aunt Pet, Miss Jakes, Ramona or the megaphone; yet I reverse him finally, Billy, on no evidence but braggadocio, and I declare that though my inner organs were devoured long ago, the worm which swallowed down my parts still throbs and glows like a crystal palace.

Yes, you were younger. I was Uncle Halley, the museum man

and infrequent meteor. Here is my first piece of ass. They weren't so flat in those days, had more round, more juice. And over here's the sperm I've spilled, nicely jarred and clearly labeled. Look at this tape like lengths of intestine where I've stored my spew, the endless worm of words I've written, a hundred million emissions or more: oh I was quite a man right from the start; even when unconscious in my cradle, from crotch to cranium, I was erectile tissue; though mostly, after the manner approved by Plato, I had intercourse by eye. Never mind, old Holsclaw, you are blind. We pull down darkness when we go to bed; put out like Oedipus the actually offending organ, and train our touch to lies. All cats are gray, says Mr. Tick; so under cover of glaucoma you are sack gray too, and cannot be distinguished from a stallion.

I must pull myself together, get a grip, just as they say, but I feel spilled, bewildered, quite mislaid. I did not restore my house to its youth, but to its age. Hunting, you hitch through the hollyhocks. I'm inclined to say you aren't half the cripple I am, for there is nothing left of me but mouth. However, I resist the impulse. It is another lie of poetry. My organs are all there, though it's there where I fail—at the roots of my experience. Poet of the spiritual, Rilke, weren't you? yet that's what you said. Poetry, like love, is—in and out—a physical caress. I can't tolerate any more of my sophistries about spirit, mind, and breath. Body equals being, and if your weight goes down, you are the less.

household apples

I knew nothing about apples. Why should I? My country came in my childhood, and I dreamed of sitting among the blooms like the bees. I failed to spray the pear tree too. I doubled up under the mat first, admiring the sturdy low branches I should have pruned, and later I acclaimed the blossoms. Shortly after the fruit formed there were falls—not many—apples the size of goodish stones which made me wobble on my ankles when I walked about the yard. Sometimes a piece crushed by a heel would cling on the shoe to track the house. I gathered a few and heaved them over the wires. A slingshot would have been splendid. Hard, an unattractive green, the worms had them. Before long I realized the worms had them all. Even as the apples reddened, lit their tree, they were being swallowed. The birds preferred the pears, which were small—sugar pears I think they're called—with thick skins of graying green that ripen on toward violet. So the fruit fell, and once I made some applesauce by quartering and pairing hundreds; but mostly I did nothing, left them, until suddenly, overnight it seemed, in that ugly late September heat we often have in Indiana, my problem was upon me.

My childhood came in the country. I remember, now, the flies on our snowy luncheon table. As we cleared away they would settle, fastidiously scrub themselves and stroll to the crumbs to feed where I would kill them in crowds with a swatter. It was quite a game to catch them taking off. I struck heavily since I didn't mind a few stairs; they'd wash. The swatter was a square of screen bound down in red cloth. It drove no air ahead of it to give them warning. They might have thought they'd flown headlong into a summered window. The faint pink dot where they had died did not rub out as I'd supposed, and after years of use our luncheon linen would faintly, pinkly, speckle.

The country became my childhood. Flies braided themselves on the flypaper in my grandmother's house. I can smell the bakery and the grocery and the stables and the dairy in that small Dakota town I knew as a kid; knew as I dreamed I'd know your body, as I've known nothing, before or since; he knew as the flies knew, in the honest, unchaste sense: the burned house, hose-wet, which drew a mist of insects like the blue smoke of its smolder, and gangs of boys, moist-lipped, destructive as its burning. Flies have always impressed me; they are so persistently alive. Now they were coating the ground beneath my trees. Some were ordinary flies; there were the large blue-green ones; there were swarms of fruit flies too, and the red-spotted scavenger beetle; there were a few wasps, several sorts of bees and butterflies—checkers, sulphers, monarchs, commas, question marks—and delicate dragonflies . . . but principally houseflies and horseflies and bottleflies, flies and more flies in clusters around the rotting fruit. They loved the pears. Inside, they fed. If you picked up a pear, they flew, and the pear became skin and stem. They were everywhere the fruit was: in the tree still—apples like a hive for them—or where the fruit littered the ground, squashing itself as you stepped . . . there was no help for it. The flies droned, feasting on the sweet juice. No one could go near the trees; I could not climb; so I determined at last to labor like Hercules. There were fruit baskets in the barn. Collecting them and kneeling under the branches, I began to gather remains. Deep in the strong rich smell of the fruit, I began to hum myself. The fruit caved in at the touch. Glistening red apples, my lifting disclosed, had families of beetles, flies, and bugs, devouring their rotten undersides. There were streams of flies; there were lakes and cataracts and rivers of flies, seas and oceans. The hum was heavier, higher, than the hum of the bees when they came to the blooms in the spring, though the bees were there, among the flies, ignoring me—ignoring everyone. As my work went on and juice covered my hands and arms, they would form a sleeve, black and moving, like knotty wool. No caress could have been more indifferently complete. Still I rose fearfully, ramming my head in the branches, apples bumping against me before falling, bursting with bugs. I'd snap my hand sharply but the flies would cling to the sweet. I could toss a whole cluster into a basket from several feet. As the pear or apple lit, they would explosively rise, like monads for a moment, windowless, certainly, with respect to one another, sugar their harmony. I had to admit, though, despite my distaste, that my arm had never been more alive, oftener or more gently kissed. Those hundreds of feet were light. In washing them off, I pretended the hose was a pump. What have I missed? Childhood is a lie of poetry.

the church

Friday night. Girls in dark skirts and white blouses sit in ranks and scream in concert. They carry funnels loosely stuffed with orange and black paper which they shake wildly, and small megaphones through which, as drilled, they direct and magnify their shouting. Their leaders, barely pubescent girls, prance and shake and whirl their skirts above their bloomers. The young men, leaping, extend their arms and race through puddles of amber light, their bodies glistening. In a lull, though it rarely occurs, you can hear the squeak of tennis shoes against the floor. Then the yelling begins again, and then continues; fathers, mothers, neighbors joining in to form a single pulsing ululation—a cry of the whole community—for in this gymnasium each body becomes the bodies beside it, pressed as they are together, thigh to thigh, and the same shudder runs through all of them, and runs toward the same release. Only the ball moves serenely through this dazzling din. Obedient to law it scarcely speaks but caroms quietly and lives at peace.

business

It is the week of Christmas and the stores, to accommodate the rush they hope for, are remaining open in the evening. You can see snow falling in the cones of the street lamps. The roads are filling—undisturbed. Strings of red and green lights droop over the principal highway, and the water tower wears a star. The windows of the stores have been bedizened. Shamelessly they beckon. But I am alone, leaning against a pole—no . . . there is no one in sight. They're all at home, perhaps by their instruments, tuning in on their evenings, and like Ramona, tirelessly playing and replaying themselves. There's a speaker perched in the tower, and through the boughs of falling snow and over the vacant streets, it drapes the twisted and metallic strains of a tune that can barely be distinguished—yes, I believe it's one of the jolly ones, it's Joy to the World. There's no one to hear the music but myself, and though I'm listening, I'm no longer certain. Perhaps the record's playing something else.

Faith: In a Tree

GRACE PALEY

JUST WHEN I MOST NEEDED important conversation, a sniff of the man-wide world, that is, at least one brainy companion who could translate my friendly language into his tongue of undying carnal love, I was forced to lounge in our neighborhood park, surrounded by children.

All the children were there. Among the trees, in the arms of statues, toes in the grass, they hopped in and out of dog shit and dug tunnels into mole holes. Whenever the children ran, their mothers stopped to talk.

What a place in democratic time! One God, who was King of the Jews, who unravels the stars to this day with little hydrogen explosions, He can look down from His Holy Headquarters and see us all: heads of girl, pony tails riding the springtime luck, short black bobs, and an occasional eminence of golden wedding rings. He sees South into Brooklyn how Prospect Park lies in its sand-rooted trees among Japanese Gardens and police, and beyond us North to dangerous Central Park. Far North, the deer-eyed eland and kudu survive, grazing the open pits in the Bronx Zoo.

But me, the creation of His second thought, I am sitting on the twelve-foot high, strong, long arm of a sycamore, my feet swinging, and I can only see Kitty, a coworker in the mother trade—a topnotch craftsman. She is below, leaning on my tree, rumpled in a black cotton skirt made of shroud remnants at about fourteen cents a yard. Another colleague, Anna Kraat, is close by on a hard park bench, gloomy, beautiful, waiting for her luck to change.

144

Although I can't see them, I know that on the other side of the
dry pool, the thick snout of the fountain spout, hurrying along the
circumference of the parched sunstruck circle (in which, when
Henry James could see, he saw lilies floating), Mrs. Hyme Cara-
way pokes her terrible seedlings, Gowan, Michael, and Christopher, astride an English bike, a French tricycle, and a Danish
tractor. Beside her, talking all the time in fear of no response,
Mrs. Steamy Lewis, mother of Matthew, Mark, and Lucy, tells of
happy happy life in a thatched hotel on a Greek island where
total historical recall is indigenous. Lucy limps along at her skirt
in muddy cashmere. Mrs. Steamy Lewis really swings within the
seconds of her latitude and swears she will have six, but Mr.
Steamy Lewis is not expected to live.

I can easily see Mrs. Junius Finn, my up-the-block neighbor
and evening stoop companion, a broad barge, like a lady, moving
slow—a couple of redheaded cabooses dragged by clothesline at
her stern; on her fat upper deck, Wyltwyck,[1] a pale three-year-
old roaring captain with smoky eyes, shoves his wet thumb into
the wind. "Hurry! Hurry!" he howls. Mrs. Finn goes puff puffing
toward the opinionated playground, that sandy harbor.

Along the same channel, but near enough now to spatter with
spite, tilting delicately like a boy's sailboat, Lynn Ballard floats
past my unconcern to drop light anchor, a large mauve handbag
over the green bench slats. She sighs and looks up to see what (if
anything) the heavens are telling. In this way, once a week, toes
in, head high and in three-quarter turn, arms at her side, graceful
as a seal's flippers, she rests, quiet and expensive. She never grabs
another mother's kid when he falls and cries. Her particular Michael on his little red bike rides around and around the sandbox,
while she dreams of private midnight.

"Like a model," hollers Mrs. Junius Finn over Lynn Ballard's
head.

I'm too close to the subject to remark. I sniff, however, and
accidentally take sweetness into my lungs. Because it's the month
of May.

Kitty and I are nothing like Lynn Ballard. You will see Kitty's
darling face, as I tell her, slowly, but me—quick—what am I?

---

[1] Wyltwyck is named for the school of his brother, Junior, where Junior, who
was bad and getting worse, is still bad, but is getting better (as man is perfect-
ible).

Not bad if you're a basement shopper. On my face are a dozen messages, easy to read, strictly for friends. Bargains Galore! I admit it now.

However, the most ordinary life is illuminated by a great event like fame. Once I was famous. From the meaning of that glow, the modest hardhearted me is descended.

Once, all the New York papers that had the machinery to do so carried a rotogravure picture of me in a stewardess's arms. I was, it is now thought, the third commercial air-flight baby passenger in the entire world. This picture is at the Home now, mounted on laundry cardboard. My mother fixed it with glass to assail eternity. The caption says: One of our Youngest. Little Faith Decided to Visit Gramma. Here she is Gently Cuddled in the Arms of Stewardess Jeannie Carter.

Why would anyone send a little baby anywhere alone? What was my mother trying to prove? That I was independent? That she wasn't the sort to hang on? That in the sensible, socialist, Zionist world of the future, she wouldn't cry at my wedding? "You're an American child. Free. Independent." Now what does that mean? I have always required a man to be dependent on, even when it appeared that I had one already. I own two small boys whose dependence on me takes up my lumpen time and my bourgeois feelings. I'm not the least bit ashamed to say that I tie their shoes and I have wiped their backsides well beyond the recommendations of my friends, Ellen and George Hellesbraun, who are psychiatric social workers and appalled. I kiss those kids forty times a day. I punch them just like a father should. When I have a date and come home late at night, I wake them with a couple of good hard shakes to complain about the miserable entertainment. When I'm not furiously exhausted from my low-level job and that bedraggled soot-slimy house, I praise God for them. One Sunday morning, my neighbor, Mrs. Raftery, called the cops because it was 3 A.M. and I was vengefully singing a praising song.

Since I have already mentioned singing, I have to tell you: It is not Sunday. For that reason, all the blue-eyed, boy-faced policemen in the park are worried. They can see that lots of our vitamin-enlarged high school kids are planning to lug their guitar cases around all day long. They're scared that one of them may strum and sing a mountain melody or that several, a gang, will gather to raise its voice in medieval counterpoint.

Question: Does the world know, does the average freedman realize, that except for a few hours on Sunday afternoon, the playing of fretted instruments is banned by municipal decree? Absolutely forbidden is the song of the flute and oboe.

Answer (Explanation): This *is* a great ballswinger of a city on
the constant cement-mixing remake, battering and shattering,
and a high note out of a wild clarinet could be the decibel to
break a citizen's eardrum. But what if you were a city-loving
planner leaning on your drawing board? Tears would drop to the
delicate drafting sheets.

Well, you won't be pulled in for whistling and here come the
whistlers—the young Saturday fathers, open-shirted and ambitious. By and large they are trying to get somewhere and have to
go to a lot of parties. They are sleepy but pretend to great energy
for the sake of their two-year-old sons (little boys need a recollection of Energy as a male resource). They carry miniature footballs
though the season's changing. Then the older fathers trot in, just a
few minutes slower, their faces scraped to a clean smile, every
one of them wearing a fine gray beard and eager eyes, his breath
caught, his hand held by the baby daughter of a third intelligent
marriage.

One of them, passing my tree, stubs his toe on Kitty's sandal.
He shades his eyes to look up at me against my sun. That is Alex
O. Steele, who was a man organizing tenant strikes on Ocean
Parkway when I was a Coney Island Girl Scout against my moth-
er's socialist will. He says, "Hey, Faith, how's the world? Heard
anything from Ricardo?"

I answer him in lecture form:

"Alex Steele. Sasha. Yes. I have heard from Ricardo. Ricardo even
at the present moment when I am trying to talk with you in a
civilized way, Ricardo has rolled his dove-gray brain into a glob of
spit in order to fly secretly into my ear right off the poop deck of
Foamline's World Tour Cruiseship *Eastern Sunset*. He is stretched
out in my head, exhausted before dawn from falling in love with an
Eastern Sunset lady passenger from the first leg of her many-mast-
ed journey round the nighttimes of the world. He is *this minute*
saying to me,

'Arcturus Rise, Orion Fall . . . '
'Cock-proud son of a bitch,' I mutter.

'Ugh,' he says, blinking.

'How are the boys?' I make him say.

'Well, he really wants to know how the boys are,' I reply.

'No, I don't,' he says. 'Please don't answer. Just make sure they don't get killed crossing the street. That's your job.'"

"What?" says Alex Steele. "Speak clearly, Faith, you're garbling like you used to."

"I'm joking. Forget it. But I did hear from him the other day. Out of the pocket of my stretch denims I drag a mashed letter with the exotic stamp of a new underdeveloped nation. It was a large stamp with two smiling lions on a field of barbed wire. The letter says, "I am not well. I hope I never see another rain forest. I am sick. Are you working? Have you seen Ed Snead? He owes me $180. Don't badger him about it if he looks broke. Otherwise send me some to Guerra Verde c/o Dotty Wasserman. Am living here with her. She's on a Children's Mission. Wonderful girl. Reminds me of you ten years ago. She acts on her principles. I *need* the money."

"That is Ricardo. Isn't it, Alex? I mean there's no signature."

"Dotty Wasserman!" Alex says. "So that's where she is . . . a funny plain girl. Faith, let's have lunch sometime. I work up in the East Fifties. How're your folks? I hear they put themselves into a Home. They're young for that. Listen, I'm the executive director of Incurables, Inc., a fund-raising organization. We do wonderful things, Faith. The speed of life-extending developments. . . . By the way, what do you think of this little curly Sharon of mine?"

"Oh, Alex, how old is she? She's darling, she's a little golden baby, I love her. She's a peach."

"Of course! *She's* a peach, you like anyone better'n you like us," says my son Richard, who is jealous—because he came first and was deprived at two and one-half by his baby brother of my single-hearted love, my friend Ellie Hellesbraun says. Of course, that's a convenient professional lie, a cheap hindsight, as Richard, my oldest son is brilliant, and I knew it from the beginning. When he was a baby all alone with me, and Ricardo his daddy was off exploring some deep creepy jungle, we often took the ferry to Staten Island. Then we sometimes took the ferry to Hoboken. We walked bridges, just he and I, I said to him, Richie, see the choo choos on the barges, Richie, see the strong fast tugboat, see the merchant ships with their tall cranes, see the *United States* sail away for a week and a day, see the Hudson River with its white current. Oh, it isn't really the Hudson River, I told him, it's the North River; it isn't really a river, it's an estuary, part of the sea, I told him, though he was only two. I could tell him scientific things like that, because I considered him absolutely brilliant. See how beautiful the ice is on the river, see the stony palisades, I said, I hugged him, my pussycat, I said, see the interesting world.

So he really has no kicks coming, he's just peevish.

"We're really a problem to you, Faith, we keep you not free," Richard says, "anyway it's true you're crazy about anyone but us."

It's true I do like other kids. I am not too cool to say Alex's Sharon really is a peach. But you, you stupid kid, Richard! who could match me for pride or you for brilliance? Which one of the smart third-grade kids in a class of learned Jews, Presbyterians, and Bohemians? You are one of the two smartest and the other one is Chinese—Arnold Lee who does make Richard look a little simple, I admit it. But did you ever hear of a child who, when asked to write a sentence for the word "who" (they were up to the hard "wh"s), wrote and then magnificently, with Oriental lisp, read the following: "Friend, tell me WHO among the Shanghai merchants does the largest trade?"[2]

"That's a typical yak yak out of you, Faith," says Richard.

"Now Richard, listen to me, Arnold's an interesting boy; you wouldn't meet a kid like him anywhere but here or Hong Kong. So use some of these advantages I've given you. I could be living in the country, which I love, but I know how hard that is on children—I stay here in this creepy slum, I dwell in soot and slime just so you can meet kids like Arnold Lee and live on this wonderful block with all the Irish and Puerto Ricans although God knows why there aren't any Negro children for you to play with . . ."

"Who needs it?" he says, just to tease me. "All those guys got knives anyway. But you don't care if I get killed much do you?"

[2] The teacher, Marilyn Gewirtz, the only real person in this story, a child-admirer, told me this.

How can you answer that boy?

"You don't," says Mrs. Junius Finn, glad to say a few words. "You don't have to answer them. God didn't give out tongues for that. You answer too much, Faith Asbury, and it shows. Nobody fresher than Richard."

"Mrs. Finn," I scream in order to be heard, for she's some distance away and doesn't pay attention the way I do, "What's so terrible about fresh. EVIL is bad. WICKED is bad. ROBBING, MURDER, and PUTTING HEROIN IN YOUR BLOOD is bad."

"Blah, blah," she says, deaf to passion. "Blah to you."

Despite no education, Mrs. Finn always is more in charge of word meanings than I am. She is especially in charge of Good and Bad. My language limitations here are real. My vocabulary is adequate for writing notes and keeping journals, but absolutely useless for an active moral life. If I really knew this language, there would surely be in my head, as there is in Webster's or the Dictionary of American Slang, that unreducible verb designed to tell a person like me what to do next.

Mrs. Finn knows my problems because I do not keep them to myself. And I am reminded of them particularly at this moment, for I see her roughly the size of life, held up at the playground by Wyllie, who has rolled off the high ruddy deck of her chest to admire all the English bikes filed in the park bike stand. Of course that is what Junior is upstate for: love that forced possession. At first his father laced him on his behind, cutting the exquisite design known to generations of daddies who labored at home before the rise of industrialism and group therapy. Then Mr. Finn remembered his childhood, and that it was Adam's Fall not Junior who was responsible. Now the Finns never see a ten-speed Italian racer without family sighs for Junior who is still not home as there were about 176 bikes he loved.

Something is wrong with the following tenants: Mrs. Finn, Mrs. Raftery, Ginnie, and me. Everyone else in our building is on the way up through the affluent society, putting five to ten years into low rent before moving to Jersey or Bridgeport. But our four family units, as people are now called, are doomed to stand culturally still as this society moves on its caterpillar treads from ordinary affluent to absolute empire. All this in mind, I name names and dates. "Mrs. Finn, darling, look at my Richard, the time Junior took his Schwinn and how Richard hid in the coal in

the basement thinking of a way to commit suicide," but she coolly answers, "Faith, you're not a bit fair, for Junior give it right
back when he found out it was Richard's."

OK.

Kitty says, "Faith, you'll fall out of the tree, calm yourself."
She looks up, rolling her eyes to show direction, and I see a handsome man in narrow pants whom we remember from other Satur-
days. He has gone to sit beside Lynn Ballard. He speaks softly to
her left ear while she maintains her profile. He has never spoken
to her Michael. He is a famous actor trying to persuade her to
play opposite him in a new production of *SHE*. That's what Kitty, my kind friend, says.

I am above that kindness. I often see through the appearance of
things right to the apparition itself. It's obvious that he's a weekend queer, talking her into the possibilities of a neighborhood
threesome. When her nose quivers and she agrees, he will easily
get his really true love, the magnificent manager of the Supermarket, who has been longing for her at the check-out counter.
What they will do then, I haven't the vaguest idea. I am the child
of puritans and I'm only halfway here.

"Don't even think like that," says Kitty. No. She can see a con-
tract in his pocket.

There is no one like Kitty Skazka. Unlike other people who
have similar flaws that doom, she is tolerant and loving. I wish
Kitty could live forever, bearing daughters and sons to open the
heart of man. Meanwhile, mortal, pregnant, she has three green-
eyed daughters and they aren't that great. Of course, Kitty thinks
they are. And they are no worse than the average gifted, sensitive
child of a wholehearted mother and half-a-dozen transient fathers.

Her youngest girl is Antonia, who has no respect for grown-ups.
Kitty has always liked her to have no respect; so in this, she is
quite satisfactory to Kitty.

At some right moment on this Saturday afternoon, Antonia decided to talk to Tonto, my second son. He lay on his belly in the
grass, his bare heels exposed to the eye of flitting angels and he
worked at a game that included certain ants and other bugs as
players.

"Tonto," she asked, "what are you playing, can I?"

"No, it's my game, no girls," Tonto said.

"Are you the boss of the world?" Antonia asked politely. "Yes," said Tonto.

He thinks, he really believes, he is. To which I must say, Righto! you *are* the boss of the world, Anthony, you are prince of the day-care center for the deprived children of working mothers, you are the Lord of the West Side loading zone whenever it rains on Sundays. I have seen you, creepy chief of the dark forest of four ginkgo trees. The Boss! If you would only look up Anthony and boss me what to do, I would immediately slide down this scabby bark, ripping my new stretch slacks and do it.

"Give me a nickel, Faith," he ordered at once.

"Give him a nickel, Kitty," I said.

"Nickels, nickels, nickels, whatever happened to pennies?" Anna Kraat asked.

"Anna, you're rich. You're against us," I whispered, but loud enough to be heard by Mrs. Junius Finn, still stopped at the mouth of the playground.

"Don't blame the rich for everything," she warned. She herself, despite the personal facts of her economic position, is disgusted with the neurotic rise of the working class.

Lynn Ballard bent her proud and shameless head.

Kitty sighed, shifted her yardage, and began to shorten the hem of the enormous skirt, which she was wearing. "Here's a nickel, love," she said.

"Oh boy! Love!" said Anna Kraat.

Antonia walked in a wide circle around the sycamore tree and put her arm on Kitty who sewed, the sun just barely over her left shoulder—a perfect light. At that very moment, a representational artist passed. I think it was Edward Roster. He stopped and kneeled, peering at the scene. He squared them off with a film-maker's viewfinder and said, "Ah, what a picture!" then left.

"Number one!" I announced to Kitty, which he was, the very first of the squint-eyed speculators who come by to size up the stock. Pretty soon, depending on age and intention, they would move in groups along the paths or separately take notes in the shadows of the statues.

"The trick," said Anna, downgrading the world, "is to know the speculators from the investors. . . ."

"I will never live like that. Not I," Kitty said softly.

"Balls!" I shouted, as two men strolled past us, leaning toward

one another. They were not fairies, they were Jack Resnick and
Tom Weed, music lovers inclining toward their transistor, which
was playing the *Chromatic Fantasy*. They paid no attention to us
because of their relation to this great music. However, Anna
heard them say, "Jack, do you hear what I hear?" "Dammit yes,
the over-romanticizing and the under-Baching, I can't believe it."

Well, I must say when darkness covers the earth and great
darkness the people, I will think of you: Two Men with smart
ears. I don't believe civilization can do a lot more than educate a
person's senses. If it's truth and honor you want to refine, I think
the Jews have some insight. Make no images, imitate no God.
After all, in His field, the graphic arts, He is preeminent. Then let
that One who made the tan deserts and the blue Van Allen belt
and the green mountains of New England be in charge of beauty,
which He obviously understands, and let man who was full of
forgiveness at Jerusalem, and full of survival at Troy, let man be
in charge of Good.

"Faith, will you quit with your all-the-time philosophies," says
Richard, my first- and disapproving-born. Into our midst, he'd
galloped, riding an all-day rage. Brand new ball bearings, roller
skates, heavy enough for his big feet, hung round his neck.

I decided not to give into Richard by responding. I digressed
and was free: A cross-eyed man with a red beard became president of the Parent-Teachers Association. He appointed a committee of fun-loving ladies who met in the lunchroom and touched
up the coffee with little gurgles of brandy.

He had many clever notions about how to deal with the money
shortage in the public school. One of his great plots was to pro-
mote the idea of the integrated school in such a way that private
school people would think their kids were missing the real thing.
And at 5 A.M., the envious hour, the very pit of the morning of
middle age, they would think of all the public school children
deeply involved in the urban tragedy, something their children
might never know. He suggested that one month of public school
attendance might become part of the private school curriculum,
as natural and progressive an experience as a visit to the boiler
room in first grade. Funds could be split 50–50 or 30–70 or 40–60
with the Board of Education. If the plan failed, still the projected
effort would certainly enhance the prestige of the public school.

Actually something did stir. Delegations of private progressive school parents attacked the Board of Ed for what became known as the Shut-Out, and finally even the parents and teachers associations of the classical schools (whose peculiar concern always had been educating the child's head) began to consider the value of exposing children who had read about the horror at Ilium to ordinary street fights, so they could understand the *Iliad* better. Public School (in Manhattan) would become a minor like typing, required but secondary.

Mr. Terry Koln, full of initiative, energy, and lightheartedness was reelected by unanimous vote and sent on to the United Parents and Federated Teachers Organization as special council member, where in a tiny office all his own he grew marihuana on the windowsills, swearing it was deflowered marigolds.

He was the joy of our PTA. But it was soon discovered that he had no children, and Kitty and I have to meet him now surreptitiously in bars.

"Oh," said Richard, his meanness undeflected by this jolly digression:

> "The ladies of the PTA
> wear baggies in their blouses
> they talk on telephones all day
> and never clean their houses."

He really wrote that, my Richard. I thought it was awfully good, rhyme and meter and all, and I brought it to his teacher. I took the afternoon off to bring it to her. "Are you joking, Mrs. Asbury?" she asked.

Looking into her kind teaching eyes, I remembered schools and what it might be like certain afternoons and I replied, "May I have my Richard please, he has a dental appointment. His teeth are just like his father's. Rotten."

"Do take care of them, Mrs. Asbury."

"God, yes, it's the least," I said, taking his hand.

"Faith," said Richard, who had not gone away. "*Why* did you take me to the dentist that afternoon?"

"Why? Why? Why?" asked Richard, stamping his feet and shouting. I didn't answer. I closed my eyes to make him disappear.

"Why not?" asked Phillip Mazzano, who was standing there looking up at me when I opened my eyes.

"Where's Richard?" I asked.

"This is Phillip," Kitty called up to me. "You know Phillip that I told you about?"

"Yes?"

"Phillip," she said.

"Oh," I said and left the arm of the sycamore with as delicate a jump as can be made by a person afraid of falling, twisting an ankle, and being out of work for a week.

"I don't mind school," said Richard, shouting from behind the tree. "It's better than listening to her whine."

He really talks like that.

Phillip looked puzzled. "How old are you, sonny?"

"Nine."

"Do nine-year-olds talk like that? I think I have a boy who's nine."

"Yes," said Kitty. "Your Johnny's nine, David's eleven, and Mike's fourteen."

"Ah," said Phillip, sighing; he looked up into the tree I'd flopped from—and there was Judy, Anna's kid, using my nice warm branch. "God," said Phillip, "More!"

Silence followed and embarrassment, because we outnumbered him, though clearly, we tenderly liked him.

"How is everything Kitty?" he said, kneeling to tousle her hair. "How's everything my old honey girl? Another one?" He tapped Kitty's tummy lightly with an index finger. "God!" he said, standing up. "Say Kitty, I saw Jerry in Newark day before yesterday. Just like that. He was standing in a square scratching his head."

"Jerry?" Kitty asked in a high loving squeak. "Oh, I know. Newark all week . . . Why were you there?"

"Me? I had to see someone, a guy named Vincent Hall, a man in my field."

"What's your field?" I asked.

"Daisies," he said. "I happen to be in the field of daisies."

What an answer! How often does one meet in this black place, a man, woman, or child who can think up a pastoral reply like that?

For that reason I looked at him. He had dark offended eyes deep in shadow, with a narrow rim of whiteness under the eyes, the result, I invented, of lots of late carousing nights, followed by eye-wrinkling examinations of mortalness. All this had marked him lightly with sobriety, the first enhancing manifest of ravage.

Even Richard is stunned by this uncynical openhearted nota-tion of feeling. Forty bare seconds then, while Jack Resnick puts his transistor into the hollow of an English elm, takes a tattered score of the *Messiah* out of his rucksack, and writes a short Eliza-bethan melody in among the long chorus holds to go with the last singing sentence of my ode to Phillip.

"Nice day," said Anna.

"Please, Faith," said Richard. "Please. You see that guy over there?" He pointed to a fat boy seated among adults on a park bench not far from listening Lynn Ballard. "He has a skate key and he won't lend it to me. He stinks. It's your fault you lost the skate key, Faith. You know you did. You never put anything away."

"Ask him again, Richard."

"You ask him, Faith. You're a grown-up."

"I will not. You want the skate key, you ask him. You have to go after your own things in this life. I'm not going to be around forever."

Richard gave me a gloomy, lip-curling look. No. It was worse than that. It was a baleful, foreboding look; a look which as far as our far in the future relations were concerned could be named ill-auguring.

"You never do me a favor, do you?" he said.

"*I'll* go with you, Richard." Phillip grabbed his hand. "We'll talk to that kid. He probably hasn't got a friend in the world. I'm not kidding you, boy, it's hard to be a fat kid." He rapped his belly, where, I imagine, certain memories were stored.

Then he took Richard's hand and they went off man and boy to tangle.

"Kitty! Richard just hands him his skate, his hand and just goes off with him. . . . That not like my Richard."

"Children sense how good he is," said Kitty.

"He's good?"

"He's really not *so* good. Oh he's good. He's considerate. You know what kind he is, Faith. But if you don't really want him to be good, he will be. And he's very strong. Physically. Someday I'll tell you about him. Not now. He has a special meaning to me."

Actually everyone has a special meaning to Kitty, even me, a dictionary of specific generalities, even Anna and all our children.

Kitty sewed as she spoke. She looked like a delegate to a Conference of Youth from the People's Republic of Ubmonsk from Lower Tartaria. A single dark braid hung down her back. She wore a round-necked white blouse with capped sleeves made of softened muslin, woven for aged bridesbeds. I have always listened carefully to my friend Kitty's recommendations for she has made one mistake after another. Her experience is invaluable.

Kitty's kids have kept an eye on her from their dear tiniest times. They listened to her reasons, but the two eldest, without meaning any disrespect, had made different plans for their lives. Children are all for John Dewey. Lisa and Nina have never believed that Kitty's life really worked. They slapped Antonia for scratching the enameled kitchen table. When Kitty caught them, she said, "Antonia's a baby. Come on now girls, what's a table?"

"What's a *table?*" said Lisa. "What a nut! She wants to know what a table is?"

"Well, Faith," said Richard, "*he* got the key for me."

Richard and Phillip were holding hands, which made Richard look like a little boy with a daddy. I could cry when I think that I always treat Richard as though he's about forty-seven.

Phillip felt remarkable to have extracted that key. "He's quite a kid, Faith, your boy. I wish that my Johnny in Chicago was as great as Richard here. Is Johnny really nine, Kitty?"

"You bet," she said.

He kept his puzzled face for some mysterious eventuality and folded down to cross-legged comfort, leaning familiarly on Nina and Lisa's backs. "How are you two fairy queens?" he asked and tugged at their long hair gently. He peeked over their shoulders. They were reading *Classic Comics*, "Ivanhoe" and "Robin Hood."

"I hate to read," said Antonia.

"Me too," hollered Tonto.

"Antonia, I wish *you'd* read more," said Phillip. "Antonia, little beauty. These two little ones. Forest babies. Little sunny brown creatures. I think *you* would say, Kitty, that they understand their bodies?"

"Oh, yes, I would," said Kitty, who believed all that.

Although I'm very shy, I tend to persevere so I said, "You're pretty sunny and brown yourself. How do you make out? What are you? An actor or a French teacher, or something?"

"French . . ." Kitty smiled. "He could teach Sanskrit if he wanted to. Or Filipino or Cambodian."

"Cambodge . . ." Phillip said. He said this softly as though the wars in Indochina might be the next subject for discussion.

"French teacher?" asked Anna Kraat, who had been silent, grieved by spring, for one hour and forty minutes. "Judy," she yelled into the crossed branches of the sycamore. "Judy . . . French. . . ."

"So?" said Judy. "What's so great? 'Je m'appelle Judy Solomon. Ma pere s'appelle Pierre Solomon.' How's that folks?"

"Mon pere," said Anna. "I told you that before."

"Who cares?" said Judy, who didn't care.

"She's lost two fathers," said Anna, "within three years."

Tonto stood up to scratch his belly and back, which were itchy with wet grass. "Mostly nobody has fathers, Anna," he said.

"Is that true, little boy?" asked Phillip.

"Oh yes," Tonto said. "My father is in the Equator. They never even had fathers," pointing to Kitty's daughters. "Judy has two fathers, Peter and Dr. Kraat. Dr. Kraat takes care of you if you're crazy."

"Maybe I'll be your father."

Tonto looked at me. I was too rosy. "Oh no," he said. "Not right now. My father's name is Ricardo. He's a famous explorer. Like an explorer I mean. He went in the Equator to make contacts. I have two books by him."

"Do you like him?"

"He's all right."

"Do you miss him?"

"He's very fresh when he's home."

"That's enough of that!" I said. It's stupid to let a kid talk badly about his father in front of another man. Men really have too much on their minds without that.

"He's quite a boy," said Phillip. "You and your brother are straight boys." He turned to me. "What do I do? Well I make a living. Here. Chicago. Wherever I am. I'm not in financial trouble. I figured it all out ten years ago. But what I really am, really . . ." he said, driven to lying confidence because he thought he ought to try that life anyway. "What I truly am is a comedian."

"That's a joke, that's the first joke you've said."

"But that's what I want to be . . . a comedian."

"But you're not funny."

"But I am. You don't know me yet. I want to be one. I've been a teacher and I've worked for the State Department. And now what I want to be's a comedian. People have changed professions before."

"You can't be a comedian," said Anna, "unless you're funny."

He took a good look at Anna. Anna's character is terrible, but she's beautiful. It took her husbands about two years apiece to see how bad she was, but it takes the average passer, answerer, or asker about thirty seconds to see how beautiful she is. You can't warn men. As for Kitty and me, well, we love her because she's beautiful.

"Anna's all right," said Richard.

"Be quiet," said Phillip. "Say, Anna, are you interested in the French tongue, the French people, French history, or French civilization?"

"No," said Anna.

"Oh," he said, disappointed.

"I'm not interested in anything," said Anna.

"Say!" said Phillip, getting absolutely red with excitement, blushing from his earlobes down into his shirt, making me think as I watched his blood descend from his brains that I would like to be the one who was holding his balls very gently, to be exactly present so to speak, when all the thumping got there I felt his keenness, though the cutting edge was standing over that nice white airy spongy loaf, my pal Anna.

Aquarius Obscured

ROBERT STONE

In the house on Noe Street, Big Gene was crooning into the telephone.

"Geerat, Geeroot. Neexat, Nixoot."

He hung up and patted a tattoo atop the receiver, sounding the cymbal beat by forcing air through his molars.

"That's how the Dutch people talk," he told Alison.

"Keroot. Badoot. Krackeroot."

"Who was it?"

He lay back on the corduroy cushions and vigorously scratched himself. A smile spread across his face and he wiggled with pleasure, his eyelids fluttering.

"Some no-nut fool. Easy tool. Uncool."

He lay still with his mouth open, waiting for rhyming characterizations to emerge.

"Was it for me?"

When he looked at her, his eyes were filled with tears. He shook his head sadly to indicate that her questions were obviated by his sublime indifference.

Alison cursed him.

"Don't answer the fucking phone if you don't want to talk," she said. "It might be something important."

Big Gene remained prone.

"I don't know where you get off," he said absently. "See you reverting to typical boojwa. Reverting to type. Lost your fire."

His junky mumble infuriated Alison. She snorted with exasperation.

"For Christ's sake!"

"You bring me down so bad," Gene said softly. "I don't need you. I got control, you know what I mean?"

"It's ridiculous," she told him. "Talking to you is a complete waste of time."

As she went into the next room she heard him moan, a lugubrious, falsetto coo incongruent with his bulk but utterly expressive of the man he had become. His needles had punctured him.

In the bedroom, Io was awake; her large brown eyes gazed fearfully through crib bars at the sunlit window.

"Hello, sweetie," Alison said.

Io turned solemnly toward her mother and yawned.

A person here, Alison thought, lifting her over the bars, the bean blossomed. Walks and conversation. The end of our madonna and child number. A feather of panic fluttered in her throat.

"Io," she told her daughter, "we have got to get our shit together here."

The scene was crumbling. Strong men had folded like stage flats, legality and common sense were fled. Cerebration flickered.

Why me, she demanded of herself, walking Io to the potty. Why do I have to be the only one with any smarts?

On the potty, Io delivered. Alison wiped her and flushed the toilet. By training, Alison was an astronomer but she had never practiced.

Io could dress herself except for the shoes. When Alison tied them, it was apparent to her that they would shortly be too small.

"What'll we do?" she asked Io with a playful but genuinely frightened whine.

"See the fishies," Io said.

"See the fishies?" Alison stroked her chin, burlesquing a thoughtful demeanor, rubbing noses with Io to make her smile. "Good Lord."

Io drew back and nodded soberly.

"See the fishies."

At that moment, Alison recalled the fragment of an undersea dream. Something in the dream had been particularly agreeable and its recall afforded her a happy little throb.

"Well that's what we'll do," she told Io. "We'll go to the aquarium. A capital idea."

"Yes," Io said.

Just outside Io's room, on the littered remnant of a sundeck,
lived a vicious and unhygienic doberman, who had been named
Buck after a dog Big Gene claimed to have once owned in Aruba.
Alison opened the sliding glass door to admit it, and watched
nervously as it nuzzled Io.

"Buck," Io said without enthusiasm.

Alison seized the dog by its collar and thrust it out the bedroom
door before her.

In the living room, Big Gene was rising from the cushions, a
cetaceous surfacing.

"Buck, my main man," he sang. "Bucky bonaroo."

"How about staying with him today?" Alison said. "I want to
take Io to the aquarium."

"Not I," Gene declared. "Noo."

"Why the hell not?" Alison asked savagely.

"Cannot be."

"Shit! I can't leave him alone here, he'll wreck the place. How
can I take him to the goddamn aquarium?"

Gene shrugged sleepily.

"Ain't this the night you get paid?" he asked after a moment.

"Yeah," Alison said.

In fact, Alison had been paid the night before, her employer
having thrown some 80 dollars' worth of half-dollars into her
face. There had been a difference of opinion regarding Alison's
performance as a danseuse, and she had spoken sharply with Mert
the Manager. Mert had replied in an incredibly brutal and hostile
manner, had fired her, insulted her breasts, and left her to peel
coins from the soiled floor until the profile of Jack Kennedy was
welded to her mind's eye. She had not mentioned the incident to
Gene; the half-dollars were concealed under the rubber sheet beneath Io's mattress.

"Good," Gene said, "Because I got to see the man then."

He was looking down at Io, and Alison watched him for signs
of resentment or contempt but she saw only sadness, sickness in
his face. Io paid him no attention at all.

It was startling the way he had mellowed out behind smack.
Witnessing it, she had almost forgiven him the punches, and she
had noticed for the first time that he had rather a kind heart. But
he stole and was feckless; his presence embarrassed her.

"How'm I going to take a dog to the aquarium, for Christ's sake?"

The prospect of having Buck along irritated Alison sorely. In her irritation, she decided that the thing might be more gracefully endured with the white-cross jobbers. The white-cross jobbers were synthetics manufactured by a mad chemist in Hayward. Big Gene called them IT-^{390} to distinguish them from IT-^{290} which they had turned out, upon consumption, not to be.

She took a handful from the saki jar in which they were stored and downed them with tap water.

"All right, *Buck*," she called, pronouncing the animal's name with distaste, "goddamn it." She put his leash on, sent Io ahead to the car, and pulled the reluctant dog out behind her.

With Io strapped in the passenger seat and Buck cringing under the dashboard, Alison ran Lombard Street in the outside lane, accelerating on the curves like Bondurant. Alison was a formidable and aggressive driver, and she drove hard to stay ahead of the drug's rush. When she pulled up in the aquarium's parking lot, her mouth had gone dry and the little sanctus bells of adjusted alertness had begun to tinkle. She hurried them under wind-rattled eucalyptus and up the massive steps that led to the building's Corinthian portico.

"Now where are we going to put this goddamn dog?" she asked Io. When she blinked, her eyeballs clicked. I've done it, she thought. I've swallowed it again. Vandalism.

After a moment's confused hesitation, she led Buck to one side of the entrance and secured his chain round a brass hydrant fixture with a carefully worked running clove hitch. The task brought to her recollection a freakish afternoon when she had tied Buck in front of a bar on El Camino. For the protection of passersby, she had fashioned a sign from the cardboard backing of a foolscap tablet and written on it with a green, felt-tipped pen—DO NOT TRY TO PET THIS DOG. Her last memory of the day was watching the sign blow away across the street and past the pumps of an Esso station.

Buck's vindictive howls pursued them to the oxidized-copper doors of the main entrance.

It was early morning and the aquarium was uncrowded. Liquefactious sounds ran up and down the smooth walls, child voices ricocheted from the ceiling. With Io by the hand, Alison wandered through the interior twilight, past tanks of sea horses, scorpion fish, African *Tilapia*. Pausing before an endlessly gyrating school of salmon, she saw that some of the fish were eyeless, the sockets empty and perfectly cleaned. The blind fish swam with the rest, staying in line, turning with the school.

Io appeared not to notice them.

In the next hall, Alison halted her daughter before each tank, reading from the lighted presentation the name of the animal contained, its habitat and Latin name. The child regarded all with gravity.

At the end of the East Wing was a room brighter than the rest; it was the room in which porpoises lived in tanks that were open to the sky. As Alison entered it, she experienced a curiously pleasant sensation.

"Look," she said to Io. "Dolphins."

"Dolphins?"

They walked up to the glass of the largest tank; its lower area was fouled with small handprints. Within, a solitary blue-gray beast was rounding furiously, describing gorgeous curves with figure of eights, skimming the walls at half an inch's distance. Alison's mouth opened in awe.

"An Atlantic Dolphin," she told Io in a soft, reverential voice. "From the Atlantic Ocean. On the other side of America. Where Providence is."

"And Grandpa," Io said.

"And Grandpa is in Providence, too."

For the space of several seconds, the dream feeling returned to her with an intensity that took her breath away. There had been some loving presence in it and a discovery.

She stared into the tank until the light that filtered through the churning water began to suggest the numinous. Io, perceiving that her mother was not about to move on, retraced her steps toward the halls through which they had come, and commenced seeing the fish over again. Whenever an aquarium-goer smiled at her, she looked away in terror.

Alison stood transfixed, trying to force recall. It had been something special, something important. But silly—as with dreams. She found herself laughing and then, in the next moment, numb with loss as the dream's sense faded. Her heart was racing with the drug.

God, she thought, it's all just flashes and fits. We're just out here in this shit.

With sudden horror, she realized at once that there had been another part of the dream and that it involved the fact that she and Io were just out there and that this was not a dream from which one awakened. Because one *was*, after all.

She turned anxiously to look for Io and saw the child several galleries back, standing in front of the tank where the blind fish were.

The dream had been about getting out of it, trying to come in and make it stop. In the end, when it was most terrible, she had been mercifully carried into a presence before which things had been resolved. The memory of that resolution made her want to weep.

Her eye fell on the animal in the tank; she followed its flights and charges with fascination.

There had been some sort of communication, with or without words.

A trained scientist, Alison loved logic above all else; it was her only important pleasure. If the part about one being out there was true—and it was—what then about the resolution. It seemed to her, as she watched the porpoise, that even dreamed things must have their origin in a kind of truth, that no level of the mind was capable of utterly unfounded construction. Even hallucinations—phenomena with which Alison had become drearily familiar—needed their origins in the empirically verifiable—a cast of light, a sound on the wind. Somehow, she thought, somewhere in the universe, the resolving presence must exist.

Her thoughts raced, she licked her lips to cool the sere dryness cracking them. Her heart gave a desperate leap.

"Was it you?" she asked the porpoise.

"Yes," she heard him say. "Yes, it was."

Alison burst into tears. When she had finished sobbing, she took a Kleenex from her bag, wiped her eyes, and leaned against the cool marble beside the tank.

Prepsychosis. Disorders of thought. Failure to abstract.

"That is ridiculous," she said.

From deep within, from the dreaming place, sounded a voice.
"You're here," the porpoise told her. "That's what matters now."

Nothing in the creature's manner suggested communication or even the faintest sentience. But human attitudes of engagement, Alison reminded herself, were not to be expected. To expect them was anthropocentrism— a limiting, reactionary position like ethnocentrism or sexism.

"It's very hard for me," she told the porpoise. "I can't communicate well at the best of times. And an aquarium situation is pretty weird." At a loss for further words, Alison fell back on indignation. "It must be awful for you."

"It's somewhat weird," she understood the porpoise to say. "I wouldn't call it awful."

Alison trembled.

"But . . . how can it not be awful? A conscious mind shut up in a tank with stupid people staring at you? Not," she hastened to add, "that I think I'm any better. But the way you're stuck in here with these slimy, repulsive fish."

"I don't find fish slimy and repulsive," the porpoise told her.

Mortified, Alison began to stammer an apology, but the creature cut her off.

"The only fish I see are the ones they feed me. It's people I see all day. I wonder if you can realize how *dry* you all are."

"Good Lord!" She moved closer to the tank. "You must hate us."

She became aware of laughter.

"I don't hate."

Alison's pleasure at receiving this information was tempered by a political anxiety. The beast's complacency suggested something objectionable; the suspicion clouded her mind that her interlocutor might be a mere Aquarium Porpoise, a deracinated stooge, an Uncle . . . .

The laughter sounded again.

"I'm sorry," Alison said, "My head is full of such shit."

"Our condition is profoundly different from yours. We don't require the same things. Our souls are as different from yours as our bodies are."

"I have the feeling," Alison said, "that yours are better."

"I think they are. But I'm a porpoise."

The animal in the tank darted upward, torpedo-like, toward the fog-colored surface—then plunged again in a column of spinning, bubbling foam.

"You called me here, didn't you?" Alison asked. "You wanted me to come."

"In a way."

"Only in a way?"

"We communicated our presence here. A number of you might have responded. Personally, I'm satisfied that it was yourself."

"Are you?" Alison cried joyfully. She was aware that her words echoed through the great room. "You see, I asked because I've been having these dreams. Odd things have been happening to me." She paused thoughtfully. "Like I've been listening to the radio sometimes and I've heard these wild things—like just for a second. As though there's been kind of a pattern. Was it you guys?"

"Some of the time. We have our ways."

"Then," she asked breathlessly, "why me?"

"Don't you know why?" the beast asked softly.

"It must have been because you knew I would understand."

There was no response.

"It must have been because you knew how much I hate the way things are with us. Because you knew I'd listen. Because I need something so much."

"Yet," the porpoise said sternly, "you made things this way. You thought you needed them the way they are."

"It wasn't me," Alison said. "Not me. I don't need this shit."

Wide-eyed, she watched him shoot for the surface again, then dive and skim over the floor of his tank, rounding smartly at the wall.

"I love you," she declared suddenly. "I mean I feel a great love for you and I feel there is a great lovingness in you. I just know that there's something really super-important that I can learn from you."

"Are you prepared to know how it is with us?"

"Yes," Alison said. "Oh, yes. And what I can do."

"You can be free," the animal said. "You can learn to perceive in a new way."

Alison became aware of Io standing beside her, frowning up at her tears. She bent down and put her head next to the child's.

"Io, can you see the dolphin? Do you like him?"

"Yes," Io said.

Alison stood up.

"My daughter," she told her dolphin.

Io watched the animal contentedly for a while and then went to sit on a bench in the back of the hall.

"She's only three-and-a-half," Alison said. She feared that communication might be suspended on the introduction of a third party. "Do you like her?"

"We see a great many of your children," the beast replied. "I can't answer you in those terms."

Alison became anxious.

"Does that mean that you don't have *any* emotions? That you can't love?"

"Were I to answer yes or no I would deceive you either way. Let's say only that we don't make the same distinctions."

"I don't understand," Alison said. "I suppose I'm not ready to."

"As your perception changes," the porpoise told her, "many things will seem strange and unfamiliar. You must unlearn old structures of thought that have been forced on you. Much faith, much resolution will be required."

"I'll resist," Alison admitted sadly. "I know I will. I'm very skeptical and frivolous by nature. And it's all so strange and wonderful that I can't believe it."

"All doubt is the product of your animal nature. You must rise above your species. You must trust those who instruct you."

"I'll try," Alison said resolutely. "But it's so incredible! I mean for all these centuries you guys and us have been the only aware species on the planet, and now we've finally come together! It just blows my mind that here—now—for the first time . . ."

"What makes you think it's the first time?"

"Good Lord!" Alison exclaimed. "It's not the first time?"

"There were others before you, Alison. They were weak and fickle. We lost them."

Alison's heart chilled at his words.

"But hasn't it ever worked?"

"It's in the nature of your species to conceive enthusiasms and then to weary of them. Your souls are self-indulgent and your concentration feeble. None of you has ever stayed with it."

"I will," Alison cried. "I'm unique and irreplaceable, and nothing could be more important than this. Understanding, responding inside—that's my great talent. I can do it!"

"We believe you, Alison. That's why you're here."

She was flooded with her dreaming joy. She turned quickly to look for Io and saw her lying at full length on the bench staring up into the overhead lights. Near her stood a tall, long-haired young man who was watching Alison. His stare was a profane irritation and Alison forced it from her mind, but her mood turned suddenly militant.

"I know it's not important in your terms," she told the porpoise, "but it infuriates me to see you shut up like this. You must miss the open sea so much."

"I've never left it," the animal said, "and your pity is wasted on me. I am here on the business of my race."

"I guess it's the way I was brought up. I had a lousy upbringing, but some things about it were good. See, my father, he's a real asshole but he's what we call a liberal. He taught me to really hate it when somebody was oppressed. Injustice makes me want to fight. I suppose it sounds stupid and trivial to you, but that's how it is with me."

The dolphin's voice was low and soothing, infinitely kind.

"We know how it is with you. You understand nothing of your own behavior. Everything you think and do merely reflects what is known to us as a Dry Posture. Your inner life, your entire history are nothing more than these."

"Good Lord!" Alison said. "Dry Posture."

"As we work with you, you must bear this in mind. You must discover the quality of Dry Posture in all your thoughts and actions. When you have separated this quality from your soul, what remains will be the bond between us. At that point your life will truly begin."

"Dry Posture," Alison said. "Wow!"

The animal in the tank was disporting itself just below the surface; in her mounting enthusiasm Alison became increasingly frustrated by the fact that its blank, good-humored face appeared utterly oblivious of her presence. She reminded herself again that the hollow dissembling of human facial expression was beneath its nature, and welcomed the opportunity to be divested of a Dry Posture.

The silence from which the dolphin spoke became charged with music.

"In the sea lies our common origin," she heard him say. "In the sea all was once One. In the sea find your surrender—in surrender find victory, renewal, survival. Recall the sea! Recall our common heartbeat! Return to the peace of primordial consciousness!"

"Oh, how beautiful," Alison cried, her own consciousness awash in salt flumes of insight.

"Our lousy Western culture is worthless," she declared fervently. "It's rotten and sick. We've got to get back. Please," she implored the dolphin, "tell us how!"

"If you receive the knowledge," the animal told her, "your life will become one of dedication and struggle. Are you ready to undertake such striving?"

"Yes," Alison said. "Yes!"

"Are you willing to serve that force which relentlessly wills the progress of the conscious universe?"

"With all my heart!"

"Willing to surrender to that sublime destiny which your species has so fecklessly denied?"

"Oh, boy," Alison said, "I surely am."

"Excellent," said the porpoise. "It shall be your privilege to assist the indomitable will of a mighty and superior species. The natural order shall be restored. That which is strong and sound shall dominate. That which is weak and decadent shall perish and disappear."

"Right on!" Alison cried. She felt her shoulders squaring, her heels coming together.

"Millennia of usurpation shall be overturned in a final solution!"

"Yeah," Alison said. "By any means necessary."

It seemed to Alison that she detected in the porpoise's speech a foreign accent; if not a Third World accent, at least the accent of a civilization older and more together than her own.

"*So,*" the porpoise continued, "where your cities and banks, your aquaria and museums now stand, there shall be rubble only. The responsibility shall rest exclusively with humankind, for our patience has been thoroughly exhausted. What we have not achieved through striving for equitable dialogue, we shall now achieve by striving of another sort."

Alison listened in astonishment as the music's volume swelled behind her eyes.

"For it is our belief," the porpoise informed her, "that in strife, life finds its purification." His distant, euphonious voice assumed a shrill, hysterical note. "In the discipline of ruthless struggle, history is forged and the will tempered! Let the craven, the once-born, shirk the fray—we ourselves shall strike without mercy at the sniveling mass of our natural inferiors. Triumph is our destiny!"

Alison shook her head in confusion.

"Whoa," she said.

Closing her eyes for a moment, she beheld, with startling clarity, the image of a blond-bearded man wearing a white turtle-neck sweater and a peaked officer's cap. His face was distended with fury; beside him loomed a gray cylindrical form which might have been a periscope. Alison opened her eyes quickly and saw the porpoise blithely coursing the walls of its tank.

"But that's not love or life or anything," she sobbed. "That's just cruelty."

"Alison, baby, don't you know it's all the same? Without cruelty you can't have love. If you're not ready to destroy someone, then you're not ready to love them. Because if you've got the knowledge—you know, like if you really have it—then if you do what you have to do that's just everybody's karma. If you have to waste somebody because the universe wills it, then it's just like the bad part of yourself that you're wasting. It's an act of love."

In the next instant, she saw the bearded man again. His drawn, evil face was bathed in a sinister, submarine light, reflected from God knew what fiendish instruments of death.

"I know what you are," Alison called out in horror. "You're a fascist!"

When the beast spoke once more, the softness was vanished from its voice.

"Your civilization has afforded us many moments of amusement. Unfortunately, it must now be irrevocably destroyed."

"Fascist!" Alison whimpered in a strangled voice. "Nazi!"

"Peace," the porpoise intoned, and the music behind him turned tranquil and low. "Here is the knowledge. You must say it daily."

Enraged now, she could detect the mocking hypocrisy in his false, mellow tones.

> *"Surrender to the Notion*
> *Of the Motion of the Ocean."*

As soon as she received the words, they occupied every cubit of her inner space, reverberating moronically, over and over. She put her hands over her ears.

"Horseshit!" she cried. "What kind of cheapo routine is that?"

The voice, she suspected suddenly, might not be that of a porpoise. It might be the man in the turtleneck. But where?

Hovering at the mouth of a celestial Black Hole, secure within the adjoining dimension? A few miles off Sausalito at periscope depth? Or—more monstrous—ingeniously reduced in size and concealed within the dolphin?

"Help," Alison called softly.

At the risk of permanent damage, she desperately engaged her linear perception. Someone might have to know.

"I'm caught up in this plot," she reported. "Either porpoises are trying to reach me with this fascist message or there's some kind of super-Nazi submarine offshore."

Exhausted, she rummaged through her knit bag for a cigarette, found one, and lit it. A momentary warp, she assured herself, inhaling deeply. A trifling skull pop, perhaps an air bubble. She smoked and trembled, avoiding the sight of the tank.

In the next moment, she became aware that the tall young man she had seen earlier had made a circuit of the hall and was standing beside her.

"Fish are groovy," the young man said.

"Wait a minute," Alison demanded. "Just wait a minute here. Was that . . . ?"

The young man displayed a woodchuck smile.

"You were really tripping on those fish, right? Are you stoned?"

He carried a camera case on a strap round his shoulder, and a black cape slung over one arm.

"I don't know what you're talking about," Alison said. She was suddenly consumed with loathing.

"No? 'Cause you look really spaced out."

"Well, I'm not," Alison said firmly. She saw Io advancing from the bench.

The young man stood by as Io clutched her mother's floor-length skirt.

"I want to go outside now," Io said.

His pink smile expanded and he descended quickly to his haunches to address Io at her own level.

"Hiya, baby. My name's Andy."

Io had a look at Andy and attempted flight. Alison was holding one of her hands; Andy made her fast by the other.

"I been taking pictures," he told her. "Pictures of the fishies." He pursued Io to a point behind Alison's knees. Alison pulled on Io's free hand and found herself staring down into the camera case.

"You like the fishies?" Andy insisted. "You think they're groovy?"

There were two Nikon lenses side by side in the case. Alison let Io's hand go, thrust her own into the case and plucked out a lens. While Andy was asking Io if she, Io, were shy, Alison dropped the lens into her knit bag. As Andy started up, she seized the second lens and pressed it hard against her skirt.

Back on his feet, Andy was slightly breathless.

"You wanna go smoke some dope?" he asked Alison. "I'm goin' over to the art museum and sneak some shots over there. You wanna come?"

"Actually," Alison told him, "I have a luncheon engagement."

Andy blinked. "Far out."

"Far out?" Alison asked, "I'll tell you something far out, Andy. There is a lot of really repulsive shit in this aquarium, Andy. There are some very low-level animals here and they're very frightening and unreal. But there isn't one thing in this place that is as repulsive and unreal as you are, Andy."

She heard the laughter echo and realized that it was her own. She clenched her teeth to stop it.

"You should have a tank of your own, Andy."

As she led Io toward the door, she cupped the hand that held the second lens against her hip, like a mannequin. At the end of the hall, she glanced back and saw Andy looking into the dolphin's tank. The smile on his face was dreadful.

"I like the fish," Io said, as they descended the pompous stone steps outside the entrance. "I like the lights in the fish places."

Recognizing them, Buck rushed forward on his chain, his tongue dripping. Alison untied him as quickly and calmly as she could.

"We'll come back, sweetie," she said. "We'll come back lots of times."

"Tomorrow?" the child asked.

In the parking lot, Alison looked over her shoulder. The steps were empty; there were no alarums or pursuits.

When they were in the car, she felt cold. Columns of fog were moving in from the bay. She sat motionless for a while, blew her nose, and wrapped a spare sweater that was lying on the seat around Io's shoulders.

"Mama's deluded," she explained.

The Universal Fears

JOHN HAWKES

MONDAY MORNING, bright as the birds, and there he stood for the first time among the twenty-seven girls who, if he had only known, were already playing the silence game. He looked at them, they looked at him, he never thought of getting a good grip on the pointer laid out lengthwise on that bare desk. Twenty-seven teen-age girls—homeless, bad-off, unloved, semi-literate, and each one of their poor unattractive faces was a condemnation of him, of all such schools for delinquent girls, of the dockyards lying round them like a seacoast of iron cranes, of the sunlight knifing through the grilles on the windows. They weren't faces to make you smile. Their sexual definition was vague and bleak. Hostile. But even then, in their first institutional moment together, he knew he didn't offer them any better from their point of view—only another fat man in the mid-fifties whose maleness meant nothing more than pants and jacket and belted belly and thin hair blacked with a cheap dye and brushed flat to the skull. Nothing in the new teacher to sigh about. So it was tit for tat, for them the desolation of more of the same, for him the deflation of the first glance that destroyed the possibility of finding just one keen lovely face to make the whole dreary thing worthwhile. Or a body promising a good shape to come. Or one set of sensual lips. Or one sign of adult responsiveness in any of those small eyes. But there was nothing, except the thought that perhaps their very sullenness might actually provide the most provocative landscape for the discovery of the special chemistry of pain that belongs to girls. Still he was already sweating in the armpits and going dry in the mouth.

"Right, girls," he said, "let's come to order."

In a shabby display of friendliness, accessibility, confidence, he slid from behind the desk and stood leaning the backs of his upper thighs against the front edge of it. Through the south window came the sounds of whistles and windlasses, from closer came the sounds of unloading coal. It made him think of a prison within a prison. No doubt the docks were considered the most suitable context for a school, so-called, for girls like these. Yes, the smells of brine and tar and buckets of oil that rode faintly in on the knifing light were only complementary to the stench of the room, to the soap, the thick shellac, the breath of the girls, the smell of their hair. It was a man's world for an apparently sexless lot of girls, and there was only one exotic aroma to be caught on that tide: the flowery wash of the sweet bay rum that clung to the thick embarrassed person of their old teacher new on the job.

"Right, girls," he said, returning warm glance for hostile stare, tic-like winks for the smoky and steady appraisal of small eyes, "right now, let's start with a few names. . . ."

And there they sat, unmoving, silent, ranked at three wooden benches of nine girls each, and all of their faces, whether large or small, thin or broad, dark or light, were blank as paper. Apparently they had made a pact before he entered the room to breathe in unison, so that now wherever he looked—first row on the left, first on the right—he was only too aware of the deliberate and ugly harmony of flat chests or full that were rising and falling slowly, casually, but always together.

Challenging the prof? Had they really agreed among themselves to be uncooperative? To give him a few bad minutes on the first day? Poor things, he thought, and crossed his fatty ankles, rested one flat hand on the uphill side of the belly, and then once more he looked them over at random, bearing down on a pair of shoulders like broken sticks, two thin lips bruised from chewing, a head of loose brown hair and another with a thin mane snarled in elastic bands, and some eyes without lashes, the closed books, claw marks evident on a sallow cheek.

"Girl on the end, there," he said all at once, stopping and swinging his attention back to the long black hair, the boy's shirt buttoned to the throat, the slanted eyes that never moved, "what's your name? Or you," he said, nodding at one of the younger ones, "what's yours?" He smiled, he waited, he shifted his glance from girl to girl, he began to make small but comforting gestures with the hand already resting on what he called his middle mound.

And then they attacked. The nearest bench was going over and coming his way like the side of a house undergoing demolition, and then the entire room was erupting not in noise but in the massed and silent motion of girls determined to drive their teacher out of the door, out of the school, and away, away, if they did not destroy him first right there on the floor. They leaped, they swung round the ends, tight-lipped they toppled against each other and rushed at him. He managed to raise his two hands to the defensive position, fingers fanned out in sheer disbelief and terror, but the cry with which he had thought to stop them merely stuck in his throat, while for an instant longer, he stood there pushing air with his trembling outthrust hands. The girls tripped, charged from both sides of the room, swarmed over the fallen benches in the middle, dove with undeniable intent to seize and incapacitate his person.

The pointer, yes, the pointer, it flashed to his mind, invisibly it hovered within his reach, burned like a long thin weapon with which he might have struck them, stabbed them, beaten them, fended them off. But of course the pointer was behind him and he dared not turn, dared not drop the guard of his now frenzied hands. In an instant he saw it all—the moving girls between himself and the door, the impenetrable web of iron battened to each one of the dusty windows, and he knew there was no way out, no help. A shoe flew past his ear, a full-fifty tin of cigarettes hit the high ceiling above his head and exploded, rained down on him in his paralysis and the girls in their charge. No pointer, no handy instrument for self-defense, no assistance coming from anywhere.

And then the sound came on, adding to that turbulent pantomime the shrieks of their anger, so that what until this instant had been impending violence brimming in a bowl of unnatural silence, now became imminent brutality in a conventional context of the audionics of wrath. His own cry was stifled, his head was filled with the fury of that small mob.

"Annette . . . !"

"Deborah . . . !"

"Fuck off . . ."

"Now . . . now . . ."

"Kill him . . . !"

Despite their superior numbers they were not able to smother him in the first rush, and despite his own disbelief and fear he did not go down beneath them without a fight. Quite the contrary, because the first to reach him was of medium height, about fourteen, with her ribs showing through her jersey and a cheap bracelet twirling on her ankle. And before she could strike a blow he caught her in the crook of his left arm and locked her against his trembling belly and squeezed the life from her eyes, the breath from her lungs, the hate from her undersized constricted heart. He felt her warmth, her limpness, her terror. Then he relaxed the pressure of his arm and the slight girl sank to his feet, he drove a doubled fist into the pimpled face of a young thick-lipped assailant whose auburn hair had been milked of its fire in long days and nights of dockyard rain. The nose broke, the mouth dissolved, his fist was ringed with blood and faded hair.

"You fucking old bastard," said a voice off his left shoulder, and then down he went with a knee in his ribs, arms around his neck and belly, a shod foot in the small of his back. For one more moment, while black seas washed over the deck and the clouds burst, the pit yawned, the molten light of the sun drained down as from a pink collapsing sack in the sky, he managed to keep to his all-fours. And it was exactly in this position that he opened his eyes, looked up, but only in time to receive full in the mouth the mighty downward blow of the small sharp fist of the slant-eyed girl whose name he had first requested. The black hair, the boy's gray workshirt buttoned tight around the neck, a look of steady intensity in the brown eyes, and the legs apart, the body bent slightly down, the elbow cocked, and then the aim, the frown, the little fist landing with unexpected force on the loose torn vulnerable mouth—yes, it was the same girl, no doubt of it.

Blood on the floor. Mouth full of broken china. A loud kick driven squarely between the buttocks. And still through the forests of pain he noted the little brassy zipper of someone's fly, a sock like striped candy, a flat bare stomach gouged by an old scar, bright red droplets making a random pattern on the open pages of an outmoded Form One Math. He tried to shake a straddling bony tormentor off his bruised back, bore another shock to the head, another punch in the side, and then he went soft, dropped, rolled over, tried to shield his face with his shoulder, cupped both hurt hands over the last of the male features hiding down there between his legs.

They piled on. He saw the sudden blade of a knife. They dragged each other off, they screamed. He groaned. He tried to worm his heavy beaten way toward the door. He tried to defend himself with hip, with elbow. And beneath that struggling mass of girls he began to feel his fat and wounded body slowing down, stopping, becoming only a still wet shadow on the rough and splintered wood of the classroom floor. And now and then through the shrieking he heard the distant voices.

"Cathy . . ."

"Eleanora . . ."

"Get his fucking globes . . ."

"Get the globes . . ."

They pushed, they pulled, they tugged, and then with his eyes squeezed shut he knew suddenly that they were beginning to work together in some terrible accord that depended on childish unspoken intelligence, cruel cooperation. He heard the hissing of the birds, he felt their hands. They turned him over—face up, belly up—and sat on his still-breathing carcass. One of them tore loose his necktie of cream-colored and magenta silk while simultaneously his only white shirt, fabric bleached and weakened by the innumerable Sunday washings he had given it in his small lavatory sink, split in a long clean easy tear from his neck to navel. They flung his already mangled spectacles against the blackboard. They removed one shoe, one sock, and yanked the shabby jacket off his right shoulder and bounded up and down on his sagging knees, dug fingernails into the exposed white bareness of his right breast. Momentarily his left eye came unstuck and through the film of his tears he noted that the ringleader was the girl with the auburn hair and broken nose. She was riding his thighs, her sleeves were rolled, her thick lower lip was caught between her teeth in a parody of schoolgirl concentration, despite her injury and the blood on her face. It occurred to him that her pale hair deserved the sun. But then he felt a jolt in the middle, a jolt at the hips, and of course he had known all along that it was his pants they were after, pants and underpants. Then she had them halfway down, and he smelled her cheap scent, heard their gasping laughter, and felt the point of the clasp knife pierce his groin.

"He's fucking fat, he is . . ."

"The old suck . . ."

In his welter of pain and humiliation he writhed but did not cry out, writhed but made no final effort to heave them off, to stop the knife. What was the use? And wasn't he aware at last that all his poor street girls were actually bent to an operation of love not murder? Mutilated, demeaned, room a shambles and teacher overcome, still he knew in his fluid and sinking consciousness that all his young maenads were trying only to feast on love.

"Off him! Off him!" came the loud and menacing voice from the doorway while he, who no longer wanted saving, commenced a long low moan.

"Get away from him at once, you little bitches . . . !"

There he was, lying precisely as the victim lies, helplessly inseparable from the sprawled and bloodied shape the victim makes in the middle of the avenue at the foot of the trembling omnibus. He was blind. He could not move, could not speak. But in customary fashion he had the distinct impression of his mangled self as noted, say, from the doorway where the director stood. Yes, it was all perfectly clear. He was quite capable of surveying what the director surveyed—the naked foot, the abandoned knife, the blood like a pattern spread beneath the body, the soft dismembered carcass fouling the torn shirt and crumpled pants. The remnants of significant male anatomy were still in hiding, dazed, anesthetized, but the pinched white hairy groin, still bleeding, was calling itself to his passive consciousness while beckoning the director to a long proud glance of disapproval, scorn, distaste.

Gongs rang, the ambulance came and went, he lay alone on the floor. Had the girls fled? Or were they simply backed against those dusty walls with legs crossed and thumbs hooked in leather belts, casually defying the man in the doorway? Or silent, sullen, knowing the worst was yet to come for them, perhaps they were simply trying to right the benches, repair the room. In any case he was too bruised to regret the hands that did not reach for him, the white ambulance that would forever pass him by.

"Sovrowsky, Coletta, Rivers, Fiume," said the director from his point of authority at the door. "Pick him up. Fix his pants. Follow me. You bitches."

In the otherwise empty room off the director's office was an old leather couch, there not merely for the girls' cramps but, more important, for the director's rest, a fact which he knew intuitively and immediately the moment he came awake and felt beneath him the pinched and puffy leather surface of the listing couch. And now the couch was bearing him down the dirty tide and he was conscious enough of adding new blood to fading stains.

Somebody was matter-of-factly brushing the cut above his eye with the flaming tip of a long and treacherous needle. And this same person, he discovered in the next moment, was pouring a hot and humiliating syrup into the wounds in his groin.

"Look at him," murmured the thin young woman, and made another stroke, another daub at the eye, "look at him, he's coming round."

Seeing the old emergency kit opened and breathing off ammonia on the young woman's knees pressed close together, and furthermore, seeing the tape and scissors in the young woman's bony hands and hearing the tape, seeing the long bite of the scissors, it was then that he did indeed come round, as his helpful young colleague had said, and rolled one gelatinous quarter-turn to the edge of the couch and vomited fully and heavily into the sluggish tide down which he still felt himself sailing, awake or not. His vomit missed the thin black-stockinged legs and narrow flat-heeled shoes of the young teacher seated beside him.

"I warned you," the director was saying, "I told you they were dangerous. I told you they beat your predecessor nearly to death. How do you think we had your opening? And now it's not at all clear you can handle the job. You might have been killed. . . ."

"Next time they'll kill him, rightly enough," said the young woman, raising her brows and speaking through the cheap tin nasal funnel of her narrow mouth and laying on another foot-long strip of tape.

Slowly, lying half on his belly, sinking into the vast hurt of his depthless belly, he managed to lift his head and raise his eyes for one long dismal stare at the impassive face of the director.

"I can handle the job," he whispered, just as the vomiting started up again from the pit of his life. From somewhere in the depths of the building he heard the rising screams of the girl with the thick lips, auburn hair, and broken nose.

He was most seriously injured, as it turned out, not in the groin or flanks or belly, but in the head. And the amateurish and careless ministrations of the cadaverous young female teacher were insufficient, as even the director recognized. So they recovered his cream and magenta tie, which he stuffed into his jacket pocket, helped to replace the missing shoe and sock, draped his shoulders in an old and hairy blanket, and together steadied him down to his own small ancient automobile in which the young female teacher drove him to the hospital. There he submitted himself to something under two hours of waiting and three at least of professional care, noting in the midst of fresh pain and the smells of antiseptic how the young teacher stood by to see the handiwork of her own first aid destroyed, the long strips of tape pulled off brusquely with the help of cotton swabs and a bottle of cold alcohol, and the head rather than chest or groin wrapped in endless footage of soft gauze and new strips of official tape. He felt the muffling of the ears, the thickening sensation of the gauze going round the top of his head and down his swollen cheeks, was aware of the care taken to leave stark minimal openings for the eyes, the nose, the battered mouth.

"Well," muttered the medical student entrusted with this operation of sculpting and binding the head in its helmet and facemask of white bandages, "somebody did a job on you, all right."

No sooner had he entered the flat than his little dog Murphy, or Murph for short, glanced at the enormous white hive of antiseptic bandages and then scampered behind the conveniently open downstairs door of the china cabinet, making a thin and steady cry of uncommonly high pitch. He had frightened his own poor little dog, he with his great white head, and now he heard Murph clawing at the lower inside rear wall of the china cabinet and, leaning just inside his own doorway, became freshly nauseous, freshly weak.

"Come out, Murph," he tried to say, "it's me." But within its portable padded cell of bandage, his muffled voice was as wordless as Murphy's. From within the cabinet came the slow circular sounds of Murphy's claws, still accompanied by the steady shrill music of the little animal's panic, so that within the yet larger context of his own personal shock, he knew at once that he must devote himself to convincing the little dog that the man inside the bandages was familiar and unchanged. It could take days.

"Murphy," he meant to say, "shut your eyes, smell my hands, trust me, Murph." But even to his own steady ear the appeal sounded only like a faint wind trapped in the mouth of a mute.

It was dusk, his insulated and mummified head was floating, throbbing, while the rest of him, the masses of beaten and lacerated flesh beneath the disheveled clothes, cried out for sleep and small soft hands to press against him and slowly eliminate, by tender touch, these unfamiliar aches, these heavy pains. He wanted to lie forever on his iron bed, to sit swathed and protected in his broken-down padded chair with Murph on his lap. But the night was inimical, approaching, descending, filling space everywhere, and the flat no longer felt his own. The chair would be as hard as the bed, as unfamiliar, and even Murphy's latest hectic guilt-ridden trail of constraint and relief appeared to have been laid down by somebody else's uncontrollable household pet. Why did the window of his flat give onto the same dockyard scene, though further away and at a different angle, as the window of the schoolroom in which he had all but died? Why didn't he switch on a light, prepare his usual tea, put water in Murphy's bowl? A few minutes later, on hands and knees and with his heavy white head ready to sink to the floor, he suddenly realized that injury attacks identity, which was why, he now knew, that assault was a crime.

He did his clean-up job on hands and knees, he made no further effort to entice his dog from the china cabinet, he found himself wondering why the young teacher had allowed him to climb to the waiting and faintly kennelish-smelling flat alone. When he had dropped the last of poor little bewhiskered Murphy's fallen fruit into a paper sack now puffy with air and unavoidable waste, and in pain and darkness had sealed the sack and disposed of it in the tin pail beneath the sink, he slowly dragged himself to the side of the iron bed and then, more slowly still, hauled himself up and over. Shoes and all. Jacket and torn shirt and pants and all. Nausea and all. And lay on his side. And for the first time allowed the fingers of one hand to settle gently on the bandages that bound his head, and slowly and gently to touch, poke, caress, explore. Then at last, and with this same hand, he groped and drew to his chin the old yellow comforter that still exhaled the delicate scent of his dead mother.

Teacher Assaulted at
Training School for Girls

Mr. Walter Jones, newly appointed to the staff of St. Dunster's Training School for Girls, received emergency treatment today at St. Dunster's Hospital for multiple bruises which, as Mr. Jones admitted and Dr. Smyth-Jones, director of the school, confirmed, were inflicted by the young female students in Mr. Jones's first class at the school. Mr. Jones's predecessor, Mr. William Smyth, was so severely injured by these same students November last that he has been forced into early and permanent retirement. Dr. Smyth-Jones expressed regret for both incidents, but indicated that Mr. Jones's place on the staff would be awaiting him upon his full and, it is to be hoped, early recovery. "The public," he commented, "little appreciates the obstacles faced by educators at a school such as St. Dunster's. After all, within the system for the rehabilitation of criminally inclined female minors, St. Dunster's has been singled out to receive only the most intractable of girls. Occasional injury to our staff and to the girls themselves is clearly unavoidable."

With both hands on the wheel and Murph on his lap and a large soft-brimmed felt hat covering a good half of the offending white head, in this condition and full into the sun he slowly and cautiously drove the tortuous cobbled route toward Rose and Thyme, that brutally distended low-pitted slab of tenements into which his father, Old Jack, as he was known by all, had long since cut his filthy niche. The sun on the roof of the small old coffin of a car was warm, the narrow and dusty interior was filled with the hovering aroma of fresh petrol, and Murph, with his nose raised just to the level of the glass on the driver's side, was bobbing and squirming gently to the rhythm first of the footbrake and then the clutch. As for himself, and aside from the welcome heat of the little dog and the ice and glitter of the new day, it gave him special pleasure to be driving cautiously along with a lighted cigarette protruding from the mouth-slit in the bandages and, now and again, his entire head turning to give some timorous old woman the whole shock full in the face. He was only too conscious that he could move, that he could drive the car, that he filled the roaring but slowly moving vehicle with his bulk and age, that Murph's tiny pointed salt-and-pepper ears rose just above the edge of the window, and then was only too conscious, suddenly, of the forgotten girls.

Why, he asked himself, had he forgotten the girls? Why had he forced from his mind so simply, so unintentionally, the very girls whose entry into his life had been so briefly welcome, so briefly violent? Would he give up? Would he see them again? But why had he applied for that job in the first place? Surely he had not been going his own way, finally, after what his nimble old Dad called the juicy rough. All this pain and confusion for easy sex? Not a bit of it.

And then, making a difficult turn and drawing up behind a narrow flat-bedded lorry loaded down with stone and chugging, crawling, suddenly he saw it all, saw himself standing in Old Jack's doorway with Murph in his arms, saw his nimble Dad spring back, small and sallow face already contorted into the familiar look of alarm, and duck and turn, and from somewhere in the uncharted litter of that filthy room whip out his trench knife and stand there against the peeling wall with his knees knocking and weapon high and face contorted into that expression of fear and grievous pride common to most of those who lived in the ruin and desolation of Rose and Thyme. Then he heard the silent voices as the little old man threw down the trench knife and wiped his little beak and small square toothless mouth down the length of his bare arm.

It's you, is it?

Just me, Dad. Come to visit.

You might know better than to be stalking up here like some telly monster with that head of yours and that dead dog in your arms.

Murph's all right, Jack. Aren't you, Murph?

It's that school, that fucking school. My own son beaten near to death by a bunch of girls and written up in the papers. I read it, the whole sad story. And then stalking up here like a murderous monster.

They're very strong girls. And there were a lot of them. Twenty-seven actually.

Why were you there? Tell me why, eh? Oh, the Good Samaritan....

Yes, the Good Samaritan.

Or were you really after a little juicy rough?

Mere sex? Not a bit of it. Of course I wouldn't rule out possibilities, but there's more than that.

Juicy rough. Walter, juicy rough. Don't lie.

I believe I want to know how those girls exist without romance. Or do they?

Use the glove, Walter! Let me give you the old fur glove. It does a lovely job. You can borrow it. . . .

"Yes," he heard himself musing aloud from within the bundle of antiseptic stuffing that was his head, and pressing first the brake and then the accelerator, "yes, I want to be at the bottom where those girls are. Without romance."

At a faster pace now and passing the lorry, he headed the little dark blue car once more in the direction from which he and Murphy had started out in the first place. Occasionally it was preferable to meet Old Jack not in the flesh but in the mind, he told himself, and this very moment was a case in point.

"No," said the young female teacher in the otherwise empty corridor, "it's you! And still in bandages."

"On the stroke of eight," he heard himself saying through the mouth-slit, which he had enlarged progressively with his fingers. "I'm always punctual."

"But you're not ready to come back. Just look at you."

"Ready enough. They couldn't keep me away."

"Wait," she said then, her voice jumping at him and her face full of alarm, "don't go in there . . . !"

"Must," he said, and shook her off, reached out, opened the door.

The same room. The same grilled and dusty windows. The same machinery in spidery operation in the vista beyond. Yes, it might have been his first day, his first morning, except that he recognized them and picked them out one by one from the silent rows—the narrow slant-eyed face, the girl with tuberculosis of the bone, the auburn-haired ringleader who had held the knife. Yes, all the same, except the ringleader was wearing a large piece of sticking plaster across her nose. Even a name or two came back to him and for an instant these names evoked the shadowy partial poem of the forgotten rest. But named or unnamed their eyes were on him, as before, and though they could not know it, he was smiling in the same old suit and flaming tie and dusty pointed shoes. Yes, they knew who he was, and he in turn knew all about their silence game and actually was counting on the ugliness, the surprise, of the fully bandaged head to put them off, to serve as a measure of what they had done and all he had forgiven even before they had struck, to serve them as the first sign of courage and trust.

"Now, girls," he said in a voice they could not hear, "if you'll take out pencils and paper and listen attentively, we'll just begin." Across the room the pointer was lying on the old familiar desk like a sword in the light.

Swan Feast

WILLIAM MATHES

I AM NOT MUCH OF a hunter, being less interested in killing than in the places one goes to hunt, the precision and smoothness of guns and rifles, the polished surfaces of barrels and bullets, and the tight, sure thud on my shoulder. I do not especially care for rising before dawn, nor for eating something I have killed. Nevertheless, I try to apply my skill and use my weapons in actual hunting a few times each year. It seems only right to do so. But since I find most hunters a little too boring and boisterous for friendship, I seldom go hunting with the same group twice or to the same lodge. I cover the field, as it were, spending in all about six weekends each year gameshooting.

One year I went several hundred miles for bear, but was not in shape for the hills and regretted both not getting a shot and being stiff for a week after I returned. Upland game is scarce here in the tidewater; the fields are all posted (by absentee landlords) and the birds are hard to find—gun shy and usually roosting in the trees. South there is good duck and goose hunting, ideal for a weekend hunter like myself. At first I tried taking my wife and children with me, but they disliked waiting in the motel (there was nothing else for them to do in the small towns near the hunting) and they disliked even more going to the blinds: the wetness and the loud gun-blasts and the blood.

So, I began asking around the local sporting goods stores about lodges or hotels where one might go to hunt. I compiled a sizable list and proceeded to choose one in the middle-price range, thinking that both the cheaper and the very luxurious places appeal to hunters unlike myself in the extreme, and that a moderately priced one might draw moderate people with whom I would have more, if not much, in common. I was free one weekend when, as luck would have it, several men from my town were going to the lodge I had chosen. We left on a Friday night, driving in one station wagon—all six of us with our guns and gear and two dogs, a Labrador and a setter, who did not get along too well.

We took turns driving and after midnight we were creeping across the wood bridge that was the only access to the lodge; it was the one building on a small, flat island on the edge of the sound—a well-traveled flyway. The moon was full, so we had no trouble making out the place: the rather small and conventional building, the ghostly reflections on the smooth surface of the sound, and the waving marsh grass and patches of scrub pine that covered most of the island. They were expecting us. The driveway fairly swarmed with Negro help. Some were rather ragged; two at least were barefoot. The dogs ran off, but returned without a fuss: well-bred and sleepy. The accommodations were adequate, the atmosphere was cozy: a large, roaring fireplace; men in boots and hunting clothes stringing decoys and comparing shotguns; card games and whiskey.

From the great window overlooking the sound we were offered a striking view: the black water seemed split as into an abyss by the reflection of the moon; it made me think of a cold, silver knife. Several men became apparently drunk almost immediately. I found myself talking quite loudly, as was everyone else. We were all keyed up: glad to be away from home for awhile, thinking about our adventure (small as it was, we were not used to much more), and speculating about the hunting. There was some talk about having one of the Negro boys drive to a nearby town for a dozen party girls—certain kinds of men, I've noticed, seem to need women badly when they are nervous and excited; but they decided it would be too late by the time the girls got back to the lodge.

The next morning, when it was time to go to the blinds, some of the men had not slept at all; they looked slightly ill, others were ill in fact. But we all went, all but one fellow who had passed out and could not be roused. The Negroes got us into the boats, showed us how to use the hand-warmers, and fed us scrambled egg sandwiches. We ate the sandwiches in the boats on the way to the blinds. It took about an hour for all of us to be deposited in the blinds and the boats hidden. Everyone was eager—men and dogs—for the first few minutes, but by the time the sun showed we were all feeling the effects of little sleep and the bone-chilling dampness. One of the men in my blind was still drinking heavily and before long had vomited his egg sandwiches—outside the blind, fortunately. He seemed quite pleased; the activity had warmed him up.

The light showed us a wide expanse of the sound; our blind was at the top of a small hook cove and had been dug out of the swamp ooze, which dripped between the cracks in the timber lining. We could see all around us, but the ducks could not see us at all—like those one-way mirror-glasses. The hook cove was a natural shelter for the ducks; they had to fly right over our blind to land into the wind. Everything had been neatly planned. Decoys had been anchored in the cove and they looked very lifelike to me. One of them had capsized, though, and a Negro waded out and set it right. He said it was so cold that he thought the water might freeze, especially since there was no wind. This was bad news; if the decoys froze in, the hunting was apt to be poor. The ducks could tell there was something wrong about a decoy sitting motionless in ice.

Everyone began to get tired of waiting. The cold had penetrated past all our expensive and guaranteed clothing, and our eyes squinting into the low sun turned into watery, nearly sightless, red gobs. Still, the sound was beautiful, changing color as the sun developed: from gray to silver (as if the sun were the moon and the morning the night) to yellow to red, and then, suddenly, the water and everything else had its natural color—red tinted but true. The water seemed as thick and slow as gravy; and the grass dipped its tips into the brightest center of the sun. And above, the sky was crystal blue. Too blue for good hunting; the birds would be flying long distances and probably high. The best we could hope for was a tired and hungry flock, just by chance, looking for a quick feeding and rest; they might come in low enough to take a look at our hook cove. Hit-and-run shooting is better than nothing, but it takes skill. At least a breeze was building, and that would help.

Something made a great splashing noise to our left and we saw a large flock of coot walking on the surface and trying to fly.

They had hopes for the new breeze, but it folded on them and they went out of sight still splashing, still not flying. We watched them go, watched them just to see something move, watched them until they were as small as the ruffles far out on the sound. But then from our right came the sounds of shotguns firing. We waited, tense, getting warm now, moving our trigger fingers to increase circulation. The blinds had been laid out in a circle so that as the flocks were shot at from one blind, they tended to flee in the direction of the next blind—and so on, around and around until everyone had a limit or, if the flock were small, until all the birds had been killed. The next flurry of shots was closer. They would be coming out of the sun; we squinted and strained to see them and then they were on top of us: skimming the surface of the sound, searching the shoreline for a safe place, the formation already broken up and beginning to scatter. There were two wounded stragglers—sure, slow targets.

The dogs sensed their coming and our tension. Their whole life was in this brief drama: the whine of wings, the popping of shotguns, and the splashes of the birds. They waited with their legs crouched, ready to spring at the sound of the first shots. The Negro boys had to hold them back, or they would have jumped too soon. Then the ducks were upon us, spinning up out of the sun. We would have to shoot squinting into the sun. We stood and fired; six birds stopped within the haze of shot, fluttered and fell like rag dolls hung too precariously in the sky. They fell and before they hit the water the dogs were after them, leaping far out into the water, paddling intently toward the dead birds, feeling the freezing water bite their hot noses. All the prerequisites had been fulfilled; it was their time. They were more present, even, than the men with their guns. For a few minutes they comprehended fully.

The rest of the flock turned away from our fire, flew quickly out of range, and circled out over the sound, gaining altitude; they would look for a safer place now. Then the stragglers came toward us—dazed, wounded, slow—and we picked them off. The dogs were busy for the better part of a half hour; there were no cripples; even into the sun, we had shot cleanly, killing neatly. Exhausted and soaked, the dogs lay in the bottom of the blind out of the wind—flying long red tongues and rolling their eyes with delight. There was nothing to do but wait for the boat; counting the stragglers, we had taken our limit. Just before noon, the launch came to take us back; the other blinds had done well too. The bottom of the launch was packed with bloody ducks on strings like fish. One cripple had been kept alive—its wings broken; some men amused themselves with it until we were nearly to the lodge and then gave it to one of the Negro boys to kill; he took it by the feet and bashed in its skull on the gunwale. The bony head was hard, and it cracked only after repeated blows.

I slept most of the afternoon, as did everyone else. The man who could not be roused that morning was the only afternoon hunter. By dark the lodge was humming again: sleep had spurred appetites, and in back a whole army of Negro boys was plucking and cleaning our birds, dipping them into pots of boiling water. The steam and the feathers mixed; it might have been a tar and feathering. The whiskey only made us more hungry, but it was something warm in our stomachs.

By dinner most of the men were drunk again, and I was unusually flushed and gregarious from more than my usual quota of highballs. It was a grand dinner: heaps of oysters raw and baked, with red sauce and hot butter to dip them in; our ducks, stuffed with wild rice and chestnuts, were served on planks. There were two birds for each of us, and deep dishes of vegetables, fruits, and yams. The lodge proprietor served an acceptable Rhine wine: he seemed the perfect host. I thought about coming to his lodge again and told him so. The only jarring note was the ice cream for dessert; a mild cheese would have been better with the coffee and liqueur. The proprietor announced that the rest of our game had been dressed and put on dry ice in cartons, so that we could take it back with us.

The drinking after dinner was more intense and serious. We would be going home the next afternoon and, it being now or never, some of the men got to talking about bringing in party girls, but they talked themselves out of it. The consensus was that these girls, cheap as they were, would not be very attractive, although the proprietor assured us that they were young and pretty—they were merely used to a low standard of living. Finally, our perfect host suggested that we might like a "show"; his help sometimes were interested in making extra money. Everyone seemed delighted and agreed quickly to put up five dollars each. I was not especially interested (if you've seen one sex show, you've seen them all), but there was no polite way out of it and I made my contribution like everyone else.

Soon the lodge was prepared: the windows covered, the doors locked, chairs arranged around a table in front of the fireplace. The lights were turned off, but the fire gave ample illumination. The proprietor led in a naked Negro man and woman. Both were young, handsome and shapely. The man seemed the younger of the two, really just a boy. The woman had covered herself with white flour; apparently, the proprietor had a sense of humor. She was fullhipped and voluptuous, and the men whistled and called obscenities to her; used to them, she answered with a lascivious grin. The boy was not smiling, and looked uneasy. The proprietor introduced the couple and asked that everyone remain seated during the show and afterward. He said he did not want anyone getting any ideas about starting their own show. He said that the girl was not a whore and that he would not permit her to be abused. Someone in the crowd said, "You mean gang-banged!" and everyone laughed. The manager smiled, but you could see that he was not the sort to stand for any trouble, as he put it, even if we were paying for it. The men were in a good mood; they sat back, poured more drinks, and waited to be entertained. There were the usual cracks about how "Nigger women are the only ones who really like it," and about how "It takes a big man to split a black oak." The couple climbed up on a large table. The boy was a virile-looking fellow, but his long, hoselike penis was not responding to the girl; he was now visibly nervous: this was probably his debut in show business. In the red firelight both of them looked like naked devils.

The white flour made the woman look remarkably like a white woman, except that very few white women are so muscular and fully developed, or have such a marvelously beautiful body. The proprietor's sense of humor was something of an insult both to white womanhood and the white male's fear of the black male's prowess. But no one seemed to have taken this in or, if they did, be offended by it. We were all watching her closely; I could not take my eyes away from the spectacle of her, as she pranced and postured for us; her breasts were high and firm, with nipples as dark and as shiny as her eyes; her hips were full and rounded, her thighs tapered and full; her pubic hair was thin and the red lips of her labia were filling with excitement—like a vertical, red smiling mouth. She opened and closed her vagina, winking at the crowd: they howled. She seemed to like showing herself, to watch the white men looking at a real woman, comparing what they saw with their scrawny wives.

Then she flipped the boy's still limp penis, laughed, and began to dance for him. She moved her hips in and out, pulling our eyes with her body, opening herself up to the smoky air and the firelight. Cupping her breasts in her hands, she offered them to the boy. She curled around his side, parting and tangling her pubic hair on his flank, biting his hip with her vagina. The curly pubic hairs crackled in the silence. The crowd clapped to the rhythm of her dance and she gave herself to it; finally bending over backward and shuddering, she had an orgasm. A line of her juices ran down her thigh and this scent of her began to excite the boy; her dance and now her musk had blocked out the audience. His penis was filling and his eyes watered and glistened with pain and tension. Sensing him, she kneeled by him and placing his penis in her mouth, she blew it up, as if it were a balloon. It grew visibly larger, until he seemed about to burst with the feelings she had created in him. Quickly, he pulled her head away from him; her flashing white teeth delicately resisted and scraped across his penis. This pain catapulted him into action. He threw her down so hard on her back that the slapping sound reverberated in the room. He thrust himself at her as though he were using a weapon on her, but she was a willing victim and thrust herself up to meet him, to draw him into her. She opened herself up with both hands, so he would have no trouble penetrating her. They convulsed together for several minutes; we could hear the sounds of their stomachs slapping and their juices splashing. I was dry-mouthed, the other men also coughed and licked their lips. Suddenly, the boy fell off her, still pumping semen into the air; she reached for it and rubbed it all over herself, making a kind of dough from the flour: her breasts shown in the light as if they had been oiled. But there was something wrong with the boy, his eyes were rolling and his body was convulsing abnormally. Much of the white flour had smeared on to him and he tried to rub it off both of them. She was still in orgasm as he fell from her, so she took his head in her hands and pulled out his tongue before he strangled on it and shoved his convulsing head between her legs to let his erratic spasms finish the job. With him rooting in her insides, she arched her back and pounded the table with her fists until she went rigid and her fingers went from a fist to open palms and stiff fingers. Finished, her hands relaxed and she yawned and pulled him from her by twisting his ears. His head came up from her body, twisting and jerking in paroxysms of pain and confusion; his mouth wet with her juices and his tongue still out, still searching for the hot, responding knot in her. She soothed him until he was able to be led, still dazed, out of the room.

The lights were put on and the room arranged as it had been before. The talk started up again and there were a few jokes about how they had sent a boy to do a man's job. Someone said that there should be a law against "nigger women" being built like that. A ruddy man claimed to have seen a much better show in Cuba before the war. After such a performance, everyone was restless and sober—myself included. I was, frankly, a little sick from the show and most especially at myself for responding like everyone else. I had always prided myself on being civilized, somewhat more so than other men; not a prude, certainly, but still not as violent nor as perverted as the majority of men. But now, quite unexpectedly, I found that any special sensitivity and transcendence I had achieved was at best in precarious balance with the violence and prurience that I shared with all men; and that in me, as in them, sexuality and violence were intimately related. I was thoroughly shocked, not so much by what I had seen as by my reactions to it. The man and woman who had performed for us remained innocent, while we who had watched had been rendered obscene.

Our restlessness grew; the whiskey was sour to the taste and the cigarettes stifling. We followed each other around the room, turning in agitated and meaningless circles of motion, not talking very much but thinking altogether too much, and feeling our tensions build without any hope of release. The woman's musk was still evident in the room; the place had become, as her odor reminded us, the scene of our shame; it was a complex sense of shame—no one would speak of it—but it called for more, not less, perversion; it was the kind that cried for some kind of finishing, some release, some death to complete it: blood on the ground, or on hands, to cleanse it from us. What we had seen and felt had opened us up like tins of rotten meat.

I went outside with a group seeking fresh air and a different place. We felt the cold, but it was irrelevant. We were driven like holy men, searching for a sign, hoping for a miracle to release us. There was nothing to fasten on to out there: the profound isolation of the place, the distant sound and swamp, and the mysterious white light of the moon. We might have been in another world; there were no signs to remind us of the everyday, none of the features of civilization that modify the chronic insanities of the everyday. It was a different world, so it is not too surprising that we were different men in it. We were searching, at least in part, for something to bring us back. But our fatigue, the morning's blood, the feast, and the show had weakened and disoriented us. We found nothing to remind us that we were only men in a lonely place; there was nothing but the persistent moon. And the moon has seen every madness of mankind.

I was only dimly aware of these things at the time—as by a vague anxiety, a disturbance that one knows so well that it comes to mind only with great difficulty. Because of the cold, we were about to go back inside, when the moon flashed and we looked up into its whiteness that was now broken with long-necked silhouettes: swans! A swarm of these unlikely creatures was spiraling down from the center of the moon, or so it seemed from where we stood, falling down slowly and gracefully to a place about a mile distant—one of the men told us—a cove now in the lee of the brisk wind. It appeared to me that bits and pieces of the moon were flaking off, as if the moon were chipped and breaking, as if the swans were the life of the moon leaving it. The birds were more white out of the moon's light than in it; their great wings hushed the night and their long necks trembled with the fatigue of their journey.

Because deer hunting is also good in these swamps—farther inland on timbered, higher ground—several of the men had brought rifles and carbines just in case. Now they went for these weapons, stripped away their cases, and loaded them. The proprietor saw what we had in mind and tried to stop us, not out of any noble feelings but because we might bring the wardens down on him. As by common agreement, we ignored him; and silently we ran from the lodge toward the cove. Still the swans spiraled down from the moon; we could see nothing else. Like blinded men, we stumbled and fell through the swamp grass forcing a path. The tall grass hid mudholes and muskrat runs; falling repeatedly in them, we were soon covered with the black ooze and the rotten stink of the place. Looking around, I thought I was with an army of demons. And when I caught their eyes, the whiteness reflected there seemed to have eaten them hollow—like snails cleaned by salt. But we all nodded, one to the other, and went on; I doubt if there was anything on earth that could have stopped us.

The proprietor tried. Suddenly, he appeared in our path. He had come by a shorter route to head us off, to make one more appeal. There is a five-hundred-dollar fine for killing a swan— and probably that and jail too for the lodge manager who permits it on his land. At one time, flocks of swan turned the blue fall skies white, dazzling and mystifying the swamps and the people living there. But discovered to be a gourmet's delicacy—all white meat and succulent beyond compare—they were slaughtered in great numbers, nearly to the point of extinction. The proprietor held up his hands to stop us, but before he had time to speak he was shouldered aside. Off-balance in the muck and the darkness, he foundered impotently, merely watched us pass by him.

I am not sure why I went with them; perhaps it was because I had always been curious about the ways of other men—not feeling a sense of identity with many of them. While readily and even expertly participating in their games and dramas, I usually remained detached from the men themselves and uninvolved in their activities. That it should be so seemed natural to me, and yet at the same time a continuing source of mild perplexity. And my initiation was no less perplexing. As with my sense of isolation, there was no clear reason for my sudden and complete sense of belonging. As there had been a kind of pleasure in being alone, so too was there pleasure, albeit of a different sort, in the one-minded mindlessness of the group to which I so passionately and suddenly belonged. We shared something more than is required for friendship. Like a wildly oscillating pendulum, I had gone short of the mark in isolation, but past it in the mob. Still, in the mob there was a wonderfully secure feeling, as if we were all invulnerable, immortal. I a distant god had become a god among gods. Without understanding it, there was no denying the power of it. And there was no escaping it either, until it had run its course.

My quick excitement carried me to lead them to the cove, running easily through the blackness and whiteness beckoning, the grass whipping my face and hands, the grass parting before me as the Red Sea before Moses. Behind me a man stumbled and fell up to his arms in a deep hole; I grabbed his rifle and ran on as he tried to extricate himself; he understood that there was no time to lose. I was familiar with the weapon—a carbine; it felt like a short sword in my hand and I hacked the grass away with it. At the cove there was a clear place in the sound, a tidal bank exposed and solid with pine nubs and tangles of vegetation. I flew on to it and raised up the rifle; the swans were all around, their wings whistling, their white bodies catching the light. I shot against the moon, sighting on the swans as they fell across the white disk, their wings out, their necks twisting in terror at my shots. Suddenly dead they fell like stone-weights. Soon several of us were spaced along the bank firing at point-blank range, firing at the moon and chipping off pieces of it. The flock was committed to land; once they were so committed, they cannot change direction—even to evade destruction. Those of us without weapons waded into the sound and gathered the bodies. Stopping, the carbine empty, I gave it back to its owner who had finally arrived. He was whimpering as he loaded it, spilling cartridges and fumbling with the mechanism. I was quickly sated, but many of the others were not. I saw one man standing waist-deep in the water tearing a wing off a crippled swan, laughing at its efforts to fight him off, finally cutting its throat and drinking the frothy blood. Another saw him and vomited, wiping his face and going back to shooting. Others were pulling at the dead birds, trying to eat the raw flesh past the glistening down.

The pile of carcasses looked—all red and white—as if we had killed the moon, as if it had been a living thing and now it was bloody and dead. We rolled and laughed on this pile of life going cold. Men threw the bodies in the air and beat each other, as with pillows, until they were exhausted and covered with mud, feathers, and blood. The silence was broken with cheers and laughter, high and wild like mountain wind, not pleasant to hear; only gods can kill the moon; only devils would want to. Some stood on top of the pile and masturbated, others tried to use the warm bodies of the dead birds to receive them. Others were in exhausted reveries, resting in awkward positions, waiting for the rest of it to happen. There was not a man among us who would not have carved out the heart of the land, of the earth itself, had he known

how to do it, had he known the place to cut. Had we come, at
that moment, on a church picnic or a congregation of whores, we
would have torn them limb from limb. But with each other we
were safe enough; we shared the passion and the horror of shame.

Some of the men dragged the carcasses to higher ground, to a
small pine knoll where there was enough dry wood to start a fire.
We cleaned the birds—some of them at least; there were too
many to eat—and carved them and roasted the pieces over open
fires. The fires fed by the pine pitch roared quickly and high. In
the firelight we saw each other: debauched and leering faces,
some streaked with blood and some with vomit. I thought I had
wandered into Hell and had joined devils roasting souls.

Some talked of going back to the lodge for the Negro woman,
but before they had a chance—and I had no doubt they would
have killed her—one of the fires, banked too high, broke loose; it
blazed up and reached the trees and quickly spread across the
high ground. None of us were immediately aware of the danger;
everything was so wet, there was so much water and mud everywhere, that we forgot about the tinder tips of the tall grass. Soon
the knoll was all burning and we retreated back the way we had
come—some still dragging dead swans. When we were only halfway back, the lodge several hundred yards away, the fire spread
to the grass and swept down on us. Grass fires can outrun a man,
especially when the path to safety is over mud and muskrat colo-
nies. The smoke is what kills; the fire races across the dry tips and
smothers everything beneath it. Sensing the danger, the crowd of
men panicked. Several were trampled into the swamp and probably were drowned there before the fire reached them. Some of us
thought to turn quickly toward the sound and make for the safety
of the open water. It was closer than the high ground at the
lodge—and safer too—but it did not seem so to the others. Most
of the men kept on along the path we had made as we rushed to
the cove and they were killed by the smoke and fire. Those of us
who had thought of the sound just made it; falling into the icy
water and stumbling away from the grass, we looked over our
shoulders to see the smoke boiling after us and the fire spitting at
the black water.

After the fire had burned past—it took the whole island, including the bridge and the lodge—we came out shivering from
shock and from the freezing water. We found the bodies of the

men about a hundred yards from what they had thought would be the safety of the lodge. The proprietor and his help had escaped over the bridge when they saw the fire coming in the grass. The whole island was smoky and blacker than the night, like an ancient battlefield. There was nothing to do for the dead men, so we waited for someone to come and take us back to the mainland. Within an hour, the sheriff came in a launch and there were other boats to take us back. Before we left, we saw the deputies bringing out the burnt bodies. The moon was still so bright that, with all the gray ash on them, they looked like half-burned logs—all in one piece and stiff. Ice was forming in the sheltered pickets of the sound, so they were probably frozen. The light on them turned the soot ash white and they glistened in it as if they too had fallen from the moon, as if they had been brought down from some moon massacre and left behind. It was cold going back in the boats; some of the men were still shivering from more than just the cold, and I was one of them.

Robert Kennedy Saved from Drowning

DONALD BARTHELME

K. at His Desk

HE IS NEITHER abrupt with nor excessively kind to associates. Or he is both abrupt and kind.

The telephone is, for him, a whip, a lash, but also a conduit for soothing words, a sink into which he can hurl gallons of syrup if it comes to that.

He reads quickly, scratching brief comments ("Yes," "No") in corners of the paper. He slouches in the leather chair, looking about him with a slightly irritated air for new visitors, new difficulties. He spends his time sending and receiving messengers.

"I spend my time sending and receiving messengers," he says. "Some of these messages are important. Others are not."

Described by Secretaries

A: "Quite Frankly I think he forgets a lot of things. But the things he forgets are those which are inessential. I even think he might forget deliberately, to leave his mind free. He has the ability to get rid of unimportant details. And he does."

B: "Once when I was sick, I hadn't heard from him, and I thought he had forgotten me. You know usually your boss will send flowers or something like that. I was in the hospital, and I was mighty blue. I was in a room with another girl, and *her* boss hadn't sent her anything either. Then suddenly the door opened and there he was with the biggest bunch of yellow tulips I'd ever seen in my life. And the other girl's boss was with him, and he

201

had tulips too. They were standing there with all those tulips, smiling."

Behind the Bar

At a crowded party, he wanders behind the bar to make himself a Scotch and water. His hand is on the bottle of Scotch, his glass is waiting. The bartender, a small man in a beige uniform with gilt buttons, politely asks K. to return to the other side, the guests' side, of the bar. "You let one behind here, they all be behind here," the bartender says.

K. Reading the Newspaper

His reactions are impossible to catalog. Often he will find a note that amuses him endlessly, some anecdote involving, say, a fireman who has propelled his apparatus at record-breaking speed to the wrong address. These small stories are clipped, carried about in a pocket, to be produced at appropriate moments for the pleasure of friends. Other manifestations please him less. An account of an earthquake in Chile, with its thousands of dead and homeless, may depress him for weeks. He memorizes the terrible statistics, quoting them everywhere and saying, with a grave look: "We must do something." Important actions often follow, sometimes within a matter of hours. (On the other hand, these two kinds of responses may be, on a given day, inexplicably reversed.)

The more trivial aspects of the daily itemization are skipped. While reading, he maintains a rapid drumming of his fingertips on the desktop. He receives twelve newspapers, but of these, only four are regarded as serious.

Attitude Toward His Work

"Sometimes I can't seem to do anything. The work is there, piled up, it seems to me an insurmountable obstacle, really out of reach. I sit and look at it, wondering where to begin, how to take hold of it. Perhaps I pick up a piece of paper, try to read it, but my mind is elsewhere, I am thinking of something else, I can't seem to get the gist of it, it seems meaningless, devoid of interest, not having to do with human affairs, drained of life. Then, in a hour, or even a moment, everything changes suddenly: I realize I only have to *do* it, hurl myself into the midst of it, proceed mechanically, the first thing and then the second thing, that it is simply a matter of moving from one step to the next, plowing through it. I become interested, I become excited, I work very fast, things fall into place, I am exhilarated, amazed that these things could ever have seemed dead to me."

Sleeping on the Stones of Unknown Towns (Rimbaud)

K. is walking, with that familiar slight dip of the shoulders, through the streets of a small city in France or Germany. The shop signs are in a language which alters when inspected closely, MÖBEL becoming MEUBLES for example, and the citizens mutter to themselves with dark virtuosity a mixture of languages. K. is very interested, looks closely at everything, at the shops, the goods displayed, the clothing of the people, the tempo of street life, the citizens themselves, wondering about them. What are their water needs?

"In the West, wisdom is mostly gained at lunch. At lunch, people tell you things."

The nervous eyes of the waiters.

The tall bald cook, white apron, white T-shirt, grinning through an opening in the wall.

"Why is that cook looking at me?"

Urban Transportation

"The transportation problems of our cities and their rapidly expanding suburbs are the most urgent and neglected transportation problems confronting the country. In these heavily populated and industrialized areas, people are dependent on a system of transportation that is at once complex and inadequate. Obsolete facilities and growing demands have created seemingly insoluble difficulties and present methods of dealing with these difficulties offer little prospect of relief."

K. Penetrated with Sadness

He hears something playing on someone else's radio, in another part of the building.

The music is wretchedly sad; now he can (barely) hear it, now it fades into the wall.

He turns on his own radio. There it is, on his own radio, the same music. The sound fills the room.

Karsh of Ottawa

"We sent a man to Karsh of Ottawa and told him that we admired his work very much. Especially, I don't know, the Churchill thing, and, you know, the Hemingway thing, and all that. And we told him we wanted to set up a sitting for K. sometime in June, if that would be convenient for him, and he said yes, that was okay, June was okay, and where did we want to have it shot, there or in New York or where. Well, that was a problem because we didn't know exactly what K.'s schedule would be for June, it was up in the air, so we tentatively said New York around the fifteenth. And he said, that was okay, he could do that. And he wanted to know how much time he could have, and we said, well, how much time do you need? And he said he didn't know, it varied from sitter to sitter. He said some people were very restless and that made it difficult to get just the right shot. He said there was one shot in each sitting that was, you know, the key shot, the right one. He said he'd have to see, when the time came."

Dress

He is neatly dressed in a manner that does not call attention to itself. The suits are soberly cut and in dark colors. He must at all times present an aspect of freshness difficult to sustain because of frequent movements from place to place under conditions which are not always the most favorable. Thus he changes clothes frequently, especially shirts. In the course of a day he changes his shirt many times. There are always extra shirts about, in boxes.

"Which of you has the shirts?"

A Friend Comments: K's Aloneness

"The thing you have to realize about K. is that essentially he's absolutely alone in the world. There's this terrible loneliness which prevents people from getting too close to him. Maybe it comes from something in his childhood, I don't know. But he's very hard to get to know, and a lot of people who think they know him rather well don't really know him at all. He says something or does something that surprises you, and you realize that all along you really didn't know him at all.

"He has surprising facets. I remember once we were out in a small boat. K. of course was the captain. Some rough weather came up and we began to head back in. I began worrying about picking up a landing and I said to him that I didn't think the anchor would hold, with the wind and all. He just looked at me. Then he said: "Of course it will hold. That's what it's for."

K. on Crowds

"There are exhausted crowds and vivacious crowds.

"Sometimes, standing there, I can sense whether a particular crowd is one thing or the other. Sometimes the mood of the crowd is disguised, sometimes you only find out after a quarter of an hour what sort of crowd a particular crowd is.

"And you can't speak to them in the same way. The variations have to be taken into account. You have to say something to them that is meaningful to them *in that mood*."

Gallery-going

K. enters a large gallery on 57th Street, in the Fuller Building. His entourage includes several ladies and gentlemen. Works by a geometricist are on show. K. looks at the immense, rather theoretical paintings.

"Well, at least we know he has a ruler."

The group dissolves in laughter. People repeat the remark to one another, laughing.

The artist, who has been standing behind a dealer, regards K. with hatred.

K. Puzzled by His Children

The children are crying. There are several children—one about four, a boy, then another boy, slightly older, and a little girl, very beautiful, wearing blue jeans, crying. There are various objects on the grass, an electric train, a picture book, a red ball, a plastic bucket, a plastic shovel.

K. frowns at the children whose distress issues from no source immediately available to the eye, which seems indeed uncaused, vacant, a general anguish. K. turns to the mother of these children who is standing nearby wearing hip-huggers which appear to be made of linked marshmallows studded with diamonds but then I am a notoriously poor observer.

"Play with them," he says.

This mother of ten quietly suggests that K. himself "play with them."

K. picks up the picture book and begins to read to the children. But the book has a German text. It has been left behind, perhaps, by some foreign visitor. Nevertheless K. perseveres.

"*A ist der Affe, er isst mit der Pfote.*" ("A is the Ape, he eats with his Paw.")

The crying of the children continues undiminished.

A Dream

Orange trees.

Overhead, a steady stream of strange aircraft which resemble kitchen implements, bread boards, cookie sheets, colanders.

The shiny aluminum instruments are on their way to complete the bombing of Sidi-Madani.

A farm in the hills.

Matters (from an Administrative Assistant)

"A lot of matters that had been pending came to a head right about that time, moved to the front burner, things we absolutely had to take care of. And we couldn't find K. Nobody knew where he was. We looked everywhere. He had just withdrawn, made himself unavailable. There was this one matter that was probably more pressing than all the rest put together. Really crucial. We were all standing around wondering what to do. We were really getting pretty nervous because this thing was really . . . Then K. walked in and disposed of it with a quick phone call. A quick phone call!"

Childhood of K. as Recalled by a Former Teacher

"He was a very alert boy, very bright, good at his studies, very thorough, very conscientious. But that's not unusual; that describes a good number of the boys who pass through here. It's not unusual, that is, to find these qualities which are after all the qualities that we look for and encourage in them. What *was* unusual about K. was his compassion, something very rare for a boy of that age—even if they have it, they're usually very careful not to display it for fear of seeming soft, girlish. I remember, though, that in K. this particular attribute was very marked. I would almost say that it was his strongest characteristic."

Speaking to No One But Waiters, He—

"The dandelion salad with bacon, I think."
"The *rysstafel*."
"The poached duck."
"The black bean purée."
"The cod fritters."

K. Explains a Technique

"It's an expedient in terms of how not to destroy a situation which has been a long time gestating, or, again, how *to* break it up if it appears that the situation has changed, during the gestation period, into one whose implications are not quite what they were at the beginning. What I mean is that in this business things are constantly altering (usually for the worse) and usually you want to give the impression that you're not watching this particular situation particularly closely, that you're paying no special attention to it, until you're ready to make your move. That is, it's best to be sudden, if you can manage it. Of course you can't do that all the time. Sometimes you're just completely wiped out, cleaned out, totaled, and then the only thing to do is shrug and forget about it."

K. on His Own Role

"Sometimes it seems to me that it doesn't matter what I do, that it is enough to exist, to sit somewhere, in a garden for example, watching whatever is to be seen there, the small events. At other times, I'm aware that other people, possibly a great number of other people, could be affected by what I do or fail to do, that I have a responsibility, as we all have, to make the best possible use of whatever talents I've been given, for the common good. It is not enough to sit in that garden, however restful or pleasurable it might be. The world is full of unsolved problems, situations that demand careful, reasoned, and intelligent action. In Latin America, for example."

As Entrepreneur

The original cost estimates for burying the North Sea pipeline have been exceeded by a considerable margin. Everyone wonders what he will say about this contretemps which does not fail to have its dangers for those responsible for the costly miscalculations, which are viewed in many minds as inexcusable.

He says only: "Exceptionally difficult rock conditions."

With Young People

K., walking the streets of unknown towns, finds himself among young people. Young people line these streets, narrow and curving, which are theirs, dedicated to them. They are everywhere, resting on the embankments, with their guitars, small radios, long hair. They sit on the sidewalks, back to back, heads turned to stare. They stand implacably on street corners, in doorways, or lean on their elbows in windows, or squat in small groups at that place where sidewalk meets the walls of buildings. The streets are filled with these young people who say nothing, reveal only a limited interest, refuse to declare themselves. Street after street contains them, a great number, more displayed as one turns a corner, rank upon rank stretching into the distance, drawn from the arcades, the plazas, staring.

He Discusses the French Writer, Poulet

"For Poulet, it is not enough to speak of *seizing the moment*. It is rather a question of, and I quote, 'recognizing in the instant which lives and dies, which surges out of nothingness and which ends in dream, an intensity and depth of significance which ordinarily attaches only to the whole of existence.'"

"What Poulet is describing is neither an ethic nor a prescription but rather what he has discovered in the work of Marivaux. Poulet has taken up the Marivaudian canon and squeezed it with both hands to discover the essence of what may be called the Marivaudian being, what Poulet in fact calls the Marivaudian being.

"The Marivaudian being is, according to Poulet, a pastless futureless man, born anew at every instant. The instants are points which organize themselves into a line, but what is important is the instant, not the line. The Marivaudian being has in a sense no history. Nothing follows from what has gone before. He is constantly surprised. He cannot predict his own reaction to events. He is constantly being *overtaken* by events. A condition of breathlessness and dazzlement surrounds him. In consequence he exists in a certain freshness which seems, if I may say so, very desirable. This freshness Poulet, quoting Marivaux, describes very well."

K. Saved From Drowning

K. in the water. His flat black hat, his black cape, his sword are on the shore. He retains his mask. His hands beat the surface of the water which tears and rips about him. The white foam, the green depths. I throw a line, the coils leaping out over the surface of the water. He has missed it. No, it appears that he has it. His right hand (sword arm) grasps the line that I have thrown him. I am on the bank, the rope wound around my waist, braced against a rock. K. now has both hands on the line. I pull him out of the water. He stands now on the bank, breathing heavily.

"Thank you."

The Oranging of America

MAX APPLE

1

FROM THE OUTSIDE it looked like any ordinary 1964 Cadillac limousine. In the expensive space between the driver and passengers, where some installed bars or even bathrooms, Mr. Howard Johnson kept a tidy ice cream freezer in which there were always at least eighteen flavors on hand, though Mr. Johnson ate only vanilla. The freezer's power came from the battery with an independent auxiliary generator as a backup system. Although now Howard Johnson means primarily motels, Millie, Mr. HJ, and Otis Brighton, the chauffeur, had not forgotten that ice cream was the cornerstone of their empire. Some of the important tasting was still done in the car. Mr. HJ might have reports in his pocket from sales executives and marketing analysts, from home economists and chemists, but not until Mr. Johnson reached over the lowered plexiglass to spoon a taste or two into the expert waiting mouth of Otis Brighton did he make any final flavor decision. He might go ahead with butterfly shrimp, with candy kisses, and with packaged chocolate chip cookies on the opinion of the specialists, but in ice cream he trusted only Otis. From the back seat Howard Johnson would keep his eye on the rearview mirror where the reflection of pleasure or disgust showed itself in the dark eyes of Otis Brighton no matter what the driving conditions. He could be stalled in a commuter rush with the engine overheating and dripping oil pan, and still a taste of the right kind never went unappreciated.

When Otis finally said, "Mr. Howard, that shore is sumpin,

210

that one is um-hum. That is it, my man, that is it." Then and not until then did Mr. HJ finally decide to go ahead with something like banana fudge ripple royale.

Mildred rarely tasted and Mr. HJ was addicted to one scoop of vanilla every afternoon at three, eaten from his aluminum dish with a disposable plastic spoon. The duties of Otis, Millie, and Mr. Johnson were so divided that they rarely infringed upon one another in the car, which was their office. Neither Mr. HJ nor Millie knew how to drive, Millie and Otis understood little of financing and leasing, and Mr. HJ left the compiling of the "Traveling Reports" and "The Howard Johnson Newsletter" strictly to the literary style of his longtime associate, Miss Mildred Bryce. It was an ideal division of labor, which, in one form or another, had been in continuous operation for well over a quarter of a century.

While Otis listened to the radio behind his sound-proof plexiglass, while Millie in her small, neat hand compiled data for the newsletter, Mr. HJ liked to lean back into the spongy leather seat looking through his specially tinted windshield at the fleeting land. Occasionally, lulled by the hum of the freezer, he might doze off, his large pink head lolling toward the shoulder of his blue suit, but there was not too much that Mr. Johnson missed, even in advanced age.

Along with Millie, he planned their continuous itinerary as they traveled. Mildred would tape a large green relief map of the United States to the plexiglass separating them from Otis. The mountains on the map were light brown and seemed to melt toward the valleys like the crust of a fresh apple pie settling into cinnamon surroundings. The existing HJ houses (Millie called the restaurants and motels houses) were marked by orange dots, while projected future sites bore white dots. The deep green map with its brown mountains and colorful dots seemed much more alive than the miles that twinkled past Mr. Johnson's gaze, and nothing gave the ice cream king greater pleasure than watching Mildred with her fine touch, and using the original crayon, turn an empty white dot into an orange fulfillment.

"It's like a seed grown into a tree, Millie," Mr. HJ liked to say at such moments when he contemplated the map and saw that it was good.

They had started traveling together in 1925. Mildred then a secretary to Mr. Johnson, a young man with two restaurants and a dream of hospitality, and Otis, a 20-year-old busboy and former driver of a Louisiana mule. When Mildred graduated from college, her father, a Michigan doctor who kept his money in a blue steel box under the examining table, encouraged her to try the big city. He sent her a monthly allowance. In those early days, she always had more than Mr. Johnson, who paid her $16.50 a week and meals. In the first decade they traveled only on weekends, but every year since 1936, they had spent at least six months on the road, and it might have gone on much longer if Mildred's pain and the trouble in New York with Howard Jr. had not come so close together.

They were all stoical at the Los Angeles International Airport. Otis waited at the car for what might be his last job while Miss Bryce and Mr. Johnson traveled toward the New York plane along a silent moving floor. Millie stood beside Howard while they passed a mural of Mexican landscape and some Christmas drawings by fourth graders from Watts. For 40 years they had been together in spite of Howard Jr. and the others, but at this most recent appeal from New York, Millie urged him to go back. Howard Jr. had cabled "My God, Dad, you're 69 years old, haven't you been a gypsy long enough? Board meeting December 3 with or without you. Policy changes imminent."

Normally, they ignored Howard Jr.'s cables but this time Millie wanted him to go, wanted to be alone with the pain that had recently come to her. She had left Howard holding the new canvas suitcase in which she had packed her three notebooks of regional reports along with his aluminum dish, and in a moment of real despair, she had even packed the orange crayon. When Howard boarded Flight 965 he looked old to Millie. His feet dragged in the wing-tipped shoes, the hand she shook was moist, the lip felt dry, and as he passed from her sight down the entry ramp Mildred Bryce felt a fresh new ache that sent her hobbling toward the car. Otis had unplugged the freezer and the silence caused by the missing hum was as intense to Millie as her abdominal pain.

It had come quite suddenly in Albuquerque, New Mexico, at the grand opening of a 210-unit house. She did not make a fuss. Mildred Bryce had never caused trouble to anyone, except perhaps to Mrs. HJ. Millie's quick precise actions, angular face, and thin body made her seem birdlike, especially next to Mr. HJ, six-three with splendid white hair accenting his dark blue gabardine suits. Howard was slow and sure. He could sit in the same position for hours while Millie fidgeted on the seat, wrote memos, and filed reports in the small gray cabinet that sat in front of her and parallel to the ice cream freezer. Her health had always been good, so at first she tried to ignore the pain. It was gas: it was perhaps the New Mexico water or the cooking oil in the fish dinner. But she could not convince away the pain. It stayed like a match burning around her belly, etching itself into her as the round HJ emblem was so symmetrically embroidered into the bedspread, which she had kicked off in the flush that accompanied the pain. She felt as if her sweat would engulf the foam mattress and crisp percale sheet. Finally, Millie brought up her knees and made a ball of herself as if being as small as possible might make her misery disappear. It worked for everything except the pain. The little circle of hot torment was all that remained of her, and when finally at sometime in the early morning it left, it occurred to her that perhaps she had struggled with a demon and been suddenly relieved by the coming of daylight. She stepped lightly into the bathroom and before a full-length mirror (new in HJ motels exclusively) saw herself whole and unmarked, but sign enough to Mildred was her smell, damp and musty, sign enough that something had begun and that something else would therefore necessarily end.

2

Before she had the report from her doctor, Howard Jr.'s message had given her the excuse she needed. There was no reason why Millie could not tell Howard she was sick, but telling him would be admitting too much to herself. Along with Howard Johnson, Millie had grown rich beyond dreams. Her inheritance, the $100,000 from her father's steel box in 1939, went directly to Mr. Johnson who desperately needed it, and the results of that investment brought Millie enough capital to employ two people at the Chase Manhattan with the management of her finances. With money beyond the hope of use, she had vacationed all over the world and spent some time in the company of celebrities, but the reality of her life, like his, was in the back seat of the limousine waiting for that point at which the needs of the automobile and the human body met the undeviating purpose of the highway and momentarily conquered it.

Her life was measured in rest stops. She, Howard, and Otis had found them out before they existed. They knew the places to stop between Buffalo and Albany, Chicago and Milwaukee, Toledo and Columbus, Des Moines and Minneapolis, they knew through their own bodies, measured in hunger and discomfort in the '30s and '40s when they would stop at remote places to buy land and borrow money, sensing in themselves the hunger that would one day be upon the place. People were wary and Howard had trouble borrowing (her $100,000 had perhaps been the key) but invariably he was right. Howard knew the land, Mildred thought, the way the Indians must have known it. There were even spots along the way where the earth itself seemed to make men stop. Howard had a sixth sense that would sometimes lead them from the main roads to, say, a dark green field in Iowa or Kansas. Howard, who might have seemed asleep, would rap with his knuckles on the plexiglass, causing the knowing Otis to bring the car to such a quick stop that Millie almost flew into her filing cabinet. And before the emergency brake had settled into its final prong, Howard Johnson was into the field and after the scent. While Millie and Otis waited, he would walk it out slowly. Sometimes he would sit down, disappearing in a field of long and tangled weeds, or he might find a large smooth rock to sit on while he felt some secret vibration from the place. Turning his back to Millie, he would mark the spot with his urine or break some of the clayey earth in his strong pink hands, sifting it like flour for a delicate recipe. She had actually seen him chew the grass, getting down on all fours like an animal and biting the tops without pulling the entire blade from the soil. At times he ran in a slow jog as far as his aging legs would carry him. Whenever he slipped out of sight behind the uneven terrain, Millie felt him in danger, felt that something alien might be there to resist the civilizing instinct of Howard Johnson. Once when Howard had been out of sight for more than an hour and did not respond to their frantic calls, Millie sent Otis into the field and in desperation flagged a passing car.

"Howard Johnson is lost in that field," she told the surprised driver. "He went in to look for a new location and we can't find him now."

"The restaurant Howard Johnson?" the man asked.

"Yes. Help us please."

The man drove off leaving Millie to taste in his exhaust fumes the barbarism of an ungrateful public. Otis found Howard asleep in a field of light blue wild flowers. He had collapsed from the exertion of his run. Millie brought water to him, and when he felt better, right there in the field, he ate his scoop of vanilla on the very spot where three years later they opened the first fully air-conditioned motel in the world. When she stopped to think about it, Millie knew they were more than businessmen, they were pioneers.

And once, while on her own, she had the feeling too. In 1951 when she visited the Holy Land there was an inkling of what Howard must have felt all the time. It happened without any warning on a bus crowded with tourists and resident Arabs on their way to the Dead Sea. Past ancient Sodom the bus creaked and bumped, down, down, toward the lowest point on earth, when suddenly in the midst of the crowd and her stomach queasy with the motion of the bus, Mildred Bryce experienced an overwhelming calm. A light brown patch of earth surrounded by a few pale desert rocks overwhelmed her perception, seemed closer to her than the Arab lady in the black flowered dress pushing her basket against Millie at that very moment. She wanted to stop the bus. Had she been near the door she might have actually jumped, so strong was her sensitivity to that barren spot in the endless desert. Her whole body ached for it as if in unison, bone by bone. Her limbs tingled, her breath came in short gasps, the sky rolled out of the bus windows and obliterated her view. The Arab lady spat on the floor, and moved a suspicious eye over a squirming Mildred.

When the bus stopped at the Dead Sea, the Arabs and tourists rushed to the soupy brine clutching damaged limbs, while Millie pressed $20 American into the dirty palm of a cabdriver who took her back to the very place where the music of her body began once more as sweetly as the first time. While the incredulous driver waited, Millie walked about the place wishing How-

ard were there to understand her new understanding of his kind
of process. There was nothing there, absolutely nothing but pure
bliss. The sun beat her like a wish, the air was hot and stale as a
Viennese bathhouse, and yet Mildred felt peace and rest there,
and as her cab bill mounted she actually did rest in the miserable
barren desert of an altogether unsatisfactory land. When the driver, wiping the sweat from his neck, asked, "Meesez . . . pleeze.
Why American woman wants Old Jericho in such kind of heat?"
when he said "Jericho" she understood that this was a place
where men had always stopped. In dim antiquity Jacob had perhaps watered a flock here and not far away Lot's wife paused to
scan for the last time the city of her youth. Perhaps Mildred now
stood where Abraham had been visited by a vision and making a
rock his pillow had first put the ease into the earth. Whatever it
was, Millie knew from her own experience that rest was created
here by historical precedent. She tried to buy that piece of land,
going as far as King Hussein's secretary of the interior. She imagined a Palestinian HJ with an orange roof angling toward Sodom,
a seafood restaurant, and an oasis of fresh fruit. But the land was
in dispute between Israel and Jordan and even King Hussein, who
expressed admiration for Howard Johnson, could not sell to Millie
the place of her comfort.

That was her single visionary moment, but sharing them with
Howard was almost as good. And to end all this, to finally stay in
her 18th-floor Santa Monica penthouse, where the Pacific dived
into California, this seemed to Mildred a paltry conclusion to an
adventurous life. Her doctor said it was not so serious, she had a
bleeding ulcer and must watch her diet. The prognosis was, in
fact, excellent. But Mildred, 56 and alone in California, found the
doctor less comforting than most of the rest stops she had experienced.

3

California, right after the Second War, was hardly a civilized
place for travelers. Millie, HJ, and Otis had a 12-cylinder '47 Lincoln and snaked along five days between Sacramento and Los
Angeles. "Comfort, comfort," said HJ as he surveyed the redwood
forest and the bubbly surf while it slipped away from Otis who
had rolled his trousers to chase the ocean away during a stop near

San Francisco. Howard Johnson was contemplative in California. They had never been in the West before. Their route, always slightly new, was yet bound by Canada where a person couldn't get a tax break and roughly by the Mississippi as a western frontier. Their journeys took them up the eastern seaboard and through New England to the early reaches of the Midwest, stopping at the plains of Wisconsin and the cool crisp edge of Chicago where two HJ lodges twinkled at the lake.

One day in 1947 while on the way from Chicago to Cairo, Ill., HJ looked long at the green relief maps. While Millie kept busy with her filing, HJ loosened the tape and placed the map across his soft round knees. The map jiggled and sagged, the Mid- and Southwest hanging between his legs. When Mildred finally noticed that look, he had been staring at the map for perhaps 15 minutes, brooding over it, and Millie knew something was in the air.

HJ looked at that map the way some people looked down from an airplane trying to pick out the familiar from the colorful mass receding beneath them. Howard Johnson's eye flew over the land—over the Tetons, over the Sierra Nevada, over the long thin gouge of the Canyon flew his gaze—charting his course by rest stops the way an antique mariner might have gazed at the stars.

"Millie," he said just north of Carbondale, "Millie. . . ." He looked toward her, saw her fingers engaged and her thumbs circling each other in anticipation. He looked at Millie and saw that she saw what he saw. "Millie"—HJ raised his right arm and its shadow spread across the continent like a prophecy—"Millie, what if we turn right at Cairo and go that way?" California, already peeling on the green map, balanced on HJ's left knee like a happy child.

Twenty years later Mildred settled in her 18th-floor apartment in the building owned by Lawrence Welk. Howard was in New York, Otis and the car waited in Arizona. The pain did not return as powerfully as it had appeared that night in Albuquerque, but it hurt with dull regularity and an occasional streak of dark blood in her bowels kept her mind on it even on painless days.

Directly beneath her gaze were the organized activities of the golden age groups, tiny figures playing bridge or shuffleboard or looking out at the water from their benches as she sat on her sofa and looked out at them and the fluffy ocean. Mildred did not regret family life. The HJ houses were her offspring. She had watched them blossom from the rough youngsters of the '40s with steam heat and even occasional kitchenettes into cool mature adults with king-sized beds, color TVs, and room service. Her late years were spent comfortably in the modern houses just as one might enjoy in age the benefits of a child's prosperity. She regretted only that it was probably over.

But she did not give up completely until she received a personal letter one day telling her that she was eligible for burial insurance until age 80. A $1,000 policy would guarantee a complete and dignified service. Millie crumpled the advertisement, but a few hours later called her Los Angeles lawyer. As she suspected, there were no plans, but as the executor of the estate he would assume full responsibility, subject of course to her approval.

"I'll do it myself," Millie had said, but she could not bring herself to do it. The idea was too alien. In more than 40 years Mildred had not gone a day without a shower and change of underclothing. Everything about her suggested order and precision. Her fingernails were shaped so that the soft meat of the tips could stroke a typewriter without damaging the apex of a nail, her arch slid over a six B shoe like an egg in a shell, and never in her adult life did Mildred recall having vomited. It did not seem right to suddenly let all this sink into the dark earth of Forest Hills because some organ or other developed a hole as big as a nickel. It was not right and she wouldn't do it. Her first idea was to stay in the apartment, to write it into the lease if necessary. She had the lawyer make an appointment for her with Mr. Welk's management firm, but canceled it the day before. "They will just think I'm crazy," she said aloud to herself, "and they'll bury me anyway."

She thought of cryonics while reading a biography of William Chesebrough, the man who invented petroleum jelly. Howard had known him and often mentioned that his own daily ritual of the scoop of vanilla was like old Chesebrough's two teaspoons of Vaseline every day. Chesebrough lived to be 90. In the biography it said that after taking the daily dose of Vaseline he drank three cups of green tea to melt everything down, rested for 12 minutes, and then felt fit as a young man, even in his late 80s. When he died, they froze his body and Millie had her idea. The Vaseline people kept him in a secret laboratory somewhere near Cleveland and claimed he was in better condition than Lenin, whom the Russians kept hermetically sealed, but at room temperature.

In the phone book she found the Los Angeles Cryonic Society and asked it to send her information. It all seemed very clean. The cost was $200 a year for maintaining the cold. She sent the pamphlet to her lawyer to be sure that the society was legitimate. It wasn't much money, but still if they were charlatans, she didn't want them to take advantage of her even if she would never know about it. They were aboveboard, the lawyer said. "The interest on a ten thousand dollar trust fund would pay about five hundred a year," the lawyer said, "and they only charge two hundred dollars. Still who knows what the cost might be in say two hundred years?" To be extra safe, they put $25,000 in trust for eternal maintenance, to be eternally overseen by Longstreet, Williams, and their eternal heirs. When it was arranged, Mildred felt better than she had in weeks.

4

Four months to the day after she had left Howard at the Los Angeles International Airport, he returned for Mildred without the slightest warning. She was in her housecoat and had not even washed the night cream from her cheeks when she saw through the viewing space in her door the familiar long pink jowls, even longer in the distorted glass.

"Howard," she gasped, fumbling with the door, and in an instant he was there picking her up as he might a child or an ice cream cone while her tears fell like dandruff on his blue suit. While Millie sobbed into his soft padded shoulder, HJ told her the good news. "I'm chairman emeritus of the board now. That means no more New York responsibilities. They still have to listen to me because we hold the majority of the stock, but Howard Junior and Keyes will take care of the business. Our main job is new home-owned franchises. And, Millie, guess where we're going first?"

So overcome was Mildred that she could not hold back her sobs even to guess. Howard Johnson put her down, beaming pleasure through his old bright eyes. "Florida," HJ said, then, slowly repeated it, "Flor-idda, and guess what we're going to do?"

"Howard," Millie said, swiping at her tears the filmy lace cuffs of her dressing gown, "I'm so surprised I don't know what to say. You could tell me we're going to the moon and I'd believe you. Just seeing you again has brought back all my hope." They came out of the hallway and sat on the sofa that looked out over the Pacific. HJ, all pink, kept his hands on his knees like paperweights.

"Millie, you're almost right. I can't fool you about anything and never could. We're going down near where they launch the rockets from. I've heard . . ." HJ leaned toward the kitchen as if to check for spies. He looked at the stainless steel and glass table, at the built-in avocado appliances, then leaned his large moist lips toward Mildred's ear. "Walt Disney is planning right this minute a new Disneyland down there. They're trying to keep it a secret, but his brother Roy bought options on thousands of acres. We're going down to buy as much as we can as close in as we can." Howard sparkled. "Millie, don't you see, it's a sure thing."

After her emotional outburst at seeing Howard again, a calmer Millie felt a slight twitch in her upper stomach and in the midst of her joy was reminded of another sure thing.

They would be a few weeks in Los Angeles anyway. Howard wanted to thoroughly scout out the existing Disneyland, so Millie had some time to think it out. She could go, as her heart directed her, with HJ to Florida and points beyond. She could take the future as it happened like a Disneyland ride or she could listen to the dismal eloquence of her ulcer and try to make the best arrangements she could. Howard and Otis would take care of her to the end, there were no doubts about that, and the end would be the end. But if she stayed in this apartment, sure of the arrangements for later, she would miss whatever might still be left before the end. Mildred wished there were some clergyman she could consult, but she had never attended a church and believed in no religious doctrine. Her father had been a firm atheist to the very moment of his office suicide, and she remained a passive nonbeliever. Her theology was the order of her own life. Millie had never deceived herself, in spite of her riches all she truly owned was her life, a pocket of habits in the burning universe. But the habits were careful and clean and they were best represented in the body that was she. Freezing her remains was the closest image she could conjure of eternal life. It might not be eternal and it surely would not be life, but that damp musty feel, that odor she smelled on herself after the pain, that could be avoided, and who knew what else might be saved from the void for a small initial investment and $200 a year. And if you did not believe in a soul, was there not every reason to preserve a body?

Mrs. Allen of the Cryonic Society welcomed Mildred to a tour of the premises. "See it while you can," she cheerfully told the group (Millie, two men, and a boy with notebook and Polaroid camera). Mrs. Allen, a big woman perhaps in her mid-60s, carried a face heavy in flesh. Perhaps once the skin had been tight around her long chin and pointed cheekbones, but having lost its spring, the skin merely hung at her neck like a patient animal waiting for the rest of her to join in the decline. From the way she took the concrete stairs down to the vault, it looked as if the wait would be long. "I'm not ready for the freezer yet. I tell every group I take down here, it's gonna be a long time until they get me." Millie believed her. "I may not be the world's smartest cookie"—Mrs. Allen looked directly at Millie—"but a bird in the hand is the only bird I know, huh? That's why when it does come . . . Mrs A is going to be right here in this facility, and you better believe it. Now, Mr. King on your left"—she pointed to a capsule that looked like a large bullet to Millie—"Mr. King is the gentleman who took me on my first tour, cancer finally but had everything perfectly ready and I would say he was in prime cooling state within seconds and I believe that if they ever cure cancer, and you know they will the way they do most everything nowadays, old Mr. King may be back yet. If anyone got down to low enough temperature immediately it would be Mr. King." Mildred saw the boy write, "Return of the King" in his notebook. "Over here is Mr. and Mizz Winkleman, married sixty years, and went off within a month of each other, a lovely, lovely couple."

While Mrs. Allen continued her necrology and posed for a photo beside the Winklemans, Millie took careful note of the neon-lit room filled with bulletlike capsules. She watched the cool breaths of the group gather like flowers on the steel and vanish without dimming the bright surface. The capsules stood in straight lines with ample walking space between them. To Mrs. Allen, they were friends, to Millie it seemed as if she were in a furniture store of the Scandinavian type where elegance is suggested by the absence of material, where straight lines of steel, wood, and glass indicate that relaxation too requires some taste and is not an indifferent sprawl across any soft object that happens to be nearby.

Cemeteries always bothered Millie, but here she felt none of the dread she had expected. She averted her eyes from the cluttered graveyards they always used to pass at the tips of cities in the early days. Fortunately, the superhighways twisted traffic into the city and away from those desolate marking places where used-car lots and the names of famous hotels inscribed on barns often neighbored the dead. Howard had once commented that never in all his experience did he have an intuition of a good location near a cemetery. You could put a lot of things there, you could put up a bowling alley, or maybe even a theater, but never a motel, and Millie knew he was right. He knew where to put his houses but it was Millie who knew how. From that first orange roof angling toward the east, the HJ design and the idea had been Millie's. She had not invented the motel, she had changed it from a place where you had to be to a place where you wanted to be. Perhaps, she thought, the Cryonic Society was trying to do the same for cemeteries.

When she and Howard had started their travels, the old motel courts huddled like so many dark graves around the stone marking of the highway. And what traveler coming into one of those dingy cabins could watch the watery rust dripping from his faucet without thinking of everything he was missing by being a traveler . . . his two-stall garage, his wife small in the half-empty bed, his children with hair the color of that rust. Under the orange Howard Johnson roof all this changed. For about the same price you were redeemed from the road. Headlights did not dazzle you on the foam mattress and percale sheets, your sanitized glasses and toilet appliances sparkled like the mirror behind them. The room was not just there, it awaited you, courted your pleasure, sat like a young bride outside the walls of the city wanting only to please you, you only you on the smoothly pressed sheets, your friend, your one-night destiny.

As if it were yesterday, Millie recalled right there in the cryonic vault the moment when she had first thought the thought that made Howard Johnson Howard Johnson's. And when she told Howard her decision that evening after cooking a cheese-soufflé and risking a taste of wine, it was that memory she invoked for both of them, the memory of a cool autumn day in the '30s when a break in their schedule found Millie with a free afternoon in New Hampshire, an afternoon she had spent at the farm of a man who had once been her teacher and remembered her after 10 years. Otis drove her out to Robert Frost's farm where the poet made for her a lunch of scrambled eggs and 7-Up. Millie and Robert Frost talked mostly about the farm, about the cold winter he was expecting and the autumn apples they picked from the trees. He was not so famous then, his hair was only streaked with gray as Howard's was, and she told the poet about what she and Howard were doing, about what she felt about being on the road in America, and Robert Frost said he hadn't been that much but she sounded like she knew and he believed she might be able to accomplish something. He did not remember the poem she wrote in his class but that didn't matter.

"Do you remember, Howard, how I introduced you to him? Mr. Frost, this is Mr. Johnson. I can still see the two of you shaking hands there beside the car. I've always been proud that I introduced you to one another." Howard Johnson nodded his head at the memory, seemed as nostalgic as Millie while he sat in her apartment learning why she would not go to Florida to help bring Howard Johnson's to the new Disneyland.

"And after we left his farm, Howard, remember? Otis took the car in for servicing and left us with some sandwiches on the top of a hill overlooking a town, I don't even remember which one, maybe we never knew the name of it. And we stayed on that hilltop while the sun began to set in New Hampshire. I felt so full of poetry and"—she looked at Howard—"of love, Howard, only about an hour's drive from Robert Frost's farmhouse. Maybe it was just the way we felt then, but I think the sun set differently that night, filtering through the clouds like a big paintbrush making the top of the town all orange. And suddenly I thought what if the tops of our houses were that kind of orange, what a world it would be, Howard, and my God, that orange stayed until the last drop of light was left in it. I didn't feel the cold up there even though it took Otis so long to get back to us. The feeling we had about that orange, Howard, that was ours and that's what I've tried to bring to every house, the way we felt that night. Oh, it makes me sick to think of Colonel Sanders, and Big Boy, and Holiday Inn, and Best Western . . ."

"It's all right, Millie, it's all right." Howard patted her heaving back. Now that he knew about her ulcer and why she wanted to stay behind, the mind that had conjured butterfly shrimp and 28 flavors set himself a new project. He contemplated Millie sobbing in his lap the way he contemplated prime acreage. There was so little of her, less than 100 pounds, yet without her Howard Johnson felt himself no match for the wily Disneys gathering near the moonport.

He left her in all her sad resignation that evening, left her thinking she had to give up what remained here to be sure of the proper freezing. But Howard Johnson had other ideas. He did not cancel the advance reservations made for Mildred Bryce along the route to Florida, nor did he remove her filing cabinet from the limousine. The man who hosted a nation and already kept one freezer in his car merely ordered another, this one designed according to cryonic specifications and presented to Mildred housed in a 12-foot orange U-Haul trailer connected to the rear bumper of the limousine.

"Everything's here," he told the astonished Millie, who thought Howard had left the week before, "everything is here and you'll never have to be more than seconds away from it. It's exactly like a refrigerated truck." Howard Johnson opened the rear door of the U-Haul as proudly as he had ever dedicated a motel. Millie's steel capsule shone within, surrounded by an array of chemicals stored on heavily padded rubber shelves. The California sun was on her back but her cold breath hovered visibly within the U-Haul. No tears came to Mildred now; she felt relief much as she had felt it that afternoon near ancient Jericho. On Santa Monica Boulevard, in front of Lawrence Welk's apartment building, Mildred Bryce confronted her immortality, a gift from the ice cream king, another companion for the remainder of her travels. Howard Johnson had turned away looking toward the ocean. To his blue back and patriarchal white hairs, Mildred said, "Howard, you can do anything," and closing the doors of the U-Haul, she joined the host of the highways, a man with two portable freezers, ready now for the challenge of Disneyworld.

"The Oranging of America" is fiction and its content derives entirely from Max Apple's imagination. Any similarities between his story and the lives of any persons, living or dead, are unintended and coincidental. Mr. Apple wishes it to be known that he "has no personal knowledge of Howard Johnson or of his friends and relatives and only a snacking acquaintance with the establishments so named."

THE EDITOR

"I Always Wanted You to Admire My Fasting"; or, Looking at Kafka

PHILIP ROTH

To the students of English 275,
University of Pennsylvania, Fall 1972

"I always wanted you to admire my fasting," said the hunger artist. "We do admire it," said the overseer, affably. "But you shouldn't admire it," said the hunger artist. "Well then we don't admire it," said the overseer, "but why shouldn't we admire it?" "Because I have to fast, I can't help it," said the hunger artist. "What a fellow you are," said the overseer, "and why can't you help it?" "Because," said the hunger artist, lifting his head a little and speaking, with his lips pursed, as if for a kiss, right into the overseer's ear, so that no syllable might be lost, "because I couldn't find the food I liked. If I had found it, believe me, I should have made no fuss and stuffed myself like you or anyone else." These were his last words, but in his dimming eyes remained the firm though no longer proud persuasion that he was still continuing to fast.

—"A Hunger Artist," Franz Kafka

1

I AM LOOKING, as I write of Kafka, at the photograph taken of him at the age of forty (my age)—it is 1924, as sweet and hopeful a year as he may ever have known as a man, and the year of his death. His face is sharp and skeletal, a burrower's face: pronounced cheekbones made even more conspicuous by the absence of sideburns; the ears shaped and angled on his head like angel wings; an intense, creaturely gaze of startled composure—enormous fears, enormous control; a black towel of Levantine hair pulled close around the skull the only sensuous feature; there is a familiar Jewish flare in the bridge of the nose, the nose itself is long and weighted slightly at the tip—the nose of half the Jewish boys who were my friends in high school. Skulls chiseled like this one were shoveled by the thousands from the ovens; had he lived, his would have been among them, along with the skulls of his three younger sisters. Of course it is no more horrifying to think of Franz Kafka in Auschwitz than to think of anyone in Auschwitz—to paraphrase Tolstoy, it is just horrifying in its own way. But he died too soon for the holocaust. Had he lived, perhaps he would have escaped with his good friend and great advocate Max Brod, who eventually found refuge in Palestine, a citizen of Israel until his death there in 1970. But *Kafka* escaping? It seems unlikely for one so fascinated by entrapment and careers that culminate in anguished death. Still, there is Karl Rossman, his American greenhorn. Having imagined Karl's escape to America and his mixed luck here, could not Kafka have found a way to execute an escape for himself? The New School for Social Research in New York becoming *his* Great Nature Theater of Oklahoma? Or perhaps through the influence of Thomas Mann, a position in the German department at Princeton . . . But then had Kafka lived it is not at all certain that the books of his which Mann celebrated from *his* refuge in New Jersey would ever have been published; eventually Kafka might either have destroyed those manuscripts that he had once bid Max Brod to dispose of at his death, or, at the least, continued to keep them his secret. The Jewish refugee arriving in America in 1938 would not then have been Mann's "religious humorist," but a frail and bookish fifty-five-year-old bachelor, formerly a lawyer for a government insurance firm in Prague, retired on a pension in Berlin at the time of Hitler's rise to power—an author, yes, but of a few eccentric stories, mostly about animals, stories no one in America had ever heard of and only a handful in Europe had read; a homeless K., but without K.'s willfulness and purpose, a homeless Karl, but without Karl's youthful spirit and resilience; just a Jew lucky enough to have escaped with his life, in his possession a suitcase containing some clothes, some family photos, some Prague mementos, and the manuscripts, still unpublished and in pieces, of *Amerika, The Trial, The Castle,* and (stranger things happen) three more fragmented novels, no less remarkable than the bizarre masterworks that he keeps to himself out of Oedipal timidity, perfectionist madness, and insatiable longings for solitude and spiritual purity.

July, 1923: Eleven months before he will die in a Vienna sanatorium, Kafka somehow finds the resolve to leave Prague and his father's home for good. Never before has he even remotely succeeded in living apart, independent of his mother, his sisters and his father, nor has he been a writer other than in those few hours when he is not working in the legal department of the Workers' Accident Insurance Office in Prague; since taking his law degree at the university, he has been by all reports the most dutiful and scrupulous of employees, though he finds the work tedious and enervating. But in June of 1923—having some months earlier been pensioned from his job because of his illness—he meets a young Jewish girl of nineteen at a seaside resort in Germany, Dora Dymant, an employee at the vacation camp of the Jewish People's Home of Berlin. Dora has left her Orthodox Polish family to make a life of her own (at half Kafka's age); she and Kafka—who has just turned forty—fall in love . . . Kafka has by now been engaged to two somewhat more conventional Jewish girls— twice to one of them—hectic, anguished engagements wrecked largely by his fears. "I am mentally incapable of marrying," he writes his father in the forty-five-page letter he gave to his mother to deliver, ". . . the moment I make up my mind to marry I can no longer sleep, my head burns day and night, life can no longer be called life." He explains why. "Marrying is barred to me," he tells his father, "because it is your domain. Sometimes I imagine the map of the world spread out and you stretched diagonally across it. And I feel as if I could consider living in only those regions that either are not covered by you or are not within your reach. And in keeping with the conception I have of your magnitude, these are not many and not very comforting regions—and marriage is not among them." The letter explaining what is wrong between this father and this son is dated November, 1919; the mother thought it best not even to deliver it, perhaps for lack of courage, probably, like the son, for lack of hope. During the following two years Kafka attempts to wage an affair with Milena Jesenská-Pollak, an intense young woman of twenty-four who has translated a few of his stories into Czech and is most unhappily married in Vienna; his affair with Milena, conducted feverishly, but by and large through the mails, is even more demoralizing to Kafka than the fearsome engagements to the nice Jewish girls. They aroused only the paterfamilias longings that he dared not indulge, longings inhibited by his exaggerated awe of his father—"spellbound," says Brod, "in the family circle"—and the hypnotic spell of his own solitude; but the Czech Milena, impetuous, frenetic, indifferent to conventional restraints, a woman of appetite and anger, arouses more elemental yearnings and more elemental fears. According to a Prague critic, Rio Preisner, Milena was "psychopathic"; according to Margaret Buber-Neumann, who lived two years beside her in the German concentration camp where Milena died following a kidney operation in 1944, she was powerfully sane, extraordinarily humane and courageous. Milena's obituary for Kafka was the only one of consequence to appear in the Prague press; the prose is strong, so are the claims she makes for Kafka's accomplishment. She is still only in her twenties, the dead man is hardly known as a writer beyond his small circle of friends—yet Milena writes, "His knowledge of the world was exceptional and deep, and he was a deep and exceptional world in himself . . . [He had] a delicacy of feeling bordering on the miraculous and a mental clarity that was terrifyingly uncompromising, and in turn he loaded on to his illness the whole burden of his mental fear of life . . . He wrote the most important books in recent German literature." One can imagine this vibrant young woman stretched diagonally across the bed, as awesome to Kafka as his own father spread out across the map of the world. His letters to her are disjointed, unlike anything else of his in print; the word fear, frequently emphasized, appears on page after page. "We are both married, you in Vienna, I to my Fear in Prague." He yearns to lay his head upon her breast; he calls her "Mother Milena"; during at least one of their two brief rendezvous, he is hopelessly impotent. At last he has to tell her to leave him be, an edict that Milena honors though it leaves her hollow with grief. "Do not write," Kafka tells her, "and let us not see each other; I ask you only to quietly fulfill this request of mine; only on those conditions is survival possible for me; everything else continues the process of destruction."

Then in the early summer of 1923, during a visit to his sister
who is vacationing with her children by the Baltic Sea, he finds
young Dora Dymant, and within a month Franz Kafka has gone
off to live with her in two rooms in a suburb of Berlin, out of
reach at last of the "claws" of Prague and home. How can it be?
How can he, in his illness, have accomplished so swiftly and deci-
sively the leave-taking that was so beyond him in his healthiest
days? The impassioned letter-writer who could equivocate inter-
minably about which train to catch to Vienna to meet with Milena (if he should meet with her for the weekend at all); the
bourgeois suitor in the high collar, who, during his drawn-out
agony of an engagement with the proper Fraulein Bauer, secretly
draws up a memorandum for himself, countering the arguments
"for" marriage with the arguments "against"; the poet of the un-
graspable and the unresolved, whose belief in the immovable bar-
rier separating the wish from its realization is at the heart of his
excruciating visions of defeat, the Kafka whose fictions refute every easy, touching, humanish daydream of salvation and justice
and fulfillment with densely imagined counter-dreams that mock
all solutions and escapes—this Kafka, escapes! Overnight! K. pen-
etrates the Castle walls—Joseph K. evades his indictment—"a
breaking away from it altogether, a mode of living completely
outside the jurisdiction of the court." Yes, the possibility of which
Joseph K. has just a glimmering in the Cathedral, but can neither
fathom nor effectuate—"not . . . some influential manipulation of
the case, but . . . a circumvention of it"—Kafka realizes in the last
year of his life.

Was it Dora Dymant or was it death that pointed the new way?
Perhaps it could not have been one without the other. We know
that the "illusory emptiness" at which K. gazed upon first entering the village and looking up through the mist and the darkness
to the Castle was no more vast and incomprehensible than was
the idea of himself as husband and father to the young Kafka; but
now it seems the prospect of a Dora forever, of a wife, home, and
children everlasting, is no longer the terrifying, bewildering prospect it would once have been, for now "everlasting" is undoubtedly not much more than a matter of months. Yes, the dying
Kafka is determined to marry, and writes to Dora's Orthodox father for his daughter's hand. But the imminent death that has
resolved all contradictions and uncertainties in Kafka is the very

obstacle placed in his path by the young girl's father. The request of Franz Kafka, a dying man, to bind to him in his invalidism Dora Dymant, a healthy young girl, is—denied!

If there is not one father standing in Kafka's way, there is an-other—and, to be sure, another beyond him. Dora's father, writes Max Brod in his biography of Kafka, "set off with [Kafka's] letter to consult the man he honored most, whose authority counted more than anything else for him, the 'Gerer Rebbe.' The rabbi read the letter, put it to one side, and said nothing more than the single syllable, 'No.'" *No.* Klamm himself could have been no more abrupt—or any more removed from the petitioner. *No.* In its harsh finality, as telling and inescapable as the curselike threat delivered by his father to Georg Bendemann, that thwarted fian-cé: "Just take your bride on your arm and try getting in my way. I'll sweep her from your very side, you don't know how!" *No.* Thou shalt not have, say the fathers, and Kafka agrees that he shall not. The habit of obedience and renunciation; also his own distaste for the diseased and reverence for strength, appetite, and health. "'Well, clear this out now!' said the overseer, and they buried the hunger artist, straw and all. Into the cage they put a young panther. Even the most insensitive felt it refreshing to see this wild creature leaping around the cage that had so long been dreary. The panther was all right. The food he liked was brought him without hesitation by the attendants; he seemed not even to miss his freedom; his noble body, furnished almost to the bursting point with all that it needed, seemed to carry freedom around with it too; somewhere in his jaws it seemed to lurk; and the joy of life streamed with such ardent passion from his throat that for the onlookers it was not easy to stand the shock of it. But they braced themselves, crowded around the cage, and did not want ever to move away." So no is no; he knew as much himself. A healthy young girl of nineteen cannot, *should* not, be given in matrimony to a sickly man twice her age, who spits up blood ("I sentence you," cries Georg Bendemann's father, "to death by drowning!") and shakes in his bed with fevers and chills. What sort of un-Kafka-like dream had Kafka been dreaming?

And those nine months spent with Dora have still other "Kafka-esque" elements: a fierce winter in quarters inadequately heated; the inflation that makes a pittance of his own meager pension, and sends into the streets of Berlin the hungry and needy whose sufferings, says Dora, turn Kafka "ash-gray"; and his tubercular lungs, flesh transformed and punished. Dora cares as devotedly and tenderly for the diseased writer as does Gregor Samsa's sister for her brother, the bug. Gregor's sister plays the violin so beautifully that Gregor "felt as if the way were opening before him to the unknown nourishment he craved"; he dreams, in his condition, of sending his gifted sister to the Conservatory! Dora's music is Hebrew, which she reads aloud to Kafka, and with such skill that, according to Brod, "Franz recognized her dramatic talent; on his advice and under his direction she later educated herself in the art . . ."

Only Kafka is hardly vermin to Dora Dymant, *or to himself.* Away from Prague and his father's home, Kafka, in his fortieth year, seems at last to have been delivered from the self-loathing, the self-doubt, and those guilt-ridden impulses to dependence and self-effacement that had nearly driven him mad throughout his twenties and thirties; all at once he seems to have shed the pervasive sense of hopeless despair that informs the great punitive fantasies of *The Trial,* "The Penal Colony," and "The Metamorphosis." Years earlier, in Prague, he had directed Max Brod to destroy all his papers, including three unpublished novels, upon his death; now, in Berlin, when Brod introduces him to a German publisher interested in his work, Kafka consents to the publication of a volume of four stories, and consents, say Brod, "without much need of long arguments to persuade him." With Dora to help, he diligently resumes his study of Hebrew; despite his illness and the harsh winter, he travels to the Berlin Academy for Jewish Studies to attend a series of lectures on the Talmud—a very different Kafka from the estranged melancholic who once wrote in his diary, "What have I in common with the Jews? I have hardly anything in common with myself and should stand very quietly in a corner, content that I can breathe." And to further mark the change, there is ease and happiness with a woman: with this young and adoring companion, he is playful, he is pedagogical, and one would guess, in light of his illness (*and* his happiness), he is chaste. If not a husband (such as he had striven to be to the conventional Fraulein Bauer), if not a lover (as he struggled hopelessly to be with Milena), he would seem to have become something no less miraculous in his scheme of things: a father, a kind of father to this sisterly, mothering daughter. As Franz Kafka awoke one morning from uneasy dreams he found himself transformed in his bed into a father, a writer, and a Jew.

"I have completed the construction of my burrow," begins the long, exquisite, and tedious story that he wrote that winter in Berlin, "and it seems to be successful. . . . Just the place where, according to my calculations, the Castle Keep should be, the soil was very loose and sandy and had literally to be hammered and pounded into a firm state to serve as a wall for the beautifully vaulted chamber. But for such tasks the only tool I possess is my forehead. So I had to run with my forehead thousands and thousands of times, for whole days and nights, against the ground, and I was glad when the blood came, for that was proof that the walls were beginning to harden; in that way, as everybody must admit, I richly paid for my Castle Keep." "The Burrow" is the story of an animal with a keen sense of peril whose life is organized around the principle of defense, and whose deepest longings are for security and serenity; with teeth and claws—*and* forehead— the burrower constructs an elaborate and ingeniously intricate system of underground chambers and corridors that are designed to afford it some peace of mind; however, while this burrow does succeed in reducing the sense of danger from without, its maintenance and protection are equally fraught with anxiety: "these anxieties are different from ordinary ones, prouder, richer in content, often long repressed, but in their destructive effects they are perhaps much the same as the anxieties that existence in the outer world gives rise to." The story (whose ending is lost) terminates with the burrower fixated upon distant subterranean noises that cause it "to assume the existence of a great beast," itself burrowing in the direction of the Castle Keep.

Another grim tale of entrapment, and of obsession so absolute that no distinction is possible between character and predicament. Yet this fiction imagined in the last "happy" months of his life is touched with a spirit of personal reconciliation and sardonic self-acceptance, with a tolerance for one's own brand of madness, that is not apparent in "The Metamorphosis"; the piercing masochistic irony of the early animal story—as of "The Judgment" and *The Trial*—has given way here to a critique of the self and its preoccupations that, though bordering on mockery, no longer seeks to

resolve itself in images of the uttermost humiliation and defeat . . .
But there is more here than a metaphor for the insanely defended
ego, whose striving for invulnerability produces a defensive system that must in its turn become the object of perpetual concern—there is also a very unromantic and hard-headed fable
about how and why art is made, a portrait of the artist in all his
ingenuity, anxiety, isolation, dissatisfaction, relentlessness, obses-
siveness, secretiveness, paranoia, and self-addiction, a portrait of
the magical thinker at the end of his tether, Kafka's Prospero . . .
It is an infinitely suggestive story, this story of life in a hole. For,
finally, remember the proximity of Dora Dymant during the
months that Kafka was at work on "The Burrow" in the two un-
derheated rooms that was their illicit home. Certainly a dreamer
like Kafka need never have entered the young girl's body for her
tender presence to kindle in him a fantasy of a hidden orifice that
promises "satisfied desire," "achieved ambition," and "profound
slumber," but that once penetrated and in one's possession,
arouses the most terrifying and heartbreaking fears of retribution
and loss. "For the rest I try to unriddle the beast's plans. Is it on
its wanderings, or is it working on its own burrow? If it is on its
wanderings then perhaps an understanding with it might be possible. If it should really break through to the burrow I shall give it
some of my stores and it will go on its way again. It will go on its
way again, a fine story! Lying in my heap of earth I can naturally
dream of all sorts of things, even of an understanding with the
beast, though I know well enough that no such thing can happen,
and that at the instant when we see each other, more, at the
moment when we merely guess at each other's presence, we shall
blindly bare our claws and teeth . . . "

He died of tuberculosis of the lungs and the larynx a month short
of his forty-first birthday, June 3, 1924. Dora, inconsolable, whispers for days afterward, "My love, my love, my good one . . ."

2

1942. I am nine; my Hebrew school teacher, Dr. Kafka, is fifty-
nine. To the little boys who must attend his "four-to-five" class
each afternoon, he is known—in part because of his remote and
melancholy foreignness, but largely because we vent on him our
resentment at having to learn an ancient calligraphy at the very

hour we should be out screaming our heads off on the ballfield—
he is known as Dr. Kishka. Named, I confess, by me. His sour
breath, spiced with intestinal juices by five in the afternoon,
makes the Yiddish word for "insides" particularly telling, I think.
Cruel, yes, but in truth I would have cut out my tongue had I
ever imagined the name would become legend. A coddled child, I
do not yet think of myself as persuasive, nor, quite yet, as a literary force in the world. My jokes don't hurt, how could they, I'm
so adorable. And if you don't believe me, just ask my family and
the teachers in school. Already at nine, one foot in Harvard, the
other in the Catskills. Little Borscht Belt comic that I am outside
the classroom, I amuse my friends Schlossman and Ratner on the
dark walk home from Hebrew school with an imitation of Kishka,
his precise and finicky professorial manner, his German accent,
his cough, his gloom. "Doctor *Kishka!*" cries Schlossman, and
hurls himself savagely against the newsstand that belongs to the
candy store owner whom Schlossman drives just a little crazier
each night. "Doctor Franz—Doctor Franz—Doctor Franz—*Kishka!*" screams Ratner, and my chubby little friend who lives upstairs from me on nothing but chocolate milk and Mallomars does
not stop laughing until, as is his wont (his mother has asked me
"to keep an eye on him" for just this reason), he wets his pants.
Schlossman takes the occasion of Ratner's humiliation to pull the
little boy's paper out of his notebook and wave it in the air—it is
the assignment Dr. Kafka has just returned to us, graded; we were
told to make up an alphabet of our own, out of straight lines and
curved lines and dots. "That is all an alphabet is," he had explained. "That is all Hebrew is. That is all English is. Straight
lines and curved lines and dots." Ratner's alphabet, for which he
received a C, looks like twenty-six skulls strung in a row. I received my A for a curlicued alphabet inspired largely (as Dr.
Kafka would seem to have surmised from his comment at the top
of the page) by the number eight. Schlossman received an F for
forgetting to even do it—and a lot he seems to care, too. He is
content—he is *overjoyed*—with things as they are. Just waving a
piece of paper in the air, and screaming, "*Kishka! Kishka!*"
makes him deliriously happy. We should all be so lucky.

At home, alone in the glow of my goose-necked "desk" lamp
(plugged after dinner into an outlet in the kitchen, my study) the
vision of our refugee teacher, sticklike in a fraying three-piece

blue suit, is no longer very funny—particularly after the entire beginner's Hebrew class, of which I am the most studious member, takes the name "Kishka" to its heart. My guilt awakens redemptive fantasies of heroism. I have them often about "the Jews in Europe." I must save him. If not me, who? The demonic Schlossman? The babyish Ratner? And if not now, when? For I have learned in the ensuing weeks that Dr. Kafka lives in "a room" in the house of an elderly Jewish lady on the shabby lower stretch of Avon Avenue, where the trolley still runs, and the poorest of Newark's Negroes shuffle meekly up and down the street, for all they seem to know still back in Mississippi. A *room*. And *there!* My family's apartment is no palace, but it is ours at least, so long as we pay the thirty-eight-fifty a month in rent; and though our neighbors are not rich, they refuse to be poor and they refuse to be meek. Tears of shame and sorrow in my eyes, I rush into the living room to tell my parents what I have heard (though not that I heard it during a quick game of "aces up" played a minute before class against the synagogue's rear wall—worse, played directly beneath a stained glass window embossed with the names of the dead): "My Hebrew teacher lives in a *room*.'"

My parents go much further than I could imagine anybody going in the real world. Invite him to dinner, my mother says. *Here?* Of course here—Friday night; I'm sure he can stand a home-cooked meal and a little pleasant company. Meanwhile my father gets on the phone to call my Aunt Rhoda, who lives with my grandmother and tends her and her potted plants in the apartment house at the corner of our street. For nearly two decades now my father has been introducing my mother's forty-year-old "baby" sister to the Jewish bachelors and widowers of New Jersey. No luck so far. Aunt Rhoda, an "interior decorator" in the dry goods department of "The Big Bear," a mammoth merchandise and produce market in industrial Elizabeth, wears falsies (this information by way of my older brother) and sheer frilly blouses, and family lore has it that she spends her hours in the bathroom every day applying powders and sweeping her stiffish hair up into a dramatic pile over her head; but despite all this dash and display, she is, in my father's words, "still afraid of the facts of life." He, however, is undaunted, and administers therapy regularly and gratis: "Let 'em squeeze ya, Rhoda—it *feels* good!" I am his flesh and blood, I can reconcile myself to such scandalous talk in our kitchen—*but what will Dr. Kafka think?* Oh, but it's too late to do anything now. The massive machinery of matchmaking has been set in motion by my undiscourageable father, and the smooth engines of my proud homemaking mother's hospitality are already purring away. To throw my body into the works in an attempt to bring it all to a halt—well, I might as well try to bring down the New Jersey Bell Telephone Company by leaving our receiver off the hook. Only Dr. Kafka can save me now. But to my muttered invitation, he replies, with a formal bow that turns me scarlet—who has ever seen a person do such a thing outside of a movie house?—he replies that he would be *honored* to be my family's dinner guest. "My aunt," I rushed to tell him, "will be there too." It appears that I have just said something mildly humorous; odd to see Dr. Kafka smile. Sighing, he says, "I will be delighted to meet her." Meet her? He's supposed to *marry* her. How do I warn him? And how do I warn Aunt Rhoda (a very great admirer of me and my marks) about his sour breath, his roomer's pallor, his Old World ways, so at odds with her up-to-dateness? My face feels as if it will ignite of its own—and spark the fire that will engulf the synagogue. Torah and all—when I see Dr. Kafka scrawl our address in his notebook, and beneath it, some words *in German.* "Good night, Dr. Kafka!" "Good night, and thank you, thank you." I turn to run, I go, but not fast enough: out on the street I hear Schlossman—that fiend!—announcing to my classmates who are punching one another under the lamplight down from the synagogue steps (where a card game is also in progress, organized by the Bar Mitzvah boys): "Roth invited Kishka to his *house!* To *eat!*"

Does my father do a job on Kafka! Does he make a sales pitch for familial bliss! What it means to a man to have two fine boys and a wonderful wife! Can Dr. Kafka imagine what that's like? The thrill? The satisfaction? The pride? He tells our visitor of the network of relatives on his mother's side that are joined in a "family association" of over two hundred and fifty people located in seven states, including the state of Washington! Yes, relatives even in the Far West: here are their photographs, Dr. Kafka; this is a beautiful book we published entirely on our own for five dollars a copy, pictures of every member of the family, including infants, and a family history by "Uncle Lichtblau, the eighty-five-year-old patriarch of the clan. This is our family newsletter

that is published twice a year and distributed nationwide to all
the relatives. This, in the frame, is the menu from the banquet of
the family association, held last year in a ballroom of the "Y" in
Newark, in honor of my father's mother on her seventy-fifth
birthday. My mother, Dr. Kafka learns, has served *six consecutive
years* as the secretary-treasurer of the family association. My father has served a two-year term as president, as have each of his
three brothers. We now have fourteen boys in the family in uniform. Philip writes a letter on V-mail stationery to five of his
cousins in the Army every single month. "Religiously," my mother puts in, smoothing my hair. "I firmly believe," says my father,
"that the family is the cornerstone of everything." Dr. Kafka,
who has listened with close attention to my father's *spiel*, handling the various documents that have been passed to him with
great delicacy and poring over them with a kind of rapt absorp-
tion that reminds me of myself over the watermarks of my
stamps, now for the first time expresses himself on the subject of
family; softly he says, "I agree," and inspects again the pages of
our family book. "Alone," says my father, in conclusion, "alone,
Dr. Kafka, is a stone." Dr. Kafka, setting the book gently upon
my mother's gleaming coffee table, allows with a nod how that is
so. My mother's fingers are now turning in the curls behind my
ears; not that I even know it at the time, or that she does. Being
stroked is my life; stroking me, my father, and my brother is hers.

My brother goes off to a Boy Scout "council" meeting, but only
after my father has him stand in his neckerchief before Dr. Kafka
and describe to him the skills he has mastered to earn each of his
badges. I am invited to bring my stamp album into the living
room and show Dr. Kafka my set of triangular stamps from Zanzibar. "Zanzibar!" says my father rapturously, as though I, not
even ten, have already been there and back. My father accompanies Dr. Kafka and myself into the "sun parlor," where my tropi-
cal fish swim in the aerated, heated, and hygienic paradise I have
made for them with my weekly allowance and my Hanukah *gelt*.
I am encouraged to tell Dr. Kafka what I know about the tem-
perament of the angelfish, the function of the catfish, and the
family life of the black molly. I know quite a bit. "All on his own
he does that," my father says to Kafka. "He gives me a lecture on
one of those fish, it's seventh heaven, Dr. Kafka." "I can imagine," Kafka replies.

Back in the living room my Aunt Rhoda suddenly launches into a rather recondite monologue on "scotch plaids," designed, it would appear, only for the edification of my mother. At least she looks fixedly at my mother while she delivers it. I have not yet seen her look directly at Dr. Kafka; she did not even turn his way at dinner when he asked how many employees there were at "The Big Bear." "How would I know?" she replies, and continues conversing with my mother, something about a grocer or a butcher who would take care of her "under the counter" if she could find him nylons for his wife. It never occurs to me that she will not look at Dr. Kafka because she is shy—nobody that dolled up could, in my estimation, be shy—I can only think that she is outraged. *It's his breath. It's his accent. It's his age.* I'm wrong—it turns out to be what Aunt Rhoda calls his "superiority complex." "Sitting there, sneering at us like that," says my aunt, somewhat superior now herself. "Sneering?" repeats my father, incredulous. "Sneering and laughing, yes!" says Aunt Rhoda. My mother shrugs: "*I* didn't think he was laughing." "Oh, don't worry, by himself there he was having a good time—*at our expense.* I know the European-type man. Underneath they think they're all lords of the manor," Rhoda says. "You know something, Rhoda?" says my father, tilting his head and pointing a finger, "I think you fell in love." "With *him?* Are you *crazy?*" "He's too quiet for Rhoda," my mother says, "I think maybe he's a little bit of a wallflower. Rhoda is a lively person, she needs lively people around her." "Wallflower? He's not a wallflower! He's a gentleman, that's all. And he's lonely," my father says assertively, glaring at my mother for coming in over his head like this *against* Kafka. My Aunt Rhoda is forty years old—it is not exactly a shipment of brand new goods that he is trying to move. "He's a gentleman, he's an educated man, and I'll tell you something, he'd give his eye teeth to have a nice home and a wife." "Well," says my Aunt Rhoda, "let him find one then, if he's so educated. Somebody who's his equal, who he doesn't have to look down his nose at with his big sad refugee eyes!" "Yep, she's in love," my father announces, squeezing Rhoda's knee in triumph. "With him?" she cries, jumping to her feet, taffeta crackling around her like a bonfire. "With *Kafka?*" she snorts, "I wouldn't give an old man like him the time of day!"

Dr. Kafka calls and takes my Aunt Rhoda to a movie. I am

astonished, both that he calls and that she goes; it seems there is more desperation in life than I have come across yet in my fish tank. Dr. Kafka takes my Aunt Rhoda to a play performed at the "Y." Dr. Kafka eats Sunday dinner with my grandmother and my Aunt Rhoda, and at the end of the afternoon, accepts with that formal bow of his the Mason jar of barley soup that my grandmother presses him to carry back to his room with him on the No. 8 bus. Apparently he was very taken with my grandmother's jungle of potted plants—and she, as a result, with him. Together they spoke in Yiddish about gardening. One Wednesday morning, only an hour after the store has opened for the day, Dr. Kafka shows up at the dry goods department of "The Big Bear"; he tells Aunt Rhoda that he just wanted to see where she worked. That night he writes in his diary, "With the customers she is forthright and cheery, and so managerial about 'taste' that when I hear her explain to a chubby young bride why green and blue do not 'go,' I am myself ready to believe that Nature is in error and. R. is correct."

One night, at ten, Dr. Kafka and Aunt Rhoda come by unexpectedly, and a small impromptu party is held in the kitchen— coffee and cake, and even a thimbleful of whiskey all around, to celebrate the resumption of Aunt Rhoda's career on the stage. I have only heard tell of my aunt's theatrical ambitions. My brother says that when I was small she used to come to entertain the two of us on Sundays with her puppets—she was at that time employed by the W.P.A. to travel around New Jersey and put on puppet shows in schools and even in churches; Aunt Rhoda did all the voices, male and female, and with the help of another young girl, manipulated the manikins on their strings. Simultaneously, she had been a member of the "Newark Collective Theater," a troupe organized primarily to go around to strike groups to perform *Waiting for Lefty;* everybody in Newark (as I understood it) had had high hopes that Rhoda Pilchik would go on to Broadway—everybody except my grandmother. To me this period of history is as difficult to believe in as the era of the lake-dwellers that I am studying in school; of course, people say it was once so, so I believe them, but nonetheless it is hard to grant such stories the status of the real, given the life I see around me.

Yet my father, a very avid realist, is in the kitchen, *schnapps* glass in hand, toasting Aunt Rhoda's success. She has been awarded one of the starring roles in the Russian masterpiece, *The Three Sisters*, to be performed six weeks hence by the amateur group at the Newark "Y." Everything, announces Aunt Rhoda, everything she owes to Franz, and his encouragement. One conversation— "One!" she cries gaily—and Dr. Kafka had apparently talked my grandmother out of her lifelong belief that actors are not serious human beings. And what an actor *he* is, in his own right, says Aunt Rhoda. How he had opened her eyes to the meaning of things, by reading her the famous Chekhov play—yes, read it to her from the opening line to the final curtain, all the parts, and actually left her in tears. Here Aunt Rhoda says, "Listen, listen— this is the first line of the play—it's the key to everything. Listen—I just think about what it was like that night Pop passed away, how I thought and thought what would happen, what would we all do—and, and, listen—"

"We're listening," laughs my father.

Pause; she must have walked to the center of the kitchen linoleum. She says, sounding a little surprised, "'It's just a year ago today that father died.'"

"Shhh," warns my mother, "you'll give the little one nightmares."

I am not alone in finding my aunt "a changed person" during the ensuing weeks of rehearsal. My mother says this is just what she was like as a little girl. "Red cheeks, always those hot, red cheeks—and everything exciting, even taking a bath." "She'll calm down, don't worry," says my father, "and then he'll pop the question." "Knock on wood," says my mother. "Come on," says my father, "he knows what side his bread is buttered on—he sets foot in this house, he sees what a family is all about, and believe me, he's licking his chops. Just look at him when he sits in that club chair. This is his dream come true." "Rhoda says that in Berlin, before Hitler, he had a young girlfriend, years and years it went on, and then she left him. For somebody else. She got tired of waiting." "Don't worry," says my father, "when the time comes I'll give him a little nudge. He ain't going to live forever, either, and he knows it."

Then one weekend, as a respite from the "strain" of nightly rehearsals—which Dr. Kafka regularly visits, watching in his hat and coat from a seat at the back of the auditorium until it is time to accompany Aunt Rhoda home—they take a trip to Atlantic City. Ever since he arrived on these shores Dr. Kafka has wanted to see the famous boardwalk and the horse that drives from the high board. But in Atlantic City something happens that I am not allowed to know about; any discussion of the subject conducted in my presence is in Yiddish. Dr. Kafka sends Aunt Rhoda four letters in three days. She comes to us for dinner and sits till midnight crying in our kitchen; she calls the "Y" on our phone to tell them (weeping) that her mother is still ill and she cannot come to rehearsal again—she may even have to drop out of the play—no, she can't, she can't, her mother is too ill, she herself is too upset! Good-bye! Then back to the kitchen table to cry; she wears no pink powder and no red lipstick, and her stiff brown hair, down, is thick and spiky as a new broom.

My brother and I listen from our bedroom, through the door that silently he has pushed ajar.

"Have you ever?" says Aunt Rhoda, weeping. "Have you ever?"

"Poor soul," says my mother.

"*Who?*" I whisper to my brother. "Aunt Rhoda or—"

"Shhhh!" he says, "Shut *up!*"

In the kitchen, my father grunts. "Hmm. Hmm." I hear him getting up and walking around and sitting down again—and then grunting. I am listening so hard that I can hear the letters being folded and unfolded, stuck back into their envelopes and then removed to be puzzled over one more time.

"Well?" demands Aunt Rhoda. "*Well?*"

"Well what?" answers my father.

"Well what do you want to say *now?*"

"He's *meshugeh*," admits my father. "Something is wrong with him all right."

"But," sobs Aunt Rhoda, "no one would believe me when *I* said it!"

"Rhody, Rhody," croons my mother in that voice I know from those times I have had to have stitches taken, or when I awaken in tears, somehow on the floor beside my bed. "Rhody, don't be hysterical, darling. It's over, kitten, it's all over."

I reach across to my brother's "twin" bed and tug on the blanket. I don't think I've ever been so confused in my life, not even by death. The speed of things! Everything good undone in a moment! By what? *"What?"* I whisper. *"What is it?"*

My brother, the Boy Scout, smiles leeringly and with a fierce hiss that is no answer and enough answer, addresses my bewilderment: "Sex!"

Years later, a junior at college, I receive an envelope from home containing Dr. Kafka's obituary, clipped from the *Jewish News*, the tabloid of Jewish affairs that is mailed each week to the homes of the Jews of Essex County. It is summer, the semester is over, but I have stayed on at school, alone in my room in the town, trying to write short stories; I am fed by a young English professor and his wife in exchange for babysitting; I tell the sympathetic couple, who are also loaning me the money for my rent, why it is I can't go home. My tearful fights with my father are all I can talk about at their dinner table. "Keep him away from me!" I scream at my mother. "But, darling," she asks me, "what is going on? What is this all about?"—the very same question with which I used to plague my older brother, asked of me now out of the same bewilderment and innocence. "He *loves* you," she explains. But that, of all things, seems to me to be precisely what is blocking my way. Others are crushed by paternal criticism—I find myself oppressed by his high opinion of me! Can it possibly be true (and can I possibly admit) that I am coming to hate him for loving me so? praising me so? But that makes no sense—the ingratitude! the stupidity! the contrariness! Being loved is so obviously a blessing, *the* blessing, praise such a rare bequest; only listen late at night to my closest friends on the literary magazine and in the drama society—they tell horror stories of family life to rival *The Way of All Flesh*, they return shell-shocked from vacations, drift back to school as though from wars. What they would give to be in my golden slippers! "What's going on?" my mother begs me to tell her; but how can I, when I can neither fully believe that this is happening to us, nor that I am the one who is making it happen. That they, who together cleared all obstructions from my path, should seem now to be my final obstruction! No wonder my rage must filter through a child's tears of shame, confusion, and loss. All that we have constructed together over the course of two century-long decades, and look how I must bring it down—in the name of this tyrannical need that I call my "independence"! Born, I am told, with the umbilical cord around

my neck, it seems I will always come close to strangulation trying
to deliver myself from my past into my future . . . My mother,
keeping the lines of communication open, sends a note to me at
school: "We miss you"—and encloses the very brief obituary notice. Across the margin at the bottom of the clipping, she has
written (in the same hand that she wrote notes to my teachers and
signed my report cards, in the very same handwriting that once
eased my way in the world), "Remember poor Kafka, Aunt Rhoda's beau?"

"Dr. Franz Kafka," the notice reads, "a Hebrew teacher at the
Talmud Torah of the Schley Street Synagogue from 1939 to 1948,
died on June 3 in the Deborah Tuberculosis Sanitorium in Browns
Mills, New Jersey. Dr. Kafka had been a patient there since 1950.
He was 70 years old. Dr. Kafka was born in Prague, Czechoslova-
kia, and was a refugee from the Nazis. He leaves no survivors."

He also leaves no books: no *Trial*, no *Castle*, no "Diaries." The
dead man's papers are claimed by no one, and disappear—all
except those four *"meshugeneh"* letters that are, to this day as far
as I know, still somewhere amongst the memorabilia accumulated
in her dresser drawers by my spinster aunt, along with a collection of Broadway "Playbills," sales citations from "The Big Bear,"
and transatlantic steamship stickers.

Thus all trace of Dr. Kafka disappears. Destiny being destiny,
how could it be otherwise? Does the Land Surveyor reach the
Castle? Does K. escape the judgment of the Court, or Georg Bendemann the judgment of his father? "'Well, clear this out now!'
said the overseer, and they buried the hunger artist, straw and
all." No, it simply is not in the cards for Kafka ever to become
the Kafka—why, that would be stranger even than a man turning
into an insect. No one would believe it, Kafka least of all.

End of Days

M. F. BEAL

DARRELL HURT WAS HAVING A HARD TIME sawing through the tough throathide of a steer, though he had butchered more than a hundred in his life as stockman and farmer, when suddenly the white-furred skin split, his knife ripped the jugular, sending a fountain of blood over his hipboots, and he realized he would never be able to finish the butchering.

He dragged himself to one of the hewn timbers of the barn and leaned against it, head hidden in his arm, knife dripping on the floor, eyes cemented shut by a feeling just short of weeping.

It was a large barn that he and his wife and brother Ben had built in '28. The supporting timbers were logs so thick around you could barely embrace them and feel your fingertips; the floor was three-inch, end-grain, old-growth fir with concrete gutters where once he'd milked a dairy herd. The ceiling was twenty-four feet high with a loft holding racked haybales; at the very peak swung a block and tackle with its system of ropes, its singletree to be hooked where hamstring met hock of the hindlegs of the butchered steers. Through the barn doors he had left half open, the wind tossed dime-sized drops of winter rain.

Darrell tried to understand why he could not finish the butchering. His eyes were drawn to the animal's blood as it pattered the flooring, found cracks, and sought the earth below. The yarddog, Sam, left his treat of a severed hoof to lap the flow; feeling Darrell's eyes, he flagged a long tailswing, flattened his ears as he wolfishly continued. The smell of the steer, heavy with softness, grain, and the yellowness of warm fat from the steer's brisket and back, reached Darrell in wind gusts, then dragged off, up through the hay, down to the richening loam beneath the barn. Where he had skinned the belly (before the inertia set in) and cut away the long brown tasseled organ of the steer, the fat stood clumped, erect. And though he knew quite well the steer was dead of a bullet aimed downward behind the ear into the mass of its brain, he could see that when the wind touched the skinned ribs of the creature, its muscles rippled, remembering how to dislodge a fly. *It is still alive*, he thought suddenly, but he knew it was not.

He jabbed his knife into a beam with a quick snap of wrist and reached into the bucket of warm water he always had at the butchering. He rubbed his hands as if he wished he were soaping them; then, with this familiarity in his head, he told his feet to move to the next step: lifting the steer onto the singletree hoist. But they would not move. *I will have to go up to the house for a while, till this passes*, he decided.

There was a rising path leading to the house set into the top of the hill. The house was of concrete blocks; Darrell had only finished it three winters before. Sometimes when he thought of all the years he and Verna and Sally had lived in what was now the wood and tool shed, he had to stop and shake his head before he could pick up the screwdriver or hammer or stick of wood he was after.

He walked up the rising path slowly and watched the outlines of the house come clear through the rain. There were lights in the windows. A man who had stopped the summer before to ask permission to fish from their bridge said the house reminded him, somehow, of the old houses—shelters—the first settlers had built on the Great Plains. Darrell like the idea of that; he told the man he was one of the early settlers in this part of the West. No man had farmed this land before. It had been burned-over stumpland, the trees fired by the Indians so grass would grow up and give more graze for deer and elk. Then the government opened it for settlement, and some crazy old man took papers on it, built a tiny shack—even smaller than Darrell's—down by the creek, and sat there and read books till he died. Darrell bought the land from the old guy's cousin, paid the place off working on the highway crew and logging, and now, forty-one years after getting it, after yarding out stumps, plowing seeding, fencing and stocking, had almost a hundred acres of prime bottom pasture, pure-bred Hereford beefcritters, the new concrete block house.

Verna was working in the kitchen. She looked up as he undid his boots, dropped them on the mat.

"Finish the butchering? I've got something here you sure will hate to see." Her voice told him she'd baked a pie or some such treat. He gained weight now that he was getting older and she didn't bake pies for him as often.

"Whatcha got? Let's see—from the smell in here I'd say it's something pretty bad. Did you burn some grease . . . no, it's worse than that." He chuckled like crumpling paper.

"Oh, Darrell, I baked you an apple pie." She opened the oven door to show it. He couldn't get over how tired he felt, how the sight of the pie seemed suddenly to fist his stomach into a tight sour lump.

"I'm feeling a little under the weather," he said. Knowing that already, she looked up from pouring milk into a pitcher. A drop of milk fell on her apron; the fabric swallowed it. "I think I'll lie down," he said.

The livingroom was twenty-six by thirty-two. They had wanted a big livingroom and that size seemed about right. But now that the house was built, he was appalled each time he entered the room at just how enormous twenty-six by thirty-two was. Inside the room with its high ceiling and double windows, he felt somehow out of scale; as if he had grown smaller. Staring out the windows into the pastured valley he now and then was amazed to think himself a deep-sea diver; the plumed and fronded trees swayed with currents and pressures greater than any he had imagined and his eyes warily sought the warning fin of some incredible fish come to stare back. Inside this room, he could feel the weight of that different atmosphere on his shoulders, inside his head. "Like a fish out of water," he'd think to himself, the idea flowing into his head as the trees bent to the wind. But that wasn't it, exactly; he meant almost the direct opposite. Still, that was what came to mind. That these were the only words to express what he felt disturbed him, too; it made him think things inside him were folding and bending like the world outside his window. How could you admit you couldn't sometimes tell grass from water? You couldn't tolerate things going unreal like that.

Yet they did, and there were moments of panic like this afternoon in the barn when you almost thought you wanted them to.

He eased into his chair and stared at the carpet, a long, thick one that swirled into patterns as you walked through it; it was green, like his pastures, but as seen underwater. "How's that for grass?" he found himself asking each new visitor in an almost worried attempt to recover, simply, what it *must* be. But they always agreed, saying: "Best looking crop of grass I ever seen."

Verna called his chair "the cradle." It was an arc of beige moire plastic pushed into soft tufted swells. He did not sit in it but lay down, knees and head slightly raised. Under the right armrest was a switch and when he pressed it, the chair began to vibrate gently. It helped his back; it relaxed away the knot in his belly. It was hard to stay awake when the switch was on.

But even as his finger touched the switch, he noticed on the little table beside him the card they'd been given at the funeral of the Disston boy.

He and Verna had had a boy. They had Sally, and then four years later Verna got pregnant again. Everyone joked about this one being another girl, but Darrell's father—who was alive then—said, "No, by god, this one's going to have a handle on 'im." Darrell's mother had borne seven children and his father had infallibly predicted the sex of each. Well, when Verna's baby was born it was a son, all right, but it lacked calcium in its bones, the doctor said, and so when it got out of its mother it just seemed to collapse inward, a creature out of its element. The doctor said it was a rare case, that he wanted to write it up for some journal. Darrell signed papers giving permission; and then a few years later began to dream at night his son was in a bottle somewhere on some laboratory shelf, still a prisoner *inside*. But now inside glass, a prison of glass and alcohol. After her confinement, Verna never spoke of the baby at all.

The death of the neighbor's son had been, in a sense, expected. When they were told Bobby Disston had been hit and killed by a car while he was changing a tire on the roadside in the dusk everyone was shocked, but the next response was: I always suspected something would happen to that kid. He was always getting into scrapes, and had had several minor accidents. "He used his life as if all he had to do was walk into the dimestore and buy a new one," another neighbor said. Even his mother said, "I knew it. I knew it."

The funeral announcement showed a chapel window with pink and yellow shafts filtering through on a cross; it was on thin crisp paper. On the inside was a poem:

> To close the eye, to fall asleep,
> To draw a labored breath,
> To find release from daily cares
> In what we know as death . . .
>
> Is this the crowning of a life,
> The aim or end thereof?
> The totaled sum of consciousness,
> The ripened fruit of love?
>
> It cannot be, for they live on
> A little step away.
> The soul, the everlasting life,
> Has found a better day . . .

Darrell did and didn't believe any of it. He did believe the poem; he didn't believe Bobby Disston had been *headed* for a bad end. But during and after the funeral he realized something: they, all of them in the world, when such things happened, were nearing the end of days; and it was not long off now. The Last Judgment was near. He had not spoken to anyone yet of this.

His fingers touched the button on the underside of the chair-arm. With the card in his other hand he dozed and dreamt:

He was standing outside the funeral home; there was a funeral, and he had been invited. He had on his best suit, a dark blue one; he rubbed the tip of one shoe on the back of his trouserleg, then the other. He thought: this doesn't make sense; I haven't done that since I was a kid. There was difficulty getting someone to answer the door. He rang again and again; he could hear inside the music of the service, but no one answered the door. I'm late, he thought. They've gone on without me. He realized his hair was out of place and tried to smooth it with his hand, but his hair was stiff, hard like animal hair, and would not lie flat. He yanked his hand away in panic, pushed at the door.

Now suddenly the funeral director appeared and though they

were men of the same age and even had fished together, the
director didn't greet him; he said nothing, in fact, though Darrell
spoke to him somberly about being late, and how sorry he was,
and what a tragedy about Bobby Disston. Instead the director
hustled—literally shoved—him into a tiny room. It was dark, a
closet. He could hear the music, then the voice of the preacher,
but couldn't make out the words. The room, which had seemed so
tiny at first, expanded but remained dark; then it contracted, was
even smaller than at first. He couldn't stand; he lay down. He
stretched out his feet. The music had stopped now; even the
preacher's voice was fading and instead he heard a roar, a dull
heavy sound of water moving, pressing. He tried to struggle up,
to stand again. He could not.

Verna called Darrell's brother Ben to help finish the butchering
and after supper the men started down the path to the barn. It
was getting dark and Darrell had turned on the floodlight. He
couldn't get over how much the trees were like feathers. Darrell
felt he had never seen trees before. "Trees, grass—they're alive,"
he thought, unable to be more precise about his new idea than
that, but contented with the notion.

Ben talked about how the Grange needed a new roof.

"I've stuck them damn shingles down till there's nothing left of
'em but roofing tar." It was true; Darrell nodded. "I'm going into
Portland next week; I'll price them. Eleanor says burn the place
down and start right; but I think a new roof will do 'er."

"I was skinning and I got a little light feeling, you know?"
Darrell said while his head was clear. They had reached the barn.
The steer lay belly up on the floor and its flanks no longer quiv-
ered when the wind struck muscle. Its belly was enormous, reaching almost to the midleg knuckle where Darrell had sawed off the
hooves, the first task of butchering. Sam flopped his tail at them
and continued to chew one of the discarded feet. And Darrell
thought another of his unwelcome thoughts: for all the doctors'
skill in putting one man's heart into another man, or sewing in
new kidneys, some things were beyond all resurrection.

"It's funny how weak I feel when I get down here in the
wind," he said.

"There's a flu going around," said Ben, working a flap of hide
down, fleshing away with the sharp knife. The fat under the

steer's hide was white and where the capillaries to the hide had been severed, there were tiny dribbles of red, as if it had been flailed with the thorns of the running blackberry that hedged the pastures.

"Better get that blood off before it sets," Darrell said. He fixed his jaw and found he could take up the gardenhose to run jets of water on the fat, found even he could put his hand on the fat and scrub a bit to loosen the red. The steer had a different smell now, a strong thick one that fought into the nostrils even though Darrell breathed through his mouth. He heard Ben doing the same, both of them panting.

"Stiffening up now," said Ben. "Better get this damn hide off."

Darrell took up a knife then, and worked the hide with his brother.

Soon Ben was hooking the hocks to the singletree and Darrell, pulling at the block and tackle, had the hindquarters off the floor. His hands trembled as he sliced the brisket, through the heavy fat, to the ribs. Ben urged the tip of his knife under the muscle at the belly, nudging the tip in small jerks to penetrate muscle but not intestine. The fascia popped, hissed like a kid's balloon. Intestine bulged through the parting.

"Lots of gas," said Ben. There was a new odor now, a green slime smell of decay. The floodlight had become their only illumination and under it the fat sides of the critter as they parted buckled into dimples and swells, grew yellow-pink, waxy, mottled like the thighs of a fat old woman. Darrell saw fat and muscle cling to each other before this last dismemberment. He had always thought change natural before; now he suddenly saw the resistance even a dead thing could make. Then was it "natural" for one thing to be changed into another, as he and Verna might consume steak? Was it "natural" (the arithmetic leapt into his head) that in his sixty-five years almost thirty steers like this one had passed through him, that almost ten tons of critter had gone to nourish his two hundred pounds? If it happened, well then it must. Or? The intestines popped angrily from the cavity as Ben worked his incision to the clumps of fat where the steer's member had been. Pressing them back with his hands, feeling the veins of his hands and wrists knot to press, Darrell stood, feet spread, wondering whether to tell Ben they were in the end of days.

How would he say it? *The wars, the killings, young men dying, old men without energy; fighting, killing for no good reason, accidents . . . it used to happen, it all happened before but never this way, never so many, with so little sense.* And of course it was written, as well. *The prophets saw, they told us, they gave us a blueprint. How long do we have? A year? A hundred days?* It could happen tomorrow.

The lungs and stomach finally bulged out now, slipped between Darrell's hands, slapped the floor. Ben panted, stepped back, wiped his forehead, looked at Darrell, waiting. For what? There was a quizzical look in Ben's eyes. Finally Darrell saw, moved to the block and tackle, cranked the steer higher.

"You want the tail, Darrell?"

"No."

Ben found the joint, cut; the tail fell. Darrell cut a hank of twine, slid it around the tight colon as Ben held the guts aside, and cinched it up.

They began to search the entrails for the liver: Darrell, slipping again into the job, called to the dog who trotted up, took a lung-lobe with careful teeth, backed off.

"Want the sweetbreads, Darrell?"

"No."

"You got the heart there? I'll take the hanging tender."

Cutting away the heart and the shaft of muscle that held it in place, Darrell answered himself: *no, I won't say anything, no one will know.* He gripped the colon and pulled back. Ben grunted, ran his knife around the anus; there was a suck of air, the guts splayed on the floor, gleamed. The dog clicked his teeth.

And how tired Darrell was now; he himself felt flayed, taken apart. The heart lay in its bucket with the tender coiled around it; he drew kidneys from the gaping chest, sent them to rest on the heart. So much to do: hide to fist from the back, head to sever, carcass to wash again with cloths . . .

"Not much left now, Darrell," said Ben looking at him again, with that queer look. And suddenly Darrell realized what Ben saw: Darrell dying. Darrell old, tired, speechless, afraid. And when the end of days had come for him, Darrell, Ben would say: "I knew he wasn't long for this world. I could see it that night."

Verna—could she see it? Would she say "I knew it, I knew it"? Would they sit in the funeral home, in the chapel that was not really like the pink-yellow lit chapel on the card; the real chapel, and in the sanctuary, a real, vast, dark casket enclosing himself, who was really dead? Would they go *on?*

No Last Judgment, no end of days. They would go on. The huge livingroom of his new stone house would be no more or less empty. "Old Darrell died, did you hear about it?" "Is that a fact; well to tell you the truth I saw it coming."

He found himself giving Ben a look of pure hate and his brother, alarmed, took his shoulder.

"Darrell, you look bad. You go up to the house."

And as his feet lifted him up the dark path his body seethed. His face filled, his chest, his ribs lifted to hard bundles. He felt his organs had been turned to stone; his body, stiff, drum-tight, seethed and burned; molten, furious. *I want them all to come with me,* his head shouted: *I want to kill them all, kill them all, all——*

Hammie and the Black Dean

AUSTIN CLARKE

YOU WOULDN'T SEE Hammie eating with one of them. And you wouldn't see him playing Frisbee, or touch football, or softball with them. Not in the early days anyhow. No, not one brother at Berkshire College, high up in the mountains, would think of sitting down at the same table with a white student. Not if he was really *black*. But there were a few "blacks" who reasoned that Berkshire College was not set up to make the forty black students there feel as if they were back home on some street corner in Harlem or in Roxbury. These "motherfuckers," as Hammie called them, would reason that the college was indeed a white institution, that everything about it was going to remain white in spite of Hammie's black-power rhetoric and also in spite of the fact that the college had two black professors and a black dean. Those few "jive brothers" saw this clearly, and they went on sitting and talking with the white students. They even moved into the same dormitory with the white students. The *real brothers*, the "bloods," stopped speaking to them. And they called them "niggers." "Toms" was too polite a name for these motherfuckers, Hammie said.

And what made the real brothers really mad was the hurtful fact that among these "motherfuckers," there were the only two black women on campus. One of them was passably beautiful. The other was tolerably intelligent and had a lot of money and a rich daddy. The bloods would spend long hours between hands of bid whist or Tonk or penny poker plotting the murder and rape of this sister; and in more jovial movements, they would talk about "embarrassing" her in front of the white boys. She dated only white boys. The other sister said openly that in her "honest and intellectual opinion, black men are bastards, and those who aren't bastards, are children!"

The real brothers therefore stuck close together. They talked loud in their section of the dormitory, which they baptized the Black Mosque—although they drank Boone's Farm and smoked pot every night, and on weekends slept with their friends' dates— and they called one another "niggerrrr," in loving twists of endearment; rapped and rapped about their fear and discomfort and alienation from studying at a white college in such swallowing circumstances, so close to the "motherfucking honkie"; and, although they did not know it, swam together in their romantic parody of myths about white people and myths about black inferiority, like fish in a strange current, in difficulty, in a rushing mountain stream.

And the white students, the "others," *them,* watched the brothers coming and going, envied something about the way they talked and walked, and how they told the administration to "fuck off!"; about the way they spoke at dinner, loud and happy; indeed, everything that these black students did among themselves; and still the white students failed to understand the real reason for it. So the white students puzzled a little more over it, and then decided to hate the black students in return, although they didn't tell them so to their faces. But you might hear two of them in a dormitory washroom discussing blacks in words similar to the graffiti of sentiments and sexual fantasies which wallpapered the toilets in an adolescent confusion about prowess and dreams that indicated some kind of sexual lockjaw. Perhaps this was why the black students started living and eating apart. It probably began in the dormitory toilets. "Those motherfucking white boys. Always thinking about their pricks. Shee-it! when they not thinking about their pricks, they writing about it. But they sure's hell can't do much fucking with it! The motherfuckers!" This is how Hammie, the most talkative black student, put it. Whatever it was about the white students and about practically all of the white faculty which caused this deep and obsessive hatred from the black students, they always mentioned the dormitory toilets. "They bug the hell outta me, Jim!" Hammie said, meaning either the whites at Berkshire, or the toilets, or both. And whether

it was some kind of puritanical vengeance, or merely the depths
to which the blacks disdained graffiti and writing hands on the
walls of the dormitory, you could not find one smudge of sexual
fantasy or sexual jokes on the pearly white walls of the toilets in
the Black Mosque. Hammie used to yell *"damn!"* almost each
time he saw a white boy with a white girl; and straightaway,
because you might have been close to the circumstance, you knew
he was commenting upon all those hips going to waste, and on his
own ability to "outhump any white motherfucker on this motherfucking campus, Jim!" When he saw one of the two sisters with a
white boy, even in the daytime, he went wild. "Damn!" That
second "damn" told you many things about Hammie.

And the situation at Berkshire continued to be divided. The
whites went their way, many of them getting A's, because, as
Hammie put it, the university was theirs, and they were pro-
grammed from childhood to get A's; and the blacks—except those
who were integrating—roaring into the dining hall, laughing loud
like there was an epidemic of forced hilarity, at things which
normally back in the Black Mosque they would not laugh at, but
laughing loud publicly, as if with their voices they were standing
like so many cowboys rearing back on some secret inner strength
they had over these white boys; and they continued to get, mainly, C's, because, as Hammie said, "all the white profs are racist
bastards." But there was little open conflict A small conspicuous
group of whites was determined like National Guardsmen to fight
for the system and for what was right, and eventually to enter the
system at some cozy corner of its trimmed haircut of security and
of middle-class living. The others just wore their hair long, and
did their thing with pot and drugs. And the brothers were content
to "just slide, Jim, sliiiiide!"

Then, all of a sudden, something happened. No one noticed the
first indications, for no one ever expected anything like it to happen at Berkshire College. Mountain people, Hammie said, are
like farmers. They live off a land of hard and tough rules, like a
tradition. That is what Hammie said he meant when he told one
of his white professors during a seminar in political science,
"Man, this place ain't nothing but a motherfucker!" And that was
Hammie. He could translate the most complicated analytical
statement into the basest colloquialism, into the most ordinary

expletive. But whatever he said, whether you were present or you heard about it afterwards, it made you laugh. It made you laugh first, and then it made you think. And most of all, you found yourself thinking of why he so often, among his wise sayings, so blatantly said such deprecating things about himself. "I'm only a nigger from Roxbury ghetto, Jim!" was a favorite saying of his, spoken with fierce conviction, at the top of his voice, in the presence of white students even. Hammie would spit the words out, not so much as a testament to the source of his fierce militant blackness, but rather as an embarrassment to those few black students, who, Hammie reasoned, had forgotten in one of those pitiful moments of their integration, that being a college student at Berkshire was not the same thing as being white. So that, after all, if the truth was going to be faced, these "misguided" blacks had to be reminded with the pain of embarrassment, through Hammie's voice, that they were nothing more than "motherfucking niggers, too, Jim, so dig it!"

So that in this circumstance of place and in these strengths of vibrations, as Hammie liked to say, the bloods at Berkshire College came and went, went and came, carefree in their posturing, walking through the snowbound and unshoveled walks of the campus, pretending that they belonged here in the mountains; late for lectures, when they did decide to go; late for breakfast, raucous and starved by dinnertime, but leaving the uncooked, badly seasoned roast beef on the edges of their plastic trays. And no white student dared open his mouth to reproach Jack or Jim or Hammie. The bloods, the real brothers, sat by themselves, with their Afros or with Afro-hair braided in pigtails, and demonic defiance of whatever thought and suspicion and chip they might have placed upon their own worth, before and during their time at this exclusive college in the mountains. And they cut their style with combs and cake-cutters jutting from their stubborn hip pockets.

But all of a sudden, something happened. One detected the first signs when the weather became better. The bloods started to walk through the campus in sweat shirts, leaving their evil-fitting winter coats behind. They had bought them anyhow in disregard of the care and the style which they normally used for buying clothes—purple, green, or black silk trousers—as if they had all lived their lives in the deep, winterless South. At first, the change might have been seen as, and called, more of an aberration of behavior and of attitude than a change. Many had come to think of the attitude of the bloods to the white students as something fixed in the stars of their births. Anything like a change in this feeling was bound to be unthinkable. But a change it was. The bloods began sitting at tables with white students: at breakfast, at lunch, and at dinner. Those other blacks who had always done so were petrified. And the two sisters did not know what to do.

The change came first during breakfast. And it looked as if the first few bloods to sit with the whites were doing so because not many of the real brothers, and certainly not Hammie, who never awoke before midday, would see them so early in the morning. Nobody would ever see those "jive bourgeois black motherfuckers *in-tee-gratin'*, Jack!" The Black Dean happened to have got up early one morning, for some kind of administration business, and he decided to have breakfast in the student's dining hall. He saw a few bloods sitting with some white students, eating breakfast and talking. He couldn't believe his eyes. He hurriedly ate his cornflakes and french toast, having forgotten to take the five glasses of orange juice which he liked; and he rushed over to Baxter Building to meditate on the phenomenon. He was so worried about it that he took into his confidence the Dean of the college, a sallow-faced young man, with blond hair and badly fitting suits. "The black students are beginning to exploit the facilities of the college at last," he told his colleague in administration, in a whisper, in confidence. Getting the black students, the militants, and the middle-class ones, to exploit the facilities of the college to the full had been the Black Dean's aim for the two long years he was Dean of Minority Groups. During that time, he had worried about being a radical dean. Should he be a *black* dean, or a member of the administration, like the other white college employees? The bloods had, on more than one occasion, embarrassed him through small reminders that after all, not only had they made his appointment possible, but that he was just a "jive motherfucker!" Everyone, black or white, who met the enmity of these bloods, was a "jive motherfucker!" Hammie had been the mouthpiece of this ironical reassurance. "You ain't nothing but a nigger, Jim! Brother Malcolm was hip to your ass, Jack!"

But after talking to his colleague, the Black Dean, with a bit of the mission of the television white knight attached to his pride, was beginning to feel that his tough position with the bloods was the correct one: black students, whatever their social origin, in ghetto or suburbs, should have *one* motivation and *one* mission at a place like Berkshire College: "to get the best goddamn sheep-skin possible. Stop the shitting around about black nationalism. Remember that they're really white-blackmen, as the Indian chief said in the movie. And be cool. Shit, those niggers're more *white* than me, and I'm on the goddamn administration! Can you deal with that?"

The *in-tee-grating* beginning at breakfast was apparent right up until lunch, when most of the students were wide awake enough to notice the metamorphosis taking place. Word about it came to the President of the college, who made a note in his confidential file, reserved for ATTITUDES AND ETHNICAL DIFFER-ENCES OF BLACK STUDENTS AT BERKSHIRE. *TOP SECRET.* The President had become something of a figure in the Northeast by being misquoted once at a meeting of his faculty, and he made a point of writing this note himself.

What he had actually said at that meeting was, "*There is no intellectual room at Berkshire for the encouragement of black studies. We already have two black professors on faculty, one has tenure. And there is a black dean. To encourage racial view-points is not within the interpretation of the charter of this col-lege.*" His secretary had made the mistake—perhaps through fa-tigue, for it was approaching the end of fall semester—of leaving out the negatives in the first and last sentences. When the speech appeared in the Alumni Bulletin, the trustees drafted a letter of protest, and sent it to the President; but they kept a sealed enve-lope demanding his resignation, waiting to see how the alumni and the press would treat what the spokesman for the trustees termed, "this remarkable lack of prudence."

Then things began to happen. Some black students took up arms on another Eastern campus. The demonstrations spread and their demands for more black students and faculty and courses were reflected in the nation's headlines. All of which had nothing to do with the President's remarks at the faculty meeting. But, as if by magic, they were picked up and publicized as a notable example of academic realism and courage, and the President of this small exclusive college, tucked away in the forgotten moun-tains, became suddenly a national celebrity. "The most liberal and intelligent college president in the nation"—that was how the most influential newspaper in the country summed him up. The trustees suggested new ways and means for recruiting more black students to Berkshire, and they voted him a small increase in his salary. So this was why the President wrote this confidential note himself. He also called up the Black Dean, and asked him to have lunch with him in the Faculty Club that afternoon.

The Black Dean would get these invitations out of the blue, and at first they puzzled him. But it did not take him long to realize that there was a connection between each invitation and some variation in the attitudes of the college toward the black students and the faculty. All the employees of Berkshire College were white except for the two black professors, the Black Dean, and a cook for one of the fraternity houses. The Black Dean accepted the invitation in high spirits. He felt sure now he was on the right track. Only a few minutes ago the Dean of the college had assured him, "You're doing a great job," giving him the credit for this historical change. "Keep it up."

The Black Dean even was a bit disappointed that this was all the Dean could think of saying; but he had always felt that the Dean was not a very bright man. He knew he could make a much better Dean of the college. "Shit, man, I would whup those niggers' ass into such shape!" he used to tell his wife, just before they fell asleep after the Channel Seven eleven o'clock news. "Baby, those niggers' ass would be so whupped, that . . . " And he would dream of sitting in the College Dean's chair, in his office and with his private secretary; and of inviting the Assistant Dean, *and his wife,* to cocktail parties in his university-loaned house. "Shit, baby, just sit tight. For one more year! One o' these afternoons when I come home for lunch, I'll be telling you that from next month, I'll be the new . . . " The President was smiling as the Black Dean approached his table in the Faculty Club. Soon the President was talking about playing golf, that it was a shame that the Black Dean didn't make use of the facilities on the campus. "You don't mind if I call you Burt, do you? we're informal here at Berkshire, you know, and I hope you'll drop the Mr. President title you've been using to address me by, and remember always that I'm Cliff to you, that the time has come for you and me to have a little rap session, heh-heh-heh! . . . " And afterward, they walked back to the President's office. "Sit down, sit down, Burt . . . " Burt told the story to his wife that night as they pulled the blanket over their naked bodies, just after the weather. . . . "When I really dug what that motherfucker was into, I freaked out. Siddown, siddown, Burt, he says, and shit, baby, the only chair *I* could see, the only motherfucking chair I could see that he was pointing me to, was *his* chair . . . the President's chair. Ain't that a bitch? And then comes the bomb! Baby, when that bomb dropped, I thought I was in Japan. Hiroshima! The son of a bitch made me sit down, siddown Burt, and then he pulled this Polaroid camera from a drawer and took a picture of me sitting in *his* fucking chair! Then he took another one. Gave me one. Look! And kept one for him! Ain't that a bitch, though? . . . " And when he was deep into the trough of his first sleep that night, he saw Hammie appearing from behind a fence as you climb the slight grade from the students' dining hall, going up the slippery path beside the house where the football coach lives with his shaggy-haired dog which runs out at you, barking—there Hammie appeared wearing a pair of red-white-and-black trousers, red-white-and-black shirt, white tie as dazzling as the snow on the path, black socks which the Black Dean could see, because the trousers were worn high on the waist, a black jacket like an Edwardian undertaker's, and a black felt hat left over from Zorro and the days in the wild cowboy West, and pulled wickedly down a corner of his dark shades. And he could smell the grass Hammie was smoking, and could see it, at his lips. "Nigger, you smoking shit? In my motherfucking presence, nig-gerrr? 'Amma going see that your ass is kicked out of this college . . . "; and when that dream faded, the Black Dean was riding the horse of his wife's buxom thighs.

The weather turned warm. The bloods appeared on the field, on the first fine warm evening after dinner, to play touch football. Nobody had organized it. It just occurred. Hammie was naturally the quarterback, the "general" as he called it. He quarterbacked for the juniors against the sophomores. But the sophomores were stronger and keener and they hit hard and professionally, as if they knew that the white coach was watching them from his verandah with his shaggy-haired dog. The sophomores hit so hard that they caused Hammie to yell, "Do you motherfuckers think we's *white boys?* Shee-it! This is only a *game,* Jack!" But the sophomores had seen the coach in their dreams of greatness, and having a few overgrown jock-strap-full freshmen in their lineup, continued to hit hard; and once they made Hammie bend over for two minutes writhing in silent pain. "Smoking grass and playing touch football is a bitch, Jim"; and the white students on the same field, but in their own corner of the world, playing a girls' game of volleyball, stopped slapping the ball over the makeshift net and rolled on the ground in laughter. "Those motherfucking white boys!" Hammie hissed, and continued to evade the hard tackles of the misdirected, misguided but very conscientious sophomores, big as professional linebackers. That was the last game ever played on the Berkshire College campus in which all blacks or all whites played.

The very next evening the game was integrated. It began at dinner, which was veal cutlets with something on them like sawdust mixed in tomato sauce, and Hammie, always able to see the pleasanter side of college meals, roared, "This motherfucker *got* to be digested!" Leaving his dinner untouched, Hammie went on telling a joke about a white professor who had the best grass on the campus but who was still "not cool," and was a motherfucking racist, Jim! and then asked each of the bloods for a cigarette. No one had a cigarette for Hammie. Hammie then went on saying something about the "motherfucking white students who are more racist than the faculty, although they come on strong as Yippies, and shit like that," and all of a sudden, without a reason or rhyme, he got up and went to the next table where all whites were sitting, eating the veal cutlets, and said to a long-haired white student, "Gimme a cigarette!" The white boy stopped eating, dropped his knife and fork on the plate, kept the chewed veal cutlet in his mouth, some sauce dripping through his front teeth which had gaps between them, pushed his hand into the breast pocket of his green army fatigue jacket and took out a package of Kools. Before he had got the cigarettes out, each of the seven other white students sitting with him had theirs out too, and were offering them to Hammie. Hammie smiled. The white boys smiled. He took the package from the hand of the first white boy, who was now fumbling with his gold Dunhill lighter, chose one cigarette, smoothed the edge of the pack, handed it back, took one cigarette from each of the seven other white boys, put them in the pocket of his dashiki, and then held his lips squeezed tight around the first cigarette up to the hand of the white boy holding the lighter. The white boy's hand held the lighter firmly. He looked into Hammie's eyes. Hammie squinted his eyes, closed his hands over the white boy's, and said, "Thanks, Charlie." The boy's name was actually Charles. When Hammie walked back to his own table, the other bloods said, "Did ya get for us, too?" Hammie piled the glasses and the uneaten veal cutlets onto his plastic tray, got up, squeezed his lips more tightly over the cigarette, squinted his eyes in a half-smile, and said low to the table, "Cop for yourselves, niggers!" And the whole table exploded in laughter. The white boys nearby, inclined as always toward black humor, laughed also. They had not quite heard what was said, but they felt that the release in the laughter of the bloods meant it was groovy, and they themselves felt more relaxed.

Everybody on the campus was feeling more relaxed these days. The Black Dean met a black and very militant student the next afternoon in the hallway outside the office of Loans and Bursaries, and thinking that this student would, in these circumstances, and since he was alone, be more reasonable and open to less radical opinions, and thinking also of the change in the bloods, said to him, "I knew I was right, don't you think so, Brother?" The black student nodded his head, skinned a smile, and said, "Yeah, man! Yeah, you copped!" and hastily left. When the student got out of Baxter Building, where he had been to ask for a loan to pay for his long-distance telephone bill, and also to see whether the college would give him some money for his plane fare to California for the summer vacation, he wondered what the hell the Black Dean was talking about. Hammie loomed up somewhere on the campus, and when he heard about it, he said, "I *told* you that motherfucker's freaking out, Jim!" But Hammie knew what the Black Dean was talking about, and he added, "Ain't that a bitch?" The bloods were no longer seen sitting on the short wall near the dining hall where they would watch the white students of Erin House playing softball with a child's beach ball; and they were no longer standing by making ethnical and racial remarks when the whites played Frisbee, something which the bloods never did, which led Hammie to conclude that it must have been a white man's game. "Right into that shit! In-teegratin', Jack!" was the way Hammie put it, and he and the other bloods got down and did their thing with a panache and a style, as if they were eating Southern fried chicken and ribs and playing bid whist, which was *their* black thing over in the Black Mosque.

The bloods were changing. Those who had integrated before the change continued to be confused. At breakfast, which was served from seven-thirty until eight-thirty, the bloods were all there. Sitting all over the dining hall. Sitting with whichever white student they might have been in the line with, and no longer separated in a corner of the dining hall nearest to the kitchen, and occupying the three tables which they had claimed as theirs. And when not a single one of them had turned up for one of the three meals, these tables would remain empty. But the change was now like the change in the weather. In-teegratin', Jack! Like a bitch! Even at their games of boredom and ritual, bid whist and Tonk, you could see the bloods and white students sitting down around the low tables, smoking each other's cigarettes, but mostly the white boys', not that they were necessarily more generous, but because they were wealthier. Touch football had become an integrated sport, like the television version on Sunday afternoons. The bloods even got up in time for their eight-thirty classes. And some whites professors had to call the Dean of the college and inquire whether So-and-so, *a black student,* was actually registered because, "I'm sorry if I cause some feeling here, Dean, but I haven't seen that student in my class before, not even on the first day of classes, you understand of course, that I'm not implying that . . ." And the Dean of the college smiled into his voice which went over the telephone and then he called Burt. Everybody in administration was now calling him Burt. He called Burt through the thin eaves-dropping partition between their offices, and laughed with him, and made two coffees from the nearby machine, and sat down in his chair, while Burt, who was the most popular member of the administration these days, sat on the Dean's desk. The Dean of the college said, "Things are happening. We've even got the black students to go to classes at last." The Black Dean sipped his coffee hot and black, as he himself was black and now feeling beautiful, and he said, "Right on!" To himself he added, Those niggers're copping!

One afternoon soon after that, the black professor of history, a neatly dressed, moustached-cropped, short-haired middle-aged man, stopped Burt as he was getting into his car, and he said, holding onto the top of Burt's opened car door, "Could you tell me, man, I'm not sure myself, because naturally I haven't done any research on the topic in question, but it seems to me that the black students are going through some attitudinal metamorphosis, which as far as I can deduce, I mean, one couldn't conclude from this evidence that . . ." Burt cut him short happily. "Right on!" he said. But the black professor of history went on talking, ". . . now, I know, that a few days ago I personally had to take a stand with the black students in respect to their attitude toward my course . . . because some of them mistake rapping for discussing, and even although I am black like them, still I want them to understand that I am not going to give them A's in my African History course *merely because* they're black, and by the same token, I'm not going to give a white student a C because he's white. As far as I'm concerned, I'm black like them, but as an intellectual, I'm more concerned with their scholarly evaluation of the historical material . . ." "Right on," said Burt, and drove away.

The white professors spread the word throughout the campus: the black students are coming, the black students are coming. And indeed they did come: lectures were full again, the white professors saw for the first time the number of black students on campus, and their first reaction was, "Where are they coming from?" Some said, "I didn't know *we* had so many black students in this place!"; and others said, "I wonder whether we have a disproportionate number of them, to put the student population out of its national racial perspective?" One bearded white professor, known as the radical on the faculty, was worried by the relative numbers and the significance of those numbers in situations which made small numbers look like extraordinarily large and frightening numbers.

For instance, one morning, at seven-thirty, all of a sudden, all the bloods, through some luck of electronics, for some strange reason or other, turned their stereos high, almost as high as they could go, and the campus swung with "Oh Happy Day!" It was a beautiful day, a typical and beautiful New England day in spring, as many residents would describe this kind of a day to you, a day without the feeling of oppression which the bloods said they got every day of their lives at Berkshire College. Perhaps there was even a bird, which nobody saw of course, singing somewhere in some tree. And when the bloods blared this weather forecast into song, and the Edwin Hawkins Singers were happy as the birds, the four campus policemen came down on the doors and the halls in the Black Mosque, and in the black entryways over in the Freshman Dorms (although no music came from there), like thick slabby grimy hands slapping a cricket dead. One of the campus cops grew emotional and said, "Turn that fucking savage music off! You're disturbing the goddamn peace!" Hammie's record player was playing the loudest. "Dig it! the motherfucker *said*, check it out! he *said*, you niggers're disturbing the peace. *Not* the white students, he didn't say you're disturbing the white students, but *the peace*, Jack! Law and fucking order!" So they turned off their stereos, and the campus, already awake because the students were studying for exams, filed happily into the dining room for breakfast. The campus cops didn't know that the white students, those who were being disturbed, had really liked the idea of being disturbed by "Oh Happy Day!" first thing in the morning, after a hard night of studying.

With nothing else to do, since it was so early, all the bloods arranged to go to breakfast, all of them, all forty out of an enrollment of fourteen hundred, all one thirty-fifth of the student body, all three percent and a little extra bit, this "large number of blacks" lined up outside the dining hall this morning, and havoc reigned. The student at the head of the stairs as you come up into the dining hall dropped his pencil and notebook in which he checked and counted and saw to it that no student ate who shouldn't; he ran into the dining hall office at the rear of the meat cleavers and the large aluminum pots hanging like trophies, to ask the dietitian, "How many blacks registered to eat here?" She didn't know. But he made her look at the line of "cruel-looking blacks," and she changed her color. She immediately got on the telephone to check it out with somebody over in Baxter Building. The bloods kept on coming. When the first one was checking his eating credentials with the frightened student, the last one was still outside the dining hall building by the metal sculpture of something or somebody which nobody could determine. Some white students who were in the line further up ahead moved back and allowed the bloods behind them to move up in the line. The bloods were coming, and somebody called the President to ask him if he knew that there were so many black students registered here, because no one had ever seen so many of them together at one time. The President said he must check into it. "What's going on, Burt?" he demanded of the Black Dean on the telephone, even before the Black Dean had left home. When the telephone rang, the Black Dean was still lying on top of his wife; and on the radio, which came on automatically at seven, Roberta Flack was singing "Reverend Lee." The Black Dean smiled into the telephone in his hand, and said, "Mr. President, I can't tell you that." He looked at the telephone in his hand, as one would look at a ticklish problem, and afterwards he turned back to his wife and said, "White folks sure *is* crazy!"

Something had happened to their communications, but it wasn't anything which couldn't be patched up later that day, at luncheon at the Faculty Club, for instance. Or on the next day, Friday, when they now went trap-shooting together, a new experience for Burt, which he indulged in, through his love of guns and with the President's encouragement. Both he and his wife realized that something special had happened to his social prestige in the white academic community. The other two black wives on the campus heard about it. "Burt can't make it, I don't think, because as you know, Fridays is when he and the President leave to go trap-shooting," his wife would say, excusing him from a party. So the rupture in communications was nothing that could not be mended. Only last week, when news came to the President that the black students were taking part in seminar discussions and had actually started going to almost all their lectures, for the first time in the history of Berkshire College, the President had ordered a bottle of champagne from King's Liquor Store down on River Street, to decorate both the otherwise bare table in the club and to put a bouquet upon the breast of the President's "right hand man," as the President himself began to refer to the Black Dean. When the cork in the bottle went off, it sounded like a rifle shot in the peaceful dining rooms of this old sedate Faculty Club so high up in the mountains.

"What's going on, Burt?" he asked later that morning, when they were together in his office. His secretary was present and, for some reason which the Black Dean couldn't understand, was taking notes. He was standing facing the President, and the questions being fired at him. "What's really going on? What *are* they organizing?" The questions contained slight variations, but they pointed to the same implication, that the Black Dean was doing something awful behind the President's back. Into the President's mind flashed a picture of Burt and himself, walking through the wet grass, half-hidden in the fog and mist, and Burt with a gun walking behind. . . . "Burt, you can tell me what's going on, surely?" The Black Dean began to think of his wife lying under him, and of the words Roberta Flack had been saying at the very moment when the President had called; *do it to me!* . . . and he wanted to smile, but this was no time for smiling. After all, he was standing and the President was sitting in the President's chair, and Burt who was, at heart, in spite of whatever impression he made upon others, a very ambitious man, and had seen himself more than once in his imagination sitting in the President's chair, with his official capacity making it legal—Burt wanted to smile now as he was standing watching the President's chair. The President asked the secretary to leave them alone; he wanted to say something confidential to the Black Dean. "I feel as if you have betrayed me, Burt," he said, the moment the door was closed. "We have been close, you and me, we have always discussed things, like men, like brothers, as you people say. You and I. Brothers, Burt. What's going on now, therefore, all of a sudden? I have been fair to you, haven't I? You can't deny that. I have suggested your name for membership in my Country Club. I know, I know! you don't have to tell me . . . I know it's nothing like the things which still aren't done in this country or even around here. But it's a start. I know that. You are on the waiting list, and in a few more months, if everything goes well, you'll be *the first black member of this college* ever to eat his dinners at the Country Club, not that this is any great honor, as I said, but we're still in this damn country, aren't we? And I'll be there at your side! I've also nominated you to the Berkshire Gun and Rifle Club, so that you can keep your guns. Legal, you know. And you and me have been trap-shooting several times, when there were only two of us in the woods, with loaded guns, and I never *for one moment* ever thought . . . I even took your advice and built a gun panel and rack in my office, to give the place a little urbanity, as you suggested. Who did I come to? You! Your word, urbanity . . . bringing the suburbs back into the inner city, you told me that, and I did it, because it was a damn good idea. You told me that. And I did it, Burt. Because I had faith in you, because I could see that one day, not too far in the distant future, you'd be sitting right here where I am sitting now, talking to you, but you have . . ."

He left the rest of the sentiment dangling, and without any warning, he went over to the panel behind his desk and pressed a button. Part of the wall slid back and there was a gun rack with six double-barrelled shotguns and two beautifully wrought rifles. All of a sudden, it occurred to Burt that the President's building the gun rack in his office was like building an extension onto a house—it suggested permanency. The President threw one of the rifles, an M-16, at Burt. "I've never regretted taking your advice in acquiring this one. Try it out. It's your suggestion. Go on, try it out, take aim at something. Go on. Take aim at something, goddammit. You make me nervous just by the way you stand there being so goddamn cool. Burt, take aim at something . . ."

They didn't have luncheon together that day. The secretary told Burt that the President had a heavy schedule for the whole day. Burt walked over to the students' dining hall, crossing the grass lot in front of Baxter Building, which he had seen through the scope of the powerful and accurate rifle from the President's office a few minutes ago. Now from this position, he was seeing in the lens of his imagination the President's face mapped out against the rich black leather of his chair. *"Take aim at something, go on! Go on, take aim at something!"* The instructions hit against his head as he walked along the gravel path between the snack bar and the college theater building. *"Take aim at something, go on!"* But what was he going to take aim at? There was nothing he wanted to kill: hunting didn't please him all that much; no one he disliked so much that he wanted to kill him—or her: he thought, all of a sudden, of his wife, and their five children she had borne him in just under six years of their marriage, and he wondered why she couldn't go on the Pill, like any other ordinary middle-class wife. No, she believed in naturalism. Naturalism. Shee-it, I could take a shot at naturalism, right now! *"Go on, Burt, take aim at something, anything!"* He was holding the powerful weapon; and into his sights came Hammie. Yeah! Sometimes, he felt as if he could kill Hammie. Even with his bare hands. Yeah! he would like to "off" Hammie sometime. Yes! get his ass kicked and kicked out of this college, for Hammie was a pain in the ass these days: organizing the black students, organizing a back-to-lecture campaign without first having discussed the strategy with him, and he was *the* Black Dean, shee-it, who that motherfucker think he is, anyhow? He trotted down the last of the gravel incline before the parking space of the dining hall, his mind full of the meeting with the President, and he almost walked right into a pale green station wagon. He recovered from his thoughts quickly, and his disgust for Hammie shot into his mind like a bullet; and he had actually shaped the words with which he wanted to reproach Hammie, but as he was about to explode *"motherfuckerrrrrrrr!"* Hammie leaned his head and shoulders out of the window on the driver's side, and smiled. "How you doing, Dean?" All the Black Dean could see were the nicotine-stained teeth grinning at him, like a large derision. "Motherfucker," he said, not quite as harshly as he had intended. "The college should take away those cars, if y'all don't know how to drive the motherfuckers!" And he went into the dining hall, hearing Hammie's broad laugh behind just before the tires screeched.

He went in, trembling and frustrated, to have his lunch. Boston beans, wieners, bread, cole slaw, three glasses of milk, two glasses of orange juice, and a slab of cherry pie with a block of vanilla ice cream. His plastic tray was loaded down. He deliberately walked in the opposite direction from the "black tables"—although there was no such thing lately—*ain't messing with no niggers today!* He didn't look around too much as he put down his tray. So when he spread his napkin and looked up, he was slightly surprised that he was sitting at a table with white students. Suddenly, he felt relaxed: he didn't have to talk, he didn't have to rap about blackness and about the legitimacy of black students at a white college, which he found himself drawn into each time he sat with the bloods at a table. With these white students, he could just sit there and eat. This afternoon was his own. He was going to sit down and try to eat the bad food which the college dining hall served, and afterwards, he would even take a walk along the highway past the two motels, turn right, walk up the hill behind the dormitories and the dining hall, and return to his office. He didn't know what he was going to do when he got back to his office: the two secretaries in the outer office would look up at him as he entered, in that way which said they knew something was going wrong, something which involved him. So these two middle-aged and not very attractive ladies, he felt, would look at him and feel sorry for him. And the woman in the next office, the one in charge of the girls at the college (there were only about ten of them), well, this woman too would come out of her office with her coffee cup in her hand, her lipstick painted onto the white porcelain, and would find some common ground for opening a conversation with the two secretaries, which was bound to focus on the Black Dean. And he could expect that neither of the other two deans would be coming into his office this afternoon for coffee. They already would certainly know that something was wrong, because almost every day he had found some time between work and the President's invitation, to go with them to the gymnasium to play handball; and they would kid him about going trap-shooting with the President on weekends. He didn't know what he would do this afternoon. There were so many things he had to do, and none he could think of wanting to do. He couldn't even take aim when someone said, Take aim. He wondered whether he was wise in having taken this job as Dean in the first place. What was he aiming for in life? He had often looked through the lens of his conversations in bed with his wife, and he had seen himself sitting in the President's chair; and sometimes, when it seemed that just being on the campus had taken away even that ability to dream about a future, he would see Hammie in his lens and he would pull the trigger of his discontent and fire a few bullets into Hammie's body, just to show himself that he still had some guts left, and because, too, of what Hammie was doing to the less militant black students. But still he would not feel satisfied. He knew that he should not have recommended Hammie's admission three years ago, after the college had become morally bound to admit "black disadvantaged kids from the inner city." But there was one victory he did have over Hammie and all the other Hammies on the campus: not another one of them who showed any sign of becoming another Hammie, not one nigger like that would he ever again waste a word on, suggesting that he was suitable for admission to Berkshire College."This is no place for ghetto blacks, just because they are deprived," he would reason with himself, and sometimes with his wife. This college, Berkshire, was for middle-class blacks, decent people from decent homes . . . he himself had graduated from Berkshire in the days when there were only two black faces on the campus, and he didn't occupy administration buildings! . . . from decent families who could appreciate and "exploit" the facilities of Berkshire College, people with whom he would want to

drink tea on Sunday afternoons, talk with at meals when he went
to the dining hall to eat; people with whom he might even drink
a gin-and-tonic at one of the few cocktail parties he had to give in
his rented house.

He was walking now, aimlessly, to his office, and he was thinking that he should have put his hand in the money. In the petty
cash, in the funds for black students' entertainment, in some fund
for the *ABC* program at the college, and buy the Jaguar XKE he
had had his mind on for so long. But he was too honest. "You're
too goddamn honest to be a nigger!" his wife screamed at him
one night. "An honest nigger? And working for those racist bastards over in Baxter Building, shee-it. Burt, you're something else
altogether!" And this is what his wife had come to say to him, and
to regard him as, over and over. If he had only put his hand in
the money, if he had put his hand in his wife's ass more often, if
he had done this and done that, he told himself, he would not
now be walking back to his office without aim, as if he was a
black freshman again on an all-white campus.

He entered the door of Baxter Building, and he climbed the
stairs to his office. This afternoon the marble steps pounded
against the leather in his soles like a bad thought against his mind.

He reached the door of his office the same time that Hammie,
a half-mile across campus, was coming down the stairs of the
Black Mosque. Hammie was talking to two other bloods. They
were on their way to a class in Social and Environmental Psychology. It would meet only twice more that semester, and no blood
had yet attended Miss Vanderdikeman's classes, which were very
popular with the white students. Hammie had instructed the
bloods that for them to attend a class in Social and Environmental
Psychology taught by a woman from South Africa was tanta-
mount to offering themselves as guinea pigs for "that motherfucking racist bitch, a *rabbit*, Jack!" And of course, the entire
body of bloods agreed that "Social and Environmental Psychology was not *relevant*, right on!"—all the black students boycotted
Miss Vanderdikeman's class, except for the two black girls, whom
no blood on the campus regarded as redeemable or black. They
attended religiously. And they got good grades in it, too. Something had happened, therefore, for Hammie to be going with two
other bloods to Miss Vanderdikeman's class! But the whole shit
was changing, Jack! That's how Hammie had been putting things

recently: the whole motherfucking shit's changing, Jim! Jim and Jack were now going to all their classes, and the administration was more and more confused about the change in the bloods, although the administration had previously criticized the black students for not going to classes.

This afternoon was still a beautiful one. Some white students who were not hippies suddenly grew brave and walked about without shoes; and a few bloods wore waistcoats next to their skin. The grass was warm enough to sit on. There was a dryness in the air sufficient for Hammie and two bloods to enjoy a can of soda; and you could see them walking lazily across the campus, each man with a bright can of soda in his hand. And then one other *baaaad* mother came by with a paper bag in his hand and put it to his mouth, as if he was drinking something other than soda. As he joined Hammie, he passed the dripping paper bag from hand to hand, from mouth to mouth, in a perfect example of brother-hood, and then they all four began grooving and laughing and looking baaaadd and so cool.

And so Hammie and the three bloods decided to remain out-side the classroom and enjoy the day and the cans and the paper bag.

When they came to the path leading diagonally across to their lecture room, just beyond the Baxter Building, they stopped, just stopped like tired men, to catch their breath. When they first stopped, there were only four of them. When they first stopped, the President was in the middle of dictating a letter to his secre-tary about the Black Dean's application to the Berkshire Gun and Rifle Club. When they stopped and stood, as if on their haunches, rearing back like the black cowboys they had admired, tall in their hips, the Black Dean was puzzling over an admissions statis-tic that had to do with the projected increase of black students spanning the next two years, and the aims of the college concern-ing the coloring of the student body; and he was thinking of Hammie. When they first stopped, Miss Vanderdikeman was clearing her throat of the harshness from the mentholated ciga-rettes she smoked in too great numbers, like links on a long chain. Hammie was breaking up the bloods with a story about a friend of his from Roxbury, this baaad mother: "Motherfucker's slick, Jim," and they roared, the four of them roared and the noise traveled all through the business corridors of the administration building. A woman secretary looked out, and what she saw was four black students misbehaving themselves. The bloods roared because it was a good story. It was a story of a mother who was bad, a man who remained in the ghetto and copped, that's how Hammie put it. "That motherfucker *copped!* that motherfucker copped, Jim! He don't have no BA from no Ivy League college, but he's making twenty-five grand . . ." The bloods roared. They liked this story because it showed them that a man could be black and rich and remain in the ghetto, that he could be bad and remain in the ghetto. ". . . motherfucker drives a *hog*, Jim! russet-brown and *gold!*" Another blood, smelling out the rapping and hearing the laughter, joined the group below the President's window, in time to hear the word, "gold," and he screamed, "Check it out! check it out!" The bloods roared. Hammie was rearing back on his heels like a cowboy idol of his, and he was talking and acting and moving with his body in a total embodiment, in a complete involvement with the story and with the innumerable shades and nuances of the story. The bloods followed his movements with movements of their own, with harmony and rhythm. ". . . motherfucker wears only five-hundred-dollar suits, drinks Chivas Regal *straaaaaaight*, Jim! and lives in a ten-foot-square room *with a fountain!*—and colored lights flickering! Now, ain't that nigger the baddest? . . . can you dig it?" "Shee-it!" the bloods screamed at the top of their lungs; for there was not one blood among them who could look forward to this kind of living even after his graduation from Berkshire College, even after having been on the Dean's List for eight straight semesters; and they all wondered in their heart of hearts, while they laughed, whether it was worth making it through college for a diploma and recommendations and shit like that, when "this mother was so baaad," when a blood on the block was wiser, and was making it with more style than they could imagine. And their laughter had a strange ring in it, something like nostalgia, and still something like emulation, and something too like ridicule both for their position in the college and for their presence so near now to Baxter Building; and they thought, each one of them, at different times in the story, of their respective experiences walking through the corridors of Baxter Building, hat in hand in some symbolic time and circumstance, asking the Dean or the Provost for a break so that they might "slide through the course in political science one

more time, sir," or for "some bread to clear my motherfucking
head with some wine, Jim! this place is a motherfucker, and I gotta
get me some wine and some grass *this* fucking weekend!"; and
some of them thought of going mad in a place like Berkshire; and
some of them saw only the burnished hog parked beside a tene-
ment, with the blood coming out, and getting into it, and the foxes
sitting beside him, and he didn't have to crack a fucking book
studying a lot of shit like political science and social anthropology
and sociology and social psychology, when his own psychology
hadn't been conceived of yet in the textbooks and in the minds of
the nation's educators; it was better to be a motherfucking hustler,
Jim! and just sliiiide, than to be a black student at this Ivy League
institution and have to ask a white professor to *permit* you to slide!
Sliding was sliding, Hammie added, and if you was gonna slide,
you had to slide *with* style. And here was a mother who was sooooo
baaaaad, who lived in style, Jim! In style! "And a nigger ain't a
nigger 'cept he got *style!* Style, style, style, style . . . you see that
motherfucker dressed! cashmere coat draped over his shoulders
like if he is Superman, Jim. Dig it! or Zorro the Black . . ." And
they laughed even harder at this.

A white secretary looked out of a window on the second floor
and saw ten noisy niggers in the words of her heart, but in her
report to the Provost, she said there were "some black students
talking, sir." Upstairs, in his office, the President was sitting in his
deep black leather chair, rearing back, listening to classical music
on the campus radio station. It was his habit. He liked Wagner.
And he was listening to Wagner now. Somebody on the students'
announcing committee had found out the President's tastes, and
every afternoon, timed for the President's return from the Faculty Club, this enterprising student would put on his heaviest Wagner and lull the President into raptures of relaxation and of power
and of health and vigor. The small transistor radio was on the
desk and the President was listening, with his eyes closed and his
muscles completely relaxed. The gun rack was locked. His windows were slightly ajar.

Meanwhile more bloods were coming to hear Hammie. Hammie was three floors below, on the grass, telling his audience
about this "baaaad nigger who started his fortune with a half-
pound of heroin and a Greyhound bus ticket, and who got busted
once while *in transit* with the stuff," and who took the two Ital-

ian cops to his golden hog and said, "Here! here!" giving each cop a couple hundred eagles, Jim! 'cause my man was baaaaad! The bloods exploded like a volley of bullets: this was the supreme existentialist black man, able to deal with the motherfucking materialist white man, Hammie said, quoting from somewhere. Their voices reached a crescendo, and the President, just as Wagner closed his overture, just as the rolling timpani came to a peaceful end after the explosion of musical and intellectual torment and exertion. At the second roar, the voices of the bloods frightened him out of his reverie. He rushed to the window, and he saw all those blacks down there . . .

In a minute the Black Dean was summoned to his office. "What's going on?" His voice was like the clarinets in the music he had been listening to. The Black Dean looked down and saw Hammie. He saw Hammie using his arms, his mouth wide open, his brown teeth parted in a grimace of dramatization. The Black Dean didn't know the context of the grimace. "What's going on?" The President ordered Burt to tell him. Burt looked down again, and there were, all of a sudden, the forty black students gathered. The bloods and the others. To talk about the "large" number of black students on the campus was one thing: to see them gathered under the President's window was something else! Burt thought then of the students' demonstrations taking place in the country: Yale, Brandeis, Cornell, Columbia. But those were big schools and far away from the peace of the Berkshire hills. Then he thought again, or rather had the thought pushed into his head by the insistence of the President's voice behind him: yes! there was also Dartmouth and Amherst and Wesleyan, even Smith had had some black rumblings recently. And when this thought really registered, and when he realized how close he was living to the black students on campus and how far they had kept him from their deliberations, he panicked. "*What's going on?*" The President's question seemed to be a demand to know the reason, a demand that was repeating itself loudly, like a record stuck in its grooves.

The blacks were demonstrating, sir, he thought of telling the President. He even thought of exploiting his role as consultant. The President had called *him* first. The President had not called the Provost. Not the Dean of the college. Not even the campus police. Not the press. Him! He! The Black Dean! Burt looked at the President and saw only the large black leather chair in which he was sitting like some small frightened animal accustomed to being petted and being loved when it was disturbed. Burt saw the President's chair. Just then, a roar came up from the throats of the forty bloods three windows below. "What are we going to do about this, Burt?" The President got up from the chair and stood beside Burt. He was agitated. "What would you advise, Burt, in an emergency of this nature?" Burt waited. He didn't know what to advise. He didn't even know whether it was an emergency. The President walked the miles of nervousness from the door back to the window. Burt waited. Then he took up the telephone. His first thought was to call the town police. *If ever I had power on this motherfucking campus, I would've whupped these niggers' ass!* He remembered saying it, many times: he even remembered how his body became tense whenever he said it. He imagined how he would whup them; and he imagined himself cradling the telephone between his head and his shoulders, lighting a cigarette at the same time, and he waited in his mind for the answer at the other end; and as he waited, he actually walked round the desk and sat in the President's chair. The bloods were carrying on down below, "This is the President of Berkshire!" he imagined himself telling the police chief. He was talking to himself, as he swiveled in arcs, in the chair. Burt knew the chief personally. Only a few days ago he had been to the police station to get the chief to fix a parking ticket; and while he had waited, he saw a chart on the board showing the "Rise in Town Crime; a correlation between the increase in blacks at Berkshire College Campus and Local Crime." The chief didn't see him reading the chart. "Any time, Burt, boy!" the chief had said, fixing the ticket. Burt imagined the chief responding to his call to come and get the black students; and he could hear the chief's voice, *"Sure, Burt! sure! any time!"* Burt imagined the police coming. The police were coming. The police were coming. The campus cops, all four, were coming, too.

The bloods were coming to a climax in their appreciation of Hammie's supreme rapping performance. " . . . and one night, Jim, in Boston, in Roxbury, two cops came face to face with my man, and single-handed, my man *stomped their ass!"* Another blow for not attending the Man's institutions, but instead, "copping for yourself," as one of the black students, from Harlem, shouted. They were coming to the end of their entertainment, and Hammie had interposed in his narrative something about having a party later tonight at the Afro-Am House. The President heard only the words: *later tonight at the Afro-Am House.* And some of the bloods were going to go down the hill to King's Liquor Store to buy some wine, Boone's Farm Strawberry Wine and Bali H'ai, because some Smith College sisters were coming up. The sisters from Smith were coming. Burt got up from the President's chair and looked down at the bloods and focused his eyes on Hammie: "motherfucker! I could shoot your ass right now, I could take one automatic handle . . . " he said to himself, as Hammie jumped up in the air, overcome by his own glee. Motherfucker, I could take your ass right now! he was thinking, and he was imagining himself holding the President's M-16, and the police coming: *the town police were arriving stealthily; yes, they were coming through the back door, through the basement, actually, the door where supplies for the stockroom were taken in on the elevator, and he saw them mounting the marble steps as if they were wearing rubbers, and they had guns in their hands, and he imagined the campus police driving up in their campus stationwagon; yes! they drove up and parked beside the building on the other side from the bloods, and he could see them, like four thieves, which he had always called them, climb the silent stairs, and one of them would stop and drink a mouthful of water from the fountain, as he always did before climbing the stairs.*

Burt saw all this, lived all this, as he saw two bloods move off in the direction of the liquor store. The others remained laughing. A secretary from the office of admissions looked out and saw "all those blacks! oh my God, there must be hundreds of them!" and she called her unemployed husband in a neighboring town, and her husband told her it was a goddamn shame, that he was going to call the police and get them up there for those goddamn radicals. Hammie, down below, was saying, " . . . and the only thing I've learned at this motherfucking place in three years, is *three* words: *slide, rabbit* and *psychoexistentialism.* Ain't that a bitch? And I could have copped them words in Roxbury! *Shhheeeee-it!"* Niggers jumped for joy! They jumped up in the air, some of them ran to the steps of Baxter Building to sit down and recover from the exertion of laughing, and ran back; and some just jumped. And in the midst of their excitement, Hammie looked up and saw the Black Dean at the window of the President's office. He saw the Black Dean. And the Black Dean saw him. *Motherfucker, I could take your ass right now! right now!* The other bloods saw the M-16 in the Black Dean's hands. *"Crack-crack-crack-crack-crack! Crack-crack-crack!"* Somebody was screaming. *"Crack-crack-crack!"* The Black Dean held the weapon firmly in his hands, rammed into his shoulder, and screamed and screamed until he saw each one of the bloods fall to the ground. Hammie was the last one to fall. It took two rounds to put Hammie down. *Motherfucker, I got your ass, at last!* It was a happy scream, something like a hysterical laugh, something like the explosion of relief at the climax of an orgasm. The secretary on the floor of the admissions office had seen the black students jumping and laughing when she telephoned her husband, but when she came back to check, she saw them as they touched the grass, all of them, and then lie flat. She thought they were dancing. The President was at his window looking down. Burt was beside him, holding the high-powered semi-automatic weapon. He was like a man after a long-distance run: he was shaking from the exertion of his movements and emotions. I got the motherfuckers at last, he was saying to himself. The President looked at the gun and all he knew, all he was aware of, was that it was the same gun he had thrown at Burt that afternoon, demanding that he take aim at something. He was so far from the present, so far from the fact of the black students below, that he could not tell whether the noise he had heard as he watched Burt from his desk was really the noise of firing or the noise of Burt's voice. They both waited to see what the bloods would do next. "What's going on, Burt?" he asked Burt. "What are they going to do next?" Burt waited. "What's going on?" Burt put the weapon on the chair again and left the President's office. The President waited in his office window and watched, waiting for the bodies to move, and he watched and watched until it brought fuzziness and water to his vision, and in time he thought he saw blood oozing from various parts of the black students' bodies lying on the ground. But it couldn't be blood, could it? What would blood be doing down there? What was he thinking? There were only black students down there.

The two bloods came running back across the grass with four large paper bags. They had brought the wine. One of them held a bottle in his hand, and just before he reached the group, he put it to his lips. The President expected every man to jump up when they saw that. But they remained still. And just before these two bloods reached the others, they put down the paper bags, and while getting up, they happened to see the President looking down at them. He had his Polaroid camera, aiming at them. For a while they remained locked in their stares, and then they walked on to hand the wine over to the other bloods lying so still on the grass. "*Shee-it!*" one of them said, "are you niggers serious?"

Hammie lifted his head from the grass, gasped, and as though with the last breath in his body, in a dying man's voice, said, "*Playing* dead? Shit, we *be* dead! The Black Dean offed our ass from the President's office . . . " And just then, Hammie jumped up and shouted, at the top of his voice, "Motherfuckerrrrrrrrs!" The Black Dean had appeared on the steps of the administration building, and he faced, alone, the full venom of Hammie's curse.

Getting Lucky

LEONARD MICHAELS

LIEBOWITZ MAKES HIS HEAD out of cigarettes and coffee, goes to the westside subway, stands in a screaming iron box, and begins to drift between shores of a small personal misery and fantastic sex, but this morning in a dense, rigid crowd, he felt fingers and the flow of internal life forked into dialogue—himself, standing man who lived too much blind from the chest down, and the other, a soft inquisitive spider pinching the tongue of his zipper, dragging it toward the floor booming in the bones of his rooted feet, booming in his legs, sucked booming through his opened fly. "I was in the hand of an invisible stranger, with no how do you do, and Forty-second Street was minutes away." Liebowitz tried to look around. "Was everyone groping everyone else? Fads in New York spread to millions." To his left, a Negro lady with a tired sullen profile and fat neck the color of liver. Directly ahead, a man's pale earlobe; ravages of a mastoid operation; the million tension lines of an incipient scowl. Against his back, pillars and rolls of indeterminable architecture. On his right, in a miasma of deodorants and odorants, a highschoolish girl. Thick white make-up, black eyeliner, lipstick-blotched mouth. Her hair, bleached scraggle, hung. She stared up at an advertisement for suntan lo-tion, reading and reading and reading it, as if it were a letter from God. "Telling her maybe to wash the crap off her face." Her blotch hung open. She breathed through little teeth.

There were others to consider, but Liebowitz decided commu-nications issued from the girl stinking perfume, dreaming of the sun. "I didn't look down. I didn't look at her directly." Why not?

"I was ashamed." Is that any way to feel? "It's the way I felt." Besides, Liebowitz thinks a direct look would have seemed aggressive, "even threatening," and he says, "I didn't want her to stop." Of course he couldn't be sure who was doing it; and, whoever it was, perhaps couldn't be sure to whom it was being done. Did that make a difference? "Yes," says Liebowitz. "Between debauchery and election. Unsought, unanticipated, unearned. Not sullied by selfish, inadmissible need. I don't say filthy need." He makes a bland face. "It felt good. Some might call it a 'beautiful experience.'"

In effect, eight-thirty A.M., going to work, crushed, breathing poison in a screaming box, Liebowitz thought he was having what some might call a "beautiful experience." He didn't look down. He didn't look directly at the girl. Liebowitz is a native New Yorker; he retained an invulnerable core of natural sophistication. He felt hip. He felt. So many years in the subway without feeling or feeling he wasn't feeling. "Getting and spending," he says. And now he had gotten lucky. He could think of nothing he had done to account for it, which was the way it could be—"Had to be?"—if the experience were miraculous, beautiful, warm, good. Like the inexplicable sun shining in the advertisement. Or, for that matter, in the sky. Lucky, thrilled, maybe beatified, and all of it assumed with dignity. Liebowitz is no squealing TV housewife who wins two refrigerators and a week at a Mafia hotel in Vegas. "No." He got lucky and floated half-blind, delicious, cool, proud to be a New Yorker and chosen. He floated above a naked ferocity which, he admits, he couldn't call his own. "The emblem and foundation of my ethical domain—wife, child, responsibility of feeding them, the 'Mr.' on my tax forms—and yet if someone had said, 'Let's find the guy who belongs to this hardon,' I'd have led the search." Despite denials and scruples, Liebowitz says, "I had a general, friendly hardon, aimed nowhere, and even without an object, my sensations were like love."

He came.

Fingers squeezed goodbye, replaced him, zipped up, slipped away. The train stopped at Forty-second Street. Doors opened. The crowd shuffled hugger-mugger hugely to the platform. The man with the incipient scowl stepped away, a flash of camellia on his pant's leg, melting toward the cuff. Liebowitz looked elsewhere. Bleary, ringing with a chill apocalyptic sense, he was pressed loose and dopey into the crowd's motion. Once in motion, he was soon pressing himself into it, popping up on his toes, peering over heads. The girl with the deathly hair had disappeared. On the platform now, amid figures going left, right, and shoving by him into the train, Liebowitz was seized in a confusion of vectors, but, gathering deep blood force, *his* direction, himself, he thrust right, on his toes, and saw it—limp, ghoulish scraggle flying away like ghostly light. Her hair. Exhilaration building, beating in him like hawks, he felt his good luck the second time that morning. Could he do nothing wrong? "This is life," he says. Whatever it was, Liebowitz is not one for quickies. He is a serious, impressionable man. He gets involved. "It has to do with the way I was brought up. What I'm saying is that husband and father, Phillip Liebowitz, who lives in the West Nineties, who is an editor in a publishing house, who chased down the platform after a bleached, skinny, perverted bimbo, was Liebowitz, the husband and father . . . Nothing explains it if that doesn't."

To let things end in the dingy, dirty, booming oblivion of the Forty-second Street subway station would be a desecration of feelings and a mystery forever, he thought, chasing among benches, gum machines, kiosks, trashcans, and hundreds of indifferent faces.

She went up a flight of stairs, quickly, quickly, and, painful to Liebowitz, as if she didn't care to know he was chasing her. Was there nothing between them? "That's what I wanted to know," he says. Psychological consummation, now and here, in subway light, under low ceilings, in the pressure of heavy moving crowds, was imperative. He caught her. He caught her against the door of a ladies' room. The instant she pressed it he caught her arm, a thin bolt, and stopped her flight and swiveled her into his eyes. "Miss," he said, staring, beginning to say, "You know me, don't you?" A skinny, weightless, overwrought rag of girl reeking in his close, tight grip. A girl. It whispered, "Get the claws off, motherfucker, or I'll kick your balls." Whispering fire, writhing, murderous, not a girl. Liebowitz let go.

The boy twisted into the ladies' room. A dozen faces bloomed in peripheral vision. "Like vegetables of my mind," says Liebowitz. A lady in a hat said, "Creep." Beneath the hat, small, shrill eyes recognized Liebowitz. She said "Creep" as if it were his name. "Mister Creep," he muttered, pushing away through a viscous liquid of their attention. He didn't run. But he was ready, if anyone moved toward him, to run.

In the brillant, windy street Liebowitz hailed a cab. Before it stopped he had the door open. The meter began ticking. Ticking with remorseless, giddy indifference to his personal being and yet, somehow, consonant with himself. Not his heart, not the beat of his devouring viscera, yet his ticking self, his time, quickly, mercifully, growing shorter. "I'll be dead soon," he says, "tick-tick-tick."

The driver said, "*Where*, mister?"

"Nowhere," said Liebowitz from the creaks and shadows of the back.

"You can sit in the park for free. This is costing you."

To Liebowitz the smug, annoyed superiority of the driver's tone was Manhattan's theme. He ignored it, lit a cigarette, breathed in consolations of technology, and said, "I want to pay. Shut up."

In Search of a Missing IUD

ANNE HIGGINS

DEAR DR. LUNT,

You remember the other day when you had me trussed up on
the examining table like a chicken and told me for my own reassurance, peace of mind I think you said, that I should have an
abdominal X ray made; that you would write the instruction on a
slip of paper: "For the presence of a missing IUD," to be handed
to the X-ray man . . .? It struck me then, as now, as a comic line. I
wonder that you didn't see the humor of it. I suppose in your line
of work these little physical ironies cease to be funny. Or maybe
you simply deem it more politic not to snicker at your patients'
dilemmas, at least not in front of them.

To sidetrack a little bit, because I've never had the courage to
ask directly, what makes a man decide on an Ob-Gyn specialty? I
can't help but think that as a day-by-day way of making one's
living it must be a bore. To peer at nothing but the hind quarters
of trussed-up women. *Chacun à son goût*, I suppose. Still. My
apologies for getting personal, but remember that you asked a
great many personal questions of me and on the strength of my
answers made a great many personal comments and judgments. I
must confess that I was rather offended by the whole interview,
however professionally motivated your questions and well intended your advice. I suppose it's nothing more than a matter of
pride—I have an MA in English and a PhD in Comparative Literature—and I do hate to be talked down to. (You wouldn't have
expected a PhD in Comp Lit to have ended a sentence with a
preposition, would you. To down hate to be talked?) Frankly you

284

sounded like the Doctor's Advice column out of *Redbook* magazine. And I must say that your hands are unusually small. I'm not being indelicate and I'm sure that you know what you're doing, but analogously speaking, would you expect an extremely short-fingered man to go into concert-piano work? What I'm trying to say is, is it possible that you're hampered professionally by your small hands? Personally speaking, is it possible that you missed something you would otherwise have found had you been more generously endowed? Manually, that is. Look, the fact of the matter is, bluntly, this: you thought, via your probe instruments and look-see devices that the IUD was still there but you couldn't find the nylon strings that would indicate its presence to you. Now: if you think the IUD is still there then where could the nylon strings have gone? Surely they're not wafting around up there in sub-uterine breezes. All right, I'll have the X ray made to make sure of what's where. But the reason I went to you in the first place was to avoid just such an ambiguous mess as this. I have no professional quarrel with you, but at this point I do wonder about the possible professional handicap of your hands.

Dear Father Zimmel,
    Just a quick note from a former student of yours. You may remember that I took your adult theology courses off and on for five years. I was that striving, conscientious woman in the back of the room who beleaguered your life for so many years. Your eyes would shine with Holy Spirited light as you put the one of little faith in her proper place: i.e., down. Oh I know you, Father, you can't deny your venomous delight, your wicked pride in your debating skills. (Was it a subject for confession, this theological hubris?) But I know myself too, a pseudo-student of Voltaire and Diderot, a one-time admirer of Plato's Philosopher-King, a long-time disciple of Marx the Idealist, a camp follower of Dorothy Day, an early devotee of Teilhard de Chardin (did *you* ever get through him? Ah, gotcha!), an enthusiast at the same time of Catherine the Great, Hamilton, Jefferson, Walt Whitman, Ezra Pound, Henry Miller, Thérèse the Little Flower, Genet, Bertrand Russell, Dietrich Bonhoeffer, *yes* to Meister Eckhart, Phyllis McGinley, and Betty Friedan. Paradoxes, paradoxes. And guilty of rationalizations, neuroses. I never got anywhere with any of them; unlike John the Baptist I was a reed shaken by every wind,

swayed from right to left depending on the suasiveness of the breeze. How I used to pore over those books and pamphlets on the Church as Magister, the pronouncements on authority and obedience, the summonses to the logic and truth of Natural Law. In spite of them and your eloquence I remained unconvinced. Married to a Catholic, I practiced the precepts of the Church. (I'm sure you remember me now: I was that lady who was *always* pregnant.) On my own I decided to summon a different natural law into account: the one concerned with the point of diminishing returns. You would consider yourself justified in a good theologically sneering belly laugh. God is not mocked, His Law will not be abrogated by the libertine advances of twentieth-century science. Madam, I can hear you thunder, do you understand now that the Hound of Heaven will pursue you into every wickedly free-thinking gynecologist's office that you enter?

Well, Father, what is at stake? The Pascalian Wager? What it boils down to is this: candy is dandy but nothing at all would be safer. Galilean, thou hast conquered.

Dear Sister Seraphim,

I've been meaning to write for months, to tell you how much I enjoyed seeing you again; and really how impressed I am at the changes that have taken place in the last fifteen years. Nuns certainly have become swingers, haven't they? No more of those ridiculous social censures (you probably don't remember, but I do, that I spent my whole last senior semester campused as a punitive result of my contempt of those censures); full-fledged departments now in soc., psych., and poli sci.; a mixed drama department, taking advantage of nearby men's colleges (didn't you—honestly now—want to writhe at the sight of girls playing Lear and Othello?); Saul Alinsky and Paul Goodman invited to speak on campus. No administrative pronouncements on the proper length of skirts . . . Talk about progress!

Could I interject here that nineteen years ago, when I was in your freshman philosophy class, you gave one of the most brilliant lectures I've ever heard, on Augustine's concept of time. All these years and I've never told you. Ah, sins of omission.

One jarring note: it disturbed me—it bugged me, if you want to know the truth—that you referred to Alinsky as "a smart Jew." Really, I felt that was beneath you; certainly it was hitting below the ecumenical belt. I've often wondered since whether it slipped out as a remnant of preecumenical indoctrination or whether you cast it out as a barb to me. At any rate I didn't challenge it, I let it pass. I should have said something. But a first meeting in fifteen years . . . one tends to be polite, one is awed by the passage of time. And plain old nostalgia. Anyway, for the record, I object to stereotypes. Particularly, you middle-class-lace-curtain-Irish nun you, ones that refer to Jews.

One more thing for the record: if it appears in the Alumnae News that Mrs. Michael Callahan, nee Leslie Goldman, wife of the successful Omaha attorney and busy mother of eight, visited St. Rose's over the holidays and had a nice long chat with Sr. Seraphim . . . boom! There goes my annual contribution. I can see it now: "Leslie Callahan, who incidentally holds a graduate degree, is a shining example of the Educated Catholic (sic) Woman we try to turn out here at St. Rose's. Welcoming each new bundle of joy as they appear in annual succession, Leslie realizes the tremendous advantages of her educational background as a guide for teaching and nourishing these tender souls entrusted by God to her care. As she told Sr. Seraphim . . ."

Well, I won't have it. I was long gone from St. Rose's, and immersed in (and rather exhausted by) an arduous process of "finding myself" at Columbia . . . when along came Mike Callahan, that handsome Irish charmer with glittering teeth and eyes burning blue pockets of salvation and ambition. Save me from myself, would Mike Callahan. Redeem the Left-wing Jewess. Impose order on anarchy, truelove on falsesex. What could be more seductive? I fell hard and fast, swept off my feet by the passion of chaste kisses. Who needed a career, a sterile PhD, when Love beckoned in the marriage bed behind the altar? I took all the pre-Cana courses, signed everything, all the dotted lines everywhere. Sewed up everything tight. Including myself. And little heaven-sent Callahans appeared with the regularity that other women get their periods. Of course I love my children, and Mike is generous about providing a weekly cleaning woman, a personal allowance, and so on. The point is: what's the point? What's the point of enshrining a fertile woman? Fertility, like rain in season, is easy to come by. One prays against droughts but against floods too. If one prays at all and/or has any common sense. At any rate the Callahans—Successful Corporation Lawyer Michael Callahan and

His Lovely Family—appear regularly in the Omaha press. Mrs. Callahan is expecting her third child, her fifth, her seventh, her eighth. The fantastic Mrs. Callahan has just given birth to her thirty-fourth child. Mrs. Callahan, in spite of her busy schedule, finds time for community work, is active in many charitable and social organizations, and is on the board of the Omaha Arts and Culture Program. Mr. Callahan is an outstanding Catholic layman, well known in the business community, leader of the Anti-Smut Campaign, "a dabbler," he laughs modestly, "in politics," and twice voted Mr. Omaha by the Omaha Chamber of Commerce.

Dear Sister Seraphim, do you realize that some of the priests we have over for dinner are still disgruntled over the introduction of lay participation in the Mass? That Mike and I didn't speak to each other for three months before the last election? That Mike Callahan, that outstanding Catholic layman-lawyer—and *here's* a choice bit of *sub rosa* gossip for you—contributed fifteen hundred dollars toward the purchase of a neighboring house, in a nonexistent family's name, in order that it wouldn't be purchased by "undesirable elements" (read: a Negro dentist and his family).

Well. Greetings from Omaha. I didn't intend this to be so personal. I understand there are great changes going on which have not yet hit this acreage of the universe. Blessings on you and forge ahead! It was nice to be East again and to see you after so long, even under the circumstances. P.S. My late father used to ponder—with sly humor—why so many nuns took the names of male saints: Sr. Mary Michael, Sr. Francis, Sr. Paul, Sr. William Marie, etc. Frankly, if you want to know my honest opinion, I can't see names like Sr. Celestine, Sr. Illuminata, Sr. Immaculata, or Sr. Seraphim either. P.P.S. I'm sure Father, wherever he is, thanks you for your prayers. He was a secularist most of his life but he was a *good* man.

Dear Mr. Herzog,

I'll get right to the point: *don't* settle for Ramona. I know you have your needs, your faults, your weaknesses like everybody else, but the more I think about the possibility of that liaison, the more I think it would be a bad mistake. A really bad mistake. You know what would happen, she'd sap your creativity in a wink. No no, that's wrong. Gradually. You wouldn't even realize it was happening until you found yourself so thoroughly attuned to Food, to Culture, to Ramona's Orphic rites that you would never even have the desire to take up your pen again, never mind the strength. You would complain, only once, and only of a very slight headache, and there would be Ramona: "Oh no, Moses darling, don't tire yourself. Rest now." Perhaps she would put on Egyptian music to soothe you—though I have more than the suspicion that after a while the Egyptian stuff would go, you'd be getting Mantovani, don't kid yourself. Remember that Ramona is in her late thirties and that these exotic binges become tiresome, they're *wearing* on a woman that age. Ramona too will be getting headaches, but not slight ones. Huge ones. And then there will be lowered blinds and vinegar cloths for her forehead; no music at all, not even Mantovani. But for the present Ramona will soothe you, comfort you, build up your still undernourished ego. Ramona understands everything, anticipates your every desire. After a while you will want to put your *own* sugar in your coffee. You think you will scream if you hear the sympathetic assent of "poor Moses" one more time. (And you will feel guilty about that precisely because Ramona *is* a dear, good woman and undoubtedly she *does* love you and want your happiness.) But for right now, Ramona will put on her clanging Egyptian music—oh yes, I've heard those sensuous wails—and dance tenderly naked for you, clad only in Vita Dew Youth Emulsion, jingling jangling gold bracelets and her black lace underpants. (Panties to women like Ramona.) Oh God, and the high heels of course. –

Moses, that's the crux: don't marry a woman who Prepares herself. At thirty-seven or so she's a looker still with superb shoulders and good breasts—and by your own admission the shape of a woman's breasts is important to you (as appalling a weakness as I find that to be in you, still it's honest, it's an honest weakness)— but think, Moses, think that when Ramona is forty-seven and her whole life is a dedicated, consuming passion to keeping those shoulders soft, that bosom high and firm, those Orphic elements trim. Hours, whole days will be spent Preparing herself. At sixty, after a month of grim, self-disciplined Preparations, she will still be standing coyly in the bedroom door (the bedroom lighting will have been rearranged to forbid harshness at any hour) and asking, "Moses darling, do I please you?" *That* is what will become of your life, you a domesticated poodle leafing through Ramona's magazines, waiting for the mistress to appear, in order to give a few appreciative barks (quacks, the old quack-quack phenomenon, as you so well described it) and be led, sniffing tamely and with an increasing exhaustion, through the hoops of the Orphic rituals.

I sound shrill. Perhaps I am simply jealous of Ramona. Ramona, after all, is a woman of the world, perfumed, a cooker of fancy shrimp and arbiter of dry wines. She has the good sense to serve chilled grapes for dessert and not strawberry shortcake; she attends lectures and is sexually mature. (I suppose I hate her because she's a realist at heart as well as a narcissist.) Certainly Ramona regards Precautions as a necessary part of Preparations. Ramona knew that when she was sixteen. How do some women know all about these things and manage them successfully? I assure you that other women are not so fortunate in these affairs.

At any rate, I beg you not to marry Ramona. I feel no immodesty about proposing myself; on the other hand, no shame, only a little sadness knowing you wouldn't have me. I used to be one of those dungareed, flat-chested, hawk-nosed beauties that are prone to prowl around Eastern universities talking literature and art in coffee houses and crummy pubs. After eight children I am still flat-chested and hawk-nosed but I have acquired a mid-aged, mid-west spread. They like wide-hipped women out here; their greatest compliment is to ask if you are a local girl. Wealthy Nebraskan businessmen would overlook (forgive!) my Semitic nose for the pleasure of my heavy thighs. Faagh, I look down my fine curved beak at them. Go eat corn, man, you and I could make no good music together. On the other hand, I see myself clearly on the Ludeyville wavelength, attuned to your marvelous old place up there, running green through the summers, crouching low by fires in winter. The acreage, the solitude, the physical work involved in keeping up a place like that: bliss. Just that. Real work pleasures, like driving nails into hard wood and bringing an abandoned garden to ordered life. My husband calls the carpenter, the plumber, the electrician. Appliances whir softly, constantly. Things that go whir in the night. How blissful the silence of the Berkshires. How divine a stove that didn't blind you with chrome, I could be happy in Ludeyville. I repeat without shame, I could make you happy. No go, eh? Moses in the fullness of his Jewish heart may love children, but not eight little Callahans and their wide-hipped Omaha ma. I don't blame you for a minute, it's a preposterous idea.

I didn't start out intending this proposal at all. I started out giving you a little piece of well-meant advice on Ramona, which I will now (tiresomely) repeat and for the last time: don't do it. The temptation is great. But dear Moses Herzog, you are too close to sainthood to give it up now for a few years of mortal happiness. The end. And anyway you probably wouldn't even be that happy.

Dear Gypsy,

Remember that time you and Jon were living in Lima and you got stoned on pisco sours one afternoon and the Terrible Thing happened? After four years I still giggle thinking about it. There you were, smashed as could be, and in desperation hanging your head over the toilet when Jon comes staggering in, cross-eyed drunk, and says, "Gypsy darling, let me help you" and *drops the toilet seat on your nose.* I'm laughing now, just at the thought of that letter. You thought for sure your nose was broken, the poor bridge was bent all out of shape and it swelled immediately and turned seven shades of green and purple and you had dinner guests that night. And you couldn't say a word. As I remember, you made some feeble excuse about bumping into a doorway in the middle of the night, and everyone thought Jon had beaten you up and exchanged raised eyebrows over the dinner candles. You couldn't even write to anyone about it, except me. That always struck me as the funniest part, not being able to explain it. How can you say: my throbbing nose is big as a potato because my husband dropped the toilet seat on it. It's like suffering from hemorrhoids. You can complain in company about a migraine headache, about having cancer, ulcers, sinusitis, arthritis, neuralgia, neuritis. But you *can't* writhe on the edge of your chair and moan Oh my aching ass!

Which brings me to the point of this letter. To whom else could I write about this comedy of the absurd? Remember at Father's funeral when you advised me that if I didn't want to go on proliferating like a rabbit I Should Do Something About It? Well, I did. I went to the most discreet gynecologist in town and got one of those squiggly loop-de-loops. And you know what's happened to it? I don't either. Neither does the Gyn. Maybe it's there, maybe it's not. I'm supposed to get an X ray to find out. What's Mike going to say when he gets a bill for one flat abdominal X-ray plate? I can always pay cash, that's not the real problem. It's simply the psychological effect it has on me. Frankly, at this point I feel like a damned sneak. I don't agree with Mike, I think he's all wrong on a lot of issues, but there's a certain basic honesty and integrity that must be preserved in a marriage if it's going to work at all. It was bad enough having to sneak to the Gyn, but now this sneaking off to the X-ray man . . . where did I read once that guilty people get caught because they have a subconscious *need* to get caught? I feel like the unholy alliance of Freud and the Catholic church has teamed up, in a spurt of black humor, to get me. (Good grief, not only guilt but paranoia. What next?) Mike is simply intransigent on the whole issue. He was furious with me even for talking to the priest to get "permission" to use the Pill (if I never read another article or listen to another discussion on Morality and the Pill I'll die happy). His final words (cold, but concessive) (for him) were that if I wanted to take The Pill (why do they always capitalize it, like some divinity or higher institution) he wouldn't object though he certainly didn't approve of "thwarting Nature" like that. (When he had that kidney operation last year he darn well had an anesthetic and I didn't hear any objections *then* about "thwarting Nature.") Anyway, it was at that point I decided *I* didn't want to take the Pill. Talk about interfering with Nature! Why should I let my body chemistry and whole hormone system get thrown out of whack. So off I sneaked to the loop-de-loop man and only to have the Final Solution turn out like this.

What's really funny about it is that the whole thing is right out of a best-seller. Some Mary McCarthy character would get herself in a situation like this. The girl goes to the clinic and gets her device. Three months later she goes back for the routine checkup and they can't find it. Trauma. She comes home, expecting her boyfriend to take her in his arms and say something consoling like, "Never mind, love, we'll find another one." Instead, bored by her hysterics and uninterested in the femaleness of the problem anyway, he is crass, callow. He finally says something really boorish, like, "What do you expect me to do? Send up a search party?" The girl sobs, rages. She accuses him of not loving her and by then she is right, he doesn't, he couldn't care less. He takes up painting and hashish again, and she goes home to Mother. There's even material here for a television script, one of those deadly family situation comedies. Outline: everyone loses something and finds it again. Junior's lost dog finds its way home (accompanied, of course, by a litter of pups—cute!), Sister discovers the lost Atlantis (in the encyclopedia—educational!), Pop finds his misplaced pipe on the roof (hilarious!—American Pops are such sweet, inept bunglers), Mom discovers her missing IUD (in the garden? *in the asparagus patch?* We just lost the sponsor), and Grandma finds the lost chord. Sound of a great Amen as the camera pans to a long shot of the mountains.

Dear oh dear, Gypsy, how did identical twins ever turn out so different as we? You still barren after three marriages and I caught up on the proverbial horns over this idiotic birth-control business. I know your childlessness is a source of great sorrow to you but truly, Gypsy, I couldn't hand over even one of my children, not even to you who I know would love it dearly and spoil it rotten. (I'm still not sure whether when I saw you at the funeral you were serious or facetious about that proposal.) I'm a neurotic and at times a crappy mother but I have this *thing* about my kids. On the other hand, I often envy (read: turn pea-green with frustrated jealousy) your freedom to travel, to indulge your artistic and intellectual caprices, to meet the Beautiful *and* the Interesting People! (*We* are on a *tu-toi* basis with the chairman of the State Republican Club. Oh, we are *Important* People!) I could even get interested in politics—if politics were the subject at hand and not wheeler-dealer political games. These disgusting exhibitions of avarice and cynicism which we entertain in our living room are what are known as grassroots politics. Hear my cries of disavowal . . . And yet what am *I* contributing to the Betterment of Mankind? Well. More later.

Dear Father,

I've just been writing to Gypsy and wondering how the two of us, she and I, managed to turn out so unalike. But now I am thinking, No, we're not really that much different. The real mystery here is how you managed to turn out two who are so different from *you.* Also, I was writing to Sr. Seraphim and ended up with some inane postscript defending you as a "good man." I don't know why. I suppose it has something to do with the old De

Mortuis etc. theme. And in the conversation I had with Sr. S. when I went to see her after the funeral, I laid it on quite a bit thicker than merely a good man. I made you out to be one of those heart-of-gold humanists; Father, forgive me, I had you embracing Orthodoxy at the very end, and not only buried with your *tallis* in the casket but facing toward Zion with a little sack of Israeli soil under your head. I don't know what got into me. I suppose maybe I just wanted to one-up her with religion. I can hear you rattling your coffin with laughter. Even worse, and this will really tickle you, she fell for it. The only thing that would have impressed her more would have been a deathbed conversion to Catholicism. However, the Orthodoxy bit was quite dramatically correct. I conjured pictures of Yahrzeit lights and keening relatives rending their garments . . . I'm not proud of myself. I suppose deep down I always wanted you to be exactly that sort of man who would have a funeral like that.

When I was growing up—and Gypsy too—we craved the identity that other kids had. They rebelled against their immigrant parents or grandparents, when they went to college they had nose jobs done and pretended not to understand Yiddish, but Father, we were steeped in European readings, how we wanted you to grow a long patriarchal beard, to strap on phylacteries and sit swaying and wailing and muttering ancient prayers and incantations. How we used to hope that one of your silvery-laughed lady friends would turn out to be a Jewish mama and light candles on Friday nights. Your funeral, by the way, was filled with these ladies, aging now but heavily mascaraed, all with lacquered hair, both young and old—both men and women too, yes, Father, they all turned out—all trilling in their thrilling theatrical voices, a regular chapelful of preening peacocks. I think half of them came to meet their agents. If it's any comfort to you it was a grand affair. The embarrassed rabbi, wordly fellow though he was, broke out in a bad case of hives. He was assisted by a nondenominational minister whose chief claim to fame is that he once officiated at the marriage of a homosexual pair in an East Village apartment; his homily on tolerance is still widely remembered. The funeral cortege was a status admixture of limousines and roaring Hondas: who could be farther In or farther Out. At the final chapel service several ladies fainted from the heat, and Gypsy's purse got snatched. Wild. It was right up your alley.

Gypsy and I didn't think it was very funny. Gypsy, in fact, became so enraged at the oleaginous minister that she threatened to report him to the Better Business Bureau. (That *did* strike me as funny but she wouldn't laugh about it even later.)

I'm thinking that the reason "good man" sticks in my craw was not anything to do with your succession of ladies—though by what quirk of paternal tenderness did you keep them hidden from Gypsy and me for so long?—but with your diabolical refusal to make any judgments except as they concerned pleasure. You didn't mix the sacred and the profane, you refused to acknowledge any distinction. Thus you were not a bad man or a good man with a neuter neutral laughing man. I'm convinced that the only reason you honored that absurd deathbed wish of Mother's to send one of us to a Baptist and the other to a Catholic college was because you found it so outrageously funny. Ethical Culture Mother's half-Jewish daughters separated and sent off at age seventeen to cope with the formal rigors of Christian theology. And you waving a debonair handkerchief at the train station and laughing like a madman up your agnostic sleeve. Good God, what a joke. I must hand it to you, you preceded the black humorists by forty years. You were op/pop art fleshed out. Really Father, you would have enjoyed your funeral. You knew all along you were going to die. It was your best joke, your lifetime *coup*, and with unerring sense of theater you saved it for last.

The only good thing about your funeral, really the only decent thing that happened during that whole fluttering travesty of death and burial, was a meeting I had with the Anderssons. You may not even remember them; they were Ethical Culture people, friends of Mother's. I remember meeting them several times as a child, and they were old then. Gypsy and I found them fascinating because they "talked funny." They're Scandinavian, Swedes I think. Anyway, there they were at your funeral. They had kept up with your career all these years and had come to "pay their respects." In that milling mob of self-seekers these two old humble eccentrics were like a whiff of strong ozone. Gypsy and I took them out for dinner, and here comes the story: they had no children and in their later years took to breeding and raising chihuahuas. One day, close to the lying-in time of one of the females, they spent the whole afternoon and evening away from home. Came home after midnight completely exhausted, only to find carnage all over the apartment. The female had started to whelp and was whimpering and making a mess of the living room rug; in the meantime the other dogs had gotten hold of a feather pillow from the bedroom, ripped it apart, and scattered it from one end of the apartment to the other. Feathers, mounds and heaps of feathers, wet, dry, sticky, floating, clinging feathers every place they looked, and in the midst of this the mother having pups in the middle of the living room rug. Poor weary old Anderssons, to be faced with this! Mrs. A. got a cardboard box and started assisting the mother while Mr. A. began the cleanup job. He had gathered several armloads of feathers and stuffed them in a paper bag in the kitchen when he heard a squeak. He rocked back and forth thinking he had never heard that particular floorboard squeak before. And then he realized it was coming from the paper bag and he went over and began digging through the feathers and *found* it, down in the bottom of the bag, a puppy, half smothered, still wet, and completely covered by feathers. Gently he fished it out and took it to Mrs. A. who licked it clean.

Mr. A. went on with the story but I'm stopping here. Father, *she licked it clean!* That's the point. There was nothing else to be done—such a fragile newborn couldn't be exposed to the shock of water—and without thinking twice about it she did what its mother would do. Father, I was so excited by that small incident I nearly jumped up in the restaurant and cheered. (When I told the story to Mike he was so repelled he walked out of the room.) I'm sure you never read it, but in *Kristin Lavransdatter* there was one sentence which stated simply that one of Kristin's sons had trouble with his eyes and that Kristin would clear them of matter with her tongue. Father, you understand the importance of these things, don't you? In spite of, beneath your devilish laughter you understood what it meant to be human, didn't you? To perform a human act, one of service, and in loving humility? A *Chesed shel emet?*

If you don't understand these things now I suppose you never will; not that it makes any difference. Although I must admit that I would like it to make a difference.

That's about all I have to tell you right now. I'm tiring; these graphomania sieges take their toll. We're all well here, we push on from day to day. Who knows, maybe in the long run we'll find all the things we've been looking for, including our souls.

Memo: Call Dr. Lunt's office, make an appointment. Proceed directly to the drugstore, do not pass Go, do not collect two hundred dollars. Buy arsenic. Skip Lunt, just go to the drugstore. I know the symptoms, there's no sense having Lunt confirm them. And I might end up crying in his office and then he'd have to go through his male doctor comforts his female patient routine. The old pat on the shoulder, there there buck up. Followed by the slightly impatient, "Can't you gals learn to take care of yourselves we're not in the Stone Age you know." Maybe I should just wait till the last minute and then pop over to the hospital—"There's something in my stomach, I can't imagine, do you suppose it's a gall stone?" "No, lady, it's a Mound's chocolate bar, it's a Peter Paul Almond Joy." Oh Doctor, you wit, fancy that, another bundle of almond joy.

No, I've got to see Lunt. For one thing, I've got to ask him how the baby is going to turn out. It's stupid, but I can't get over the idea that the fetus is going to form itself around the loop—sort of the way an oyster forms a pearl. Imagine a baby being born in the shape of a Lippy's loop! Or being born clutching the loop in one hand. "Nurse, do me a favor, check the kid's fists before you show him to my husband."

I'm worn out with exhaustion and chronic queasiness. I wake in the middle of the night and feel hysteria all around me—not lurking, not ready to pounce, but seeping through the room like gas. I press myself into Mike's flannel-clad back and fight the urge to bite clean through his backbone. I haven't told him yet. I think about abortion but I know I couldn't go through with it— even if I could find someone who wasn't a butcher, even if I started hanging around poolrooms and downtown bars to find out a name, a referral, even if I told Mike I wanted a week's vacation in Puerto Rico by myself and he agreed to stay home with the children ha ha ha ha ha. . . . But I couldn't. The idea is too grisly. Not the idea, the reality. To rip out a life like that, to rip it out of me and rinse it down some stainless-steel drain. But suppose I were desperate enough, would I do it? Probably. I guess that's my biggest problem. I despair, but I'm not desperate. In frustration I watch my own life go down the drain but I know I can cope with that. I'll survive. I'm strong, and even now, feeling sick all the time, I get goose-pimply with the anticipation of birth. I labor easily, though under delusion. I'm a lucky woman.

Goddamn him. I'll get a full-time housekeeper out of this one. I'll fix him. Let him see if he has any extra fifteen hundred dollars from now on to keep the niggers out of the neighborhood. Or to contribute to this or that one's campaign. Or to entertain on. I'll put laxatives in the pâte and Spanish Fly in the roe. Oh he's so cool, he has everything so neatly under control. He won't even divorce me, he says children need a mother, and then he keeps giving me more children to prove it. Irrefutable logic. He and Father Zimmel, incestuous twins! Why won't rhythm work for me? I've licked the glass off half a dozen thermometers—I should have swallowed the mercury—and each time I have either a boy or a girl for my bother. Suppose I called in the carpenters and had an extra wing built onto the house. Put up a sign: No Admittance Except With Prophylactic In Hand. But he'd see me locked away in a home for the unfit, he'd have me committed to an institution before he'd walk in that door.

And me? I? What options do I have? I'm that sexually sloppy Jewess his mother warned him about. "Jews are sexually sloppy," she told him, and she pursed her lips in scorn and fear; an Irish parody of a Jewish mother. And what of it, I gloried at the time, I'm rich with the juices of honey and pressed olives. Or was . . . But that's *it*, that's what I have to guard against. Not the frustration, not even the encroaching hysteria, but the wine turning to vinegar. The slow corrosion, the final bankruptcy. Of all defeats that's the most insidious. Its tentacles are silent, it sidles up and grabs you over coffee, and you're caught. Bitterness and anger— you can hear your own death rattles.

He won't divorce me, that's sure as the night, the day. Just let me even see a lawyer, he said, and I'd rue the day forever. The children would be caught like butterflies in a net; he'd see to it that he was left with the net. The depth and breadth of his arrogance never stop surprising me. I live in the wrong century. In another time I could have hired a band of thugs to waylay him on a dark night and do their swift razor work. Poor denuded Abelard, singing mournfully to himself, No No, they can't take that away from me. Mike impotent, the loveliest of lovers. I won't hire anyone, I'll do the dire deed myself, and I won't use a razor, not even a rusty one; I'll use the goddamned pruning shears.

Maybe when I tell Mike he'll give me another diamond sunburst. Diamonds are a girl's best friend—I'll pin it between my legs. Won't he be surprised! He thinks I care about the jewelry, the furs, he honestly thinks they should make a woman happy. I could be happy in Ludeyville with Moses Herzog, that's how I could be happy. Well, it's no use. My sagging breasts wouldn't please him, neither would my reluctance to nourish his ego. My own inner house needs refurbishing; I couldn't take on the care and feeding of his. Let that fantasy go. I'll survive this baby, I'll name it Omega—just the way I named the last five. Those Greeks, they just didn't know where to end their alphabet. Should I have an abortion or a frontal lobotomy. I'm being funny again, I can't even despair properly. The odd thing is, I don't feel suicidal. I feel used, angry, vindictive—and this *will* be the last baby, I swear that—but not suicidal. Please God in my next reincarnation I'll come back as other than a cow or a dancing bear. A fish, a Clown Loach—that would suit me. An electric stargazer: I shoot out my tongue to trap my victims and emit fifty-volt charges. (Though that sounds more like Mike.) I'll be a Moray eel, ferocious; powerful jaws, strong teeth, a savage bite. I'll be a Porcupine Globefish, inflating myself when in danger, with erected spines—why hasn't anyone thought of that before as a birth-control measure? A Brown-headed Cowbird who lays her eggs in other birds' nests; nasty wily lady, she then takes off and someone else has to brood and rear her young. I'd like to be a wild horse, even a deer—but then there's hunting season and I don't want any strain on me, any tension. Not the next time around.

Once in the Baltimore zoo I saw a guanaco. Standing so close to the fence that I could have reached in and touched her eyelashes, still she didn't move and neither did I. Her eyes were extraordinarily beautiful. Deep brown, lambent. Lashes a full inch long, thick as a painter's brush. Straight. Her fur a rich red brown, whitish underneath; black forehead and head patches. For all I know guanacos are as stupid as mules, but I know this one was not. She stood poised in perfection and it didn't matter that she was behind a Baltimore fence and not roaming the Patagonian uplands and valleys. I wanted to climb inside her skin and look out at me on the other side of the fence. I ached to reach in and stroke her, but for the world I wouldn't have demeaned her with a pat. When a kid came by and threw a handful of popcorn at her she didn't move a foreleg. Not even a glance. Keep your lousy popcorn, we guanacos are an ancient race. We may not fly, or arrow through the oceans, we may not terrorize the jungle, but we copulate with gusto, we rear our young with affection, and then free them to early independence, we're agile, curious, gentle, loyal. We have our own vision. So take your popcorn and stuff it.

She wouldn't have said that: take your popcorn and stuff it. She wasn't vulgar. But I must stop this. I'm way behind on mending, on reading. I'll come back to you, guanaco, another time.

Homemade

IAN MCEWAN

I CAN SEE NOW our cramped, overlit bathroom and Connie with a towel draped round her shoulders, sitting on the edge of the bath weeping, while I filled the sink with warm water and whistled— such was my elation—"Teddy Bear" by Elvis Presley, I can remember, I have always been able to remember, fluff from the candlewick bedspread swirling on the surface of the water, but only lately have I fully realized that if this was the *end* of a particular episode, insofar as real-life episodes may be said to have an end, it was Raymond who occupied, so to speak, the beginning and middle, and if in human affairs there are no such things as episodes, then I should really insist that this story is about Raymond and not about virginity, coitus, incest, and self-abuse. So let me begin by telling you that it was ironic, for reasons which will become apparent only very much later—and you must be patient—it was ironic that Raymond of all people should want to make me aware of my virginity. In Finsbury Park one day Raymond approached me, and steering me across to some laurel bushes, bent and unbent his finger mysteriously before my face and watched me intently as he did so. I looked on blankly. Then I bent and unbent my finger too and saw that it was the right thing to do because Raymond beamed.

"You get it?" he said. "You get it!" Driven by his exhilaration I said yes, hoping then that Raymond would leave me alone now to bend and unbend my finger, to come at some understanding of his bewildering digital allegory in solitude. Raymond grasped my lapels with unusual intensity.

"What about it then?" he gasped. Playing for time, I crooked my forefinger again and slowly straightened it, cool and sure, in fact so cool and sure that Raymond held his breath and stiffened with its motion. I looked at my erect finger and said,

"That depends," wondering if I was to discover today what it was we were talking of.

Raymond was fifteen then, a year older than I was, and though I counted myself his intellectual superior—which was why I had to pretend to understand the significance of his finger—it was Raymond who *knew* things, it was Raymond who conducted my education. It was Raymond who initiated me into the secrets of adult life which he understood himself intuitively but never totally. The world he showed me, all its fascinating detail, lore and sin, the world for which he was a kind of standing master of ceremonies, never really suited Raymond. He knew that world well enough, but it—so to speak—did not want to know him. So when Raymond produced cigarettes, it was I who learned to inhale the smoke deeply, to blow smoke rings, and to cup my hand round the match like a film star while Raymond choked and fumbled; and later on when Raymond first got hold of some marijuana, of which I had never heard, it was I who finally got stoned into euphoria while Raymond admitted—something I would never have done myself—that he felt nothing at all. And again, while it was Raymond with his deep voice and wisp of beard who got us into horror films, he would sit through the show with his fingers in his ears and his eyes shut. And that was remarkable in view of the fact that in one month alone we saw twenty-two horror films. When Raymond stole a bottle of whiskey from a supermarket in order to introduce us to alcohol, I giggled drunkenly for two hours at Raymond's convulsive fits of vomiting. My first pair of long trousers were a pair belonging to Raymond which he had given to me as a present on my thirteenth birthday. On Raymond they had, like all his clothes, stopped four inches short of his ankles, bulged at the thigh, bagged at the groin, and now, as if a parable for our friendship, they fitted me like tailor-mades, in fact, so well did they fit me, so comfortable did they feel, that I wore no other trousers for a year.

And then there were the thrills of shoplifting. The idea, as explained to me by Raymond, was quite simple. You walked into Foyle's bookshop, crammed your pockets with books, and took them to a dealer on the Mile End Road who was pleased to give you half their cost price. For the very first occasion I borrowed my father's overcoat, which trailed the pavement magnificently as I swept along. I met Raymond outside the shop. He was in shirtsleeves because he had left his coat on the underground, but he was certain he could manage without one anyway, so we went into the shop. While I stuffed into my many pockets a selection of slim volumes of prestigious verse, Raymond was concealing on his person the seven volumes of the Variorum Edition of *The Works of Edmund Spenser*. For anyone else the boldness of the act might have offered some chance of success, but Raymond's boldness had a precarious quality, closer in fact to a complete detachment from the realities of the situation. The under-manager stood behind Raymond as he plucked the books from the shelf. The two of them were standing by the door as I brushed by with my own load, and I gave Raymond, who still clasped the tomes about him, a conspiratorial smile, and thanked the under-manager, who automatically held the door open for me. Fortunately, so hopeless was Raymond's attempt at shoplifting, so idiotic and transparent his excuses, that the manager finally let him go, liberally assuming him to be, I suppose, mentally deranged.

And finally, and perhaps most significantly, Raymond acquainted me with the dubious pleasures of masturbation. At the time I was twelve, the dawn of my sexual day. We were exploring a cellar on a bomb site, poking around to see what the dossers had left behind, when Raymond, having lowered his trousers as if to have a piss, began to rub his prick with a coruscating vigor, inviting me to do the same. I did, and soon became suffused with a warm, indistinct pleasure which intensified to a floating, melting sensation, as if my guts might at any time drift away to nothing. And all this time our hands pumped furiously. I was beginning to congratulate Raymond on his discovery of such a simple, inexpensive, yet pleasurable way of passing the time, and at the same time wondering if I could not dedicate my whole life to this glorious sensation—and I suppose looking back now, I suppose that in many respects I have—I was about to express all manner of things when I was lifted by the scruff of the neck, my arms, my legs, my insides, hailed, twisted, wracked, and producing for all this two dollops of sperm which flipped over Raymond's Sunday jacket—it was Sunday—and dribbled into his breast pocket.

"Hey," he said, breaking with his action. "What did you do that for?" Still recovering from this devastating experience, I said nothing, I could not say anything.

"I show you how to do this," harangued Raymond, dabbing delicately at the glistening gisum on his dark jacket, "and all you can do is spit."

And so by the age of fourteen, I had acquired, with Raymond's guidance, a variety of pleasures which I rightly associated with the adult world. I smoked about ten cigarettes a day, I drank whiskey when it was available, I had a connoisseur's taste for violence and obscenity, I had smoked the heady resin of *cannabis sativa*, and I was aware of my own sexual precocity, though oddly it never occurred to me to find any use for it, my imagination as yet unnourished by longings or private fantasies. And all these pastimes were financed by the dealer in the Mile End Road. For these acquired tastes Raymond was my Mephistopheles, he was a clumsy Vergil to my Dante, showing me the war to a Paradiso where he himself could not tread. He could not smoke because it made him cough, the whiskey made him ill, the films frightened or bored him, the cannabis did not affect him, and while I made stalactites on the ceiling of the bomb site cellar, he made nothing at all.

"Perhaps," he said mournfully, as we were leaving the site one afternoon, "perhaps I'm a little too old for that sort of thing."

So when Raymond stood before me now, intently crooking and straightening his finger, I sensed that here was yet another fur-lined chamber of that vast, gloomy, and delectable mansion, adulthood, and that if I only held back a little, concealing, for pride's sake, my ignorance, then shortly Raymond would reveal and then shortly I would excel.

"Well, that depends . . ." We walked across Finsbury Park, where once Raymond, in his earlier, delinquent days, had fed glass splinters to the pigeons, where together, in innocent bliss worthy of *The Prelude*, we had roasted alive Sheila Harcourt's budgerigar while she swooned on the grass nearby, where as young boys we had crept behind bushes to hurl rocks at the couples fucking in the arbor; across Finsbury Park then, and Raymond saying, "Who do you know?"

Who did I know? I was still blundering, and this could be a

change of subject, for Raymond had an imprecise mind. So I said, "Who do *you* know?" to which Raymond replied "Lulu Smith" and made everything clear—or at least the subject matter, for my innocence was remarkable. Lulu Smith! Dinky Lulu! The very name curls a chilly hand round my balls. Lulu Lamour, of whom it was said she would do anything, and that she had done everything. There were Jewish jokes, Elephant jokes, and there were Lulu jokes, and these were mainly responsible for the extravagant legend. Lulu Slim—but how my mind reels—whose physical enormity was matched only by the enormity of her reputed sexual appetite and prowess, her grossness only by the grossness she inspired, the legend only by the reality. Zulu Lulu! who—so fame had it—had lain a trail across North London of frothing idiots, a desolation row of broken minds and pricks spanning Shepherd's Bush to Holloway, Ongar to Islington. Lulu! her wobbling girth and laughing piggies' eyes, blooming thighs, and dimpled finger joints, the heaving, steaming leg-load of schoolgirl flesh who had, so reputation insisted, had it with a giraffe, a hummingbird, a man in an iron lung (who had subsequently died), a yak, Cassius Clay, a marmoset, a Mars bar, and the gearstick of her grandfather's Morris Minor (and subsequently a traffic warden).

Finsbury Park was filled with the spirit of Lulu Smith, and I felt for the first time ill-defined longings as well as mere curiosity. I knew approximately what was to be done, for had I not seen heaped couples in all corners of the park during the long summer evenings, and had I not thrown stones and water bombs?—something I now superstitiously regretted. And suddenly there in Finsbury Park, as we threaded our way through the pert piles of dog shit, I was made aware of and resented my virginity; I knew it to be the last room in the mansion. I knew it to be for certain the most luxurious, its furnishings more elaborate than any other room, its attractions more deadly, and the fact that I had never had it, made it, done it, was a total anathema, my malodorous albatross, and I looked to Raymond, who still held his forefinger stiff before him, to reveal what I must do. Raymond was bound to know.

After school Raymond and I went to a cafe near Finsbury Park Odeon. While others of our age picked their noses over their stamp collections or homework, Raymond and I spent many hours here, discussing mostly easy ways of making money, and drinking large mugs of tea. Sometimes we got talking to the workmen who came there. Millais should have been there to paint us as we listened transfixed to their unintelligible fantasies and exploits, of deals with lorry drivers, lead from church roofs, fuel missing from the City Engineer's department, and then of cunts, bits, skirt, of strokings, beatings, fuckings, suckings, of arses and tits, behind, above, below, in front, with, without, of scratching and tearing, licking and shitting, of juiced cunts streaming, warm and infinite, of others cold and arid but worth a try, of pricks old and limp, or young and ebullient, of coming, too soon, too late, or not at all, of how many times a day, of attendant diseases, of pus and swellings, cankers and regrets, of poisoned ovaries and destitute testicles; we listened to who and how the dustmen fucked, how the Co-op milkman fitted it in, what the coalmen could hump, what the carpet fitter could lay, what the builders could erect, what the meter man could inspect, what the bread man could deliver, the gas man sniff out, the plumber plumb, the electrician connect, the doctor inject, the lawyer solicit, the furniture man install—and so on, in an unreal complex of timeworn puns and innuendo, formulas, slogans, folklore, and bravado. I listened without understanding, remembering and filing away anecdotes which I would one day use myself, putting by histories of perversions and sexual manners—in fact, a whole sexual morality, so that when finally I began to understand, from my own experience, what it was all about, I had on tap a complete education which, augmented by a quick reading of the more interesting parts of Havelock Ellis and Henry Miller, earned me the reputation of being the juvenile connoisseur of coitus to whom dozens of males— and fortunately females, too—came to seek advice. And all this, a reputation which followed me into art college and enlivened my career there, all this after only one fuck—the subject of this story.

So it was there in the cafe where I had listened, remembered, and understood nothing that Raymond now relaxed his forefinger at last to curl it round the handle of his cup and said,

"Lulu Smith will let you see it for a shilling."

I was glad of that. I was glad we were not rushing into things, glad that I would not be left alone with Zulu Lulu and be expected to perform the terrifyingly obscure, glad that the first encounter of this necessary adventure would be reconnaissance. And besides, I had only ever seen two naked females in my life. The obscene films we patronized in those days were nowhere near obscene enough, showing only the legs, backs, and ecstatic faces of happy couples, leaving the rest to our tumescent imaginations and clarifying nothing. As for the two naked women, my mother was vast and grotesque, the skin hanging from her like flayed toad hides, and my ten-year-old sister was an ugly bat whom as a child I could hardly bring myself to look at, let alone share the bathtub with. And after all, a shilling was no expense at all, considering that Raymond and I were richer than most of the workmen in the cafe. In fact I was richer than any of my many uncles or my poor overworked father or anyone else I knew in my family. I used to laugh when I thought of the twelve-hour shift my father worked in the flour mill, of his exhausted, blanched, ill-tempered face when he got home in the evening, and I laughed a little louder when I thought of the thousands who each morning poured out of the terraced houses like our own to labor through the week, rest up on Sunday, and then back again on Monday to toil in the mills, factories, timber yards, and quaysides of London, returning each night older, more tired, and no richer; over our cups of tea I laughed with Raymond at this quiescent betrayal of a lifetime, heaving, digging, shoving, packing, checking, sweating, and groaning for the profits of others, at how, to reassure themselves, they made a virtue of this lifetime's grovel, at how they prized themselves for never missing a day in the inferno; and most of all I laughed when uncles Bob or Ted or my father made me a present of one of their hard-earned shillings—and on special occasions a half-pound note—I laughed because I knew that a good afternoon's work in the bookshop earned more than they scraped together in a week. I had to laugh discreetly, of course, for it would not do to mess up a gift like that, especially when it was quite obvious that they derived a great deal of pleasure from giving it to me. I can see them now, one of my uncles or my father striding the tiny length of the front parlor, the coin or bank note in his hand, reminiscing, anecdoting, and advising me on life, poised before the luxury of giving, and feeling good, feeling so good that it was a joy to watch. They felt, and for that short period they were, grand, wise, reflective, kindhearted, and expansive, and perhaps, who knows, a little divine; patricians dispensing to their son or nephew in the wisest, most generous way, the fruits of their sagacity and wealth—they were gods in their own temple and who was I to refuse their gift? Kicked in the arse round the factory fifty hours a week, they needed these parlor miracle plays, these mythic confrontations between Father and Son, so I, being appreciative and sensible of all the nuances of the situation, accepted their money, at the risk of boredom played along a little, and suppressed my amusement till afterwards, when I was made weak with tearful, hooting laughter. Long before I knew it I was a student, a promising student, of irony.

A shilling then was not too much to pay for a glimpse at the incommunicable, the heart of mystery's mystery, the Fleshly Grail, Dinky Lulu's pussy, and I urged Raymond to arrange a viewing as soon as possible. Raymond was already sliding into his role of stage manager, furrowing his brow in an important way, humming about dates, times, places, payments, and drawing ciphers on the back of an envelope. Raymond was one of those rare people who not only derive great pleasure from organizing events, but also are forlornly bad at doing it. It was quite possible that we would arrive on the wrong day at the wrong time, that there would be confusion about payment or the length of viewing time, but there was one thing which was ultimately more certain than anything else, more certain than the sun rising tomorrow, and that was that we would finally be shown the exquisite quim. For life was undeniably on Raymond's side; while in those days I could not have put my feelings into so many words, I sensed that in the cosmic array of individual fates, Raymond's was cast diametrically opposite mine. Fortune played practical jokes on Raymond, perhaps she even kicked sand in his eyes, but she never spat in his face or trod deliberately on his existential corns—Raymond's mistakings, losses, betrayals, and injuries were all, in the final estimate, comic rather than tragic. I remember one occasion when Raymond paid seventeen pounds for a two-ounce cake of hashish, which turned out not to be hashish at all. To cover his losses, Raymond took the lump to a well-known spot in Soho and tried to sell it to a plainclothesman, who fortunately did not press a charge. After all there was, at that time at least, no law against dealing in powdered horse dung, even if it was wrapped in tinfoil.

Then there was the cross-country. Raymond was a mediocre

runner and was among ten others chosen to represent the school
in the sub-Counties meeting. I always went along to the meetings. In fact there was no other sport I watched with such good
heart, such entertainment and elation, as a good cross-country. I
loved the wracked, contorted faces of the runners as they came
up the tunnel of flags and crossed the finish line; I found especially interesting those who came after the first fifty or so, running harder than any of the other contestants and competing de-
monically among themselves for the hundred and thirteenth
place in the field. I watched them stumble up the tunnel of flags,
clawing at their throats, retching, flailing their arms, and falling
to the grass, convinced that I had before me here a vision of
human futility. Only the first thirty runners counted for anything
in the contest, and once the last of these had arrived the group of
spectators began to disperse, leaving the rest to fight their private
battles—and it was at this point that my interest pricked up.
Long after the judges, marshals, and timekeepers had gone home,
I remained at the finish line in the descending gloom of a late
winter's afternoon to watch the last of the runners crawl across
the end marker. Those who fell I helped to their feet, I gave
handkerchiefs to bloody noses, I thumped vomiters on the back, I
massaged cramped calves and toes—a real Florence Nightingale,
in fact, with the difference that I felt an elation, a gay fascination with the triumphant spirit of human losers who had run
themselves into the ground for nothing at all. How my mind
soared, how my eyes swam when, after having waited ten, fifteen, and even twenty minutes in that vast, dismal field, surrounded on all sides by factories, pylons, dull houses, and garages, a cold wind rising, bringing the beginnings of a bitter
drizzle, waiting there in that heavy gloom—and then suddenly to
discern on the far side of the field a limp white blob slowly making its way to the tunnel, slowly measuring out with numb feet
on the wet grass its micro-destiny of utter futility. And there beneath the brooding metropolitan sky, as if to unify the complex
totality of organic evolution and human purpose and place it
within my grasp, the tiny amoebic blob across the field took on
human shape, and yet still it held to the same purpose, staggering
determinedly in its pointless effort to reach the flags—just life,
just faceless, self-renewing life to which, as the figure jackknifed
to the ground by the finishing line, my heart warmed, my spirit

rose in the abandonment of morbid and fatal identification with the cosmic life process—the Logos.

"Bad luck, Raymond," I would say cheerily as I handed him his sweater, "better luck next time." And smiling wanly with the sure, sad knowledge of Arlecchino, of Feste, the knowledge that of the two it is the Comedian not the Tragedian who holds the Trump, the twenty-second Arcanum, whose letter is Than, whose symbol is Sol, smiling as we left the now almost dark field Raymond would say,

"Well it was only a cross-country, only a game you know."

Raymond promised to confront the divine Lulu Smith with our proposition the following day after school, and since I was pledged to look after my sister that evening while my parents were at the Walthamstow dog track, I said good-bye to Raymond there at the cafe. All the way home I thought about cunt. I saw it in the smile of the conductress, I heard it in the roar of the traffic, I smelled it in the fumes from the shoe polish factory, conjectured it beneath the skirts of passing housewives, felt it at my fingertips, sensed it in the air, drew it in my mind, and at supper, which was toad-in-the-hole, I devoured, as in an unspeakable rite, genitalia of batter and sausage. And for all this I still did not know just exactly what a cunt was. I eyed my sister across the table. I exaggerated a little just now when I said she was an ugly bat—I was beginning to think that perhaps she was not so bad-looking after all. Her teeth protruded, that could not be denied, and if her cheeks were a little too sunken, it was not so you would notice in the dark, and when her hair had been washed, as it was now, you could almost pass her off as plain. So it was not surprising that I came to be thinking over my toad-in-the-hole that with some cajoling and perhaps a little honest deceit, Connie could be persuaded to think of herself, if only for a few minutes, as something more than a sister, as, let us say, a beautiful young lady, a film star, and maybe, Connie, we could slip into bed here and try out this rather moving scene, now you get out of these clumsy pajamas while I see to the light . . . And armed with this comfortably gained knowledge, I could face the awesome Lulu with zeal and abandon, the whole terrifying ordeal would pale into insignificance, and who knows, perhaps I could lay her out there and then, halfway through the peepshow.

I never enjoyed looking after Connie. She was petulant, demanding, spoiled, and wanted to play games all the while instead of watching the television. I usually managed to get to bed an hour early by winding the clock forward. Tonight I wound it back. As soon as my mother and father had left for the dog track, I asked Connie which games she would like to play, she could choose anything she liked.

"I don't want to play games with you."

"Why not?"

"Because you were staring at me all the time through supper."

"Well of course I was, Connie. I was trying to think of the games you liked to play best, and I was just looking at you, that was all." Finally she agreed to play hide-and-seek, which I had suggested with special insistence because our house was of such a size that there were only two rooms you could hide in, and they were both bedrooms. Connie was to hide first. I covered my eyes and counted to thirty, listening all the while to her footsteps in my parents' bedroom directly above, hearing with satisfaction the creak of the bed—she was hiding under the eiderdown, her second favorite place. I shouted "coming" and began to mount the stairs. At the bottom of the stairs I do not think I had decided clearly what I was about to do; perhaps just look around, see where things were, draw a mental plan for future reference—after all, it would not do to go scaring my little sister, who would not think twice about telling my father everything, and that would mean a scene of some sort, laborious lies to invent, shouting and crying and that sort of thing, just at a time when I needed all my energy for the obsession in hand. By the time I reached the top of the stairs, however, the blood having drained from brain to groin, literally, one might say, from sense to sensibility, by the time I was catching my breath on the top stair and closing my moist hand round the bedroom door handle, I had decided to rape my sister. Gently I pushed the door open and called in a singsong voice,

"Connieeeeeeee, where aaare you?" That usually made her giggle, but this time there was no sound. Holding my breath, I tiptoed over the bedside and sang,

"I knooooow where youuuu are," and bending down by the telltale lump under the eiderdown I whispered,

"I'm coming to get you," and began to peel the bulky cover

away, softly, almost tenderly, peeking into the dark warmth under-neath. Dizzy with expectation I drew it right back, and there, helplessly and innocently stretched out before me, were my par-ents' pajamas, and even as I was leaping back in surprise I re-ceived a blow in the small of my back of such unthinking vigor as can only be inflicted by a sister on her brother. And there was Connie with mirth, the wardrobe door swinging open behind her.

"I saw you, I saw you, and you didn't see me!" To relieve my feelings I kicked her shins and sat on the bed to consider what next, while Connie, predictably histrionic, sat on the floor and boo-hooed. I found the noise depressing after a while, so I went downstairs and read the paper, certain that soon Connie would follow me down. She did and she was sulking.

"What game do you want to play now?" I asked her. She sat on the edge of the sofa, pouting and sniffing and hating me. I was even considering forgetting the whole plan and giving myself up to an evening's television when I had an idea, an idea of such simplicity, elegance, clarity, and formal beauty, an idea which wore the assurance of its own success like a tailor-made suit. There is a game which all home-loving, unimaginative little girls like Connie find irresistible, a game which, ever since she had learned to speak the necessary words, Connie had plagued me to play with her, so that my boyhood years were haunted by her pleadings and exorcised by my inevitable refusals, it was a game, in short, which I would rather be burned at the stake for than have my friends see me play it. And now at last we were going to play Mummies and Daddies.

"*I* know a game you'd like to play, Connie," I said. Of course she would not reply, but I let my words hang there in the air like bait.

"I know a game *you'd* like to play." She lifted her head.

"What is it?"

"It's a game you're always wanting to play."

She brightened. "Mummies and Daddies?" She was trans-formed, she was ecstatic. She fetched prams, dolls, stoves, fridges, cots, teacups, a washing machine, and a kennel from her room and set them up around me in a flutter of organizational zeal.

"Now you go here, no there, and this can be the kitchen and this is the door where you come in and don't tread on there be-cause there's a wall and I come in and see you and I say to you and then you say to me and you go out and I make lunch." I was plunged into the microcosm of the dreary, everyday, ponderous banalities, the horrifying, niggling details of the life of our parents and their friends, the life that Connie so dearly wanted to ape. I went to work and came back, I went to the pub and came back, I posted a letter and came back, I went to the shops and came back, I read the paper, I pinched the Bakelite cheeks of my progeny, I read another paper, pinched some more cheeks, went to work and came back. And Connie? She just cooked on the stove, washed up in the sink unit, washed, fed, put to sleep, and roused her sixteen dolls, and then poured some more tea—and she was happy. She was the intergalactic-earth-goddess-house-wife, she owned and controlled all around her, she saw all, she knew all, she told me when to go out, when to come in, which room I was in, what to say, how and when to say it. She was happy. She was complete, I have never seen another human so complete, she smiled, wide-open, joyous, and innocent smiles which I have never seen since—she tasted paradise on earth. At one point she was so blocked with the wonder, the ecstasy of it all, that mid-sentence her words choked up and she sat back on her heels, her eyes glistening, and breathed one long musical sigh of rare and wonderful happiness. It was almost a shame I had it in mind to rape her. Returning from work the twentieth time that half hour I said,

"Connie, we're leaving out one of the most important things that Mummies and Daddies do together." She could hardly believe we had left anything out and she was curious to know.

"They fuck together, Connie, surely you know about that."

"Fuck?" On her lips the word sounded strangely meaningless, which in a way I suppose it was, as far as I was concerned. The whole idea was to give it some meaning.

"Fuck? What does that mean?"

"Well, it's what they do at night when they go to bed at night, just before they go to sleep."

"Show me."

I explained that we would have to go upstairs and get into bed.

"No we don't. We can pretend and this can be the bed," she said, pointing at a square made by the design of the carpet.

"I cannot pretend and show it to you at the same time." So once again I was climbing the stairs, once again my blood was pounding and my manhood proudly stirring. Connie was quite excited too, still delirious with the happiness of the game and pleased at the novel turn it was taking.

"The first thing they do," I said, as I led her to the bed, "is to take off all their clothes." I pushed her onto the bed and, with fingers almost useless with agitation, unbuttoned her pajamas till she sat naked before me, still sweet-smelling from her bath and giggling with the fun of it all. Then I got undressed too, leaving my pants on so as not to alarm her, and sat by her side. As children we had seen enough of each other's bodies to take our nakedness for granted, though that was some time ago now and I sensed her unease.

"Are you sure this is what they do?"

My own uncertainty was obscured now by lust. "Yes," I said, "it's quite simple. You have a hole there and I put my weenie in it."

She clasped her hand over her mouth giggling incredulously. "That's silly. Why do they want to do that?" I had to admit it to myself, there was something unreal about it.

"They do it because it's their way of saying they like each other." Connie was beginning to think that I was making the whole thing up, which, again, in a way I suppose I was. She stared at me wide-eyed.

"But that's daft, why don't they just tell each other?" I was on the defensive, a mad scientist explaining his new crackpot invention—coitus—before an audience of skeptical rationalists.

"Look," I said to my sister, "it's not only that. It's also a very nice feeling. They do it to get that feeling."

"To get the feeling?" She still did not quite believe me. "Get the feeling? What do you mean, get the feeling?"

I said, "I'll show you." And at the same time I pushed Connie onto the bed and lay on top of her in the manner I had inferred from the films Raymond and I had seen together. I was still wearing my underpants. Connie stared blankly up at me, not even afraid—in fact, she might have been closer to boredom. I writhed from side to side, trying to push my pants off without getting up.

"I still don't get it," she complained from underneath me. "I'm not getting any feeling. Are you getting any feeling?"

"Wait," I grunted, as I hooked the underpants round the end of my toes with the very tips of my fingers, "if you just wait a minute I'll show you." I was beginning to lose my temper with Connie, with myself, with the universe, but mostly with my underpants, which snaked determinedly round my ankles. At last I was free. My prick was hard and sticky on Connie's belly, and now I began to maneuver it between her legs with one hand while I supported the weight of my body with the other. I searched her tiny crevice without the least notion of what I was looking for, but half-expecting all the same to be transformed at any moment into a human whirlwind of sensation. I think perhaps I had in mind a warm fleshly chamber, but as I prodded and foraged, jabbed and wheedled, I found nothing other than tight, resisting skin. Meanwhile Connie just lay on her back, occasionally making little comments.

"Oh, that's where I go wee-wee. I'm sure *our* Mummy and Daddy don't do this." My supporting arm was being seared by pins and needles, I was feeling raw, and yet still I poked and pushed, in a mood of growing despair. Each time Connie said, "I still don't get any feeling," I felt another ounce of my manhood slip away. Finally I had to rest. I sat on the edge of the bed to consider my hopeless failure while behind me Connie propped herself up on her elbows. After a moment or two I felt the bed begin to shake with silent spasms and, turning, I saw Connie with tears spilling down her screwed-up face, inarticulate and writhing with choked laughter.

"What is it?" I asked, but she could only point vaguely in my direction and groan, and then she lay back on the bed, heaving and helpless with mirth. I sat by her side, not knowing what to think but deciding, as Connie quaked behind me, that another attempt was now out of the question. At last she was able to get out some words. She sat up and pointed at my still erect prick and gasped,

"It looks so . . . it looks so . . ." She sank back in another fit, and then managed in one squeal,

"*So silly it looks so silly,*" after which she collapsed again into a high-pitched, squeezed-out titter. I sat there in lonely detumescent blankness, numbed by this final humiliation into the realization that this was no real girl beside me, this was no true representative of that sex, this was no boy, certainly, nor was it finally a girl—it was my sister, after all. I stared down at my limp prick, wondering at its hangdog look, and just as I was thinking of getting my clothes together, Connie, silent now, touched me on the elbow.

"I know where it goes," she said, and lay back on the bed, her legs wide apart, something it had not occurred to me to ask her to do. She settled herself among the pillows.

"I know where the hole is." I forgot my sister and my prick rose inquisitively, hopefully, to the invitation that Connie was whispering. It was all right with her now, she was at Mummies and Daddies and controlling the game again. With her hand she guided me into her tight, dry little-girl's cunt and we lay perfectly still for a while. I wished Raymond could have seen me, and I was glad he had brought my virginity to my notice, I wished Dinky Lulu could have seen me, in fact if my wishes had been granted I would have had all my friends, all the people I knew, file through the bedroom to catch me in my splendorous pose. For more than sensation, more than any explosion behind my eyes, spears through my stomach, searings in my groin, or wrackings of my soul—more than any of these things, none of which I felt anyway, more than even the thought of these things, I felt proud, proud to be fucking, even if it were only Connie, my ten-year-old sister, even if it had been a crippled mountain goat, I would have been proud to be lying there in that manly position, proud in advance of being able to say "I have fucked," of belonging intimately and irrevocably to that superior half of humanity who had known coitus, and fertilized the world with it. Connie lay quite still, too, her eyes half closed, breathing deeply—she was asleep. It was way past her bedtime and our strange game had exhausted her. For the first time I moved gently backwards and forwards, just a few times, and came in a miserable, played-out, barely pleasurable way. It woke Connie into indignation. "You've wet inside me," and she began to cry. Hardly noticing, I got up and started to get dressed. This may have been one of the most desolate couplings known to copulating mankind, involving lies, deceit, humiliation, incest, my partner falling asleep, my gnat's orgasm and the sobbing which now filled the bedroom, but I was pleased with it, myself, Connie, pleased to let things rest a while, to let the matter drop. I led Connie to the bathroom and began to fill the sink—my parents would be back soon and Connie should be asleep in her bed. I had made it into the adult world finally, I was pleased about that, but right then I did not want to see a naked girl, or a naked anything for a while. Tomorrow I would tell Raymond to forget the appointment with Lulu, unless he wanted to go it alone. And I knew for a fact that he would not want that at all.

Little Whale,
a Varnisher of Reality

"WHAT'S THAT YOU'VE GOT THERE?" Whale asked me.

"It's a cap."

"Gimme."

He took my new leather cap in his hands and began to examine it inquisitively. In a moment or two his curiosity had grown so intense that he was quivering.

"Tolya, what is it really, eh?" he yelled.

"Just a special sort of cap," I muttered.

"It's a cap to fly in, isn't it?" he yelled still louder, and started to jump up and down with the cap in his hands.

I seized on this idea readily.

"Yes, to fly in. You and I'll fly to the North Pole in that cap."

"Hurray! To see the polar bears?"

"That's right."

"And the walruses?"

"And the walruses."

"And who else?"

My head was bursting after a day at work in the course of which I had words with several of my colleagues, received a reprimand from the director and committed several errors of judgment. The state of my temper was as black as it well could be, but I nonetheless tried to pull myself together to make a mental survey of the meager Arctic fauna.

"The sharks," I suggested disingenuously.

"No, that's not true," he protested indignantly. "There aren't

any sharks there. Sharks are fierce and all the animals at the
North Pole are friendly!"

"Yes, of course they are," I agreed promptly. "So—we'll fly
away to see the polar bears, and the walruses. . . ."

"And the whales," he prompted.

"Yup, to see the whales and those. . . ."

"To see the limpeduza!" he yelled in an ecstasy of excitement.

"What's a limpeduza?"

He looked dismayed, put the cap down on the sofa and took
himself off into the farthest corner of the room. From where he
whispered:

"A limpeduza's a sort of animal."

"Quite right," I said. "How could I have forgotten that? The
limpeduza! It's a sort of slinky, slippery little creature, isn't it?"

"No! It's big and fluffy," said Whale with confidence.

My wife came into the room and said to Whale:

"Let's get on with our work."

They went out together but my wife came back and asked:

"Did you phone him?"

"Who?"

"As if you didn't know! Do you mean to say you've let the
whole day go by without phoning?"

"All right, I'll do it now."

She went out and, for the first time that day, I was alone. Tuning in to the unusual stillness, I felt as though I were taking a bath
or a shower, a shower of solitude after a working day filled to
bursting with noisy people, friends, and strangers.

I sat down at the empty writing table and put my hands on it,
enjoying the feel of the cool surface, innocent just now of all
work, of any kind of paper, its only function to serve as a support
for my heavy hands.

Outside the window the sun, slanting soundlessly through the
yellow foliage of a nearby garden, was reaching out toward the
corner of a multistoried block of flats, a towering parallelepiped,
still unlit and, to all appearances, uninhabited.

In the yard a wild band of ten-year-old boys were swarming
over the boiler-house roof. Looking at their wide-open mouths it
was possible to imagine the bedlam of sound beyond our window-
panes. A refined-looking old woman emerged timidly from the

front garden, alert as a doe, and turned in the direction of the boiler-house. At the sight of her the boys jumped off the roof to the ground.

Every evening the old woman would come out into the courtyard for a breath of fresh air, seating her poor behind on a rubber cushion, and she was a constant victim of the boys' malicious jokes. She had long since grown accustomed to them and patiently bore with all the pranks of these baffling, perfidious, lightning-swift terrorists of the yard, through she was nevertheless afraid of them, always afraid.

This time, the boys directed a jet from the caretaker's hose across her path and amused themselves by making wild leaps, their mouths agape with laughter. The old woman shifted patiently from one foot to the other waiting for them to get tired of this game. At that juncture, the caretaker's wife, a friend of the old woman's, put in an appearance and sailed into the attack, opening her mouth wide and waving her arms.

All this scene, had it been complete with sound effects, would most likely have caused me pain or anger, but at that moment it passed before my abstracted gaze like a reel from some old silent film.

And so the old woman got safely across the yard and the terrorists went raging off back up onto the roof of the boiler-house, never suspecting that the death of the old woman, which could not now be far away, would perhaps leave the first, naturally insignificant, devastation in their young hearts.

Trying to preserve my abstracted mood and protective languor, I reached for the telephone and began to dial this accursed number as though it were just by the way, as though it were a perfectly simply thing for me to do, but by the time I had dialed the third figure, all my insides had contracted, my heart, my liver and my spleen all balled up into one wildly palpitating tangle, and I was only saved by the insistent staccato signal coming from the receiver. Busy!

I imagined him sitting in an armchair or lying on his sofa; either way he would be sure to be playing with his spectacles, twiddling them round on one finger—and talking to someone. Who would it be? Sadovnikov? Voynovsky? Ovsyannikov? I swore and, at that moment, a yell from Whale came from the kitchen. He was getting carried away in there. Sometimes that happens.

"Go away!" he was yelling at the top of his lungs. "Go away!" he was yelling at my wife. "We don't need you here!"

I heard my wife's indignant voice and then the click of the light switch. Certain measures were being taken against Whale—he was left in the kitchen alone and in the dark. He quieted down at once.

My wife had gone to the bedroom and retired into a corner. She is always very upset by quarrels with Whale, with that tiny little boy, our son, that "Tom Thumb" aged three years and a bit.

I got up and made for the kitchen, trampling the parquet like an elephant and trumpeting cheerfully and threateningly.

"Too-roo-roo! Here comes Papa Elephant! Here comes the great elephant Bimbo himself, from the depths of the jungle! Too-roo-roo, it's Papa himself! In person!"

A feeling of peace and love surged up in my heart.

In the kitchen I could make out his round head against the dusky window. He was sitting on his pot and whispering something, raising one finger to the window where the lights could already be seen coming on in the block of flats across the way.

Now, I have almost grown accustomed to Whale. Less and less frequently am I overcome by that strange feeling of unreality when he comes running into the room or riding in on his tricycle. My reverence for the mystery, the awesomeness of the first months of his life has almost vanished. Now, it is just, well, just Whale—and that's all there is to it. A little boy, my son, a whale in a pail with a great long tail—and all that sort of nonsense.

He had been six months old when I named him Whale. My wife and I used to give him his bath. He would thrash about in the soapy water with his toothless mouth wide open. My job was to hold his head and to push back the twists of cotton which would keep falling out of his ears, and sometimes he would raise his blue eyes to mine and grin knowingly, as though foreseeing the intricacy of our present relations. To begin with he reminded me of nothing so much as a frankfurter in a bowl of soup, and I told my wife so:

"Here's another sausage for the soup."

Having given this thirty seconds' earnest consideration, my wife remarked that it was scarcely an aesthetically pleasing comparison. Then I thought up another one—a whale.

"He's a baby whale," I said.

My wife said nothing.

On the evening after this particular bath, I had left for Vnukovo Airport and there taken a huge airplane for the Far East. Later, on the Island of Sakhalin, traveling from harbor to harbor and putting up in hotels and guesthouses, I used to take out his photograph and wonder: How's my little Whale getting along back there?

Of course, I had given him plenty of other nicknames later on. He had been Bighter and Muggins, and had once received the complex but impressive surname of Dufferin-Stufferin-Ladleham-Cradleham-Spoonmonger-Porringer—but all these gradually died a natural death and were forgotten, whereas the chief one— "Whale"—had stuck.

"Well, what's happened, Whale?" I asked, sitting down on the kitchen stool and lighting a cigarette.

"Look, lights!" he said, and pointed his finger at the window.

"One, two, three, eighteen, eleven, nine," he began to count the lights, but broke off suddenly. "Look, the moon!"

I turned toward the window. A pale moon with a nibbled-away side was suspended above the houses.

"Yes, the moon." I felt a faint agitation and knocked the ash from my cigarette onto the floor.

"Tolya, Tolya, there *is* an ashtray," said Whale in his mother's voice.

"You're right," I said, "I'm so sorry."

We fell silent and sat for some time—he on the pot and I on the stool—in a complete stillness broken only by my wife's sighs from the bedroom and the rustling pages of her book. Whale's eyes were sparkling mysteriously. He was clearly enjoying this lull.

"Did you know," he roused himself suddenly, "that Pilot Gagarin flies to the moon?"

"Yes," I said.

"And did you know," he went on, "that Gagarin or Titov, or Tereshkova, or John Glenn. . . ." Pause for thought.

"What?" I asked.

". . . or Cooper never put things in their mouths or up their noses," he completed his thought.

My wife came back into the kitchen and took him off the pot.

"You haven't done anything. Back you go at once and try. You don't try at all."

"Tolya, do you try when you sit on your pot?" asked Whale.

"Yes," I said, "Bimbo the Elephant always tries."

"And Toomba the She-Elephant?"

"And Toomba."

"And Koochka the Baby-Elephant?"

"Koochka tries *very* hard."

"And who else?"

"Sperm whales."

"And are sperm whales friendly?" he asked.

"Did you make that call?" asked my wife.

"The line was busy," I answered.

"Then ring again."

"Look here!" I burst out, suddenly angry. "It's my business, isn't it? I don't need you to tell me when to phone."

"You're just afraid," she replied scathingly.

I jumped up from the stool.

"Oh, go and take Vanya for a walk!" she said sharply. "Come on. Get moving!"

Whale and I left the house and made our way along our side street out to the boulevard. It was already dark. Whale was taking big, businesslike strides. His little hand held tightly on to mine.

"Well, are they?" he asked.

"What?" I was at a loss.

"Are sperm whales friendly?"

"Oh, yes. Of course they're friendly. Sharks are fierce and whales are friendly."

I wonder what he imagines the sea to be like when he's never seen it? How can he possibly imagine the depths and the boundlessness of the sea? How does he think of this town? What does Moscow mean to him? He doesn't really know anything yet. He doesn't know what a town is or what a country is. He doesn't know the world is split up into two camps. We've in fact given, to the best of our abilities, some sort of definition to almost all known phenomena, we've made up some sort of a real world to suit ourselves, but he's still living in a wonderful, strange world not a bit like ours.

"And who bit one side of the moon off?" he asked.

"The Great Bear," I said without thinking and then wished I hadn't, foreseeing at once the difficulties of explaining it all to him. By the feel of the little hand in mine I could tell he was once again trembling with curiosity.

"What's that, Tolya?" he asked wheedlingly. "What sort of a bear?"

I lifted him up and pointed to the sky.

"See the stars? Those ones there—one, two, three, four, five, six, seven . . . like a saucepan with a long, curved handle? That's called the Great Bear."

What are stars? What is the Great Bear? Why has it been hanging there above our heads from time immemorial?

"Yes, the Great Bear!" He cried out in delight and shook his finger at it reprovingly. "She's bitten the side off the moon! Isn't she *naughty*!"

Such unquestioning acceptance of all these metaphorical conventions came as a relief.

"And a bit higher up there's the Little Bear," I said. "Do you see the little saucepan—like a ladle? That's the Little Bear."

"And where's the Daddy-Bear?" he asked reasonably. He was all for organizing the bears into a proper family.

"The Daddy-Bear, the Daddy-Bear . . ." I muttered.

"Gone hunting in the forest, hasn't he?" he suggested helpfully.

"I expect so."

I lowered him down again from my shoulder.

We came out on to the boulevard. Here, the benches were all occupied by old men and nannies. Lines of 14-year-old girls strolled arm in arm along the paths, and, behind them, lines of 15-year-old boys. The whole scene was bathed in a milky, bluish light, and the luminescent street lamps shone serenely down on a Little Humpbacked Horse the size of a mammoth, on a Firebird reminiscent of an outsized turkey, on a enormous Puss-in-Boots twice the height of a man with a dissolute expression on his rounded physiognomy, on another Puss, this time of an altogether depraved appearance, tied by a gold chain to a green oak on a Curving Shore, on Prince Gvidon, the Swan Princess, a Rocket, a giant ear of corn symbolizing the Queen of the Fields, on Gulliver. . . .

This was "Dreamland"—the children's open-air bookshop

which had spread its many stalls along the whole length of our boulevard. At this hour of the evening the stalls were already shut. Only here and there a crack of yellow light was still gleaming through the shutters of some fantastic plyboard giant—indicating that the salesgirls were still counting the take.

Whale was completely dazed. He stood rooted to the ground, not knowing who to run to first—the Cat, or the Prince, or the Swan. . . . For a minute or two he appeared to have lost all power of speech and just stood there rolling his big eyes and whispering something quite soundlessly to himself. Then he gave an imperative tug at my hand, let out a chirp of delight, and we made for the stalls at a kind of skipping run. I had difficulty in warding off the hail of questions, in telling him what was what, who was friendly and who was fierce.

On closer examination it appeared that all the figures really did stand for light and goodness, for wisdom or folksy mother-wit. Only the insignificant, weedy Kite hovering over the Swan could be said to represent the forces of evil, but Gvidon's arrow was already strung and pointing at his breast.

At last my Whale grew weary and collapsed, leaning up against the Humpbacked Horse.

"Come on, Whale," I said. "It's time to go home."

"Tolya, listen, let's take them all home with us."

"How could we take them? They're too big."

"We can take them! It doesn't matter! We really can!" He clapped the Humpbacked Horse with the palm of his hand. "We've taken that one!" He ran to the Cat and clapped him. "And that one!"

In this way he rounded them all up to take to bed with him and then, perfectly content, set out for home without looking back.

As we were about to turn off the boulevard he slowed down and I stopped. What had happened?

"Look, Tolya," he said. "What a pretty lady!"

And he was right—a pretty lady was indeed making straight for us. Her walk was like a dance, but one that she could hardly restrain. The thrusting rise of her magnificent knees set the hem of her magnificent coat surging around her and the improbably pointed umbrella which she held tucked under one arm was obviously nothing more or less than a spare pivot on which to whirl round, but her eyes, secretive and cunning, blazed with pleasure when they lighted upon us. I had not seen this particular lady for three days, and, as always when I saw or thought of her, I felt slightly giddy, confused, and ill-at-ease. Just now, in front of Whale, especially so.

"Ah," she said. "So that's your little Whale, is it? Isn't he sweet!"

She bent over him and he reached out to touch her umbrella, demanding:

"What's that? An arrow? A gun?"

"It's an umbrella!" she cried, and in one second the umbrella was open. With a tiny flapping sound it unfurled above her head, lending her whole figure an additional, almost acrobatic lightness.

"Let me hold it?" yelled Whale.

She gave him the umbrella.

"It is a pleasure to see you engaged in such a peaceful occupation, Signor," she said.

"And it gladdens me to see you, Ma'mselle," I said.

On the whole, we might very well have done without this idiotic wit, which was so typical of our circle, and have entered at once into a discussion of what had been worrying us for the last few days. However, it had come to be the accepted thing to begin any kind of conversation with a similar, or preferably more successful, attempt at humor, and she and I were unable to avoid doing so.

Whale was circling round and round the umbrella and we could talk undisturbed.

"Why are you looking so sour?"

"Does it bother you?"

"You're fed up, aren't you?"

"Why?"

"You think I'll pester you?"

"Can't you stop being arch?"

She said that she wasn't being arch, that she didn't see why we should quarrel, that after all we hadn't seen each other for three days, that she understood that I was all torn up inside, that she understood everything, and thought about me all the time and, perhaps, it was a help to me.

She was lying and not lying. How easily candor and archness

get along together in a woman's heart, I thought: their eternal calm and the absurd, repulsive fussing always going on inside them. Anyway, it's easier for beautiful women, I thought. They've no fear of death, never think about it, even. They're only afraid of old age. Dopes, they're afraid of old age.

I also thought, while she was sympathizing with me, that I mustn't let myself get drawn into her world, that I hadn't the energy, that as it was my head was full of all kinds of fussing, that this was not the moment for affairs or for romance. I have such a longing for peace, and all day long my only peaceful moment had been among the plyboard monsters of "Dreamland."

"Darling," the "pretty lady" was saying, "I understand how humiliating it is, but get up your courage and phone him. You must get everything clear and then even if it turns out for the worst, it'll still be better. I promise you it will."

She raised her hand and put the palm of that hand to my cheek. And stroked it.

At that moment Whale intervened. He tugged at the "pretty lady's" sleeve.

"Here, take your umbrella and leave my daddy alone! He's my daddy, not yours."

We took leave of the "pretty lady" and went on home. For a second or two her laugh still sounded in our ears, artificially good-natured, perhaps bitter.

On the way we called a halt at the gates of the bus depot. Huge buses were passing through the gates, and middle-size buses and minibuses.

"Daddy-Bus and Mommy-Bus and Baby-Bus," announced Whale, and burst out laughing.

And so we returned home.

While Whale was having his supper and telling his mother all about our walk, I wandered about the room glancing surreptitiously at the telephone and becoming weak with anxiety.

I hate that contraption. It simply astonishes me that my wife can chat with her friends over the telephone for hours on end, that she can establish a close relationship with people over the telephone. Perhaps her liking for her friends is transferred to the receiver and at such times it is really for the phone that she feels tenderness and affection?

I lose a lot of time because I can't bear talking on the telephone. Simply to avoid picking up the receiver I am prepared to travel to the other end of town, losing time and money.

Perhaps this is because I want life to be real and when you hear a voice on the phone it seems like something made up, as though everything were make-believe, everything at one remove from reality.

Perhaps that is what I should do now? Perhaps I should not ring him today, but should go and see him tomorrow, have it out with him face to face. Then I should be able to use subtle, scarcely noticeable graduations of expression, to show him that I am not at all that simple, that it is not all that simple to humiliate me, to make him understand that I'm a man, not a mouse, and that my visit to him is, in its own way, an act of manly courage, and that I don't give a damn. A telephone conversation allows him a tremendous advantage. For me, a conversation like that is no different from one with a supernatural force.

Then the telephone gave a ring, a depressed sort of tinkle—the monster! I lifted the receiver and heard the voice of my good friend Stasik.

"You've hurt my feelings, I've hurt your feelings, I'm a swine, you're a swine," prattled Stasik.

When the overture was concluded, I asked what he was calling about.

"To tell you not to be a fool, of course, and to ring up that bigshot immediately. You know how much depends on him. I saw Voynovsky today and he'd seen Ovsyannikov who'd had a word with Sadovnikov about it yesterday. It's what they all think you ought to do. Right now I'll phone Ovsyannikov and he'll try to get on to Sadovnikov and Sadovnikov will phone you. You don't happen to know Voynovsky's number, do you?"

I put down the receiver. There was a repulsive little click. For the next 15 minutes I sat silently over the telephone, almost physically aware of the buzzing activity my friends were raising, imagining how their words, smooth and quick as mice, would slip themselves into the wires and go slithering along to meet one another in converging streams.

Then Sadovnikov rang, promised to get in touch with Ovsyannikov who would give him Stasik's number and then Stasik would put him on to Voynovsky.

"Did you get through?" asked my wife as she came into the room.

"No answer," I lied.

"I see. You've got absolutely no sense of responsibility." She left the room. I was in a state of total anguish and indecision when in came Whale, a broad grin on his face and his arms full of books.

"Let's read, Tolya."

He had brought in books by Marshak, Yakov Akim, Evgeni Reyn, Genrikh Samgir and various folktales.

We began with the folktales. Whale cuddled up against me, listening attentively and pulling at my ear in moments of excitement.

He could not stand the Indian story about the Baby Elephant. When we got to the place where a crocodile catches the Baby Elephant by the trunk he seized the book and threw it on the floor.

"It's not true!" He even went red in the face. "It didn't happen! It's a bad story!"

"Look here, Whale," I said. "It's a good story. It ends happily."

"No! No! It's nasty! Read that one!"

Out of the pile he pulled *The Wolf and the Seven Little Kids*. Oh, Lord, I thought, all sorts of frightening things in this one too, and there's the business about eating the baby kids.

It all ends well, but how can I tell that one to my Whale when he's such a little varnisher of reality?

In the meantime, Whale had been turning over the pages looking at the pictures.

"There's Mummy-Goat bringing the milk," he was explaining. "And there are the little Baby-Goats playing."

A pleasant idyll was unfolding before us and this was just what Whale liked. Unschooled as yet in the laws of drama he calmly turned over the next page to where a small white kid was disappearing into the terrible jaws of a ferociously painted wolf. I held my breath.

"And there's Daddy-Goat," said Whale, pointing to the wolf. "He's playing with his baby."

In the most serene manner he had organized a whole goat family.

"Whale, you're wrong, you know," I said gently. "That's not Daddy-Goat. It's the big, bad wolf. He's going to swallow the little kid, but it will all come right in the end! The wolf will be punished. That's the law of the drama, my little Whale."

"No!" he shouted, on the verge of tears. "It's not a wolf! It's

Papa-Goat! He's playing! You don't understand a thing, Tolya!"

"Yes, I was wrong," I said quickly. "You're quite right. It's Papa-Goat."

"Vanya, time for bed," his mother called him, and off he went, taking along with him as part and parcel of his peaceful dreams a family of celestial bears, a family of buses, a family of goats, the "pretty lady's" umbrella, the friendly wonders of "Dreamland," and my cap which, of course, would grow to the size of an airplane overnight and take him to see the North Pole, the realm of friendly animals.

Having tucked him up, my wife came back and sat down in the armchair opposite mine. We began to smoke. Usually it was a good time of the day, but today our smoke was not companionable.

"Who's that lady Vanya was telling me about?" asked my wife.

"She's from Head Office, an adviser on legal affairs."

"I see," she said. "Well, and what are you going to do now?"

"I don't know."

"What'll happen, then?"

"I don't know."

"I see," she said.

"Oh, Lord, I wish the winter would hurry up and come!" I burst out.

"What do you want the winter for?"

"I'm due for a holiday in the winter. I'll go skiing."

"Of course," she said sarcastically. "You're a splendid skier, aren't you?"

"Oh, stop it."

"No, it's not quite true. You're a first-class skier. Everybody knows that."

She caught her underlip with her teeth so as not to cry. At that, I pulled the telephone to me and, without giving myself time to think, dialed that accursed number.

As the long, well-spaced ringing notes sounded in the receiver, I saw in my mind's eye how, at this very moment, he was swinging his legs off the sofa and walking slowly toward the telephone, still absorbed in one of his books. Perhaps he was rubbing his back or his bottom, perhaps he was thinking: Who can that be calling me? Probably that pitiful character who always has some idiotic favor to ask. Now he was lifting up the receiver.

The tone he chose to adopt with me was quiet and confidential. "Listen, they tell me that you can't bring yourself to phone me. I've been expecting you to call for some time. Is it from propriety, or are you afraid? Apparently there is some misunderstanding. At our last meeting, it seemed to me that you misunderstood. I think that the decision will be favorable. Sleep well. I am with you with all my soul, with every fiber of my being; nerves, heart, liver, and spleen, all at your service. I hereby pledge my honor and dignity, fidelity, sincerity and love, all that mankind has ever held sacred, the ideals of every generation, the axis of the earth, the solar system, the wisdom of my favorite authors and philosophers, history, geography, botany and the golden sun, the blue sea, and never-never land that I will be your faithful henchman, weapon-bearer and page."

I put down the receiver, the sweat pouring off me.

"There you are," said my wife, "you see how simple it all is and not so terrible after all. It's enough just to make up your mind and . . ." She smiled at me.

I got up and made for the bathroom, splashed my face, and then went into the bedroom and looked at Whale. He was sleeping like a little hero, his arms and legs sprawling. His baby fat had not yet altogether disappeared, and still formed bracelets at his wrists and showed in his chubby little hands. He was smiling knowingly in his sleep, evidently engaged in making various comical and beneficent readjustments in his private kingdom.

When I look at him I am filled with joy, sweetness and light. I feel like drinking to the happy fate of the seven little kids.

Translated by Avril Pyman

Tinkers

J. F. POWERS

NOT COUNTING TEDDY BEARS and the like, they were seven—two teenage girls, two boys seven and nine, a girl of five, Mama, and Daddy—and after eight days over land and sea, Daddy had a great desire to be out of the public eye. So, when they landed in Cobb, though they'd intended to stay overnight there or in Cork, he phoned the hotel in Ballydoo, near Dublin, and was happy to hear that it would be all right to arrive that evening, a day earlier than planned. At Dublin, the train, to their surprise, became the boat train to Dun Laoghaire, and, since Ballydoo lay in that direction, they stayed on it—Daddy was happy to be saving a bit on taxi fares. At Dun Laoghaire, he was happy not to have to take ship again, and to find a taxi big enough (he'd been thinking they'd need two) to accommodate them and their luggage. Things, it seemed to him—after the hotel in St. Paul, the heat in Chicago, the train trip to New York (whoever heard of washing your hair on a train?), the Empire State Building, Gimbel's, Schrafft's, Hammacher Schlemmer's (for compasses), and six days at sea—were looking up.

Except for overcrowding in the taxi, there was no difficulty until they reached their destination, almost. On the road, caught just in time by the taxi's headlights, there was a noisy gathering of some kind, around a two-tone horse.

"*Tinkers,*" the driver said with contempt, and proceeded slowly, half off the narrow pavement, while the tinkers and the horse, hooves clonking, surged about in the dark.

"*Jem, don't sell that harse!*"

"'*M sellin' the bugger!*"

"Daddy," said the younger boy, who was sitting on Daddy's lap with Kitty, his stuffed cat, on his lap. "What's *wrong?*"

"Nothing's wrong. The man who owns the horse—his friend doesn't want him to sell it. That's all."

"Beebee'll buy it," said the older boy, who was sitting with Beebee, his teddy bear, on his lap, between Daddy and the driver, and gurgled at the thought of Beebee's wealth.

"Give it a rest," Daddy said.

Beebee, a millionaire (hotels, railroads, shipping, timber), had thrown his weight around on this trip, rather had had it thrown around for him. When they checked into the hotel in New York, not a bad hotel, Daddy had been told, "Beebee usually stays at the Waldorf," and when they found their cabins on the ship, "Beebee usually goes first class," and in the dining room on the first night, "Beebee usually drinks champagne"—and the wine steward, obviously a foreigner with ideas about American parents and children, had to be told no, that was not an order. Mama and Daddy were getting a little older, and had suffered a little more on this trip.

It was not their first one to Ireland. They had gone there for a year when the teenagers were small, again when the boys were smaller, and the last time the youngest child had been born there. Each time they had rented a house in Ballydoo, and were hoping to do so again. And this time they wouldn't have to settle for what was immediately available, would be able to look around for a while, because they would be staying on as sole tenants of the hotel after it closed for the winter and the proprietors, Major and Mrs. Maroon, went to London. This arrangement, initiated by Irish friends, had been concluded by correspondence, and since the rent would be reasonable, and Mama and Daddy could not recall a small hotel facing the harbor, they were anxious to see it. When they did, they recalled it, *them* rather, these Victorian terrace houses, externally two, now internally one, now the—though it, or they, looked eastward to the sea—Westward Ho Hotel.

Without too much ado, Mrs. Maroon, a fiftyish outdoors type, received and registered them as guests, which they'd be for two weeks, before coming into their tenancy, and after they were shown their rooms and given tea in the lounge (in the presence of two other guests, women such as one sees in lounges in the British

Isles, one reading a book, one knitting), Major Maroon, portly in a double-breasted blue serge jacket with one of its brass buttons, a top one, missing, so that the five remaining looked like the Big Dipper, appeared and proposed billiards—to the boys.

"Oh, I don't know about *that*," Daddy said, rising, and with visions of cues ploughing up green pastures of cloth, accompanied the boys and Major Maroon, who smelled of stout, to what he called the Smoking Room and Library, which smelled of dog.

Billiards proved to be a form of skittles, the little table to be coin-operated. Major Maroon financed the first game, Daddy the second, after which he, having looked through the Library, a bookcase containing incunabula of the paperback revolution (Jeeves, Raffles) and Aer Lingus schedules for the previous summer but one ("Take One"), said it was past bedtime. "Ah, the lads'll like it here," said Major Maroon, and showed them where they'd find the cues.

Later that night, when the children were, it was to be hoped, asleep in their rooms, and Mama and Daddy were having a duty-free drink in theirs (no bar at the Westward Ho), Daddy mentioned the little coin-operated table.

Mama said, severely, "It's something we'll have to watch."

And Daddy resented this—that she's not only taken his point and given it back to him as her own, which was one of her conversational tricks, but that she had turned it against him in the process. He was touchy on this subject, the subject of thrift. He had been profligate in the past, yes, though badly handicapped by lack of wherewithal to be profligate with. But he had learned plenty from Mama in the years since their marriage, and while he still had plenty to learn, about thrift, he did think it was time she forgot the past and saw him, if not as her equal, *as he was today*. He hadn't used shaving cream or lotion in years, and he hardly ever changed a blade. He always bought, *if* he bought, the economy size, and didn't take the manufacturer's word for it—had learned from Mama to weigh price against ounces. He saved string, wrapping paper, claret corks, and the parts of broken things that might come in handy, though many never did—pipe-stems, for instance. He kept the family in combs he found in the street and washed—how many fathers, not professional scavengers, did that? He had paid for only three deck chairs on the ship coming over. In Ireland, he always smoked pensioners' plug. In short, he was probably America's thriftiest living author. Yes, but—this was where he pooped out as a paterfamilias—he could not provide his loved ones with a lasting home. He had subjected them to too many moves, some presented as trips abroad, but still moves. And this one, at the other end, before they left, had been the worst to date.

The big old house they'd occupied as tenants had been sold, and the new owners, Mr. and Mrs. Stout, who planned to turn it into a barracks with bunk beds for college students, as they'd done with other big old houses in the neighborhood, had been underfoot constantly in the last 30 days—asking if it would be all right to have a few trees cut down, the front sidewalk taken up, the yard paved for parking, a notice posted at the college inviting students, possible occupants of the bunk beds, to drop around, and more, much more. It had been hard not to go along with all these requests, even though Mama and Daddy were free, legally, to reject them and were up to their ears in packing, for the Stouts were such pleasant people and were motivated, it seemed, by charity in their dirty work. "Golly, where will those poor kids park their cars?" Mama and Daddy had felt guilty about rejecting the paving project, even when the trees came crashing down. The Stouts had been too much.

Fifteen years earlier, when Mama and Daddy had begun their career as tenants and travelers, when they'd surrendered their house in the woods, the first and last place they'd owned, to the faceless men of the highway department for a service road, and a few years later, when they'd surrendered the beautiful old place, the oldest house in town, to the faceless men of the department of education for a parking lot (now occupied by a faceless building), there had been acrimony, arguments about the nature of progress, between usurpers and usurpees. This time, no. The Stouts, such pleasant people, had been too much. Mama and Daddy were still talking and, in the case of Mama, still dreaming about this move.

That night, at the Westward Ho, she suddenly said:

"You know who *they* are?"

"Who *who* are?"

"The Maroons."

"How d'ya mean? Who are they?"
"The Stouts."
"Oh, now, I wouldn't say that."

The hotel closed for the winter on schedule, but for some reason the Maroons were still there a week later. Mama and Daddy
then heard from the youngest child, to whom Mrs. Maroon had
confided, that London might not agree with Happy. (This was
the genius loci of the Smoking Room and Library, a hairy terrier
that looked like Ireland on the map when in motion, a very
mixed-up dog, to judge by the way, ways rather, it relieved itself.) So Mama and Daddy spoke up, and two days later the proprietors checked out.

Life in the hotel was then homier for the tenants in one respect
than it had been in any house to date, in that they had a pet, but
otherwise was much the same for them there as anywhere else
they'd settled for a time. The children, the teenagers attending
school in Dublin, the younger ones in Ballydoo, had their new
friends (the older boy often entertaining his at billiards—it had
occurred to Daddy but evidently not to Major Maroon that it
would be a good idea to leave the tenants with the key to the
little coin-operated table). Mama, of course, had her shopping,
cooking (in a kitchen caked with grease), and her house- or hotel-
keeping. Daddy had his "office," a small room in the uninhabited
part of the hotel, where he read the *Irish Times* and the *Daily
Telegraph*, listened to the BBC, and did his writing.

He was between books, preparing to strike out in a genre new
to him. What he had in mind was a light-hearted play, later to be
a musical and a movie, about a family of campers, possibly Germans, who, on arriving in Ireland and wishing to do it right,
would hire one of those colorful horse-drawn caravans, but make
the mistake of pulling into a bivouac of tinkers for the night.
There would be singing, dancing, drinking, and fighting around
the campfire, a nice clash of life-styles (*these*, in the end, would
be exchanged!), with plenty of love interest along the way—German boy, tinker girl, or vice versa, maybe several of each for
more love interest. He couldn't overdo it, since he was writing for
the theater, but there *were* problems. He knew nothing about
tinkers or Germans or, they might be, French, and if he got them
acting and talking right, would they, particularly the tinkers, be

intelligible to an American audience? Would this audience—as it must—immediately grasp what the Germans, French, or, they might be, Japanese, would not, namely, that the tinkers were not proper campers like themselves? He was afraid he'd have to do the whole damn thing in basic American first, then do a vivid translation, thoughts of which, since he was still in several minds as to the campers' nationality—*Wunderbar! C'est magnifique! Banzai!* —turned his stomach slightly. He had once read that nobody ever wrote a best-seller, however bad, without believing in it, but he doubted this, and even if it was true, he doubted that it was true of a smash-hit play, however bad. And what had struck him as a good idea for one ("This one will run and run") continued to do so.

But he wasn't getting on with it. Hoping to see or hear something he could use, perhaps another line of tinkerese to go with those he had ("A few coppers, sor" and "I'll pray for you, m'lord"), he would take the train into Dublin, visit the junky auction rooms on the Quays, the secondhand bookshops, just wander around—too bad, what was happening to Dublin's fair city—and come home tired, with a few small purchases, always pastry from Bewley's, cherry buns, shortbread, barmbrack (at Halloween), or fruitcake (as Christmas approached).

This they'd have that evening in the lounge, some with tea, some with cocoa and wearing their pajamas—a nice family scene, yes, but one of those was an imposter, Daddy would think, considering his responsibilities and how he'd shot the day. On some evenings, while Mama was reading aloud from Captain Marryat, one of the few clothbound authors in the Library, Daddy would have a new chapter from Beebee's family history to read, which was then in the writing and remarkable in one respect: the Beebee of the period (eighteenth century) had had a wife, children, and business associates with names like Kitty, Pussy, Toydy, Lion, Bear, Dragon, and Owl, whose present-day descendants were in precisely the same relationship to the present-day Beebee!

Stability, Daddy would think.

On some evenings, when the younger children were in bed and he was saying good night to them (another nice family scene) he would hear something to his credit, that the little girl liked living so close to the sea, the boys so close to the trains—sea and trains, thanks to him, he'd think then, though the railway was now

owned by Beebee, he understood. He was wary of Beebee. The
millionaire had such a poor opinion of the Westward Ho that he
wouldn't buy it, he said—when Beebee spoke, it was through the
older boy, dryly, rather like Mama's father—but Beebee wasn't in
such good shape himself. He was worn smooth in places, and had
a new nose (thanks to Mama) of different material which he was
sensitive about, withdrawing from the conversation if it was mentioned, as he did when frivolous remarks were made about his
extreme wealth. "Well, good night, Millions," Daddy would
say—and might be told that Beebee (though present) was somewhere in the Indian Ocean, aboard *Butterscotch*, his yacht, on a
trip around the world, and on his return would be buying new
motorbikes for Lion and Bear who, being teenagers, had crashed
theirs. "On the yacht?" "They're not with Beebee now. They ra-
dioed him about it." "What'd Beebee say?" "'Crazy kids. Just
have ta buy 'em new ones.'" The older boy would gurgle, and
Daddy would shake his head in wonder at Beebee's magnanimity.
"Lion and Bear—they're back at the ranch?" "Um." "That's the
one in Colorado?" "Partly." "It's a big ranch." "Um."

Daddy would then retire to the same room he and Mama had
occupied on the first night, where they now had two relatively
easy chairs and special lighting—they now sat by two brass table
lamps that he'd picked up at an auction, instead of under the
traditional bulb suspended from the ceiling—and there, with the
radio and the electric fire playing between them, with their reading matter and drinks, they'd spend the long evening.

By the middle of December they were talking more about their
problem. They had looked at a couple of houses that were too
small, and one just not what they'd come to Ireland to live in (a
30's period "villa" of poured concrete spattered with gravel—the
agent had called it "pebbledash"), and one very nice place,
"small Georgian," with a saint's well on the grounds, but unfur-
nished and rather remote *and*, it then came out, not for rent, the
agent having presumed that they, as Americans, might buy it.
That was all they'd done about their problem by the middle of
December.

They weren't worried yet. They had the hotel, if need be,
through January, and felt secure there, so secure that on some
evenings they were inclined—at least Daddy was—to feel sorry
for their home-owning friends in America. He wouldn't, he'd tell

Mama, want to be *Joe* out there in the country with the highway, perhaps, to be rerouted through his living room, or *Fred* by the river with the threat of floods every spring (the American Forces Network, Europe, reporting six-foot drifts in the Midwest), or *Dick* in town with that big frame house to paint every five years and those big old trees that, probably now heavy with snow and ice, might *not* fall away from the house if they fell.

One evening, after doing a spot of plumbing—Ireland, the land of welcomes, is also the land of running toilets—he told Mama that hard though it was to go through life making repairs in other people's houses and hotels, knowing that whatever you did you'd probably be doing again somewhere else, it was better than making repairs in your own home, knowing that THIS IS IT, that the repairs might well outlast you, or the dissolution of your household. This was one of the consolations of vagrancy that he hadn't heard about until he heard it from his own lips, and he liked it very much. Mama took exception to it.

One evening he told her that he'd heard a man on the BBC, on "Woman's Hour," say that mobile families were superior families—and she took exception to it. He hadn't been listening carefully until it was too late, so couldn't give her the details, only remembered that mobile families were more . . . couldn't remember exactly what, only that they were superior, that the man, who was the spokesman for some association or group that had carried out a survey and issued a report, had said that mobile families were more . . .

"*More mobile?*"

One of her conversational tricks.

One morning, about a week before Christmas, they had a letter from Mrs. Maroon. She thanked them for sending on the mail, said that cabbages were very dear in London, and asked to be remembered, as her husband did, to the children and Happy. In a postscript, she said not to send on the mail for the time being, as she and her husband would be at the hotel shortly.

Mama and Daddy then had a lengthy discussion about "shortly," about whether it only meant *soon* or could conceivably mean *briefly*.

That evening the Maroons returned.

Happy was glad to see them, and others were too. "How long you staying?" the older boy asked them right away—a good question, but lost in the excitement. "*Daddy* calls Happy *Slap!*" the youngest child informed them, and Mama quickly offered them tea.

With the proprietors in residence again, the hotel wasn't what it had been for the tenants—their relationship to the dog, for instance, wasn't the same. No, even though proprietors and tenants went their own way, ate at opposite ends of the dining room, and in the evening at different times (like first and second sitting at sea, parents with small children at the first), it wasn't the same. And again, as before the proprietors left for London, there was a certain amount of overlap and flap in the kitchen. (Mama had once expected to have her very own.) Daddy was in trouble too. After two days, he moved from the part of the hotel now occupied by the proprietors—lest his typing disturb them, his playing the radio during working hours scandalize them—to the part occupied by the tenants.

The next morning, in his new office, listening to "Music While You Work" on the BBC and reading the *Irish Times* before getting to grips with the lighthearted play (in which the campers were now Americans), he came upon an item of professional interest to him. *County councils and urban district councils throughout Ireland are awaiting the publication of a report prepared by the Government Commission on Itineracy*—shouldn't that be Itinerancy? *It is expected that the report will contain several broad proposals for integrating intinerants into the normal life of the community. Their presence has often caused friction, particularly in Limerick and Dublin suburbs, where residents claim that they indulge in fighting and leave a large amount of litter.* Yes, he'd seen some of it, and while the women, babes in arms, begged in the streets, the men, as somebody had said in a letter to the *Irish Times*, drank and played cards in a ditch. *During the winter, the tinkers usually camp at sites in these suburbs, or at sites in provincial towns, but some caravans stay on the road all the year round.* Nothing new here, nothing for him. *There are six main tinker tribes.* Oh? *The Stokes, Joyces, MacDonaghs, Wards . . .* now wait a minute . . . *and Redmonds.*

So the odds against him were greater than he'd thought.

He took the next train into Dublin, left the *Irish Times* on it, and gave the first tinker woman he met a coin, wanting and not wanting to know her name.

On the Quays, he found some secondhand paperbacks for the younger children, and was tempted by a copper-and-brass ship's lamp, not a reproduction and not too big, to be auctioned that afternoon ("about half-four," he was told). He bought a French paring knife for Mama in a restaurant supply place—he liked doing business in such places.

He then had a pot of tea and two cherry buns at the nearest Bewley's, selected a fruitcake, and, to pass the time until half-four, just wandered around, window shopping and making a few small purchases: a couple of ornaments for their Christmas tree, which was now up in the lounge and rather bare; a tool, with a cloven end and an attractive hardwood handle, to remove carpet tacks and also suitable for upholstery work, should the need arise for him to do either; some brass screws that might come in handy and were, in any case, nice to have; a hardcover notebook (they did these very well in the British Isles) such as he already had several of, with inviting cream paper that he couldn't bring himself to violate; more soft lead (3B) pencils.

For some time, he stood looking in a seedman's window. Quite an idea, he thought, having a selection of a real tree there so one could see the various kinds of branches, the various kinds of saws required to get at them, saws shown cutting into them, and one, an ordinary carpenter's saw, shown cutting into a sign, just a plank, that asked the question: "WHY NOT HAVE THE RIGHT SAW FOR THE JOB?" Since on the property one might own someday, there would be many trees, wood being the fuel of the future, and one would spend so much time up on an extension ladder (shown) doing surgery, and might otherwise fall and kill oneself, and with no insurance and six dependents, why not—except for the expense—have the saw for the job? (Beebee would.)

On his way back to the Quays, he booked two seats to a coming play, and because the tickets hadn't been printed yet, and would be posted to him, he was asked to give his name and address (was suddenly sensitive about the former), and was told when he asked for a receipt, "Ah, that's all right." This he accepted, after a moment, remembering where he was (Ireland) and an attendant at this same theater one night not undertaking to tap him on the shoulder when the time would come to leave (early, to catch the last train) but giving him his watch to hold. And also remembering the fruit huckster at the Curragh on Derby Day short of change so early in the afternoon and on whose wares they'd lunched to economize, telling him to come back and pay later. And the bellboy at the old hotel in Dublin on their first visit to Ireland who, after making several trips up to their room to call them to the phone in the lobby—they were running an ad for a house—had politely declined to be tipped further for such service, which had continued. "Ah, that's all right." That was the beauty of, and the trouble with, Ireland.

He was early for the ship's lamp, and thought the prices made by the lots before it rather low, but saw right away that this was not going to be the case with the lot he wanted—a familiar feeling at auctions. He came into the bidding at the first pause, and after the figure he'd had in mind had been passed, the maximum figure, which was subject to revision in the event, he was still in it. And money talks! He arranged to take the ship's lamp with him, rather than come back for it the next day, saying he lived "down the country" and had to catch a train.

He returned to Ballydoo tired, took the shortcut from the station, and entered the hotel by the rear, expecting to find Mama in the kitchen, but didn't. He assumed that something was taking too long in the oven. He went upstairs, expecting to find her in their room having a glass of stout by the electric fire, and perhaps reading the *Daily Telegraph*, but found her lying on the bed, face down, in the cold and dark.

"What's *wrong?*"

"Look in the lounge."

"What d'ya mean?"

"*Look in the lounge.*"

He threw a blanket over her, and hurried downstairs.

The younger children were in the lounge, as he'd expected they would be, but somebody else was there too, a woman—he'd seen her there before, three months before—knitting.

So Daddy, right away, got on the phone, and during the second sitting (there wasn't a first one), with the help of the local taximan, who also did light hauling, they moved themselves and their effects, including groceries and Christmas tree, out of the hotel and into a house down the road. The agent was there, waiting for them with a temporary lease, which was signed by flashlight—the only hitch (a blow to Mama) was the electricity was off in the house. But the agent had already called the Electricity Supply

Board, and the teenagers, who had been dispatched to the shop that kept open, were soon back with a bundle of turf and a dozen candles. And a candle, as Daddy pointed out, gives a surprising amount of light for a candle. There was coal in the shed, enough for two or three days, also kindling, and the kitchen range only smoked at first. They had their meal of baked beans and scrambled eggs by candlelight in the kitchen. Then they had their dessert—the fruitcake from Bewley's—by firelight in the parlor, some with tea, some with cocoa and wearing their pajamas, and talking about the ship's lamp, which there hadn't been time to examine until then.

Mama explained its red and green windows and its internal parts—apparently all there except for the wick. Daddy was interested in the manufacturer's name and address (Telford, Grier & Mackay, Ltd., 16, Carrick St., Glasgow), almost invisible from polishing. He pointed out that copper and brass (and silver) looked better when slightly tarnished, better still when seen, as now, by firelight. No, he didn't know where the ship's lamp's *ship* was (the younger boy wanted to know), probably it *wasn't*, and no, didn't know what he was going to do with the ship's lamp. Just liked it, just liked looking at it, he said, and, seeing that that wasn't enough, said he might put it over the front door of the house they might have in America someday. They wouldn't have to worry about it, he said—these old ship's lamps were made to be out in all kinds of weather.

"Will we get to keep it, Daddy?" said the younger boy.

"Yes, of course."

"Daddy, he means the house," said one of the teenagers.

"Oh."

"The house in America," said the younger boy. "Will we get to keep it?"

"Yes, of course—when we get it." And Daddy remembered the paperbacks—one of them, actually, and then the others—still in his coat. Taking a candle, he went to the cloakroom (good idea, having a cloakroom in a house), and while there, heard a knock at the front door—hoped it was the Electricity Supply Board. It was a man in blue, a grayhaired *garda,* who had believed the house to be vacant, he said, until he saw the wee light from the fireplace.

"We're waiting for the ESB."

"Ah. You and your family were at the hotel, sir."

"We were, yes."

"And now you're here."

"We are, yes."

"And will you be here long, sir?"

"Six months. Have a six-months' lease. May be here longer. Probably not. It's hard to say. We never know."

"Ah, indeed. We never know. Good night, sir."

No, not the ESB, Daddy said, returning to the parlor, and gave the younger children the paperbacks, saying of one (*The Market: The Buying and Selling of Shares*, in which subject the older boy had shown an encouraging interest—Beebee's influence?), "If you have any questions, ask Millions." And noticed how quiet it was then, so quiet the turf could be heard burning, puffing.

"Beebee's gone," said the youngest child.

Daddy looked at the older boy.

"Sold Beebee."

"Now, *wait* a minute."

"A friend wanted to buy him. One of my friends."

It was painful to hear the pride in the boy's voice, in having friends, and Daddy knew what Mama was thinking, that this is what comes from being a mobile family. "*What* friend? What's his *name?* Where's he *live?* What *kind* of boy is he? Do *I* know him? It doesn't matter. You can't *sell* Beebee."

"I can always buy him back. That's part of the deal."

"*You can't sell Beebee.* Go get him. *Now.*"

"In the morning," Mama said.

"No, *now.*"

"He's got his pajamas on," Mama said.

"He can take 'em off."

Mama said nothing.

"O.K., *I'll* go."

So Daddy went, and, at the friend's house, a cottage, did *not* say that the older boy missed his teddy bear, or that others did, but still told the truth. "Beebee was a gift from my mother"—his mother whose funeral he, in Ireland then, had been too broke to attend—"and I don't think she'd like it if he left us." The friend, his mother, his older sister, his two small brothers, they all seemed to understand. No trouble. Ten bob. And after a cup of tea, Daddy and Beebee—who looked the same, grumpy, stuffy, and still sure of himself—came home.

The electricity was on when they got there, the Christmas tree was going, and the younger children were in bed.

When Daddy put Beebee in with the older boy and said, "Good night, Millions," there was a gurgle in the dark that made him wonder if he'd been taken.

"Where's the money?"

"Spent it."

"*What?* Already? All of it? On *what?*"

"Billiards."

Mama and Daddy had work to do, but were tired, and spent the evening in the parlor before the fire (it and the tree gave enough light to talk by), with their drinks. There hadn't been enough time until then for him to tell her what Mrs. Maroon had said: that it hadn't originally been the plan to open the hotel for the Christmas season, that unforeseen requests for bookings (she had thanked him again for sending on the mail) and the dearness of things in London had combined to change the plan, and that she and her husband had hesitated to inform the tenants, for fear of upsetting them.

"We're well out of that," he said.

"Yes," she said.

They talked about the house, about the carved mahogany chimney piece, which, though, was spoiled by glazed tiles (these reminding him of the men's room at the Union Station in Chicago), and about what they'd need in the way of equipment—different plugs for the brass lamps, for instance, for there were a number of types in use in Ireland and they had the wrong type for this house, which, though, had to be expected.

"The odds are three or four to one against you whenever you move," he said.

"Yes," she said.

He tuned in the American Forces Network, Europe, for the home news, and heard that there was a blizzard sweeping across the Midwest. Then "Mr. Midnight" came on with his usual drivel about "Music for night people, romance, and quiet listening . . . lonesome sounds of a metropolitan city after dark"—and they discussed "metropolitan city," Mama saying that it was redundant, Daddy that he didn't like the sound of it but pointing out that it might not be redundant in certain circumstances, citing bishops who were metropolitans, whose seats, sees, or see cities, were rightly called metropolitan seats, sees, or cities. But Mama still took exception to it.

After that, they talked—he did—about their friends in America, about Joe and the highway, about Fred and the river, more about Dick and those big old trees that were probably heavy with snow and ice now, and about that big frame house that had to be painted every five years.

"That's one good thing about a house like this," he said. "Pebble-dash."

"Yes," she said.

Acknowledgments

"The Universal Fears" by John Hawkes first appeared in *American Review 16*; copyright © 1973 by John Hawkes.

"Swan Feast" by William Mathes first appeared in *New American Review 1*; copyright © 1967 by William Mathes.

"Robert Kennedy Saved from Drowning" by Donald Barthelme was reprinted from *Unspeakable Practices, Unnatural Acts* by Donald Barthelme; copyright © 1968 by Donald Barthelme. It first appeared in *New American Review 3*; reprinted by permission of Farrar, Straus & Giroux, Inc.

"The Oranging of America" by Max Apple was reprinted from *The Oranging of America* by Max Apple; copyright © 1974 by Max Apple. It first appeared in *American Review 19*; reprinted by permission of Viking Penguin Inc.

"'I Always Wanted You to Admire My Fasting'; or, Looking at Kafka" by Philip Roth was reprinted from *Reading Myself and Others* by Philip Roth; copyright © 1973, 1975 by Philip Roth. It first appeared in *American Review 17*; reprinted by permission of Farrar, Straus & Giroux, Inc.

"End of Days" by M. F. Beal first appeared in *New American Review 7*; copyright © 1969 by M. F. Beal.

"Hammie and the Black Dean" by Austin Clarke first appeared in *New American Review 14*; copyright © 1972 by Austin Clarke.

"Getting Lucky" by Leonard Michaels was reprinted from *I Would Have Saved Them if I Could* by Leonard Michaels; copyright © 1971, 1975 by Leonard Michaels. It first appeared in *New American Review 10*; reprinted by permission of Farrar, Straus & Giroux, Inc.

"In Search of a Missing IUD" by Anne Higgins first appeared in *New American Review 15*; copyright © 1972 by Anne Higgins.